MW01205272

FROM THE LAND OF TOO LITTLE OR TOO MUCH

A NOVEL

ROBERT CORY

Copyright © 2023 Robert Cory
All rights reserved.

PREFACE

I am grateful to the first readers who provided thoughtful, constructive feedback on my manuscript as it transitioned into book form: Eileen Cunningham, John Hart, Sue McKinney, John Brown, and William Hart. To my son, Christian, whose tech savvy proved invaluable. My most sincere, heartfelt thank you goes to my most exacting critic and editor of every draft, my wife, Artie Anne. Cover photo by Roger Ellis, with permission.

"Let your fiction grow out of the land beneath your feet."
- Willa Cather

Also by Robert Cory

Small Worlds

They Say the Storm Will Pass

Katarina Knobolloffskeeter and the Kingdom of Moonlight

Pas De Deux

Confessions of a Las Vegas Cocktail Waitress

Char in a Barrel

PROLOGUE

Jake's father Emerson Book called it the land of too little or too much. A boundless landscape encircled the Ormestrong County community of Waltsburg, Kansas. The county's eastern boundary overlapped the Flint Hills' Nemaha Ridge that defined this nook of The Great American Desert. A land reliably called upon by stars, moon, wind, and sun where people from all around come and go, driven by routine. A place they called home; bound by the spirit of something shared, something rooted, or something gone.

FOREWORD

June 27, 2017

Dear Mr. Cory:

Thank you for your letter of inquiry. Those who could provide more detail about our town's history have since passed on. Here is what I know about how Waltsburg came into being.

It was originally known as Pierce Village. A man by the name of Remus Pierce established a dugout trading post on the Orme River at the most fordable location for miles. By all accounts, he was a shrewd businessman. He reportedly staked Shortcut, River Crossing, and Scenic Route signs at strategic junctions along the Smoky Hill, Santa Fe, and Kaw Trails. He traded with Plains Indian tribes for buffalo hides, wolf pelts, handcrafted wares, jewelry and, on occasion, for captive white women and children. The lore of Mr. Pierce and an unidentified white woman found with multiple gunshot wounds on the bank of the Orme River in 1859 has been reduced to two versions: a band of Potawatomi Indians whom he had cheated one too many times, or pro-slavery partisans from the settlement of Whitfield at odds with his Free Stater bent. When the Atchison, Topeka & Santa Fe Railway built a branch line through Pierce Village around 1881, the Postal Service required the community to rename itself. Pierce Village was too analogous to Pierceville, already an established Finney County town in western Kansas. During the railroad's construction, the young urbane enigma Walter Bruno arrived on the scene. Not long after came the post office designation: Waltsburg.

I hope this helps. I wish you the best of luck with your novel. My wife and I are looking forward to reading it.

Very truly yours,

Jacob Ulysses Book, President (Ret.)
Waltsburg State Bank

CHAPTER 1
PAN-FRYING BACON NAKED

Saturday – January 3, 1970

"Jake! Your dad's on the phone."

... "Hi dad!"

"Jake ...hi. I just wanted to call to wish you a Happy New Year."

"Thanks."

"You doing okay?"

"Yes."

"Think the Orioles will make it to the World Series this year?"

"Hope so."

"You given any more thought to coming to Seattle?"

"No."

"I'd pay your airfare."

"I know."

"Boeing's hiring. I can pull some strings. Get you a good paying job. And, like I told you last time we talked, you could stay with us till you get your feet on the ground."

"Us?"

"Oh ...guess we haven't talked in a while, have we? I got remarried last May. I'll send you a photo from our honeymoon in Hawaii."

"D'you ever hear from mom?"

"No. What makes you think I would?"

"Just wondering."

"Have you?"

"No."

"Last time I saw her, she was fixing us some bacon and eggs after her morning shift at Barney's before I had to drive back to Wichita. I came up behind her, slipped my arms around her waist, and whispered she should try pan frying bacon naked sometime. She elbowed me so hard she bruised three of my ribs. What are you up to today?"

"Donna's on her way over to fix *huevos rancheros* for breakfast."

"Doyle tells me she's quite the cook. Is he still there?"

"Yessir."

"Put him on for me, would you?"

CHAPTER 2
WE DIE THREE TIMES

Sunday – February 1

Jake blew warm air into his cupped hands, stomped his feet, and turned his back to a wintry gust of wind shoving its way through the shelter belt. His father's New Year's call popped into his head again. He tried to imagine what it would be like to live somewhere else. Waiting at the base of the tree for John Griever's instructions from above, he noticed something out of place, perhaps a good-sized toadstool cap poking out of the ground. Kneeling and venturing a tentative touch, he guessed the hard surface to be a rock or shell. When he scraped away the hardpan topsoil with a small branch, he discovered skeletal contours and fissures. Too big to be deer and too round to be cattle, it had to be human, a human skull. He called up to John, "Hey, look what I just found." John climbed down from the crow's nest; his partially constructed deer stand. Together, they removed more dirt, more rocks, and twigs. Tilted a bit sideways, the skull seemed to be staring them in the eye. Its forehead abnormally marred with cracks wide enough to let light in.

"I'll be damned," John exclaimed.

"Creepy," said Jake.

"Yep. Ponderable, ain't it? Let's cover 'im back up and call it a day."

"Aren't we gonna dig him up?"

"Maybe after a good spring rain. Ground's hard as nails now."

Jake had a strong urge to fetch a shovel as they meandered back to John's place. The thought of dying crept in. It was a birthright, was it not? Something we all had to do someday. He remembered his father telling him we die three times. First, when our heart stops. Next, when we're buried. Finally, when no one remembers us.

CHAPTER 3
HUMDRUM

Tuesday – February 3

Donna asked Jake to clean the shop for Natalie, who was away caring for her flu-addled parents. The outside temperature was a chilly 18°; the salon's thermostat read 48° when they entered shortly before eight a.m. A cursory check of the furnace indicated the pilot light was lit and the thermostat kicked in the burners. Heat was available, no circulation. Time to call Henry, the local handyman.

Chores complete, Jake stood at the front window inside Hair by Pileaux salon. His breath fogged up a spot on the glass. He deliberately enlarged the blur and traced his initials, J U B. He noticed Donna's red neon SALON sign in her center display window had a glitch. Only the ON remained constant. He wondered if she noticed. If one were the least bit superstitious, misfortune occurred in sets of three, did it not? Furnace, neon sign, what next? Lights were on inside the barber shop across the street and Jake knew his uncle Doyle and Jimmy Baguelt were locked in ping-pong combat in the back room. Only Jimmy and Wild Bill Stimka gave his uncle a game. Wild Bill had long since crowned Doyle DeCritt the Waltsburg King Pong.

Traffic at the Beau Coup Café was sporadic. Ginny's Fashions storefront was dark. She opened at ten. The former Bakery and Confectionery Shoppe a/k/a Gibby's and its faded FOR RENT sign caught his eye. Jake remembered standing in front of its display cases as a young boy, holding his mother's hand, ogling a variety of American and continental pastries, cookies, cakes, and fresh baked breads and his uncle's comment that you could gain weight just breathing the air inside

8

Gibby's. He remembered, too, the low ceiling over the customer area that felt like it was on top of them. His most lucid memory of the bakery, however, was the mechanical action of the taffy-pulling machine in the front window and how he watched interminably, trying to guess which flavor it might be judging by its color. The morning he was led there specifically to buy molasses-flavored saltwater taffy to effect what his father termed a *coup de grâce* on his loose baby teeth stood out as well.

Upon inspection, Henry declared the fan motor *kaput*. The nearest source of a replacement part for her aging equipment was Auggie's Heating and Cooling in Granfield. Henry repeated the advice he had given Donna for the past three years. She needed a new furnace, one that would be vented properly, more efficient and cost less to operate. Donna thought all the furnace repairs made to date were the equivalent of a new furnace in an old shell. It was cheaper to fix than buy new and, in another sixty days, the need for heat would not be an issue. Henry acquiesced. He suggested she keep the portable floor heater on in the back room and a couple of faucets dripping to prevent pipes from freezing. Donna phoned Valoise Bruner and two others to reschedule their appointments. Henry left for Granfield to fetch the needed parts. Ladonna Ramirez Pileaux joined Jake at the window.

A run-down '54 Ford Crestliner pulled up in front of the barber shop. Hazel Friscote, a silver-haired woman in a pink floral head scarf and knee-length wool coat got out the driver's side. She retrieved a wheelchair from the trunk and assisted her husband, T. Robert Friscote, a World War II navy veteran who witnessed the surprise attack on Pearl Harbor firsthand. Over the years, Jake raptly listened to Mr. Friscote's tales of his experience the morning of December 7, 1941, as a Carpenter's Mate 2nd Class aboard the light cruiser USS Helena. Mr. Friscote's wheelchair status was due, however, to an inadvertent slip into a combine's blades during harvest many years after the war. His left leg, amputated above the knee, turned into a source of pride for the man who now referred to himself as a one-legged ass-kicker.

"Did I tell you Natalie's going to start doing pedicures March 1st?" Donna mentioned. "She's good company. Some days in here by myself, I think I might be going crazy."

"Crazier?"

"Is that Bob Friscote?"

"None other."

"It's cold in here! You want anything from Luci's?"

"No. I better go help her."

Jake dashed out the door to help Mrs. Friscote cart her husband into his uncle's shop. Minutes later, Donna pulled up and parked her red Chevelle SS in front of Doyle's. Curled up on his loveseat blanket, Wally did not so much as twitch his tail as Donna came in. She asked Jake if he noticed her salon sign malfunctioning. He said he first noticed it last Saturday.

"Why didn't you say something?"

"I meant to this morning but…"

"If it isn't one damn thing, it's another," she huffed.

"What'd you bring me?"

"Thought you said you didn't want anything from Luci's."

"I changed my mind."

"What would you like?"

"One of her wheat germ waffles with blackberry syrup and whipped cream topping would-a been nice."

Mr. Friscote wore a faded plaid wool shirt under flannel-lined overalls. Jake wondered aloud if he owned a winter coat. T. Robert said yes, he did, but it was not cold enough to wear it. He could get by with his long johns on a day like this. He asked if they saw all the crows swarming Barney's trash container this morning. He snorted he had no use for the critters. "Few years back," explained Robert, "couple hundred of 'em started roostin' in a shelter belt on our place. We dynamited the sons-a-bitches. They ain't not come back since."

"That legal?" Donna probed.

"Don't know."

"D'you go by Robert or Bob?"

"Depends. I hear they're thinkin' a tearin' down the ol' hotel."

"They should've done that twenty years ago," Donna groused, as she grabbed a magazine with a Johnny Carson cover and sat down next to Jake.

"It's a landmark," noted Jake.

"It's a rat-infested, pigeon roost."

10

"I remember eatin' a meal there once," Robert said. "I think it might-a been our preacher's fiftieth weddin' anniversary they had there."

"You might tell Hazel we'll be offering pedicures starting March first."

"We gotta pair-a nail clippers at home," Robert mumbled.

"A pedicure treats the whole foot, not just the nails."

"You treat men, too?"

"Of course."

"Could a man like me get it for half price off?"

"Uhh...sure. Of course. Why not?" sputtered Donna.

Marti Baguelt pulled up in front of the shop to deliver six pairs of her husband's dress shoes to be shined. Allen would pick them up over the lunch hour if that was okay. T. Robert Friscote wheeled himself over to the front windows, his seed corn-logoed ball cap crooked a bit to one side. Like a wound-down manual alarm clock, he seemed content to watch the world go by. He exhibited no emotion whatsoever when his wife returned and pulled in next to Donna's Chevelle.

"Bet I forgot to give 'er the grocery money," he said, reaching into his pocket.

In her haste, Hazel Friscote flung open the driver's door, striking Donna's vehicle with such force it rocked perceptibly. Jake glanced at Donna. She folded up her magazine and mumbled "*Una vida chingada.*" Mrs. Friscote plucked the cash from her husband's hand and left without uttering a word.

Wally noiselessly shifted position, lying on his back with all four legs in the air. T. Robert waved to his wife as she backed out on to Main. Jake moved the push broom to the front of the shop, retied one of his shoelaces, and sat down beside Donna who abruptly stood up.

"Does Doyle even know Bob's here?"

'How should I know?' Jake shrugged.

She handed Jake her front door key. "Tell Henry I'll be at Charlene Stuber's. I can do her and her sister's hair today."

Jake watched Donna stoop and finger the metal on the passenger side door of her car, then impetuously back out onto Main, rev her engine, pop the clutch, and leave two, two-foot trails of Firestone rubber on the pavement. Bob Friscote probed for ear wax with a house key as he and Jake observed Percy Zepp, the town's pharmacist, buy a newspaper from the coin-operated bin at the front of the Beau Coup Cafe and hazard a long glance before going inside.

Déjà vu! From Jake's days as a paperboy when the bundles of newspapers were dropped curbside in front of the barbershop, Jake scanned the front page of the *Granfield Daily Dispatch.* By doing so, he might be the first in town to know what no one else knew.

Four chairs away sat Allen Baguelt's neatly stacked shoe boxes. Jake knew from experience that each contained a pair of dress shoes with shoe trees. He could make out two of the brand names, Bass Weejuns and Cole Haan. He recalled last fall when Allen brought in two pairs to be shined and Jimmy happened to be in the barber chair. After Jake finished putting a shine to them, Jimmy stuffed paper in the toes, mismatched the shoes in the boxes, and taped the lids shut on all four sides. Jake yawned, stretched his arms over his head and moved the shoe boxes out of sight before Jimmy spotted them. His reflected image in the backbar mirror across the room sparked a sudden awareness of his milieu. The scene reminded him of an American artist's work he studied during a History of Western Art II survey course at Ormestrong County Community College four years ago. He wondered if Sharon DeCritt, his uncle's wife, ever attempted to capture on canvas the ennui of a wintry day in a small Kansas prairie town. He helped himself to a Coke from the machine, placed the *LIFE* Donna was reading back in the magazine rack, and sauntered over to the front window next to T. Bob Friscote.

"Bet a haircut she don't bring you your waffle."

The effervescence of the carbonated drink tickled the lining of his throat. The clock on the Waltsburg State Bank read 9:25. The hollow hummingbird feeder seesawed with the wind.

Jake's memory revisited Edward Hopper textbook images as they languished inside the barber shop where it was warm, resigned to listen to the never-ending pick-pocks, score calls, and expletives emanating from the back room, waiting for Jimmy to call it quits.

CHAPTER 4
THE MAN
WITH THE IMPERFECT HALO

Monday – March 23

"I appreciate you doing this," Gene said.

"You know I charge double on my days off."

"For a man with a monk's tonsure? I should get half-off your regular rate all the time."

"Such a clever way of saying almost bald," chuckled Donna.

Doyle prepped Waltsburg's Police Chief Eugene Lasslo Lassiter for his monthly trim. Donna Pileaux sat across from them and browsed the latest Avon cosmetics catalog. Outside, a steady drizzle prevailed, soundless as catfish navigating downstream.

"Any plans for Easter?" Doyle asked.

"Two-a my officers want Easter weekend off."

"What happens if the Easter Bunny reports its eggs stolen?" Donna posed.

"You still believe in the Easter Bunny?"

"Don't you?"

"I assume you want the usual?"

"Yeah. The horseshoe Mohawk, as you call it."

"Gene, be positive," said Donna. "Think of it as an imperfect halo with hair on it."

"So, you going to Parise and Jimmy's wedding Saturday? They've been going together since fourth grade."

"Plannin' on it. They're a perfect couple if you ask me. Kind-a like you two. You set a date yet?"

"We're still in the dating phase," Doyle grinned.

"You know what they say about buyin' the cow if the milk's free."

"Trust me, Gene. You <u>do</u> <u>not</u> want to go there," said Donna, setting her magazine aside.

"This rain could save the wheat crop," Doyle remarked.

"They won't be burning pasture this week," Gene interjected.

"I love this time of year. I love the smell of the burning hills," Donna smiled.

"Air was ripe with it last week," said Doyle.

"What's Jake up to on a day like this?"

"He's sleeping in. Went fishing last night with John and Deke. Got home late."

"They catch anything? I heard the crappie was bitin'."

"Don't know. We were already in bed."

"Doyle, do you have an emery board handy?"

He plucked one from a drawer and handed it to Donna. She ambled in the direction of the shop's front windows, filing a nail. "D'you notice our redbud and Bradford pears in bloom?"

"My granddaughter calls the white ones snowball trees," said Gene. "What're you two up to today, besides gettin' wet?"

"Headed to Hutch to check on Donna's dad."

"How old's that ol' boy now?"

"He turned seventy-something last month," Donna said.

"Still at home?"

"Yup. Still doing yard work for a dozen or so customers."

"He retired from the railroad, didn't he?"

"Yes. But he'll work till he drops. Keeps his mind off Mama passing away last year."

"Railroad worked them Mexicans hard."

"Papa says it was like workin' on a chain gang without the chain, but he'd tell you the Indians had it worse."

#

The youngest of four brothers, Miguel Ramirez, Donna's father, walked off the family farm near Arandas, Jalisco, Mexico, in 1915 and purchased a one-way rail ticket to Laredo Nuevo. The State of Jalisco was in continuous civil unrest after the turn of the century, caught between one warring faction after another. Its government changed hands a dozen times. More than once, Miguel witnessed impromptu firing squads execute citizens in the streets for the crime of distributing opposition literature.

Miguel was eighteen years old, 5' 4" tall, and strong as a team of oxen. He walked across the iron truss bridge spanning the Rio Grande into Laredo, Texas, where he found work with the Southern Pacific Terminal Company as a laborer for twenty-eight cents an hour. A year later, he headed north seeking a better wage. Rumors spread that the Atchison, Topeka, and Santa Fe Railroad in Kansas City was paying thirty-one cents an hour for laborers. On the way, he found work in Hutchinson, Kansas, first with the AT&SF, then the Missouri-Pacific. He ventured no farther. Miguel made Hutch his home, roving among neighboring towns wherever work as a *traquero*, or common laborer, was available. If the railroad was not hiring, he worked twelve-hour shifts washing dishes and bussing tables at a Chinese café for ten cents an hour to make ends meet. His fair complexion earned him the nickname *güero*, white boy, and granted him uncontested access to regular seating in movie theaters, not the balconies reserved for Mexicans and Negroes. He married a local *senorita* and fathered eight children. Donna was the oldest of five girls. Miguel never went to school a day in his life, became a citizen, or left home without his straw fedora.

#

"You know we didn't officially grant Indians citizenship till 1924?" Doyle said.

"Bet that made a big difference in their lives overnight," snorted Donna.

"Greevy said you used the word retirement the other day," Doyle said to Gene.

"Gettin' closer every day."

"Set a date yet?"

"Nope. Not till I find somethin' else to keep busy."

"None of your girls want to go into law enforcement, I take it."

"Nope. The Lassiter legacy ends with me, I guess."

"D'you ever talk to any of your girls about it?" Donna asked.

"No. A man needs to be chief."

15

"Why would that be?"

"Common sense would tell you that."

"Whose? The conventional myth that only men can do this, and women that?"

"It's a man's job, if you ask me."

"Some of the most prominent hair stylists in the world are men."

"When's the last time one of your people showed up drunk and threatened you with a broken whiskey bottle?"

"How often does that happen?"

"A week ago Saturday soon enough?"

Donna conceded the point, but added, "I just think there are lots of jobs women can do as well as men, given half a chance. I mean, look at how well women performed man-jobs during the war. Not all of us grew up wanting to be housewives, secretaries, librarians, or school teachers."

"Can you face me toward the street?"

"Keeping an eye out for Waltsburg's ten most wanted?" Donna asked.

"Didn't Wild Bill Hickok say …never turn your back to a barber."

"D'you know he was marshal in Abilene for a short time? Got into a gunfight with some gambler and killed one-a his own deputies."

"Kind-a like the irony of your grandfather and his new bride," said Doyle.

#

A favorite of Kansas Law Enforcement Association old timers, the story was published statewide. Gene's great-grandfather, L. L. Lassiter, was Waltsburg's marshal in 1873. Pierce Village got its start as a trading post, do-it-yourself livery stable, and stagecoach stop on the Orme River. The stagecoach route south through Whitfield, Houray Springs, and Calvin was fraught with risk and prone to hold-ups. After one such event, Marshal Lassiter, a father, and recently remarried widower, received a tip that the bandits were holed up at the head of Minnie's Creek. He and an eight-man posse surrounded the site at sun-up the next day. A prolonged gun battle ensued, and two outlaws were wounded, one mortally. Three others escaped on horseback, riding south directly toward Marshal Lassiter and his brother-in-law, Will Copeland. As the story goes, Will rode head-on toward the fleeing bandits. In an exchange of gunfire,

Will's horse was killed, but his spirited charge split up the three outlaws. Marshal Lassiter crouched low in the tall prairie grass as one of the riders passed within ten paces of him at a full gallop. He rose, aimed his Sharps rifle, and fired once. The rider flinched, straightened, and before the marshal could fire a second shot, slumped to one side and tumbled to the ground. Minutes later, when the marshal and Will cautiously approached the fallen rider and removed the mask, they gaped at the motionless figure lying in a dark stain of blood. Roxanne (Roxie) Copeland Lassiter, the marshal's new bride from Whitfield, stared back, her wound fatal.

A day later, the wounded outlaw from the skirmish at Minnie's Creek identified the two who got away as the notorious Xidis brothers from Nevada, Missouri. Both rode with Quantrill and Bloody Bill Anderson's gangs before the start of the Civil War and had a price on their heads. Marshall Lassiter and newly deputized Will Copeland rode south. They expected to catch up with the brothers in Whitfield, a town with a history of abetting lawbreakers. The lawmen missed them there but were able to pick up their trail leading farther south and west. They caught up with Dimitris, the younger Xidis brother, in a brothel in Delano Village. As Delano had no law enforcement, the lawmen jailed him across the river in Wichita. An entertainment district, Delano Village was a cluster of notorious saloons, gambling dens and brothels. It catered to untold numbers of *vaqueros* fresh off Chisholm Trail cattle drives from Texas.

When Marko Xidis learned of Dimitris's fate, he bribed a dance hall girl to lure Lassiter and Copeland to his hideout. Marko bushwhacked the two lawmen behind the same brothel where his younger brother had been apprehended. Marshal Lassiter, shot twice in the back, died straight away. Will Copeland, wounded in the leg and left ear, reached cover and returned fire. He hit Marko in the throat and groin. Will survived his wounds; Marko did not. Will hung around Wichita long enough to collect the one-thousand-dollar reward money and return to Delano on Sunday afternoon to watch the Running of the Doves. Upon his return to Pierce Village, Will became town marshal. Six years later, at the age of twenty-six, Eugene's grandfather and L. L. Lassiter's only son Leopold was appointed marshal. Will was eager to retire and reopen his blacksmithing business.

#

"Any evil lurking about we need to be aware of?" Donna asked.

"Just your neighbor up the street."

"Icky?" Doyle guessed. "Now what's he done?"

"I heard about Mrs. Dillker's wedding ring," Donna said.

"Last Saturday, I got a call from Buck Swanson's wife sayin' she was positive her husband's gold watch fob was on one-a his overalls. People've lost all kinds-a jewelry, coins, keepsakes, what-have-you. They stick something in one-a their pockets, forget it's there, take their laundry to Icky's, and think they might-a lost whatever it was in one-a his washers or dryers. Who knows? Maybe they did. Maybe they didn't. But one thing's for sure, Icky wouldn't own up to it. He's a finders-keepers man if there ever was one."

"He's such a jerk," she said.

"I heard he's in charge of the club's golf tournament this year," said Gene. "And he'll probably run for City Council again this year, too."

"How many votes did he get last time?" Doyle queried.

"I heard you could stuff a flute with the ballots he got and still play all the notes."

"Overall, it's been pretty quiet around here, hasn't it?" Doyle remarked.

"Thank you very much."

"It hasn't always been that way," Donna said.

"Nope. Since Woodrow Wilson, we've had four unsolved murders and twice that many go missin', that we know of. Like John Griever's father."

"John rarely mentions it," said Doyle.

"He was just a kid, down with the chickenpox when his ol' man disappeared. It happened 'fore my time," Gene said. "First case I really got wound up in was Robert Muldoon. Dad and I worked our asses off on that one and come up empty. It was a day like this, spittin' rain, when we discovered the body in his temple on the third floor of the house. He'd been dead for at least two days, maybe three. Double ten-gauge shotgun blast in the back from about three paces. Blew his whole chest cavity out. He was prob'ly dead 'fore he hit the floor."

"Good riddance, from what I've heard," said Donna.

"Only ten-gauge we knew of at the time was mounted above the fireplace in the parlor of the Bruno mansion. We figured at least twenty people around here had motive enough to wanna see 'im dead. I don't think anyone cared whether we caught the shooter or not. Most people thought whoever done it did the town a big favor."

"He fancied himself an evangelist, didn't he?" questioned Donna.

"He was one strange goose," said Gene. "My dad frequently confronted him and his followers at the train depot handing out religious pamphlets. Some say he murdered his first wife and child before he moved back here in '44. The official report said they drowned, but the circumstances was suspicious."

"Hanky's older sister, Bernadette, wasn't it?" said Doyle.

"We did solve one mystery though. Winter of 1945 someone broke into the Bruno mansion and stole seven paintings, part-a the collection ol' Bruno left behind. We found four of 'em on the third floor of the Doona Falls house. We figured Robert must-a been sellin' 'em off on the sly to bankroll his lifestyle since the Muldoons' will put everything in a trust and he had to live off what Bruner called a stipend."

"You ready for a look in the mirror?" Doyle asked.

#

Doyle adjusted the windshield wiper speed as they crossed the AT&SF tracks and headed to Hutchinson. Soon, the rhythmic scrape of the wipers, drone of the engine, and jostle of the highway caused Donna's eyelids to droop.

Doyle asked, "What're we doing for Jake's birthday? Anything?"

"Falls on Easter Sunday this year, doesn't it? If Jake had a girlfriend, we could all go out to the country club for prime rib."

"Good thought, but that only gives us five days to find him one."

Donna yawned, "Is the Easter Bunny a girl?"

CHAPTER 5
TILT!

Easter Sunday – March 29

After the lunch hour, the Beau Coup Café was the ideal place to celebrate a birthday. Jake informally invited about a dozen people. Though not invited, Darcy Cage showed up early bearing a small, wrapped gift, saying she could not stay long, and helped herself to a slice of the twenty-four-inch oatmeal cookie Luci baked for the occasion. Eric Carver turned up, although he and Jake chatted briefly outside the café as Rocky, Eric's dog, was not allowed inside. Eric begged off Jake's offer to join the others, saying he was headed back to the laundromat for another round of pinball. Darcy joined them on the sidewalk. She gravitated to Eric's side, looping her arm through his, and offered him what was left of her cookie. Eric roughly pulled away. Darcy stomped off. Halfway across the boulevard she turned and shouted, "I hate you, Eric Carver!"

Backing away, Jake bought a newspaper from the rack at the curb and scanned the headlines: PARIS PEACE TALKS [Nixon Threatens to Resume Bombing of the North]; MY LAI MASSACRE? [Letter from Veteran Sparks Investigation]; BUMPER WHEAT AND CORN CROPS FORECAST [Ormestrong County Farmers Optimistic]; SUNSET DRIVE-IN TO BE SOLD [Des Moines Developer Reveals Plans]; BOAT CAPSIZES, GIRL DROWNS [Near dam at state lake. Eyewitness accounts.]

"I'll be at Icky's," Eric said and meandered off.

John Griever and Nonny pulled up. "Feel any older?" Nonny asked.

"All I know is when I crawled in bed last night, I was a year younger."

20

Jake held the door open and they filed inside, along with another scatter of Bradford pear flower petals jitterbugging like craps dice.

"What was that all about?" Donna asked.

"What?" said Jake, setting the newspaper on the table.

"Darcy and Eric."

"Beats me."

"I need to talk Darcy into doing something with her hair. The only style she knows is that dorky Sixties flip."

"Aren't you going to open it?" asked Doyle, referring to Darcy's gift.

"Not now," said Jake, helping himself to a slice of birthday cookie.

"Where did Parise and Jimmy go on their honeymoon?" Donna asked of the group.

"Tablerock Lake. Right?" said Dan, looking to his wife.

Valoise nodded. "Paul and Nadine were there a couple years ago with some friends."

"Lovely wedding," said Donna.

"Indeed, it was," agreed Nonny.

Donna leaned toward Jake and whispered, "You looked like a movie star in that tux."

Luci busied herself making sure everyone had something to drink. Francisco and Diego walked in followed by Conger and Merry Belle. Minutes later, Kirk Michaels and his four-year old niece joined the group. "Sorry I'm late," said Kirk. "Babysitting this afternoon."

Doyle presented Henry's gift, a carpenter's belt, along with Henry's regrets; he was headed to Moundridge to spend time with his mother at the nursing home. Conger handed Jake a birthday card and asked if the Knaakt twins were invited. Jake ignored him. Within thirty minutes, the party broke up. Jake was glad no one thought to sing Happy Birthday and there was enough cookie left over to last him another day or two and nibbles for Wally. On his way out the door, Jake invited Kirk to play pinball with Eric and him at Loads of Fun, like old times when the three and Jimmy played for bragging rights. Kirk declined. He promised to take his niece to the Lions Club Easter egg hunt at three.

Jake stopped by the barber shop to grab a roll of quarters on his way to Loads of Fun. It was heartening to Jake to witness signs of a pre-military Eric Carver. He smiled to himself at Eric's "Hi-Ho, Silver!" every time he hit the double multiplier target, and "Flat Tire!" at Jake's every screw-up. Eric commented he had a rocky relationship with his dog. Jake groaned at the old joke. Together they laughed and reminisced over Knaakt twin's antics at Camp TaWaKoNi and the Sunset Drive-In, late night spin-tumbling in one of Icky's commercial dryers with Jimmy and Kirk, and the who could belch the loudest contests at Perky's Burger Stand.

As they took turns on the vintage single-player machine, Jake became aware of an Eric Carver he did not know. Scarcely a sentence crossed Eric's lips without the word fuck or some variation. He called Jake Buddy, in place of the more familiar Jay-cob, and openly offered him a joint. When Francisco and Diego showed up to do their laundry, Cisco lamented that Natalie, his sister, announced she was not his wife; it was high time he learned to launder his own clothes. Eric commented, if it were him, he would tell the bitch to move out.

Cisco challenged, "You say my sister's a bitch?"

"Gimme me a break," Eric said, not distracted from his game.

Cisco seized a handful of Eric's tattered Army field jacket. "Who's the bitch?!"

Eric jerked loose from the grip and shoved Cisco backward. "You just fucked up my game, Pancho!"

Cisco took a step toward Eric, fists clenched, "That ain't all I'm gonna fuck up."

Jake interceded, jumping between them, arm extended, the flat of his hand on Cisco's chest. "He didn't mean anything by it."

Game aborted, Eric kicked the machine and muttered, "Fuck this shit," abruptly wheeled around, and stalked out with Rocky at his heel. Cisco called after him in Spanish.

"You owe me a fuckin' quarter!" Eric yelled back over his shoulder, flying out the door and waving his middle finger.

"Come and get it, bitch!"

"Hey!" said Jake, "let 'im be. Okay?"

"He still think he *El Chingon*," said Cisco. "He need to shower, shave and get a haircut," which Diego emphatically seconded. "Sorry, *amigo*. He piss me off some."

"We're better off just lettin' him be."

"That ain't the Eric Carver I watch play football," Cisco imparted. "He somebody else."

"How come he called you Pancho?"

"He call us all Pancho," Cisco fumed, then rattled off something in Spanish.

"*Ay!* He possessed by demons," Diego added.

Jake noticed Rocky's leash and a Zap Comix book on the seat of a folding chair. "Got two free games. They're yours if you want 'em. I'm out-a here."

"*Feliz cumpleaños, amigo*," said Cisco, with a quick smile.

"*Gracias* for the cookie," Diego said.

"*De nada*. Next year Donna said she and Luci would make *flan* for everyone."

"Natalie makes great *flan*," said Cisco. "How come you don't ask her out and show her a good time?"

"Been dating her pin-up for a year already."

"C'mon, Jake. She might say yes for you."

"Ha! I'm too old to die young."

CHAPTER 6
KENTUCKY PIE

Sunday – April 4

Lucille Bertolini stood at the window. Her first out-of-town booking, a chartered tour bus carrying twenty-four passengers arrived shortly after 2 p.m. Watching them disembark, she felt the hot flush of embarrassment at a glaring flaw in her meal plan: her wholly unintentional, inappropriate choice of dessert.

The seniors group, sixty-five-and-overs from the True Gospel Calvary Baptist Church, were on the home stretch of a guided outing. They came armed with canes, prescription meds, craven bladders, bifocals, amens, I told you sos, and cholesterol counts higher than a cat's back. Most counted their blessings on calloused hands, ran on about their grandchildren, and held close their world views. Their weeklong, history-based itinerary traversed five states.

While the diners found their places, Luci called her staff together in the kitchen and advised them in a low voice that today's dessert, should anyone ask, was Kentucky Pie. From small dinner salad served through tables bussed, she experienced an unsettling range of emotions, worry to fret to dread and back. She later confided to her husband, Anthony, that her anxiety was, metaphorically speaking, not unlike Daniel being cast into the lion's den. Tony responded that irony always led to reality, did it not? Today's *faux pas* had, in fact, produced a mutually beneficial result: She did not get eaten, but the Jefferson Davis Pie did, ravenously.

Recruited a week in advance, Jake helped serve the meal, kept water, iced tea glasses, and coffee cups filled, and bussed tables afterward. Five bucks and free Coca Cola for less than two hours work he considered

24

good wages. Jake stashed his bow tie and server's apron in the utility room and donned his Baltimore Orioles ball cap. The sporadic clatter of pots, pans, and dinnerware echoed across the dining area. Only one traveler remained in a booth with a Main Street view, a toothpick jutting out one side of his mouth, a pair of Foster Grants consigned to his forehead. The man asked Jake if he could talk him out of one more caffeine jolt. Jake obliged, returned the coffee pot to the service window, and refilled his Coke cup. As he sauntered toward the front door on his way out, the man motioned him over and asked how long he had been working at the café.

"I don't work here. Just filling in this afternoon."

"Bes' meal we had the whole trip," the man said with a sniffle. "Service was good, too."

"Thanks. I'll tell Luci."

"She the owner?" he said, sipping at his hot coffee. "Dat Kentucky Pie-a hers' rich. Kind-a taste to me like pee-can pie without the pee-cans. Whip cream topping had a little whiskey flavor to it. Umm-mm."

"I like her big oatmeal cookies best."

"Son, don't think I got room for 'nother bite," the man said. "Sorry 'bout Misses Dunbar," he continued, snuffling, and wiping his nose with a paper napkin. "The big lady in the purple dress. Dat be her third episode this trip. To my way-a thinkin', she gobbles up too many-a doze Carter's Little Liver Pills. Eats 'em like candy."

Gene Lassiter and Davis Spellmeier walked in.

"Hi. I'm Eugene Lassiter," Gene said, fronting the man. "You related to these folks walkin' around town?"

"I'm their driver. Somethin' wrong, officer?"

"No. Just gettin' calls about people no one knows walkin' up n' down Main Street."

"You heard-a Flopsy, Mopsy and Pete Cottontail? We the Topsy-Turvy Don't Look So Pale Folks," the driver grinned.

"Out-a where?" Gene asked.

"We Ar-kin-saw sharecroppers here for the cotton pickin' convention," the man said without skipping a beat, exaggerating his accent. "We hear-day also givin' out free wattamelon." Gene, taken aback, was momentarily at a loss for words. He looked the man square in the eye, read the crooked smile, and then laughed aloud. "Where at? I love watermelon. I take it you're just passing through?"

"Dat's the plan."

"Sorry to bother you."

"You ain't botherin' nobody. They juss out walkin' off some-a 'diss dee-licious lunch." The man glanced at his watch, "We be gettin' on down the road here in fifteen, twenny minutes."

"No need to rush off," said Gene. "We're just responding to the calls about all the strangers in town."

"Fine-a place as any to grab a bite," said the man, sniffling again. "We might come back one-a deeze days."

"You are welcome any time. Luci does know how to rustle up somethin' good to eat."

"A-men to that."

"You should try her green eggs and ham next time," quipped Jake.

The man and Gene genially shook hands. Gene and Officer Spellmeier left.

"Have a seat, young man."

"Well, I..."

"Tell me 'bout doze green eggs and ham."

Jake sat. He glanced out the window and saw an older gentleman across the street, hands folded atop his cane, sitting on the pew in front of Doyle's shop. Five women from the tour group were peering in Ginny's Fashions display windows. Four more strolling by nodded and smiled at the man with the toothpick.

"What part-a Ar-kin-saw you from?" Jake jibed.

"We ain't. Hee-hee. Ya see ...everywhere we go, people wanna-a know what we be doin' in their place. Where we be from. Some I tell Mississippi. Lookin' for a mo' righteous place to live since the Klan burned down our house-a worship. Others, I tell we out-a work Freedom Riders from Alabama lookin' for a place to practice marchin'."

"Where you headed next?"

"Home."

According to Mr. Louis Reynard Jarbois, the first stop of the tour was Lawrence, Kansas, to see the Robert Miller home and lunch at the Castle Tea Room. Next, Nebraska City, Nebraska, to see the John Brown Cave and Mayhew Cabin, relics of the abolitionist-backed Underground Railroad. A highlight of the journey included an evening at the theater in Omaha for a road production of *A Raisin in the Sun*. Headed west, they lunched at Uncle Buck's Lodge in Brewster, Nebraska (Population: 54) and drove through the Sand Hills along Hwy 2 to tour Fort Robinson, Nebraska, once home to a cavalry regiment of Buffalo Soldiers. A drive across the Pine Ridge Reservation and through the Badlands took them to Wall Drug in Wall, South Dakota, and on to Mount Rushmore "to pay our respects to Mista Lincoln." They then drove to Crook County, Wyoming, to see Devil's Tower. On the way home they stopped in Nicademus, Kansas, and the Garden of Eden in Lucas.

"Danged if I know why they scheduled us a stop in Nicko-deemus," the man said. "Ain't nothin' left-a dat place. Hardly nothin' to look at."

"Never heard of it," said Jake.

"The I-tinerary they give us say…" the man pulled a tri-folded sheet of paper from inside his jacket pocket. "…it be the only survivin' settlement wes' of the Mississippi River established by former slaves durin' the Re-construction period after the Civil War."

"Really?"

"Dat's what it say. And I tell 'em next time they wanna go someplace north-a here, day better off doin' it in summer. Day got snow on the ground in places up where we pay visit to. It still big coat weather and the wind blow too much like it do here. Dat's where deeze sniffles come from."

The telephone rang six times before Luci hustled out to answer. She dried her hands on her apron, wrote something down, and disappeared back to the kitchen.

"You like driving a bus?" Jake asked.

"Beats drivin' a towmotor."

"A what?"

"Forklift. Worked for The Coleman Company for twenny-two years. Worked my way up to operatin' one a doze my last years there."

"You like this better?"

"I like seein' God's country."

"I'm Jake, by the way," he said, offering his hand.

"Friends call me Ray. At your service," he said, shifting the toothpick to the other side of his mouth. "When you not bussin' tables what you do?"

"Shine shoes. Sweep floors. Wash windows. Go fishing once in a while."

"Where you fish at 'round here?"

"State lake. You fish?"

"Use to with my daddy, weekends. I 'member the bess spot bein' Lewis Street Bridge. Right where Lawrence Stadium at."

"In Wichita?"

"Yessir. Channel cat alley. Over the Ar-kansas River."

"Ever go to games at Lawrence Stadium?"

"Naw. But me and a fren' climb up top a box car one afternoon. One-a doze dat gets itself parked just ova the right field fence to see Satchel Paige pitch."

"When was that?!"

"Let's see…," he started, pausing to grab more napkins from the table dispenser and wipe his nose. "…dat might-a been summer-a nineteen…thirty…nineteen and thirty-five. Prob'ly 'fore you was born, young man. Basketball is my like. Few years back, we got us tickets to see Dave the Rave do his thing."

"Stallworth?"

"He. Was. The Man."

"Out-a Wichita State, right?"

"Ever been to The Roundhouse?"

"No. Stallworth plays for the Knicks now, right?"

"He do. Din along come the Armstrong kid. Change his name to Jabali when he make pro. He Rookie-a the Year in the ABA lass year. He only six-foot-two but some say he ken touch his fo'head to the rim if 'e of a mind to."

"That would be worth the price of a ticket," said Jake.

"Can't see all dat good from where we sittin' 'cause we doan be gettin' the bess seats in the house. We sits way up top where what some call nigga heaven. But, like we figure, if we's in heaven …where the rest of 'em at?"

Jake noticed Natalie Martinez enter and disappear into the kitchen. Ray ran on about his love of the game, but Jake was no longer paying close attention. Momentarily, Natalie reappeared carrying a plate covered in foil. Jake waved hello. She detoured over to their table.

"Kind-a late for lunch, isn't it?" said Jake.

"It's not for me. Anything for Allen, you know?" she said in a quiet voice, bending forward, placing her hand lightly on Jake's forearm, revealing a munificent cleavage. "Sorry I missed your birthday party."

"Allen's working today? It's Sunday."

"No. I am. Spiffing up the offices, as usual," she responded.

"What's Allen doing?"

"Someone's gotta let me in. Allen won't trust me with a key. Had to wait till they got back from Kansas City. Who's your friend?"

Jake introduced Ray. Natalie ever so lightly clasped Ray's hand.

"Nice to meet you," she said. "Oo!" she proclaimed, inspecting his fingers, "we need to make you an appointment to get those nails worked on. I better get back before this goes cold."

As they watched her leave, Ray muttered, "Damn! Thass got to be jelly 'cause jam doan wiggle like dat."

Ray grinned and sipped noiselessly at his coffee. He asked Jake what was being torn down on Main Street just the north of the tracks. Jake told what he knew about the Atlantic Hotel; it had once been the finest, most majestic accommodation in a five-county area. An arson fire gutted the top two floors and five died: two teenage girls and three businessmen from Chicago. A wealthy rancher by the name of Bearnard Muldoon bought the property a year or so later but plans to renovate and refurbish were placed on hold when the war started. In the late 40's, the Muldoon estate sold the property to a Kansas City restaurant consortium that stripped away all its salvageable chattels, but otherwise did nothing, allowing it to further deteriorate.

Ray and Jake gazed out the window. Their conversation interrupted; attention diverted by rumble and sensation. An endless stream of covered deuce-and-a-halfs, transport trailers hauling APC's, armored cars, Jeep M-37 cargo trucks, and Dodge half-ton ambulances passed by.

"You gotta Army base here?" Ray asked, above the diesel din of the olive drab pageant.

"Prob'ly on their way to Fort Riley."

"Got two cousins in the Army. One be over dare in V'etnam. Not sure where t'other is right diss minute."

"War's on, all right," Jake commented, rising from the table. "Want-a watch outside?"

Ray accompanied Jake outside, pausing briefly to restock his toothpick supply from the dispenser next to Luci's cash register. This was the first military convoy Jake ever saw pass through Waltsburg. Onlookers spontaneously gathered up and down Main as if watching a parade. Some waved to the soldiers, a few waved back. Ray said he was glad they were not going his way. With that, it was time for him to herd the folks back onto the bus and head home.

In parting, he told Jake he might be back one day for some of those green eggs and ham.

"And a manicure, right?"

"Now you talkin', son."

"How'd it go?" Doyle asked, beholding the world from the first barber chair.

"Bus driver saw Satchel Paige pitch a game in Wichita in 1935."

"No kidding? So, that's where they're from? D'you see that ol' gent sitting out front on the bench? I asked him if he wanted to come inside and sit in a friendlier chair. He said, "No, not this time." Claimed that sitting on that pew he considered make-up time for not getting his halo adjusted of late. Said them being on the road, he hadn't been to church the last couple Sundays."

Deke Stuber walked in and apologized for running late, explaining he had to wait for Anthony to finish feeding lunch to that bus load-a Samboes. Minutes later, the silver and blue charter parked parallel in front of the Beau Coup Café. Jake watched the sightseers board. The bus's emergency flashers blinked off as it pulled away.

Ray had a nose for basketball and a grand sense of humor, Jake thought. He wondered what Ray thought of Lew Alcindor, Pistol Pete Maravich, and Jo Jo White. He wished he had asked him who his favorite comedian was. Wilson, Gregory, Cosby, Pryor, Foxx? He guessed Ray liked them all. What was not to like?

CHAPTER 7
A NIGHT TO REMEMBER

Saturday – April 18

Four years earlier, the school district consolidated several Ormestrong County community high schools into Unity High and established its identity as the Warriors. Same as the first year after the merger, an oil and water mindset lingered. The hundred or so gathered for the senior prom segregated themselves by former district, by upbringing, and gender. Though the familiar faces were amicable toward one another; reserved waves, nods, and smiles freely exchanged, the overall imprint was insular. Dress ranged from rented tuxedos to bib overalls, formal satin gowns and spike heels to homemade cotton dresses complete with sashes and bows. An area garage rock band, Cal and the Callithumpers, performed for the Class of 1970. Crepe paper streamers, glitter, and helium balloon clusters festooned the hospitality room in Granfield's new Shade Tree Inn. The parquet dance floor filled only when the lights dimmed for a slow dance. When the band took a break, many attendees headed to the parking lot where booze was stashed in farm trucks and family sedans.

Jake and Conger were five years older than most prom-goers. Natalie invited Conger two months in advance. Jake was Darcy's eleventh-hour choice. The week before the event, Eric Carver reneged on his promise to escort her. When Jake and Conger arrived at Natalie's house, it was obvious the girls had spent some very long-drawn-out minutes in wardrobe and make-up. Jake hardly recognized Darcy Caitlynn Cage. The Cherries in the Snow lipstick, the bling, the coiffed hair, and spaghetti-strapped dress accentuating her bare, white shoulders created a nearly unrecognizable image. She asked why he had not worn the Jade East cologne she gave him for his birthday. He opted not to tell Darcy of his aversion to the scent; the Knaakt twins routinely used Jade East in the high school gym's locker room to treat their athlete's foot fungus.

The drive to Granfield in the front seat of Conger's Baguelt Custom Homes pickup was snug. The buffet style dinner, yearbook signing, and dance began at six p.m. By 9:45, many exchanged their prom apparel for casual attire to attend the post-prom bowling party at Granfield's Bowl-O-Rama under watchful chaperones' eyes. Conger dropped Jake and Darcy off at Jake's car in front of the barber shop. Darcy Cage's curfew was midnight; it was ten minutes till. Darcy directed Jake to park behind her father's church. When the initial riffs of Creedence Clearwater Revival's *Lookin' Out My Back Door* aired on the car's radio, Darcy rolled up her window, cranked up the volume and, in sync with her air guitar antics, sang along. At song's end she said, "Shut the engine off. You'll save gas," Jake turned the key. Instantly, it was dark enough for potatoes to sprout eyes.

"Why didn't <u>you</u> drive tonight?" Darcy asked. "It would-a been a lot more comfortable."

"I need new tires. Didn't want-a chance a flat."

"How come you didn't dance with me more tonight?"

"I'm not much of a dancer."

"I could teach you," she said, tucking one leg up on the bench seat, her back against the passenger door. "There's the big spring street dance at the community college next month that's always fun. Would you take me?"

"Maybe."

"How come you don't go out on dates more often?"

"I stay pretty busy working."

"There's more to life than work."

"I know, but…"

"Call me. I'll go out with you. Know who you look like? Little Joe Cartwright."

"From *Bonanza*?"

"Yeah. I think you look a lot like him.

Darcy's upper and lower body types were something of a mismatch. She had piano legs and a generous, shapely rear end. From her twenty-inch waist up, however, she was a well-proportioned female with an attractive face, piercing hazel eyes, and a clear complexion. It was as if Incredible Hulk and Barbie doll halves were mixed up at a Mattel factory and shipped to a small town in Kansas where they grew into one adult form.

"It's almost midnight," Jake reminded.

"Aren't you going to kiss me or try and feel me up or nothin'?" Darcy leaned forward and raised her KU sweatshirt with the colorful red, blue, and yellow Jayhawk up to her neckline. "See. I'm not wearing a bra." She scooted next to him, softly kissed his cheek, his ear and neck, and guided his left hand to one of her bare breasts. Her right hand caressed his upper thigh, then his crotch. Her tongue painstakingly explored the inside of his mouth. She began to make soft, guttural noises. His hands instinctively became quick learners. "Oo. Be gentle," she said. "I know how strong you are." Possessed by desire, any thoughts belying his captivation digressed *en route.* "This isn't your first time, is it?" she queried. As Darcy lightly nibbled on his ear she whispered, "Want me to suck you?"

Conger caught himself staring at the spiraling coil of the shop's barber pole. The only other distractions on Main Street were the Beau Coup's wind chimes jingling, the time and temperature readings on the Waltsburg State Bank, and the blinking red light on the water tower. Technically, he and Natalie were negotiating, not arguing.

"Please," Natalie begged. "I brought my swimsuit."

"You wouldn't need it," Conger responded.

"But I'm modest."

"Natalie, I worked from seven this morning till after one this afternoon at the motel site.

When I got home, Mom had a list of spring cleaning chores for me to do. I'm dead-ass tired."

"It's a perfect evening. Why waste it? You can relax in the pool, can't you?"

"I'd prob'ly fall asleep and drown."

"C'mon. I've never been there."

"Not tonight."

"We could play Marco Polo."

"Pool's not that big. It would hardly be a contest." Natalie flashed an impish ear to ear grin. "Come out tomorrow. You can have it all to yourself."

"It is tomorrow."

Conger drove up Main Street and turned the corner onto Abasto Street where Natalie, Diego and her brother Francisco lived in a small, two-bedroom rental adjacent to the long-dormant AT&SF tracks. He pulled into the drive and shut off the engine.

"It's not fair," Natalie managed, brushing the hair from her forehead.

"What isn't?"

"There's not a lot to choose from in this part of the world."

"Regarding...?"

"There isn't a boy in our senior class I would go out with. You're not like them."

"I take that as a compliment." After an awkward pause, Conger sighed, "Natalie, I need to get going."

"I don't have a curfew." She let out a sigh. "Would you take me to the ranch for a dip in the pool if I showed you these?" she said, twisting in his direction, her hands cupped under her breasts.

"No. But you can show me anyway, if you like."

She grinned furtively, "On one condition."

"I'm not taking you out there tonight."

"You show me yours," she said, unbuttoning her blouse.

"Mine aren't anywhere near as big as yours."

"Silly, you know what I mean."

In no time at all, hesitancy shifted into an unspoken, unconditional why not? He watched as she shed her blouse, reach both hands behind her back, and disentangle her arms from the straps of her bra, holding the unsecured undergarment in place with one hand. "Ready?" she said. She watched his face as she lowered the garment. She had his full attention. He casually reached up and turned on the dome light. He leaned back in the seat and watched as she reached both hands behind her back to unfasten her brassiere.

Natalie shed her blouse and disentangled her arms from the straps of her bra. She turned to face him, her back against the door, still holding the unsecured undergarment in place with one hand. "Ready?" she said. Natalie watched his face as she lowered the garment and allowed it to fall into her lap. She had his full attention. He casually reached up and turned on the dome light.

"God damn you!" she shrieked, slumping lower in the seat, reflexively folding her arms across her chest. "Turn it out!"

"Couldn't see much in the dark," he said, with a big grin.

"Don't be a jerk."

"It's dark out here." In deference, he flipped off the light. He shifted position and discreetly adjusted the denim fabric in his crotch to accommodate the stir of his manhood.

"It's hot in here," she said.

Conger rolled down his window; Natalie did likewise and slipped out of her Keds.

"Your turn."

Conger worked his jeans and briefs half-way down his thighs. Natalie reached up and turned on the dome light.

"Oh, my God!" she exclaimed in her loudest whisper. "May I?" she said, her hand already on his upper thigh. Natalie scooted closer, hovered, and groped. Conger flipped off the light and swiveled toward her to satisfy his own curiosity.

"Mmm...go easy," she whispered, "They're tender."

The genteel combat of touch drove both to shift position to heighten the pleasure. The two torchbearers of self-gratification explored without speaking, primordial as two snakes sloughing their skins on a dark stage. Natalie presumed she could swing her leg around, front him, and nestle in his lap to take him inside her. She rose, nursed his face, and maneuvered her right leg under the steering wheel. Conger intercepted her leg halfway. She pulled back.

"You don't want-a do it with me?" she said.

"Not tonight," he responded.

"Why? It's safe."

"No such thing as safe."

"Beg your pardon. It is." She leaned forward and lightly kissed his mouth. "I missed my period the last two months."

"Mmm ...who's the lucky guy?"

"Can't say yet."

"Won't say, you mean?"

"Either way, both ways, what's it matter?" Natalie said, continuing to lightly brush against Conger's cheek and gently fondle his manhood that rigidly pointed in the general direction of the dome light. "Pretty please?" she continued. Her directness, her glib commentaries combined the best of dumbfound and tantalize. Seasoned beyond her seventeen years, he mused. The narcotic warmth of her shape, a nubile frontier impossibly uneven, and a summoning tone, all resonated from an eponymous *Lorelei* siren.

"Not tonight," he repeated.

"I want your juice," she prodded.

This attractive, ready, willing, and able young woman knew which buttons to press.

"You can still have it," he said.

She looked him directly in his good eye. After several moments of reflection, she said,

"Okay. But I have conditions."

"Which are...?"

"You invite me out for a soak in the pool some night soon."

"And..."

"You don't tell nobody about tonight. About us."

"Okay by me, but that's a two-way street."

"Don't worry."

"What else?" he said.

"Pinky promise? I know how you guys like to brag."

#

Conger spotted Jake's car parked by the barn as he circled the English turnabout. Blanco came running from the direction of the pool. He quietly slipped into the house and stripped naked except for his work boots. He slung his favorite Hawaiian bath towel over his shoulder and stepped out into the star-packed black sky of a new morning. Jake was already in the pool. Only the sustained splash of the Falls broke the silence.

"Jake?"

"I'm here."

Conger kicked off his boots and submerged.

"Hope you don't mind me being here. How'd it go with Natalie?"

"Remarkable," Conger answered.

Jake abruptly climbed out. "Be right back," he said.

"Mother Nature call?

"Yup!"

"Front door of the house is open."

"Too late," Jake hollered back, disappearing into the dark, "I already got a turtlehead."

The two basked in the warm water under a crescent moon. Conger's comment that the *Playboy* pin-up on the back of the barbershop's bathroom door did not do Natalie justice was as tell-tale as either of them ventured on the evening's classified events. The courses of circumstance, the champagne moments, archived as souvenirs.

CHAPTER 8
LIKE A NEW DIME
IN A GOAT'S ASSHOLE

Saturday – May 23

Bill Stimka declared "Will Rogers never met Leland Skalicky." Others designated Allen Baguelt an also-ran. Donna Pileaux's pet theory: Allen's mother showered entirely too much praise on him during potty training. While Leland maintained an active, shameless presence within the community, Allen was wholly detached.

Allen, his wife Marti, and two children, Kristie and Jonathan, lived across the river in Waltsburg Heights, a Baguelt Custom Homes upscale residential development. He was responsible for office management, supplier relations, accounts payable, payroll and book-keeping for the firm. Truth be known, once both children were in school, Marti did the company's books from home. Allen's Ivy League attire, aloofness, and 'no dirt under these fingernails' attitude set him apart from the others in this rural community. "You know Allen" was a common aphorism heard about town. "Good morning, Allen" was most often met with a startled "Oh. Hi." Chit-chat was not his *forte*. According to his brother Jimmy, Allen simply could not resist himself.

On this spring Saturday, Allen's only transportation to John Griever's place was his most recent indulgence, a new, custom-ordered white-on-white Monte Carlo SS 454. The odometer read less than two hundred miles. He had no intention of driving it much, especially on dirt roads, until after the 4th of July car show, but circumstances left him no choice. Marti drove Allen's company pickup that morning to take Kristie to Camp Wood, a rustic YMCA youth camp tucked away in the sylvan hills west of Elmdale. Her Ford Torino sat idle inside Stuber's Garage waiting for a part. At the camp, she ran into a sorority sister from college she had not seen in ages. They stopped at Bummies in Elmdale for a ham sandwich and chocolate malt and lost track of time catching up on recent histories. He could think of no one he might ask for a favor, and he was running late.

John Griever liked his world as it was and did not clean house prior to a visit from Waltsburg's resident neatnik. If hell was a prepared place for unprepared souls as Reverend Cage espoused, then one ought to seriously consider bracing oneself for a variant of Kingdom Come, an Allen Baguelt visit. By Griever's watch, he should have arrived thirty minutes ago. John had things to do. Second-guessing Allen was not one of them. Jake promised to show up before noon. They planned to search for more bones belonging to the unknown person discovered earlier in the year. Outside his singlewide abode, John fired up two fifty-five-gallon-drum smokers he had customized for his venerated lake fish, game birds, and venison. As he watched the pre-soaked mesquite wood chips smolder, a variable breeze lifted the whitish smoke in all directions. Satisfied everything was in order, John headed back inside then, heard a vehicle pull in. Nine-year old Jonathan was first one out.

"Can I pet the goats?!" Jonathan called out.

"Okay by me," John shouted back. Jonathan ran for the barn where several of John's nannies were milling about.

"We don't have time for that!" Allen yelled from inside the car, then clambered out.

"JONATHAN! Come back here!" The boy made a U-turn and walked slowly back to the car; head hung.

Jonathan wore his little league baseball uniform. The second game of the season loomed in less than an hour at Haymaker Field in Waltsburg's Memorial Park, the Waltsburg All Stars' perfect record of 1-0 on the line. As a utility right fielder, Jonathan spent nearly all his time on the bench. Uncle Jimmy worked with him on his hitting and fielding skills half-a-dozen times with little improvement. That coaching came to an abrupt halt one evening after Jimmy taught Jonathan how to slide into a base. Arriving home with a skinned knee, a limp, and a tear in a pair of very dirty jeans was not well received. The Baguelts investigated activities other than sports. Knowing Jonathan spent inordinate periods of time in his bedroom, door closed, strumming the guitar he had received as a Christmas gift, it stood to reason that maybe, just maybe, he had natural ability.

John Griever reluctantly agreed to give Jonathan elementary guitar lessons explaining, to no avail, he was no instructor. John was introduced to string instruments by Zander Rhoades, a transient, Welsh/Cherokee half-breed who showed up at Doona Falls Ranch in the spring of 1932 looking for work, having given rail yard bulls the slip in Kansas City three days prior. He claimed to be from eastern Tennessee along the Pelisipi River. Other than a change of clothes, a bone-hafted knife, tin coffee cup, and bedroll, Zander bore only a five-string banjo. One early November morning, Mr. Rhoades hitched a ride as far as Waltsburg and then hopped a rail in the direction of warmer weather. He left a Martin OM-28 acoustic pawn shop guitar he had purchased for a song to Griever as a gift, a token of their friendship, of musical moments shared.

John's advice that they first buy Jonathan a basic instructional guidebook at the music store in Granfield was met with indifference. Neither parent was musically inclined.

"Get your guitar and shut the door," Allen instructed.

"That new?" Griever nodded toward Allen's car.

"Yes. Kind-a resembles a new dime in a goat's asshole, doesn't it?" snickered Allen, flicking a dead bug from the windshield.

"You might want-a make sure yer windows are rolled up tight," Griever advised. "'less you want that interior to smell like smoke."

"Okay to leave it parked here?" he asked, straightening the tails of his crisp, flashy Madras shirt.

"Good-a place as any. C'mon in," John said, leading the way. 'Typical Allen,' Griever thought to himself. 'No handshake, sorry we're late, or hi, how are ya?'

"We only got twenty-two minutes," Allen said, stepping inside the trailer, wrinkling his nose at the stink of cigarette smoke.

"You want somethin' to drink? Got some frozen orange juice I fresh-mixed up this mornin'."

Allen declined. He plucked a framed photograph from an end table and asked, "Where was this taken?"

"City Hall in Granfield. At my retirement party."

"Retired from what?"

"County maintenance crew. I was the guy what kept roadsides mowed. Snow plowed. Potholes filled. Roads graded. That kind of stuff."

John had Jonathan sit on the davenport while he fetched his git-tar. Like his father, Jonathan was as groomed as a standard Schnauzer competing in the Westminster Kennel Club Show. The kid had an annoying habit. His glasses were in desperate need of adjustment.Invariably his right middle finger shoved the black rimmed specs back up on the bridge of his nose. Moments later, he shoved them up again.

John had never seen a pinkish-orange, maroon-red plastic, 4-string guitar not much bigger than a ukulele. No question it was used. All four celebrity faces and their respective autographs were worn bare in spots. "Let's see what we got here," Griever said, making a show of studying the instrument. "Ah-ha! A Beatles Maestro Junior. First time I ever seen one-a these." He went through the motions of pretending to play something, then tinkered with the tuning pegs. "When's the last time you tuned this thing?" Jonathan shrugged his shoulders and pushed his glasses back up on his nose. A further complication, Griever plucked right-handed; Jonathan was a southpaw. Each time Jonathan looked down at the strings to see what he was doing his glasses slid down his nose. Up came the right middle finger for the fix. Always, he lost his Griever-directed finger placement on the neck of the little device.

Allen stood the whole time, discreetly glancing at his watch every few minutes. Hands in his pockets, hands out, rocking to and fro on his heels. He fidgeted with the change in his pocket, his shirttail, or car keys. He shed one of his penny loafers and turned it upside down to remove an irritant of some sort, balancing, not allowing his bare foot to touch the threadbare carpet. Griever invited him to pull up a chair, but Allen turned down all offers of hospitality.

At long last, scarcely fifteen minutes, Allen announced it was time for them to go. Jonathan needed to be there in time to warm up with his teammates.

"What do you think?" Allen queried.

"Too early to tell, if you ask me," Griever said, with the straightest face he could muster.

"Can I pet the goats? Please?!" Jonathan begged.

"No. Maybe next time."

"Watch your step," Griever said, as they headed out the door.

The air was rife with the aroma of smoldering mesquite wood. The fifty-five-gallon drums were scarcely visible from the smoke pouring out the numerous holes John had drilled. Allen paused briefly to button the top button of Jonathan's jersey. Jonathan middle-finger punched his glasses. Allen half-raised his hand as if to wave to John as they turned toward the car. The trio stopped in their tracks, stunned, slack-jawed.

Griever's billy and several of his brood were standing atop and around the new Monte Carlo. The billy was munching on the roof, the vinyl already devoured down to the metal. One nanny stood on the trunk and two others on the hood, one chewing on a windshield wiper blade; the wiper arm contorted beyond repair.

CHAPTER 9
SITTING DUCK

Friday – May 29

For more than thirty years, Ben Whitewater showed up at the Waltsburg barbershop this time of year. His visits preceded the Kickapoo Nation's annual powwow where dance competitions in native dress attracted tourists who spent liberally on traditional foods, artisan craftwork, and ornamental trinkets. Ben was the eldest member of the Kickapoo Tribal Council and still lived on the reservation five miles west of Horton, Kansas. Ben's affinity to Waltsburg ran deep, not unlike indigenous Indiangrass with roots up to twelve feet in length. This year, he was accompanied by his granddaughter, Portia, a recent Stanford graduate, and designated driver for the trip to Waltsburg, her first since her early teens. She sat with her arms folded, perfectly still, across from her grandfather.

#

In the summer of 1930, driving back from visiting relatives in Texas and Oklahoma, Ben's caravan of family and friends broke an axle on one of their Model A Fords on the road to Waltsburg, just a mile from Doona Falls Ranch. A young cowhand, Jack Nagel, discovered their plight and offered to help. He presumed Bearnard Muldoon would welcome the strangers as distinguished guests. The group spent three days at the ranch while repairs were made, an interlude they never forgot. They were graciously housed, fed, and given the run of the estate. They bathed in the soothing geothermal waters of the Doona Falls natural spring pool, marveled at the petroglyphs on nearby rock outcroppings, and lingered long at the Indian burial ground on the property. The visitors revealed the origin of the name Minnie's Creek. In Kaw Indian-speak, it was a combination of two words, *Mi* – sun and *Ni* – water, or sun water as the water flowed from the earth at body temperature and eventually streamed into the Orme River.

Merry Belle did the guests' laundry and made Indian fry bread fresh daily with instructions from Ben's oldest sister at her side. The guests, in turn, held a big smoke out, demonstrating how the mesquite wood they brought with them from Texas enhanced the flavor of Muldoon's Angus beef grilled over an open fire. Upon parting ways, Bearnard made it clear they would be welcome to return to the ranch any time.

#

A practiced raconteur, Ben Whitewater was full of good-natured stories that warped one's sense of history and the world. Jake remembered the yarn Mr. Whitewater spun sitting in the very same barber chair. He was eight and had recently moved in with his Uncle Doyle. Jake's impression of Indians came from stereotypes portrayed in movies and television shows. Onscreen, they spoke in curious, broken English, fought endlessly with the U.S. Cavalry, wore feathers, breastplates, and bear claw jewelry. They lived in teepees, rode bareback, and liked to take scalps. Mr. Whitewater spoke in complete, grammatically correct sentences and seemed at peace with the world at large. In retrospect, Ben may have taken advantage of Jake's naiveté. When Jake asked him if he had a real Indian name, Ben rattled off a name in the Kickapoo language. Doyle asked him for the English equivalent; Ben replied, "Sitting Duck." Jake asked why he walked with a stiff leg. Ben told him it was the result an injury he sustained on a trip with his family the summer he was sixteen years old.

"Nine of us were on a summer vacation. We rode through the Nebraska Sand Hills, then the Black Hills, and into Wyoming. Along our route, we encountered natives migrating north toward Montana to an enormous encampment along the Greasy Grass River later known as the Little Bighorn. Thousands of Northern Cheyenne, Lakota, Arapaho, seven separate tribes of Teton Sioux, Hunkpapa, Sans Arc, Brule, all peacefully gathered there. We camped overnight along the perimeter, intending to rest our horses before continuing our journey to Yellowstone

Park to see Old Faithful. The following day, mid-afternoon, we hadn't anymore digested our lunch and joined in a very promising dice game when the encampment was attacked by mounted soldiers. Panic set in. Bullets were whizzing all around us. I ran as fast as I could at my horse to vault-mount him from behind for a quick getaway, a maneuver I had been practicing at home on the reservation in my spare time. My adrenaline rush carried me clear over the horse. I landed sprawled on my belly. The horse spooked, reared up, and stomped on my left knee. It never healed properly. I've been stiff legged ever since. Having to double-clutch those Model A's didn't make it better."

#

For the second consecutive day, Waltsburg's female cottonwood tree population showered the town with its perennial fluff. A light breeze swirled the feathery matter into drifts, sending thin waves of it crisscrossing Main Street. Jake browsed the *Daily Dispatch* newspaper. Doyle unbraided and combed Ben's waist length hair.

"I trust all is well at home?" Doyle said.

"Natives restless these days. Don't want-a get drafted to fight white-man's war. Jake, what lottery number you get?"

"362."

"You have lucky numbers. Bet on those next time you go to Vegas."

"I'm seeing a lot more gray than last time."

"Clairol wearing off. Need to make appointment with your woman across street. Need to look *macho* for powwow."

"Did I hear you say Portia just graduated from Stanford? That is quite an achievement. Congratulations."

"Thank you," said Portia.

"What was your major?"

"Native American Studies."

"I tell her all along she could stay home and learn that stuff. Save big bucks. Family dead broke now. Tuition, books, room, board, travel expenses, new clothes, spending allowance, booze, dope, beach parties..."

"I had a full scholarship and worked part-time in the library year-round."

"She come of age now. Need to find husband. Jake, you have girlfriend?"

"No, sir."

"As you can see, my granddaughter very attractive. Make good squaw. Firm breasts. Round bottom. Full hips. Good hand-eye coordination. She make good children. Good for five, maybe six. Another year, she will be overripe."

Portia spewed a scold in her native *Algonquian* dialect.

"She also very spirited."

"What would you look for in a mate for Portia?" asked Doyle.

"Sense of humor. Number one factor in any relationship. Everything else second. Reserve privilege of interviewing all suitors. Have questions that must be answered correctly."

"Like what?" Doyle prodded.

"Jake, you ever run with scissors?"

Jake looked up from his newspaper, glanced at Ben, then Portia. "You're asking me?"

"Yes. Have you ever run with scissors?"

"Only if they were in my mouth."

Ben Whitewater's toothy grin waxed like a Wurlitzer keyboard. Portia's countenance transitioned instantly from glower to dazzling smirk.

"Jake, you are qualified," Ben chortled.

"What else you got planned today?" Doyle asked.

"Ping-pong Olympics next. Visit your woman across street. Get bear hug. Have color and braid put back in hair. If Natalie there, glimpse Grand Tetons. See if car ready at Stuber's. Luci making us special lunch of roasted red chili pepper corn chowder with *pugna* and mesquite-smoked buffalo strips at Beau Coup. Drive out to Merry Belle's. Pay respect to wife in Cemetary. Then, long, jaybird-naked soak in the Falls pool after dark. Have confidential chat with Great Spirit, *Kisiihiat.* Spend night at ranch."

"I can braid your hair," Portia offered.

"Have more fun across street."

Familiar chants and drumbeats were overheard. Portia noiselessly shuffled hop-step to the shop's front windows. Wally sat up, then bolted from his loveseat to join her. Jake set the newspaper aside. Anthony Bertolini a/k/a Lone Cloud set the parking brake on his converted, snub-nosed Divco milk truck in front of DeCritt's Barber Shop. Its colorful side panel read:

POPSICLES
ESKIMO PIES
FUDGESICLES
ICE CREAM SANDWICHES
ICE COLD POP

The truck's speakers blared drumbeats and chants. He dressed and played the part of an Indian. The music, however, was particularly Kickapoo he had recorded at their annual powwow three years earlier, with permission, of course. His muted bronze skin, large nose with a bend, deep brown eyes, and black hair lent credibility to his Native American role playing. In reality, he was a third-generation Italian American. He was lean, six-foot tall, an auto mechanic by trade, and married to Luci, the owner/operator of the Beau Coup Café. Afternoon drives about Waltsburg on hot summer weekends were his avocation. Once in costume and face paint, Anthony morphed into an entertainer, a local celebrity of sorts.

#

Anthony Bertolini showed up at Stuber's Garage in 1965 looking for work. Deke hired him on the spot. Born and raised in Buffalo, New York, young Anthony was introduced to his family's auto repair business at age eight, washing, waxing, and detailing customer vehicles. Four years after graduating from high school, Anthony had a falling out with his oldest brother. Anthony sold his share to his brother, socked the money away, and enlisted in the U. S. Army for a chance to get paid to see the world and broaden his mechanic skills on diesel engine trucks and heavy equipment. He volunteered for an overseas assignment as an advisor to teach his trade to South Vietnamese army (ARVN) recruits just outside Cam Rahn Bay.

In the summer of 1963, he was in Australia on a one-week pass. Anthony spent the first two evenings with his buddies carousing in the King's Cross District of Sydney. Day three, he set out to explore the city on his own. A long-lost uncle owned and operated an eating and drinking establishment in Rushcutters Bay. The city map indicated it was only a klick or so east of King's Cross. How long had it been since his last home-cooked Italian meal?

BERTOLINI'S RISTORANTE ITALIANO on Old Chum Road was closed. The shop owner next door said they were on holiday visiting relatives in the United States. Only slightly disappointed, Anthony asked for suggestions of a good place to eat. The man pointed up the street toward Wooly's Edge pub, can't miss it, a local favorite known for its outstanding seafood.

There, Anthony met bartender Lucille Grace Carpenter. A petite five-foot five in heels, her Asian and Caucasian features were the consequence of an American missionary father from Kansas and Chinese mother. The happenstance encounter culminated in dinner and drinks the last evening of his R & R. Their short-lived relationship was excruciatingly platonic, even business-like, but their conversation was lively and deep. Uncharacteristically, he talked as much as she did. Her dream was to own and operate her own eating establishment; his, he decided, was that she would write back. On the flight back to Saigon, Anthony sorted through some truly diverse thoughts: 'Why am I here?', 'I'm nearly a foot taller than she is,' and 'She's nine years older than me.'

#

Ben directed Doyle to swivel the chair to face outside.

"Who wants ice cream?" Jake asked. Wally barked and waited expectantly at the door.

"That's two. Anyone else?" Jake fetched Wally's aluminum water bowl, took three ones from the cash register and stood by the door. "Anyone?" The sounds that heralded Lone Cloud's arrival abated.

"I would have a strawberry soda if he has one," Ben said.

"Nothing for me," answered Doyle.

Wally barked again. As they walked out the door, Portia followed.

"Was pew out there last time I was here?"

"No," said Doyle. "We picked that up at an estate sale in March."

They watched as Jake set Wally's bowl of ice cream down on the sidewalk. Lone Cloud waved. Ben waved back. Portia sat at one end of the bench and unwrapped her ice cream sandwich. Jake poked his head in the door.

"He says your Pontiac's ready. He didn't have strawberry."

Jake plopped down in the middle of the bench and took the first bite of his Eskimo Pie.

"No touching," said Portia.

Jake inched to the opposite end of the bench. They noshed in silence as Wally scooted his bowl every which way around the walk, trying to lick it clean. Lone Cloud boosted the volume and slowly edged away.

"He's one heck of a good mechanic," Doyle said.

"I find that out several years ago. He come to reservation wanting to record powwow music. We work out some deal. I ask him to look at Pontiac. Had not started for two weeks. Nobody could solve problem."

"He fixed it?"

"Took him three minutes. Found potato stuffed in tailpipe."

Portia came back inside followed by Wally and Jake. She asked if there was a bathroom to wash her hands. Wally hopped up on his loveseat, licking his chops. Jake rinsed his hands in the sink behind Doyle.

"I see we have a distinguished visitor about to join us," Doyle said.

John Griever crossed the street toting a supermarket-sized brown paper sack.

"Who's that?" Ben said.

"John Griever. You know John," said Doyle.

"No. Blond. Walking dog. In front of post office."

"That's Catharine and Sherman."

"Have I met her?"

"No. Need your glasses?"

"Please."

Ben followed the pair till they were out of his line of sight then handed his glasses back to Doyle.

"Not bad. She from here?"

"No. Moved here two, maybe three years ago. Worked part-time for Karl Albrecht originally. Sells real estate full time now."

Doyle swiveled Ben to face Griever.

"Take any scalps yet, Chief?" Griever greeted.

"Just getting started."

"Thought I'd go ahead an' bring you yer jerky."

"How much I owe?"

"Ten even."

"Sit. Have chair. We can tell some lies."

"Can't. Got one-a Nonny's quilts an' three-a her afghans tumblin' in dryers over at Icky's. Them things take forever to get dry."

"Should hang on clothesline. Hot as hair dryer today. Smell like fresh air."

"She don't have a line anymore," Griever said, setting the sack on the chair next to Jake.

Wally immediately sniffed and pawed at the sack. Portia reappeared, sat next to the cash register, and browsed the shop's latest issue of *LIFE*.

"Business hoppin' at Icky's?" Ben asked.

"Naw. Just Eric and Jimmy playin' pinball. And Icky tryin' to talk me into sellin' some-a that Amway soap for him again."

"Maybe see you Sunday after church?" Ben said.

"At Merry Belle's? Nonny's planning on it."

"Oh, sweet Nonny," Ben reminisced. "Her favorite thing, strip naked and soak in Doona Falls pool. Which reminds me of second most important question."

"How come you talkin' like some TV Indian?" Griever asked.

"Oh. Sorry about that. Been practicing in front of mirror too much lately. Tourist season right around corner."

"This second most important question of yours would be regarding what?" Doyle solicited.

"Prospective husband for granddaughter."

"By all means. Let's hear it."

"Is a naked woman intelligent?"

Portia lowered her magazine and scowled at her grandfather.

"Jake," Ben said, "Do you think a naked woman is intelligent?"

"Does she have to be?"

Portia turned toward Jake. "Good answer," she smiled. Ben Whitewater flashed another big grin. "Have you met my grand-daughter, Portia?"

"Been a while. Nice to see ya again."

"We're trying to find her a husband."

"Not much to choose from around here," Griever said. "Mind if I use the facilities? Icky's men's room is out of order."

"Six dozen jerky sticks, huh? How long will that many last you?" Doyle asked Ben.

"Week or two, maybe."

"Your whole family must like them!"

"No. Make good dog treats."

Moments later, Jack Nagel and Bill Stimka showed up.

"Saw that clunker of yours parked over at Stuber's. Figured you'd be on the loser's side of the pong table by now," Jack said to Ben.

"How, to you too," Ben countered.

Jack extended his hand. "How've you been?"

"Without," said Ben.

"No women up there on the reservation?"

"Plenty. I'm down here looking for a white woman to kidnap. You remember my granddaughter, Portia?"

Jack and Bill both tipped their cowboy hats.

"Table open?" Jack asked.

"Always," said Doyle.

"Me and Bill gonna try an' squeeze in a game 'fore Claire catches up to us."

"Where's she?"

"Vet's office. Gettin' the dogs their annual shots."

"I'd kidnap Claire."

Jack said, "Catch her on the right day, she might go with you. <u>Without</u> a struggle."

Jack and Bill headed for the back room. They met Griever halfway and exchanged nods. John Griever paused long enough in front of Ben to come to attention, doff his ball cap, and in one fluid motion, bow reverently as if in the presence of royalty, "Catch ya later, Chief Whitewash."

As John walked out the door, Ben hollered, "Skunk mouth!" Doyle handed Ben the mirror. "How about just a skosh more off the top."

"Going to the Strong City rodeo this year?" Doyle asked.

"When is it?"

"First week of June, like always."

"No time off till pow-wow over. You?"

"Donna and I are going for the parade but not sticking around for

51

the rodeo."

Claire pressed her nose against the window then popped in the door.

"Hi, Doyle," she said. "Seen my husband?"

"They're in back. You met Ben Whitewater?"

"Yes. Some years ago, at the ranch." She gave Wally a pet as he sniffed her boots. "Hi, Jake. Has Anthony been by here already?"

"Yes, ma'am," Jake answered.

"Bet I can still catch him. Be right back."

Doyle suggested Jake fill Wally's water bowl and see if Claire's dogs might like a drink.

The two German Shepherds were, indeed, thirsty. As Greta lapped the last drops of water from the bowl, Hans came alive, barking. Catharine Mixx and her female boxer, Sherman, approached. Catharine slowed her pace and came to a halt in front of the barber shop. She restrained the dog on a short leash and sat on the bench.

"Would Sherman like some water?" Jake asked.

"Oh, yes. I'm sure she would."

Jake fetched another bowl of water and set it on the walk. The dog drank heartily as Wally stared through the window, tail wagging like a metronome set at *allegro* tempo.

"How sweet. Thank you, Jake," she said, popping her knuckles.

"You ever met Ben Whitewater?"

"Who?"

"Kickapoo Chief. He's inside."

"I'm all sweaty. And…"

"He won't care."

Catharine peered inside and saw Doyle, who waved, and a man seated in the first barber chair with dark rimmed glasses.

"Well…"

"Just take a minute. You should meet him."

Catharine Mixx clad in her favorite jogging outfit of athletic shorts, a lightweight Texas A&M tee, a white sweat band, and Adidas running shoes stepped into the cool shop and shivered slightly. Wally and Sherman tangled playfully. In the brief time Catharine lingered out front with Jake, Doyle informed Ben of her background as he knew it. Mid-thirties, Army brat, only child, two math degrees from Texas A&M,

taught math at Ormestrong County Community College. She sold real estate part-time in Granfield till Karl Albrecht wooed her into working for him full-time there and in Waltsburg. When Karl died, she renamed 'Albrecht Realty, Auction & Insurance Company' to 'All Bright Realty.' Married once for less than a year in her mid-20's, no children.

"Hi, Doyle," she said. "Can I borrow a towel?"

"Of course."

"This is Chief Ben Whitewater," Jake said.

"Catharine Mixx. Pleased to meet you," she replied, offering her hand.

"My pleasure," smiled Ben.

Catharine toweled off her face, neck, and arms. "Sorry I'm not very presentable. I usually jog in the mornings when it's cooler, but I had a showing in Granfield at eight this morning."

"Business before pleasure," said Ben.

"Right. Unfortunately."

"How's business?" Doyle asked.

"Not happening here. Been busy in Granfield, though."

Wild Bill and Jack reappeared from the back room.

"Did you know Karl well?" asked Ben.

"From a business standpoint, yes."

Claire returned, licking a fudgsicle. Having an audience was a temptation Ben Whitewater could not resist. Jake sat back down. He had seen the look in Ben's eyes before. He hoped it was a story he had not heard.

#

"Karl was quite a character," Ben began. "He never shook his accent. Certain parts of speech sounded as if his mouth was full of *schnitzel*. His parents spoke only German in their home. And that greeting of his: "*Grüss Gott!*" Ben told how Karl Otto Albrecht came to America with his Bavarian-born parents in 1905, typical hard-working immigrants determined to succeed. His father, Adolphus, opened a small butcher shop next door to the Atlantic Hotel and prospered. By age thirty, Karl was a trusted protégé of Walter Bruno, assisting with all types of land acquisition, disposition, and development in and around Waltsburg. It was Karl, with his trademark Cuban cigar, who introduced Bearnard Muldoon to the half section that included the natural spring source. Though it was not for sale, Bearnard, seeing its potential, offered the owner thrice its appraised value in gold coin. At its peak, Doona Falls Ranch encompassed more than 12,000 acres of pristine, protein-rich Bluestem grassland and was larger than the Rockefeller ranch in Kiowa County.

"I believe the year was 1931. A month or so after Knute Rockne was killed in that plane crash near Bazaar. Bearnard invited me to ride along with him and Karl and Karl's mother to see the crash site and look at some Flint Hills land for sale. Karl's mother was in her late 80's and spoke very little English. Karl and Bearnard sat in the front seat, matching *sombreros* pulled down over their ears, puffing on Havana cigars, and blowing smoke rings. I sat in the back seat of Karl's Packard automobile with *Frau* Albrecht who silently fanned herself without end. What should have taken two hours stretched to more than three when we had to change a flat, a common occurrence driving area roads in those days. On our way back to the ranch, Bearnard was crowing about the incomparable beauty of the Flint Hills and quoting Walt Whitman. Karl's mother finally broke her silence, "You vaunt to gid out undt yodel?"

#

Darcy Cage popped in the door. "Oh, hi everybody! This is for you," she gushed, handing Jake an envelope. "Later. Bye!"

Doyle handed Ben the mirror again. Ben nodded his approval. Jake sprang from his chair, set the envelope by the cash register, and began to sweep.

"Did you ever see the pinto that was Mary's horse?" Claire asked Ben.

"Many times," Ben said. "Mary and I used to take rides together. Sheba was a very devoted animal. No one was allowed to ride the horse but Mary."

"I believe I saw it this past spring."

"Then you have been blessed," Ben said. "You should pass that on to Merry Belle. She may still have some pendants left."

After the gathering broke up, Jake opened the envelope Darcy delivered. On the back of their photo taken at the senior prom, she'd written: There's more to life than work. x o x o – D.

CHAPTER 10
JIMMY HEADS FOR HOME

Saturday – June 20

Haymaker Field, Waltsburg's baseball diamond in Memorial Park, was home to little league teams and men's slow pitch softball. Developed by the WPA in the 30's, the park was bounded on the north and east by a boomerang-shaped mound that was a raised bed for a rail spur never completed. Beyond lay a small Mennonite cemetery and several idle pump jacks surrounded by meadows of the rolling Flint Hills as far as the eye could see. The tin-roofed, limestone remnants of the two-story Croeh Brothers grist mill and icehouse moldered on the river beside the area's most prominent hill, Jenkins Knob.

Jimmy Baguelt was a born athlete and consummate competitor. In high school, he quarterbacked the football team, started at point guard in basketball, and played shortstop on the baseball team. After high school graduation, Jimmy, Jake, Kirk Michaels, and Eric Carver joined the Waltsburg Demons slow-pitch team. All four had played baseball together since they were seven years old. In '68, Eric Carver volunteered for service in the Navy that, as it turned out, was just as well. His draft lottery number the following year was 4. Jimmy was out for the season; he had hyperextended both knees, dislocated his left shoulder, and totaled his new car out near Ormestrong County State Lake. Jake, on the other hand, was having his best year ever, thanks to some advice from Jimmy who improved his own hitting the previous year by a simple adjustment to his grip on a tip picked up at a summer baseball camp: Line up your door knocking knuckles. Jake raised his batting average over two hundred percentage points and by mid-season moved up to third in the batting order.

Consumption of alcoholic beverages was banned from the park after a close game in '64 with Waltsburg's archrivals, the Whitfield Rebels. That game, decided by a controversial call at home plate, resulted in a brawl that sent the umpire, four players and seven fans to the hospital. Since that time, fans determined to drink during a game parked themselves atop what they dubbed the Upper Deck, the old rail bed outside the ballpark's left field boundary.

Saturday's weather forecast called for evening thunderstorms. The threat of storms, however, did not deter hometown fans from showing up. The Demons' side of the bleachers was full. John Griever, Bill Stimka, Lyla Witte and her two young adult children, Indy and Briley, watched the game from the Upper Deck beyond the snow fence that defined home run territory. The radiant glow of the ball park's pole lights attracted swarms of moths, millers, and other winged insects to the delight of swooping brown bats, swallows and nighthawks, aerial acrobats devouring their fill at a potluck buffet on a breezy summer's eve. A churning blanket of low clouds blotted out all but a thin wedge of western horizon that shone like the crack of light under a bathroom door in the middle of the night.

The Demons season was off to a lackluster start. They had a 2-3 win-loss record going into the game with the Cruppley's Bend Badgers who were 5-0. By the bottom of the 4th inning, the Badgers had already established an 8-0 lead. Nothing was going right for the Demons. Their best pitcher and two other starters were working harvest. Eric Carver assumed pitching duties and throw-left/bat-right Jake moved to Carver's spot on first. Carver walked in four runs. The wind, gusting to thirty mph, played havoc with the underhand, high-arching pitches. Mid-fourth inning, Carver declared he had had enough and walked off leaving the Demons exactly ten players. Weather conditions and attitude notwithstanding, Jake suspected Eric's *esprit de corps* fell victim to harassment by Badger players; his tangle of shoulder length hair elicited a relentless barrage of gender slurs.

Jimmy Baguelt led off the 4th. First pitch, he ripped a line drive over the pitcher's head into center field for a single. Jake stepped up to the plate. Just as he got set, a prolonged gust of wind blew a blur of dust across home plate. He, the catcher, and the umpire reflexively turned their backs. Jake wiped his eyes and stepped back into the batter's box.

Four pitches in, the count was 3 and 1. Fifth pitch, Jake drove the ball down the base line over the third baseman's head. Jimmy wheeled around second and made for third. When the left fielder muffed the ball, Jimmy decided to try and make it all the way to home. As he sprinted toward third, the third base coach raised his arms signaling Jimmy to hold up: the throw was on its way. Jimmy's momentum carried him three strides beyond the bag, his left leg slipped out from under him, tearing skin off one knee. He could not scramble back in time, so he sidled toward home. The third baseman gave chase. Jimmy's three step dart toward home made the third baseman commit to making the first throw of the rundown. Jake scooted down to second base while no one was paying attention.

The third baseman flipped the ball to the catcher waiting two steps up the line from home plate. Jimmy headed back to third. The catcher chucked the ball back to the third baseman. Jimmy wheeled back toward home. The Badgers' pitcher slipped into the mix between Jimmy and the catcher. Third quickly threw the ball to the pitcher to cut Jimmy off half-way. The pitcher chased Jimmy, intent on making the tag. Jimmy was quicker, wheeled about, and feigned a convincing four step sprint toward third. But Jimmy's mind was already made up. He abruptly stopped, reversed direction, and dashed toward home. His impulsive *ruse de guerre* worked. The pitcher, fooled into thinking Jimmy was all-out trying to make it back to third, let the ball fly from his hand just as Jimmy about-faced. Right or wrong, Jimmy reasoned if he ran at top speed directly in line with the angle of the anticipated throw from the third baseman, it would take a near-perfect throw to nail him. The bamboozled Badger pitcher froze, straddling the baseline in disbelief. They collided. The pitcher took the brunt of their collision and was brashly shoved aside. Having come to a near full stop, losing both momentum and surprise, Jimmy knew his chances of beating the throw home was highly improbable. He halted his run short of home plate. The catcher took the throw from third and delivered a punishing revenge tag. The umpire called Jimmy out.

Jimmy immediately took issue with the call. The Badger pitcher blocked his path of travel; Jimmy, as base runner, owned the baseline. The umpire reasoned the pitcher was part of the play, their happenstance collision incidental. An altercation ensued. In less than a minute, it turned ugly. Jimmy knew he was right. The Demon's coach, score keeper, and utility player, Dan Bruner, intervened to reinforce Jimmy's case. The umpire held his ground. Jimmy's insults got personal; the ump ejected him from the game. Dan lingered, trying to reason with the umpire. Jimmy strode to the dugout, gathered his things, and plopped down next to his pregnant bride on the bottom row of the bleachers.

"That ump's a fucking idiot," Jimmy harped.

"Get over it. It's only a game," she said.

Jimmy glanced at his knee. Two streaks of dark strawberry blood ran down his shin onto his sock. He took off his cleat and sock and used the sock to daub the blood.

"If I had a rule book, I'd shove it up his ass."

"I said get over it!"

Behind Parise on the second row of bleachers huddled Merry Belle, Valoise Bruner, Conger, Doyle, and Donna. Conger leaned forward. "I've never seen this guy umpire before."

"READ YOUR FUCKIN' RULE BOOK, ASSHOLE!" Jimmy shouted.

Parise abruptly stood and walked off.

"Take my place," Jimmy said to Conger.

"I can't field worth a crap."

"So? I've seen you hit with your good eye. Bruner can pitch if he moves Kirk to second. Put you in right."

"I'd screw something up."

"Can't screw up any worse unless you're the umpire."

Jimmy stepped over to the dugout, conversed with his father-in-law then waved Conger over. Dan handed him a spare team jersey, size XL that fit snug as a leotard. Jimmy loaned him his ball glove and ball cap and selected a bat for him.

To add insult to injury, the Badgers coach protested Jake moving to third during the rundown. He claimed Jake had done so during the altercation at home plate, although that was not true. He argued that time was out during that pause and a runner could not legitimately advance. The ump sent Jake back to second base. Jake and Dan kept silent, relieved Jimmy followed Parise into the parking lot and was not present for another meritless call.

CHAPTER 11
WHUMPF!

The driver of the Meadowlark Yellow 1968 fastback Mustang backed out, shifted gears, revved the engine, and popped the clutch in the park's pea-graveled lot, showering the vehicles behind it with jagged pebbles. Parise yelled at Jimmy to stop acting like a child. If he wanted to fuck up somebody's transmission, he could do it in <u>his</u> truck, not her car.

Following Jimmy's departure, the Demons rallied and scored three runs. Top of the fifth, the Badgers got those runs back and two more to boot. 13 – 3. If the Demons did not score during their next at bat, they would be run-ruled, officially ending the game. As the two teams exchanged places mid-inning, a brief surge of rain mixed with a scatter of marble-size hail caused a five-minute delay. The squall brought an appreciable temperature drop. Erratic bolts of lightning and distant peals of thunder ranged from south to southwest. The umpire conferred with both coaches. Neither showed any interest in calling it a night. The pole lights surrounding the field blinked off, and then came back on. Lyla and her son Briley thought better of finishing the game from their exposed Upper Deck spot. John Griever and Wild Bill stayed; the beer was still cold. They shared a blanket pulled over their shoulders. Contrary to the admonitions of her mother, Indy remained. She occupied herself by repeatedly rehearsing dance steps acquired in pursuit of her ballet degree, insisting she was choreographing her *grand jetés, fouettés en tournants* and *entrechat-quatres* in harmony with the mood of the weather.

Bottom of the 5th, the first Demons hitter grounded out to short. Conger was up. He took his last two-bat practice swing and snugged his ballcap. Jimmy loved to annoy not only his older brother Allen, but Conger as well. Scarcely a workday went by that Jimmy did not go out of his way to pester Conger about his congenital *exotropic strabismus,* saying something like 'Where do I get the impression I do not have your full attention?' Conger thought the bat he was given seemed odd but if it was the one Jimmy used, so what? Jimmy's batting average was over .700. Dan Bruner, Jake, and other team members were certain the fungo bat Conger took to the plate was Jimmy's way of saying "to hell with it."

The umpire's attempt to dust off the plate left dark smears. Conger could not remember the last time he stood in a batter's box under game conditions. He heard the voices of encouragement from the dugout, the bleachers, and Jake coaching at first base. "Bend your knees!" "Swing level!" "Wait for a good pitch!" "Just meet the ball!" "You can do it!" …amid a mix of hoots and whistles. From the Badgers' bench, he picked out the words: ringer, walleye, and nice boots. Size fourteen cleats were hard to come by.

The first high arcing pitch with extreme back spin landed short, in front of the plate; the second, a perfect strike. A dwarf dust devil swirled across the infield. The setting sun defied the overcast and day-lighted the landscape, highlighting the scudding, ragged white and gray roiling clouds. Patches of outfield dandelions and white clover posed as bright, misshapen throw rugs. The pitcher reversed the bill of his ball cap and stepped forward, delivering the third pitch at a much lower trajectory. Conger let it pass for a called second strike over the inside corner. Next pitch was a clone of the previous one. Conger swung. The ball dribbled foul along the ground, caroming off the Badgers dugout fencing. The Demons bench went silent. The pitch to follow was a rainbow. He made good contact but was way out in front. A towering foul ball arced out of bounds disappearing into the untamed grass and weeds beyond the raised rail bed. Enthusiastic shouts erupted from the Demons bench. The umpire handed the catcher a new ball. Conger subconsciously picked up Jake hollering, "Count two Mississippi's before you swing!"

A skein of lightning appeared to the southwest; its rolling trail of thunder warned the storm moved closer. John Griever and Bill Stimka snapped up their lawn chairs and cooler of beer and ran for cover. Conger heard car engines starting in the parking lot as he silently counted one Mississippi, two Mississippi, and took a practice swing before stepping back into the batter's box. Next pitch came in like a knuckleball, chin high. The umpire finger-flashed the count, two and two. The next pitch floated toward him like a dare, big as a Texas Ruby Red grapefruit. As Conger counted, he drew the fungo back, lowered to hip level, and swung.

WHUMPF!

The squarely struck ball rocketed up toward left-center field at an angle that suggested a routine fly ball. The left, short, and center fielders searched skyward. The new white ball, blending with the twilight patina of sun-varnished overcast, was nowhere to be seen. Five seconds passed. Conger rounded second base. Ten seconds passed.

Jake yelled, "Home run! IT'S A HOME RUN!"

No one argued the point. The Demons' celebration was abruptly cut short. Waltsburg's tornado siren sounded just as the sun disappeared. Torrents of cold rain enveloped the park. Jake, Kirk, and Dan scrambled to bag the team's equipment. A jagged cloud-to-ground lightning bolt flashed close-by. Waltsburg's electrical grid went dark, the siren silent mid-wail. Vehicle engines fired up, one after another, their headlights flickering, crisscrossing the pitch-black landscape like a dysfunctional zoetrope. Dan slung the equipment bag over his shoulder and made a dash for the parking lot. As Jake snatched up his ball glove, back-to-back skeins of lightning lit up the park. For a fleeting moment, he thought he caught a glimpse of someone leaping along the top of the rail bed beyond the left field fence.

CHAPTER 12
2 CORINTHIANS 4:18

Sunday – June 21

Father's Day

Contrary to their public personas and antics, John and Nonny were as close as melon and rind. Nonny, born Olga Tatiana Kravchuk, was the only child of her Russian-born parents who emigrated from the steppes of the Ukraine following two successive years of famine. They homesteaded a 160-acre plot of unrefined land northeast of Waltsburg and eked out a hardscrabble living but never went hungry. Like most prairie immigrants, they gardened, raised chickens, and purchased a couple of cows for meat, milk, and butter. Nonny's father, a skilled carpenter, made furniture he sold in town. Her childhood memories consisted mostly of morning chores, school, after-school chores, and listening to her mother read scripture. When Nonny was nine, her father was fatally bitten by a rattlesnake while clearing rocks from their land. Her mother remarried within four months. An Irishman eight years her junior, Fergus Griever was a straw boss for the Union Pacific railroad. Less than a year later, Nonny had a little brother.

"We look not at the things which are seen, but at the things which are not seen." The oxymoronic Bible verse from Second Corinthians was their mother's favorite. A deeply religious woman, Nonny's mother devoted nearly all her spare time to reading the family Bible. Most evenings were spent reading scripture together before bedtime by the light of a kerosene lamp. Burning kerosene or candles for the sole purpose of reading scripture did not sit well with Fergus. Most Saturday evenings, after a beer or two with his fellow workers at O'Sullivan's across from the Jupiter Dance Hall in Waltsburg, Fergus Griever walked home. The family silently braced themselves for his arrival. Sober, Fergus was a decent man, but alcohol brought out the brute in him, a brute who launched into spontaneous rage over trivial issues.

#

Fergus arrived home late that Saturday evening having dallied longer than usual with his railroad pals at Sully's saloon. Upon the requisite number of states ratifying the 18th Amendment to the Constitution, the manufacture, transportation, and sale of intoxicating liquors was banned. Though the ban would not take effect until the following year, the men at the bar cursed the goddamned politicians. That led to more drink, stronger talk, and firmer resolve to ignore the law when the time came. Fergus purchased two quarts of German recipe dark wheat beer from the speakeasy behind the Jupiter Dance Hall and walked the mile and a half home. A brisk north wind turned his face and jug handle ears red but kept his beer cold. Upon arrival, he expected a hot meal and water heated for his bath.

Ten-year-old Johnny Griever had chicken pox. He was running a fever and had been bed-ridden for three days. His older half-sister, nicknamed Nonny, a child's conflicted pronunciation of Mommy, tended to John's needs. She awoke to the sound of something breaking and the raised voice of her stepfather. He was livid there was no paper in the outhouse. Wasn't that little Johnny's responsibility?

Nonny slipped into the kitchen and found Fergus with one hand at her mother's throat and a boning knife in the other. When Nonny made her presence known, he shoved her mother aside and turned his full attention toward her. As he approached, Nonny's mother screamed he would not lay a finger on her daughter. Reeking of alcohol, a fistful of her nightgown in one hand, the knife held close to Nonny's face, he demanded to know what other chores had been shirked. Nonny's mother could bear no more. She snatched the iron skillet from the wood-burning stove and struck Fergus across the side of the head with all her might, knocking him and Nonny over a kitchen chair onto the floor. As he raised up on his hands and knees, she delivered an uppercut to his forehead that sent him backward over the same fallen chair. He cursed them both as he struggled to get up. Amid Nonny's protests, she landed more skillet blows to his head till Fergus Griever lay inert as roadkill.

Nonny and her mother lugged the body outside and harnessed their mule. They dragged Fergus to the shelter belt and buried him in a hastily dug shallow pit. Their story: He never came home. Nonny and her mother never revealed to John the truth about his father's disappearance. So, it was. Neither John, nor Nonny, nor their hapless mother would again suffer the bully of his temper or the wallop of his belt. On a bright, crisp Sunday morning six weeks after the cathartic event, Nonny mustered the courage to assemble a bouquet of late blooming wildflowers to place on her stepfather's unmarked grave. What she found in the grove was a crude depression in the earth and a partial skeleton. They had not buried him deep enough to thwart scavengers from digging him up.

The following year, Nonny left for nursing school in Lincoln, Nebraska. She longed to escape the confines of her rudimentary rural upbringing. She imagined there was more to life than menial chores, Bible verses, wind, dust, pollen, cow flop, insect bites, and idle yak about the weather. John Griever stayed close to home. He and his mother were left to carry on as best they could. He never married though there were some close calls: The World War II widow in Granfield, the big-headed Swedish farmer's daughter with twelve toes, and a taxidermist named Lyla. His fierce, independent spirit trumped any yearnings for domesticated bliss. In his words, if he had wanted to mate in captivity, he would have built a zoo cage.

#

It was a picture-perfect *Home on the Range* morning, not a cloud in the sky; in John Griever parlance "a bluebird day." In keeping with his Sunday custom, John shaved a six-day beard, donned his dress-up black cowboy hat, bolo tie, and splashed on English Leather cologne just to irritate Nonny. John picked Nonny up for church at 9:30 sharp. She immediately rolled down her window and told him for the umpteenth time that the scent ranked as one of the most imperious of all time. He had no idea what the word meant. To him, it was just another one of her Brit-reformation words. Nonny sat as always in the first row, alongside Merry Belle and William. John took his place among the choir in the sanctuary of the Methodist church. After, they ate breakfast at the Beau

Coup Café or lunch at Barney's Restaurant, depending on whose whim was more persuasive. John would take Nonny home and always ask if she needed him to do anything around the house.

This Sunday, after dropping Nonny off, he stopped and picked up Jake. Wally stayed home. Given half a chance, he loved chasing Griever's goats. Anything upsetting the quiet enjoyment of the nannies these days was fair game for Pee Wee, John's recently acquired rescue donkey. Earlier in the week, Eric Carver had agreed to help with some chores requiring four hands and some farm-boy muscle. Friday evening, Carver opted out, deciding instead to spend the weekend with his mother in Lawrence.

"Why would he spend Father's Day with his mother?" Jake remarked, noting Griever had added a new ball cap to his dashboard collection.

"Don't know that."

"Told me he's going to college on the G.I. Bill."

"He ain't cut out for college.

Griever's old pickup squeaked, rattled, and kicked as they crossed the railroad tracks. He beeped his horn at Jack and Claire Nagel, Bill Stimka, and Lyla Witte about to enter Barney's Restaurant. "Nothin' better than Barney's chicken fried steak smothered in white gravy and pan-fried potatoes," John said. He lit up a Camel and plucked a couple of tobacco shreds from the tip of his tongue. Jake noticed the hand-lettered sign curbside in front of Stuber's Garage:

OUT OF MINNOWS

"Why do you think he's not for college?"

"He might enroll but he won't finish. Not sayin' his intentions ain't right. He's got things too good as it is. He don't have to work for nothin'. Ever since his folks divorced, he plays both sides from the middle. His ol' man tries to lay down the law, set some rules, but his mother lets him pretty much do as he likes." He took a long drag off his cigarette. "Eric sees Lawrence as his Disneyland. I've talked to his ol' man several times. He's a decent fella, as lawyers go."

"He ever talk about his bad experiences in Vietnam."

"No such thing as a good experience when it comes to war. Can't change what happened to 'im."

"You advised him to enlist, didn't you?"

"Yup. If you think yer gonna git drafted, you might as well pick what you might like. Don't never let Uncle Sam do it for ya."

"Still think it was good advice?"

"If you enlist in the Navy hopin' to avoid combat and they put ya on a supply boat on the Mekong River, it's bad luck. That's all."

"He told me they got shot at almost every day."

"Gettin' shot at wasn't his worst enemy." Griever took another drag and crushed out his cigarette in the ashtray. "He survived it." John made the last turn before they reached his place. He watched the dust swirl in the rearview mirror. Jake stared idly at the distorted tic-tac-toe grid of crisscrossing jet contrails.

John pointed toward the dashboard. "Like my new hat?"

"Cool," said Jake, inspecting a bright red Kansas City Chiefs ball cap.

"Bruner give it to me. Bank's givin' 'em away to customers."

"Looks to me like you might want to leave it out in the weather. Maybe run over it a few times so it matches the rest of 'em."

"Uh-oh," John said. "Smell that?"

"Skunk?" guessed Jake.

As they turned into Griever's place, the odor was strong.

"Where's the damn wind when you could need it?" Griever grumbled.

John knew immediately something was amiss. The barn doors were closed. He always left them open so his small herd of goats could shelter in bad weather. John brought the truck to a halt in front of the barn, got out, and hopped up on the truck's bed. The small herd was grazing with Pee Wee in the pasture beyond the weathered box elder trunk.

"Somethin's not right," John said, looking about then jerked the barn doors open. "Well, ah'll be damned," he muttered. He stepped around to one side of the old structure. The ancient wood planking on that side was stripped off to a height of six feet. They saw footprints, square nails, and splintered wood.

"I read somethin' on this in the *Dispatch*. Past year or two somebody's been thievin' old barn wood. Last one I read about was up by Bremen in Marshall County." He swatted at a fly, stepped back inside, arms akimbo, sizing up his disbelief. "They took all-a my old license tags and the antique butter churn."

"Better check your trailer."

John did a quick walk through but did not find anything missing.

"You gonna call Gene?"

"Prob'ly should, shouldn't I?"

"Maybe Roger saw something. You want-a check the house?"

"Ain't nothin' in it worth stealin'."

"May be. But the front door's open."

Approaching the house, they saw the two boards nailed across the main entry were pried off, the door forced open. Jake pinched his nostrils together. The skunk odor was strongest on the porch. John pulled the door shut.

"PHEW! Whoever it was got skunked good," John said.

"We're gettin' skunked now. They live in there?"

"I've seen 'em goin' 'round the outside and under the porch. They could-a found a way in, I guess."

By late afternoon, a freshening breeze dispersed the lingering odor. Jake hitched a ride back to town with Officer Spellmeier, all windows rolled down. Once home, he immediately stripped, started a load of laundry using an extra measure of soap, and jumped in the shower. That same evening, John Griever phoned Gene Lassiter to report his 30's-vintage, cathedral-shaped Philco radio missing from the trailer.

CHAPTER 13
BELIEVE IT OR DON'T!

Monday – June 22

Parise Baguelt rapped on her father's office door and then stuck her head in. "Mr. Zimmerman is here to see you."

Dan Bruner took a sip of his coffee and went to greet Isaac Zimmerman in the outer reception area. "What brings you to our neck of the woods?"

"Found somethin' that might belong to you." Mr. Zimmerman held out what appeared to be a near pristine MacGregor softball with the Demons name and logo. "This one-a yers?"

"Looks like it. Yes."

"Found it yesterday mornin' half buried top-a my father's grave."

'No way!' Dan thought to himself. Last Saturday afternoon, Zimmerman's father was formally laid to rest in the Mennonite cemetery east of Waltsburg Memorial Park's ball field. As he described his find, Dan imagined it akin to a golf shot, a high arcing ball that plugged itself in its own divot. Dan assured him it was an anomaly, a freak happenstance, and not some malicious form of vandalism. Convinced the man was not upset, he thanked him for the ball's return. Their conversation turned to the severe storm Saturday evening that dumped as much as four inches of rain in some areas, spawning minor flooding and two funnel clouds, one of which touched down a mile west of Waltsburg. As they strolled through the bank lobby, Isaac Zimmerman remarked that the hail had not damaged his corn crop.

Back in his office, Dan rolled the ball slowly across his desktop. The ball had a slight wobble to it. He glanced at his watch: quarter after nine.

His first appointment was not till ten. He grabbed his car keys and told Parise he needed to run a quick errand. Minutes later, Dan Bruner stood atop the Upper Deck. As posted, the distance from home plate to the fence was three hundred feet and as stepped off, another twenty-four feet to where he stood. He shaded his eyes and gazed eastward toward the Mennonite cemetery across a stretch of fallow pasture. The distances appeared to be nearly equal. He glanced at his watch. Just enough time to pace it off and be back at the bank in time for his appointment. Eight steps into the field, Dan's wingtips sank two inches into the rain-soaked soil. He backtracked and again eye-balled the distances. Bottom line of his windshield appraisal: It was six hundred feet or more from home plate to the cemetery's gated entrance. Conger hit a home run that belonged in Ripley's Believe It or Not. Over his lunch hour, Dan walked down to the Crème de la Crème antiques shop and asked if they had a candlestick with a spike for sale.

CHAPTER 14
RED & TEX

Saturday – June 27

During the Christmas holidays in 1930, Doyle's father struck a deer on Highway 50 and was killed. Doyle, the only son, dropped out of school to work and help support the family.

Jobs were in short supply thanks to the ripple effects of the stock market crash of 1929. A co-worker of Doyle's father called a few days after his father was laid to rest to say he knew of a job opportunity in Waltsburg. The town's barber, Boyd "Red" Ridder, needed an "able and dependable" individual "with good references" to assist with his growing practice. After a home-cooked meal and a candid chat, Doyle was offered the job, if he could start the following Monday. It was menial work. Doyle shined shoes, swept floors, and ran errands mostly. The previous year, Mr. Ridder developed an allergic reaction to some unidentified ingredient in popular tonsorial products such as Lucky Tiger, Brilliantine, and Kreml. Periodically, his hands and forearms broke out with bright red splotches, a condition that was more embarrassing than painful. Other barbers he knew did not experience the same or similar reactions; he rightly concluded it was his own sensitivity. Doyle's introduction to barbering began with the application of pomades, oils, and tonics after the cut. Walter Bruno, his manservant/chauffeur Stefan, and black Doll Face Persian cat, Josephine, showed up as a *triumvirate*, by standing appointment every other Thursday evening well after closing time. It was normally a one-hour affair. Stefan, or Stevie as he was called by Bruno, would park the Pierce-Arrow limousine behind the shop. Stevie was a talker, a gregarious sort who also served as a bodyguard. At least, that was Doyle's assessment as he never shed his vertical shoulder holster cosseting a Colt M1911 .45 caliber handgun. Bruno said little as he browsed a Barron's newspaper through his gold-rim *pince-nez*, aloof as an ice sculpture. First, a styled haircut, then scalp, neck, and shoulders massaged until he declared "That will do." Next, an application of pomade he, himself, provided. The pencil mustache, nose hairs, and eyebrows snipped with the same precision one would prune a Bonsai tree required a sober hand. Doyle shined his shoes and always addressed Bruno as Sir. In tandem with those services, Boyd's wife manicured his nails. She was also in charge of suitable treats for the cat. Doyle's first impression of Mr. Bruno: He was a fop. Over time, he decided he was just a very wealthy, eccentric old man who got a kick out of being indulged.

One evening when the world appeared poised to plunge itself headlong into war, Boyd informed Doyle that he had accepted a field sales position with a veterinary supply company in Nebraska. He had wearied of jokes related to the devil, the plague, and had never been fond of the nickname Red; twice in the past month, that redness revealed itself on his shoulders and neck. Was Doyle interested in becoming the town barber? Doyle's answer was "Yes, but…." Boyd anticipated his answer. He had already made an appointment with Archibald Bruner at Waltsburg State Bank first thing Monday morning.

#

"…then the rabbi picks up the collection plate and, with all his might, flings the contents toward Heaven and says, 'Whatever He needs, He keeps. What comes down is mine.'"

"Hadn't heard that one," Doyle said to Alex Ridder. "You want it the same length all the way around?"

"Yes. Is there a carwash in town? Grasshoppers were thick on the highway last night."

"Stuber's Garage up the street has a portable power wash back of his place he might let you use. That a CB antenna on the side of your truck?"

"Yep. Only way we can communicate out in the sticks."

"How's Boyd gettin' along these days?"

"Great. You know dad retired?"

"What's he do with himself now that he's not working?"

"He watches a lot-a sports on the TV. Loves playin' golf with his buddies and goin' pheasant huntin' up in South Dakota around Mott."

"He still go by Red?"

"Nope. Once he got out-a the barbering business, it went away."

"Long drive from Garden City?"

"Yep. I'm used to long hours on the road but not at night."

"D'you come in on Fifty?"

"Nope. Too many eighteen wheelers on that road."

"The service at Saint Mary's is at ten, right? Know how to get there?"

"Yes and yes. Paul gave me directions."

"You staying with Paul?"

"Yes. Dad cut his hair when he was a boy. He's got a nice place in that development of his across the river."

"He's still got lots available. Got a nice one left overlooking the town."

"He gave me a glimpse of that this morning after breakfast. By the way, I meant to ask Paul. Who lives in the big house on the river, west edge of town?"

"You probably mean the old Bruno mansion. It's the town museum now. Paul's done well. He has the best reputation in the county as a homebuilder."

"He says he's got all the business he wants."

"That's an odd way of saying his business is down fifty per cent this year. With the recession, Paul's been keeping his guys busy doing other things. He was low bidder on a bunch of sidewalk and curb repair work let by the town council. A year ago, he bought the Ormecrest Riverside Motel at a sheriff's sale that was abandoned after the flood of '51. He's converting it to efficiency apartments for senior citizens. Is he going to the service?"

"He and his wife are on their way to Topeka for a homebuilder's gathering of some sort."

"So, you're not sticking around?"

"Can't. It's crunch time in our business."

"How'd you get into the custom cutting business anyway, if you don't mind my asking?"

"Dad got a call from a friend in Stockville the spring of my sophomore year in high school. He had a son same age as me who'd lined up a summer job with a custom cutting outfit out-a McCook, Nebraska. They were looking for workers. Before I could even think about it, Dad told 'em I'd be there. I'd get room and board and ninety-five bucks a week. I thought I was gonna be rich. Not many jobs paid that much in North Platte when I was sixteen. All I needed was a valid driver's license."

"You ever done that kind-a work before?"

"Nope. Little did I know."

Jake walked in, clad in a dark suit, button-down shirt, tie, and sneakers, his dress shoes in hand. Doyle introduced Jake to Alex.

"Jake went to school with the twins."

"Tragic," said Alex. "We've had our share of mishaps over the years, but nothing compared to this." Jake concentrated on detailing his shoes lest his *Schadenfreude* rear its head.

"Anyway, my first week on the job, down around Alva, Oklahoma, I got a taste of what I was in for. They'd had quite a bit of rain the week before. Fields were still soggy in spots, but the wheat was dry and needed cut. The wet weather triggered a toad hatch. Thousands of the little jumpers everywhere. Like a plague. Every so often we had to stop combining 'cause the grain sieves got plugged up. Next thing I know, I'm flat on my back scrapin' toad guts and wheat dust. My face was covered in it. Got it in my hair. My mouth. My clothes. My eyes."

"Real man stuff," Doyle laughed. "What else did you learn?"

"How to reheat a hamburger on a combine's manifold till it's like fresh off the griddle."

"Can't get through life not knowin' that."

"Anyway, we worked our way north. After we shut down one evening and finished servicing the equipment, I tagged along with some of the crew into Kinsley, thinkin' we might catch the late movie just for something to do. We were an hour too late, so they decided to go have a beer, instead. I tried to beg off since I was underage. They told me not to worry. We wound up in this little honky-tonk beer joint. The place is packed. Nowhere to sit. I'm standin' near the front door sippin' on a beer when this stranger in a cream-colored Stetson walks up, gets right in my face, and says something like, "I hear your name's Tex Ritter." The crew called me that because they already had another guy named Alex. Anyway, he said his name was Tex Ritter; I couldn't be Tex Ritter. Only room for one Tex Ritter in this town. Tex Ritter wasn't no Nebraska Cornhusker and wouldn't be caught dead in no dime store cowboy hat. This ol' boy is about thirty, shorter than me, and at least three sheets to the wind. At first, I thought he was just funnin' with me. Then, he starts pokin' his finger hard into my chest sayin' I needed to get the fuck out-a his sight. Pardon my French. To make matters worse, my buddies are right there tellin' him yes, I was Tex Ritter; I was the Real McCoy. I stood my ground. It went downhill from there. The long and short of it, he wanted to fight me for the title."

"Good pun."

"Next thing I knew, we're in the parking lot, *mano a mano*. Uh, you got a bathroom I could use real quick? This mornin's coffee's run right through me."

"Sure. Through that door, on your right."

Alex bolted out of the chair toward the back room at a trot. Doyle plucked the fly swatter from its hook and stalked a wasp in the front window.

"Donna's makin' up some *enchiladas*, *charro* beans and Spanish rice for supper tonight.

"We'll eat at her place around six-thirty."

[SWAK!]

"D'you hear me?"

[SWAK! SWAK! SWAK!]

"I'll be there."

"What're you doing after the funeral?"

"John wants me to help dig nightcrawlers for Stuber's bait shed."

"You don't <u>have</u> to go this morning, you know?" Jake did not respond. "There's a couple things need done around here," Doyle suggested, replacing the swatter. "And Bruner called. Asked if you had time today to do the bank's windows."

"Sorry about that. Couldn't hold it any longer."

"So, how'd the fight turn out?"

Alex chuckled. "He was so darn drunk he didn't know when to quit. I'd knock him down; he'd get back up. Charge back at me, swingin' away. Kickin' every chance he got. I think everyone in the bar come outside to watch."

"Small town spectator sport on a hot Saturday night."

"He didn't know when he was beat, neither. Wouldn't stay down.

My nose was bleedin', drippin' all over my shirt. My fists hurt like hell. Knuckles were so raw I was on top of him punchin' with my elbows."

"How'd it end?"

"Town cop came by and broke us up."

"You get in big trouble?"

"Nope. Had me sit in his car for a few minutes. Checked my driver's license. I thought sure he'd say something 'bout me bein' underage age but didn't. Told me this other Tex guy gets in fights all the time. Same time, same place, usually. Said he could damn near set his watch by it. Bad part was havin' to spend half my week's pay gettin' patched up in the emergency room. Had to pay cash. And they threw out what was left of my favorite Cornhuskers t-shirt."

"Learn as you go, huh? Anyone still call you Tex?"

"Just my wife."

Jake put on his fresh shined shoes and disappeared into the back room. Doyle fronted Alex to view his handiwork and repositioned the rubber mat under his feet.

"Word goin' around town is the twins were killed when they wrecked one-a your grain trucks. Is that right?"

"We sent 'em to town with a full load of wheat just before the noon hour with everybody's hamburger order. Gave 'em directions as best we knew them. There aren't many road signs out where we work, only landmarks to go by like farmhouses, old silos, creeks, and some such. Anything that might get you goin' in the right direction. Can't tell you if they got lost or tried takin' a shortcut. But drivin' a loaded grain truck weighing ten ton or so over a posted 3-ton limit podunk county bridge is asking for trouble."

"No kidding!"

"From all appearances, they were going too fast and, for some reason, braked hard just before they reached the crossing. Skid marks told us that. The bridge buckled and they did a header about ten feet into the creek bottom. The truck plugged itself nose down against the opposite bank. The grain flipped forward and buried the cab. The impact must-a jammed the doors. The grain cut off their air. They suffocated."

"They couldn't crawl out the windows?"

"They might-a tried that, but grain would-a just kept comin'

75

through. It would-a been pitch dark inside that cab and any air pocket would-a been full-a grain dust. Doubt either of 'em would-a fit through one anyway."

"So, the crash itself didn't do 'em in?"

"Nope. They'd both moved around in the cab. I didn't get to the site till after they pulled 'em out. Highway patrolman told me they were clutched up in each other's arms."

"Oh, sweet Jesus!" moaned Doyle. "Who found 'em?"

"Farmer and his wife on their way to town. Your next customer wants in," Alex said, nodding toward the door. Wally was standing on the walk outside, wagging.

"Jake!" Doyle hollered but got no response. He stepped over to the door and let the dog in. "Find your chair." Wally detoured to sniff Alex's boots. "Wally. Go on. Find your chair."

"Sorry. That's Wally. Jake's dog. He must've jumped the fence."

"Good dogs, labs."

"Wally's been one heck of a good dog. He just showed up one morning, three, four years ago. The world wouldn't be the same around here without 'im."

"Did you know the twins?" Alex asked.

"Cut their hair every six weeks or so for years."

"Champ was the dominant one."

"Yep. Always got his haircut first."

"Hope his folks don't blame me for what happened."

"Why would they?"

"Because I was their boss. You never know what or, rather, <u>who</u> people might want to blame for something."

Wally barked, leaped to his feet, and dashed to the front door.

"Your dog's been looking for you," Doyle said. "Where'd you go?"

"For a walk."

"You want me to put anything on top 'fore you take a look in the mirror?"

"What would you put on hair this short?"

"Gotta ask. Some do. So they smell like a new haircut."

Doyle brushed the hair from his neck and shoulder area then handed him the mirror. He looked sideways in the mirror and ran his free hand back and forth over the top of his head.

"I gotta know," Doyle said. "What made you go back to that kind-a work?"

"Owner's daughter."

"Ah-ha!" Doyle exclaimed.

"It looks great. Thanks," Alex said, handing the mirror back. "To make a long story quick, I met her the morning right after my knock-down, drag-out in Kinsley. I had me one hell of a shiner, cuts, bruises, face was swollen, and my nuts were sore from him landing a kick. Didn't tell her that part. She was the prettiest fifteen-year-old girl I'd ever seen. Bar none. Very mature for her age."

"Big chest?" Doyle asked, as he removed tissue and cape.

"Yep. Not as well-endowed as that pin-up on your bathroom door, but darn near.

Anyway, I was only around her that one day. Her dad docked my pay for sleepin' in and put me on light duty till I healed up. I made it back home mid-August just in time to start football practice. Told Dad there wasn't a snowball's chance in hell of me doin' that kind-a work again. First week of school, a two-page, perfumed letter came in the mail with my final paycheck. Main thing she said, she hoped I'd come back next summer and work for her dad."

CHAPTER 15
INDEPENDENCE DAY

Saturday – July 4

To Jake, it was Susie Olsen Day. The fireworks show at the country club conjured up a memory he had held close since he was fifteen. Jake and blond, blue-eyed Susie Olsen had been classmates since kindergarten. Her family dry-farmed 640 acres of land several miles west of Waltsburg. She could hit and throw a baseball as well as any of the boys in their class and run nearly as fast. Why they were drawn to each other in 9th grade had always been a mystery. Their friendliness took a very pleasant turn at a 4-H Club sponsored event just before school let out for the summer. She invited Jake to come, to meet her at a private lake owned by one of their members. There would be a cook-out, a bonfire, and hayrack ride. The handholding began as they stood around the bonfire at twilight. During the hayride, the kissing was non-stop, the petting, cautiously inventive, till one of her older brothers broke them up.

Soon after school let out for the summer, harvest was in full swing, and Susie was expected to pull her weight. Though they had stayed in touch, they were able to be together only once on a Saturday evening. Doyle allowed Jake, learner's permit in his wallet, to drive to Barney's where her family was having supper, pick her up, and take her to Perky's. Less than an hour later, he had to take her back. She told Jake they planned to be in town the 4th of July and spend the day. She and her mother would tend their display of home-grown produce and baked goods in harmony with other local vendors at the old railroad depot. When that day arrived, she and Jake were able to resume their dalliance. They held hands on and off, ducked down alleys and hid behind buildings to thieve a kiss or a cop a feel during the parade. Over the noon hour they went their separate ways, agreeing to meet up later at the country club fireworks show.

#

Waldoon Days, inaugurated in 1926 as a post-wheat harvest festival the last week of June, was as popular in Waltsburg as the Christmas holidays. Forty-four years ago, a carnival troupe staked out its Big Top, amusement rides, midway, freak show, and bawdy cooch tent attractions for a ten-day stand. Four years after the fateful deaths of Bearnard and Mary Muldoon, the festival's primary backers, and a year after Sean Robert Muldoon's murder and Sharon DeCritt's untimely accident, the Waltsburg town council voted to merge Waldoon Days with its traditional Fourth of July celebration. Over time, most Waldoon Days' traditions were replaced with more contemporary or budget-friendly ones. The contract with the carnival troupe was terminated. A car show and a small Best of Show trophy replaced the scarecrow contest with its 1st, 2nd and 3rd place chalices and cash prizes. Its free mesquite-grilled Angus steak dinner was replaced by all you can eat ten-cent hot dogs and cut-rate beer.

By its size and resources, Granfield, the county seat, drew the largest crowd for an Independence Day parade. The number of participants in Waltsburg's parade was just enough for it to still be viable. Waltsburg's long-established farmers market, its peddlers arrayed around the defunct train depot, experienced its most lucrative weekend of the year.

Conspicuous displays of the red, white, and blue bedecked Waltsburg's facades. Parade participants assembled on land north of the tracks next to the abandoned cattle pens overgrown with sunflowers and pigweed. Today's pageant commenced mid-morning and took nearly an hour to run its course, looping the double-wide boulevard. Traditionally, a high school band playing John Phillip Sousa's *Stars and Stripes Forever* led the parade. This year, however, a Willy's Jeep with a tape deck and two large amps replaced the marching band. Its lone passenger was the town's most identifiable *cause célèbre*, Violet Brisby in early twentieth century garb bearing her placard:

Tremble
King
Alcohol

Trailing the jeep came Catharine Mixx in her 4-door, white 1961 Lincoln Continental convertible with red, white, and blue pleated fan bunting and signs proclaiming All Bright Realty. In lieu of a Wheat Harvest Queen, four men named Bob rode with her. The Waving Bobs, as it were, included Mayor Bob Copeland wearing an Uncle Sam high hat. Beside her, riding shotgun, Pearl Harbor vet T. Robert Friscote who preferred being seen with a blond in a convertible over being shepherded in his wheelchair by fellow VFW members. They tossed Jolly Rancher candies at bystanders.

The unrehearsed start-stop-crawl spectacle concluded with a last-minute entry. The Knights of Nazareth, a group of Harley-Davidson We Ride for Jesus motorcycle enthusiasts astonished onlookers. Nonny talked one of the Knights into giving her a joy ride afterward. Jake added a new term to his vocabulary: Ape-hangers. The car show, in front of the Waltsburg State Bank, had eleven entrants with one notable no-show: Allen Baguelt's new Monte Carlo SS 454 coupe. As the finale, a spectacular fireworks display was staged at the country club after dark.

Late afternoon, Jake joined Henry and others at the country club to prepare. They assembled the sizeable concessions tent, set up tables and folding chairs, off-loaded deliveries, and placed double-faced yard signs at strategic locations on the golf course:

DO NOT WALK
STAND OR SIT
ON GREENS

Spectators came by the pickup load filling the country club's parking lot beyond capacity. The shoulders of the roads defining the club's boundaries were lined with vehicles on both sides as far as the eye could see. Club members manned golf carts loaded with snacks, coolers of beer and soft drinks to peddle. Lone Cloud trolled the area in his ice cream truck, hoping as always for his best sales day of the year.

Revelers set off celebratory strings of ladyfingers and Black Cats that hop-skipped every which way, contrasted by the rhythmic cadence of twelve-shot Roman candles. Volcanoes spewed brilliant, whistling geysers of sparks. Bottle rockets zip-flared in all directions. The smell of gunpowder, the *eau de toilette* of war, permeated the warm twilight air. The evening was made-to-order for aerial fireworks. Jake, Donna, Doyle, Merry Belle, Conger, Nonny, and John Griever sat in lawn chairs on the slightly elevated tee box of hole Number 1 surrounded by a sea of spectators waiting for the exhibition, a durable sacred cow in the town's budget.

Twenty minutes before showtime, a barefoot Darcy Cage sashayed up to Jake as he emerged from the concessions tent balancing a makeshift tray of bottled soft drinks and canned beer. "Can I have a sip?" Darcy begged, adjusting the stars and stripes headband garnishing her forehead. "Uh…s-sure," Jake stuttered. She helped herself to the icy bottle of Coke. She asked if he had seen Eric. He had not. He caught himself staring at her taut, hominy-size nipples, audacious as skyscrapers, through her lightweight, ribbed men's undershirt. She hinted she knew of a perfect spot on the golf course to view the aerial display. Jake hesitated, but she insisted it was positively the perfect spot and enticed him to meet her here at the concessions tent after he delivered the drinks. Jake said he would be back. The no-bra look, he decided, is how the trap finds a mouse.

When he returned, only a swallow of his Coke remained. "C'mon," Darcy said, leading him by the hand. "They're gonna start any minute." As they wove their way through the throng of spectators, away from the crowd into the pitch dark of the golf course, Darcy maintained her half-step lead. Jake heard the P.A. system voice of Waltsburg's mayor reverberating across the course. "Here we are," Darcy announced. "Have a seat." Bordered on three sides by creek-nurtured trees and gnarly shrubs, they were on Number 7 green in isolated harmony with nature's noisemakers and hosts of fireflies under a star-stippled night sky. Darcy sat and tugged at Jake's pant leg to sit him down beside her. Together, alone in the dark, was it prom night again? Jake's manhood speculated yes, initiating an intuitive rouse.

"I love this spot," said Darcy. "Don't you?"

"Never been here," said Jake, restively shifting position.

"It's so peaceful," Darcy sighed. "Sometimes you can hear the creek trickling."

At that moment, half a dozen aerial bombs exploded. Cheers and applause erupted in the distance as Jake downed the last swallow of his fizzless cola. He gazed skyward, tracking the gravity defying plumes as they rose above the treetops and burst into color. *America the Beautiful* blared over loudspeakers. Jake lip-synced its opening lyric.

"Ready when you are," a quiet voice suggested.

Jake turned toward Darcy. Close enough to touch; she was naked from the waist down, her jean shorts discarded off to one side. The small of her back flush with the green, her upper torso propped only as high as her elbows permitted. Straight away, Jake's attention was drawn to the dark triangle.

"I said, I'm ready. C'mon, Jaykee," she cajoled. "We don't have all night."

Ben Whitewater's question 'Is a naked woman intelligent?' flashed across his mind. Jake burst out laughing, stood, and strode off.

"Jacob Book! Have you forgotten? We're more than friends, you know?" she called after him. "I thought you liked me!" Jake kept moving, his path through the dark guided by bursts of light and sound. "Jake…! I need to tell you something!" he heard her call out. Moments later, he thought he heard her scream "Hate you!" Jake picked his way through the lawn chair and blanket-bound spectators haphazardly scattered along his way to Number One tee box. As he saw him approach, Eric Carver rose out of the lawn chair set aside for Jake.

"I'm looking for Darcy. You seen her?"

Jake shook his head no.

"If you do, tell 'er I'm looking for her."

"Got a game Tuesday night in Cass City," said Jake.

"Won't be there. Tell Bruner for me. Okay? Driving back to Lawrence tonight."

Eric wandered off in the direction of the concessions tent. Jake plopped down next to John Griever. John leaned toward him and asked if he had been following the news lately and commented to Jake, he would not want to be in Lawrence right now. If things there did not calm down, right quick, he would not be surprised if the governor called in the National Guard.

Another patriotic song kicked in: '*Mine eyes have seen the glory….*' Ooo's and aahs followed each resounding burst coupled with folks singing along. At the conclusion, the #1 tee box group decided to wait till the worst of the traffic cleared. Doyle offered to fetch a drink for anyone who wanted one. Jake said he would like a Coke.

Drink in hand, Jake wandered through the parking lot to the backside of the clubhouse. Eight years ago, to this day, he and Susie Olsen discovered the New World. The dark hid the fact that, in no time, they were naked below the waist. Their novice status surrendered, apprenticed in the moment. She guided his hand to that place, to that cleft between her legs and directed his finger movement till she whispered "Oo, there. Right there." She cooed like a roosted pigeon and fondled his manhood till he was momentarily overwhelmed by his first jolts of wonder. Clinging to the release and each other, sweaty, and breathing as though winded from a 100-yard dash, they remained locked in an embrace for what seemed like an eternity to Jake. Neither realized the fireworks had ended. The sound of someone retching startled them. A figure, arms outstretched, head bowed, leaning against the near corner of the building, moaned, and retched again. During their scramble to get dressed, the person disappeared.

As they kissed and explored one last time before separating, she whispered "I love you, Jake Book." Jake walked to the opposite end of the clubhouse, she to the near side to avoid any hearsay. Jake yearned to meet up again, sooner than tomorrow. Though they talked by phone several times, Jake debated with himself as to why she had not told him they sold their farm and were moving to Minnesota, or even said good-bye. Ultimately, he had to believe she did not want to.

CHAPTER 16
NATALIE LUISA MARTINEZ

Thursday – July 9

Father McKnight presided, endeavoring to bridge the gap between formulaic and the ineffable. Attendance was light. Of the fifty memory cards printed, nineteen disappeared.

In Loving Memory of
Natalie Luisa Martinez
August 2, 1952 - July 6, 1970

Rosary
St. Mary's Catholic Church
Waltsburg, Kansas
Friday, July 10, 1970
7:00 PM

Mass of Christian Burial
Our Lady of Guadalupe Church
Hutchinson, Kansas
Saturday, July 11, 1970
10:00 AM

Graveside Services
Fairlawn Cemetery
Hutchinson, Kansas
Saturday, July 11, 1970
2:00 PM

The rosary and memorial service at St. Mary's Catholic Church in Waltsburg were symbolic. The empty casket, on loan from Kendall & Hoch Funeral Home, was topped with an eye-catching floral arrangement and a framed eight by ten photo, her high school senior portrait, a community's remembrance. Paul Baguelt paid for all expenses associated with the occasion. Natalie's older sister, Ramona, worked for Baguelt Custom Homes for three years while attending Ormestrong County Community College. Her brother, Francisco, had worked for Paul for twelve years and was Baguelt's lead framing carpenter, dry wall, and tile man. Natalie had been a part-time receptionist. The ties were strong.

Jake wondered if others present shared the half full/half empty feeling like his. He had not known Natalie well. His best memories of her were those from the senior prom in April. She was a toucher, often placing a finger or hand on one's arm when conversing. Once he returned to the shop, he brooded, should he remove the Playmate of the Month pin-up on the back of the bathroom door, her name, and all the hand-written gratuitous comments? Out of respect? Or just leave it in place, a fanciful memory preserved?

It was Jake's first encounter with a Catholic service. The reds and yellows of the sanctuary's stained glass windows glowed bright as bonfires in the evening sunlight. John Griever dubbed the church a postage stamp cathedral. It was a modest but noteworthy example of Gothic Revival architecture with its lantern tower, steep roofs, and ornate spires. Its lone gargoyle nicknamed Viktor was thought by many to be the inspiration for the Demons moniker adopted by the town's sports teams.

As John Jefferson Griever sang *Ave Maria*, Donna Pileaux knelt on the kneeler, made the sign of the cross, fidgeted with a string of beads, and softly recited Hail Marys. Her eyes appeared more red than brown. The 'she's in a better place' amens were non-consoling. Donna was confident that Natalie had a future in the salon business and had high hopes that one day Natalie would take over her business when she was ready to give it up.

Guests at social gatherings in private homes characteristically gravitate toward the kitchen. The shade-sheltered steps outside the main entrance of St. Mary's served a similar purpose after the formal proceedings. Jake was introduced to Angela Parker, the oldest Martinez sister once voted into the Camp TaWaKoNi Walhalla of Big Tits, who attended the service with two of her children. Happily married, heavier than Jake remembered, now living in Austin, Texas, she too was a toucher. Neither a reference to Natalie's most apparent physical features nor her pregnancy was overheard. The straightforward chatter centered on details of the tragic accident, the highway's reputation for such events, and her congeniality.

#

Natalie's parents moved from Hutchinson to Peabody, Kansas, in June. Aging empty nesters, they desired something smaller, simpler to maintain. Lower taxes, less bustle, and being closer to their three grown children were also considerations. When Natalie confided that she was pregnant, her mother made an appointment with her OB-GYN in Hutchinson. Their 4 p.m. appointment ran late. It was 7 p.m. when they arrived back in Peabody. They ate a bite at Cora's Corner Cafe and chatted about what the future might bring. After their meal, Natalie's mother suggested they take a windshield tour of the mostly unfamiliar town. She and her mother were in complete agreement that Peabody, like Newton, Waltsburg, and damn near every other small town in this reach of the world looked much the same, day or night, rain or shine. Like reading a book you had read before, was it not? At 8:35, Natalie stopped at the stop sign on North Maple Street and Highway 50. She shaded her eyes and looked west, directly into the setting sun and saw no oncoming vehicles. She glanced to her right, asking her mother to move her head back so she could see, no traffic apparent from the east either. She engaged her left-hand turn signal, repositioned her sun visor and pulled out. Neither she nor her mother spotted the flatbed semi-trailer hauling a load of rebar barreling eastward. Her Corvair was no match for the behemoth or the big rig following close behind. The highway patrol measured only five feet of skid marks before the rig, attempting to avoid a collision, jack-knifed, and flipped on top of the compact car; its occupants crushed, dead within moments of impact. It took two hours to extract the bodies of Natalie and her mother from the vehicle. High beam headlights and emergency flashers highlighted the scene like the stage-set for a rock concert well into the night. The extra traffic diverted through town alerted residents to the calamity. Peabody and other towns along the highway were all too familiar with such disconcerting events. Some referred to the highway as a death trap, the more cynical insisted practice makes perfect.

#

Jake lingered long on the church steps. Bunched like poorly racked billiard balls, the attendees shared random remembrances about the deceased. Heading home, that gnawing half-empty feeling, the remote non-specific ache of the bereft, eerily similar to the baby bird episode of his childhood, lingered like an unrequited appetite. He stopped by the post office. Quickly flipping through the mail, an envelope addressed to him, postmarked Seattle, Washington, displaced the evening's afterthoughts. The greeting card contained a photo of his father and new bride honeymooning in Hawaii. To Jake, she appeared to be much younger than his dad. He tossed it and the other mail on the car seat. The Beau Coup Café was bustling with activity. The double-sided, hand-lettered portable sign on the sidewalk proclaimed:

GERMAN BUFFET SUPPER
$5.95
All you can eat
Drink & dessert included
FRIDAY & SATURDAY
6 – 9 P.M.

When Jake got home, Doyle was watching TV.

"Why's the sound so low?" Jake asked.

"Donna's asleep in the bedroom. She did not want to be home alone tonight. I have a job for you."

"What?"

"Repaint the bathroom door at the shop."

"Tonight?"

"No. Tomorrow. There's a can of white paint in the garage next to that stack of old *Boys' Life* magazines. Donna and I are closing up shop at noon tomorrow. Going to the funeral in Hutch."

CHAPTER 17
ON THE ROAD TO OKLAHOMA

Sunday – July 19

Merry Belle's hands gripped the steering wheel at nine and three. She would not, under any circumstance, exceed fifty miles per hour on the highway. She had driven to Redmond's Peach Haven Farm in Nowata County, Oklahoma, annually for years. Either Jake or Conger had accompanied her for the last five. The arrangement: Merry drove to their destination, her companion back home.

Jake knew there was always a surprise, secondary destination. As a former high school history and social studies teacher, Merry was keen to instruct any who would listen or were, as in this case, held captive. She had not outgrown the desire to learn of new places and people as related to Kansas. Last year's peach picking journey included a detour through Crawford County, Kansas, with its rich coal mining heritage, Big Brutus, and courageous women of the Amazon Army. Today, their return trip home included a detour through Wichita to pick up some beauty items for herself, Nonny, and Donna, so any history jog would be an abbreviated one.

"Have I ever told you about my first trip to Wichita?" Merry Belle asked.

"No, ma'am." Jake knew little about the big city. Other than his confinement in St. Francis Hospital during his bout with polio, he had been there only four times: Once to a movie, The 7th Voyage of Sinbad, with his Cub Scout Troop, an air show at McConnell AFB, a semi-pro baseball game, and a jaunt to its Joyland Amusement Park.

"As you know, I was plucked off an orphan train in Waltsburg in the spring of 1922," she began. "I wasn't an orphan. I had a mother and father, but I was branded as such and treated as such. Walter Bruno arranged an unscheduled late-night train stop as a favor to Bearnard and Mary Muldoon who settled in the area three years prior. Mary wanted a girl to help with the domestic chores. The children on that train were destined for somewhere else; I never knew where. When the Children's Aid Society agent realized why the train had stopped, an argument ensued. I remember seeing him accept an envelope. After inspecting its contents, the agent slipped it in his breast coat pocket and said, "Make it quick. We have a schedule to keep.""

"How old were you?"

"I believe I was fourteen the day I was whisked off to my new life. He and Mary had a five-year-old son, Sean Robert, when they immigrated to this country from Scotland. When I arrived at the ranch, the interior of the Empire-style manse was still under construction. Its corner stone, already in place, read MCMXXI. While crossing the Atlantic, Mary took ill with the Spanish flu and gave birth to their second child four months prematurely. The ship's staff was ill-equipped to handle such an emergency. The newborn, a girl, survived less than a day. By the time the ship docked in New York, Mary O'Shae Muldoon was in a great deal of pain and horribly depressed. It took a month for her to recover sufficient strength to travel west with her husband. Bearnard was anxious to pursue his dream of finding a suitable place to raise the Angus cattle he would import from Scotland."

"Was Annabel the baby who died?" Jake asked.

"Yes. That's what Mary named her. Annabel O'Shae Muldoon. Her name is engraved on the statue in front of the house."

Jake shifted in the seat and rolled up the crack in his window.

"I was immediately in awe of the prairie. I never imagined such openness. A horizon in every direction where you can see just as far as you please. I was accustomed to the cramped and cluttered like-what-you-get living conditions. Staten Island was a peculiar blend of smells and noise spawned by factories and machines belching smoke and fumes of every sort, further convoluted by assorted cooking odors and deplorable sanitation. Factor in the distinctive ethnic customs and garb brought here from the Old World, I lived in a soup. Germans, Poles,

Jews, Bohemians, Italians, the Irish…all contributed something. Add Chinese and Russians into the mix, the broth was uniquely American. Its ingredients, say, a slice of carrot, still tasted like a carrot. An onion, like an onion. Lentils, beets, rice, all retained their flavor, not a melting pot at all. My surroundings were man-made clamor and calamity. Overnight, I was swept away like Dorothy in the Wizard of Oz and set free on a cattle ranch. The neighs, bawling, and lows of domesticated animals replaced the clang of trolley bells and the bellow of ships' horns. Fresh air filled my lungs with every breath. A wind might last for days. Incomparable sunrises and sunsets tinted clouds a regal assortment of colors that last for only minutes."

"Ah-choo!"

"Bless you!"

"Sorry. Hay fever," Jake snuffed.

"There's a Kleenex box behind my seat. Anyway, as I was saying, the morning after my arrival, Mary led me to the natural spring pool where we bathed. That afternoon we rode to Waltsburg, and she bought me a trunk full of new clothes. I pinched myself more than once to make sure I wasn't dreaming. I lived under a whole new set of rules. I was baptized and given a new name, Merry Belle O'Shae Muldoon. I learned a lot of new words, too, like yonder."

The eastern horizon glowed as the two sojourners approached the first small town along their route. Streetlights, porch lights, and a dimly lit billboard greeted them.

WHITFIELD, KANSAS
Founded 1855
Home of the Rebels
We have most services

At the junction of its main east-west avenue, Merry slowed to a crawl. "Bear with me," she said. "I'm going to make a quick run through town." Two blocks west, Merry circled ever so slowly around Whitfield's town square cluttered with construction barricades and blinking flashers. "Like threading a needle, isn't it?"

"That where they're going to put the statue?" Jake asked, ducking, and turning his head.

"I believe so. Has Doyle ever mentioned eating at Maggie's? Maggie

Charles ran a restaurant called the Stonewall House. It used to be right there, on the corner," she said, pointing. "She had a colored cook named Beulah who made the best hoecake skillet bread and red-eye gravy I ever tasted. Best place to eat breakfast in the county. Beulah's fried chicken drew a crowd Sundays after church."

"What happened?"

"When Beulah died, the quality went downhill. I heard she never wrote down her recipes. Maggie ran a tight ship. She did take good care of her customers, though. Rumor had it she allowed the Klan to meet at her place after hours."

At the edge of town, Merry accelerated to her customary fifty mph. Jake felt the air buffet the car as it strove headlong into a south wind.

"I was thinking we might stop at Daisy Mae's in Ar-kansas City for breakfast. Do pancakes sound good to you?"

"Always. Did you know who your parents were?" Jake asked.

"Yes. They were too poor to care for little Frances. That was me. My father was a hopeless drunk who could not keep a job. How I avoided scarlet fever, diphtheria, and whooping cough in those days, God only knows. First, we were moved into what was called a poor house. Then, some other children and I were separated from our families and placed in a large Catholic orphanage. It was quite regimented. And I do mean regimented. We marched to meals. We ate in silence but were hungry all the time. We girls spent our days in the sewing room. Basically, we were warehoused. The bigger children preyed on the weaker ones every chance they got."

"Law of the jungle," Jake interjected. "Were you maybe Irish?"

"Yes. I'm sure I was. The Irish back then were outsiders, marginalized by society. We were bottom of the barrel, shabby little waifs with no future so far as all the do-gooder Protestants were concerned."

"So, the train to Kansas was a good thing."

"I had no idea what I was in for."

The sun cleared the horizon, illuminating a cloudless sky. Jake glimpsed the familiar red wing blackbirds, mourning doves, and yellow-breasted meadowlarks posed on barbed wire fences and hedge posts. The occasional red-tail hawk soared on a thermal, scouting for a meal. Tall, roadside bromegrass twirled with the wind and sweeps of passing vehicles.

"My, how I'm running on! I haven't spoken of this for decades."

"What about Wichita?"

"Oh, yes," she began. "A few weeks after I arrived, the Muldoons caravanned with four other carloads of people from Waltsburg to Wichita on the Friday before Mother's Day to hear evangelist Aimee Semple McPherson preach the Gospel. Mary Muldoon was still not fully recovered from the flu and premature birth episode. She hoped to ask Sister Aimee for a personal word or moment of prayer. She longed to be among those who were healed. Or, claimed to be.

We arrived in Wichita an hour before the mid-afternoon prayer meeting. By the time we found parking and made our way to the Forum, the civic auditorium, it was filled to capacity. The entrance doors were secured, and police stood guard. Around the corner, a few able-bodied people climbed through one of the building's windows. Though it was very faint, I heard singing from inside. I thought it just a bit crazy. A second meeting was scheduled that same evening. If our group attended the evening meeting it meant an overnight stay. Mary Muldoon was adamant. She would attend the evening session. Bearnard was not happy. He and Mary had words. They decided to leave the area and find a suitable place to enjoy the basket lunches Mary brought and decide what to do. Someone in our group knew of a park north of downtown where there was a new zoo." Merry went silent for a moment. "Is this boring for you, Jacob?"

"Not at all. Wally was an orphan. I am too, sort of."

She slowed as they approached Houray Springs. The only signs of life were pervasive VHF bowtie TV antennae and tree limbs swaying in the stiff breeze.

"Gonna be hot and windy today," she said.

"Supposed to be up near a hundred," added Jake.

"Where was I?"

"You were going to the park with a zoo."

"Oh, yes. I loved everything about the zoo until we entered the monkey house. The caged varieties, the noise, the stench reminded me of Staten Island. Otherwise, the park was a beautiful place. Two carloads of our group decided not to stay so they could drive home before dark. We headed back to the central business district in plenty of time, we thought, for the evening revival. There was nowhere near the crowd we experienced earlier in the day. Determined to receive the throngs turned away earlier, Sister Aimee decided to hold the evening session in Riverside Park, where we just spent our afternoon. Bearnard was really upset. But back we went. My feet hurt from walking so much in my Sunday shoes. Thousands turned out, many of whom were sick or incapacitated. Invalids in wheelchairs, others on crutches, some transported by stretcher, their escorts shouting GANGWAY! Jake-legs, palsy, rheumatism, and gout sufferers, the blind, the deaf, the terminally ill, you name it, they came, most of them dressed in their Sunday best. I saw two mounted policemen but was not tall enough to see much else. Above the din, I heard a woman's voice off and on. I heard Amen, Praise the Lord, and Bless you, Sister, time and again, all around me. Then Sean Robert Muldoon went missing."

The skyline of another small town's water tower, grain elevator, and a church steeple rose above the treetops. In the distance, a cloud of dust trailed a farmer discing his field. Jake glanced at the signs racing past in the opposite direction: Speed Zone Ahead, Green River Ordinance Enforced, JESUS SAVES, and ads: Citizens Bank, Hay 4 Sale, First Presbyterian Church, and CALVIN CO-OP.

WELCOME to
CALVIN
Pop: 344

The one traffic light flashed yellow. At the south edge of the town, they rumbled over railroad tracks unmarked by warning signs or signals.

"So, what happened to Robert?" Jake asked.

"Oh, yes. He was nowhere to be seen. No one knew how long he'd been gone. To make matters worse, less than an hour of daylight remained. Bearnard was furious. Mary was fit to be tied; she imagined the worst. She held my hand like a vise. One of their friends suggested we split up to look for him and meet back up at the boathouse below the Murdock Street Bridge. I never thought of myself as the sharpest knife in the drawer, but it occurred to me that plan was flawed. If one party found him, how would the others know to stop? What time would we all meet at the boathouse? Suppose we didn't find him? I kept it to myself. Mary making personal contact with Sister Aimee was no longer a priority. Anyway, it turned out well. A widow with our group found

Robert at the front of the make-shift tabernacle among a band of gypsies. Safe and sound. No worse for the wear, as they say. Do you drink coffee?"

"I'm not old enough."

"Fiddlesticks! Whatever gave you that idea? I'd like to stop somewhere and get a cup to go. There's a map in the glove box."

Jake sifted through the crammed compartment. "It's all Colorado maps and stuff in here."

"Oh, I need to weed through that and toss some of it out. Are my sunglasses in there?"

"There's these."

"Could you clip those on for me, please?"

Jake obliged and resumed his search. "Found it. Let's see…, you could jog over to Leon."

"Let's do that. Surely there's something open this time of morning."

Minutes later, Merry turned toward Leon where a locally owned service station afforded drinks and a bathroom break for them both. Jake bought a cheap pair of sunglasses.

"That kid at the gas station did a crummy job on the windshield," said Jake.

"We'll do it ourselves next time. Where did I leave off?"

"They found Robert."

"Yes, we did, but it was getting late. Bearnard telephoned several hotels. With Sister Aimee's entourage, assorted religious dignitaries and pilgrims in town, and Sunday being Mother's Day, we were out of luck. We drove to Newton and spent the night in a roadside motor court of small, individual cabins. Robert <u>did</u> <u>not</u> want to stay in a cabin with his father, but Bearnard made it clear that he would make the decisions from there on out. Next morning, from Robert's bloodshot eyes, ashen face, and ginger step, it was obvious he got a severe hiding the night before. He clung to Mary for the remainder of the trip. Bearnard led the way in his Cadillac Suburban to a place called Coronado Heights. Enamored with Kansas prairie-scapes, he intended to be there before sundown the previous evening to see a prairie sunset from its summit before returning to Waltsburg. The views were magnificent."

At the intersection of Highway 160, she turned east rather than toward Ar-kansas City. 'Surely there's a decent place to have breakfast along this stretch of highway.' In the heart of Chautauqua Hill and Osage *Cuesta* country, the Curly Q Café in Moline proved her right.

CHAPTER 18
THE GIRL ON THE LADDER

Laid out on a fertile strip of bottomland in the Verdigris River Valley of northeastern Oklahoma, Redmond's Peach Haven Farm, the Peach Capital of Nowata County, grew the clingstone variety of peach Merry preferred for canning, cobblers, and pies. Past Coody's Bluff, she took the first left-hand turn then followed the handmade signs to the rustic Redmond Country Store that silently begged PAINT ME! An upright Coca Cola machine and baskets brimming with ripe, fresh-picked peaches flanked the main entrance. The air was oven-like. Not a breath of Kansas's wind. Beads of sweat formed on Jake's brow as they climbed aboard the hay wagon destined for the orchard. The rhythmic snorts of the Allis-Chalmers WD tractor filled the air with diesel fumes as it trundled pickers at a three-mph clip. Merry snugged her broad-brimmed straw hat and calculated aloud it would take two hours to handpick three bushels.

Merry began selecting peaches. Squeeze, symmetry, size, color, and so forth. Jake thought the only thing missing from her ritual was a stethoscope. Once she found a few that met her criteria, she instructed, "This is what we're looking for." He separated a bushel basket from the stack of three and set off on his quest for likely candidates. It was an August-hot day in July. Sweat trickled down his temples as he avoided the grounded fruit rotting underfoot. He stripped off the t-shirt already clinging to his chest. As he began to prospect, he felt the all too familiar tickle in his throat. Five sneezes followed. He had taken Benadryl; but something in the air was stronger.

Jake picked a half-bushel of peaches then spotted a promising, untouched tree. He scrutinized the fruit, picking as he went. He heard a groan, then another. He moved to the opposite side of the tree and saw a girl leaning at an odd angle, balanced precariously near the top of a ten-foot platform ladder dangling a peck basket off to one side. He watched the base of the ladder wobble with her every stretch. He cradled three picked peaches with one arm and grasped a leg of the ladder to steady it. He looked up. Whoever she was appeared to not be wearing any underwear. The roundest, most symmetrical little rump and shapely legs he had ever seen. Her mini skirt was the color of the sky, her worn, white cowboy boots decorated with silver stars, and her head covered by a snug fitting cloche. Warily, Jake moved around to her front side.

"Aren't you afraid of falling?"

His voice startled her. She straightened and looked down at him but did not speak.

"Your ladder was wobbling. I can hold it for you."

She shook her head no. As Jake headed around the tree he glanced back and found her still watching him. He tossed the fruit into the air and began to juggle, slowly pivoting to face the girl who remained expressionless.

"Jacob!" Merry called out.

Jake stopped juggling, took a bow, sheepishly waved to the girl, and said, "Bye."

"JACOB! Where are you?" By the sound of Merry's voice, he located her two rows over.

"There you are. How are you progressing?"

"I found a really good tree."

Jake helped Merry separate her basket of picked peaches molded to the empty one and relocate both to the next tree she chose to work. Walking where he thought was correct, one row this way, two, three rows that way to find his basket, he recalled Merry saying she did not consider herself the sharpest knife in the drawer. Turning in circles, he imagined he might be the dullest. And his spontaneous juggling act, how pointless was that? His mind was not on picking. It was looking up the girl's skirt. Minutes later, he spotted the ladder *sans* the girl and his basket on the opposite side of the tree. He wondered who she was and where she went.

It was 2 p.m. when they hitched a ride back to the country store. The oversized thermometer next to the front entrance read 96°. Jake dropped the straps of his bib overalls and wrestled into his t-shirt before going inside. A large woman with a crooked jaw, wearing a Redmond's apron, prepared to transfer the fruit to brown paper sacks. Merry informed her they would take the produce home in the baskets.

"They're two dollars more apiece that-a way," said the woman, gruffly.

The woman loaded the baskets of peaches onto a dolly before Jake could offer a hand. Merry stood at the checkout counter with her pocketbook open. A girl with jet-black hair standing on the opposite side of the counter wore a white peasant blouse, a cerulean blue skirt, and a name tag: KIMMY. Jake stared. It was her! The girl on the ladder without the hat! Her eyes were burnt umber and slant, her cheeks dimpled, and her skin very tan. She was shorter than Merry and wore a colorful beadwork bracelet. He surmised she had Indian blood.

"Are you from around here?" he asked.

She looked at him but did not answer.

"She's very shy, especially around strangers," said the large woman. "She has a speech impediment."

"A peach what?" Jake questioned.

"Speech impediment. She stutters. Been that way ever since we've known her."

Jake glanced at the girl. She shifted her eyes away from him.

Merry asked for a receipt. He noticed the girl wrote left-handed.

"I'm left-handed, too," he gushed.

She gave him a quick glance but kept writing, then handed the receipt to Merry.

"You ready?" Merry asked.

"Yes, ma'am."

He directed the squeaky four-wheeler toward the front entrance where Merry held the door open.

"Just a minute." He stepped back to the counter. "Can I have a receipt, too?" he asked.

She cocked her head sideways.

"A blank one."

She tore one from the pad and scooted it across the counter.

"Can I borrow your pen?"

Jake jotted a note on the back of the form and handed it to her. After loading up their pick, Jake vended a Coke. He adjusted the seat and rearview mirror. As he wove through the crowded parking area, he thought he glimpsed the young girl standing just inside the front entrance. He pivoted his head to verify, but customers at the door, parked cars, and then the tractor and hay wagon obscured his view. The aroma of fresh picked peaches filled his nostrils.

CHAPTER 19
THE RITE OF MEMORY

Jake knew the way: West to Bartlesville, gas up, then north into Kansas, and west through the rural hamlets of Niotaze and Peru.

"Cute girl," Merry said.

"Yes. She was."

"I think she was here last year."

"I don't remember seeing her. Is she an Indian?"

"Possibly. Today, we'll stop in Sedan," she announced. "They have a museum I would like to visit. It's specifically dedicated to the life and career of Emmett Kelly."

Jake knew Emmett Kelly with his sad face was perhaps the world's most recognizable circus clown. He liked the change of pace. People were infinitely more interesting than events, places, or things, in his opinion. Much to Merry's disappointment, the museum was closed.

#

As they neared Wichita, Jake reflected on his bout with polio. In late September 1952, a peripatetic school nurse alertly recognized Jake's lethargy and fever as possible signs of poliomyelitis. The Books' family physician, Trevor Sisk Patterson, M.D., challenged Jake to pinch a pillow between his chin and chest as if putting on a pillowcase. He failed the test. At Doc Patterson's suggestion, Jake's mother whisked him off to Wichita's St. Francis Hospital where he spent the next forty-one days as a nationwide polio epidemic raged.

For years afterward, a fellow patient haunted his dreams, a young man roughly the age Jake was now, encased in an iron lung, his face known to Jake only by way of the mirror attached to the apparatus. Occasional glances in the Impala's rearview mirror brought back the memory. Other memories came, too: spinal taps, confinement in a cage-like crib, the hospital's hallways lined with crib-bound victims, the nun in a white habit who sowed a dour variety of good cheer, and a comely black nurse with vivid red lipstick who administered hypodermic injections in his rump, always with the same counsel to assuage his conspicuous anxiety, "Diss be over fo' you kin say Jackie Robinson."

Jake shared his hospital room with three other polio patients, so it was SRO where only a crucifix served as décor. Jake's father worked at Boeing in Wichita and made periodic visits to the hospital. His self-taught juggling and amateur sleight-of-hand illusions were a welcome distraction to the bleak backdrop. Jake looked forward to Emerson's visits as did staff and other children in the ward. His uncle Doyle showed up one evening and brought him a stuffed Winnie-the-Pooh bear and an illustrated, hard bound copy of A. A. Milne's book. His speech was slurred, and he seemed wobbly on his feet; a dark-haired woman Jake did not recognize clutched tightly to his arm.

Though he was deemed well enough to return home by Thanksgiving, he remained bedridden most days and became a chronic bed-wetter. After months of prescribed exercises and a regimented diet, Jake fully recovered, but was held back a year in school. As fate would have it, his Kindergarten Class of '53 included the Knaakt twins, Champ Jr. and Chase; Jimmy Baguelt, Kirk Michaels, Susan Olsen, Eric Carver, Ramona Martinez, and Parise Bruner.

#

The transaction at the Avon consultant's home in the small bedroom community of Kechi, two miles north of the big city, took all of five minutes. They stopped in El Dorado to eat a quick bite. On the drive north, the vision of the girl on the ladder skipped in and out of Jake's thoughts. They arrived at Doona Falls just before sundown. As they approached the turnabout, they were met by Blanco. Conger sat on the front steps reading a book.

"How was the trip?" Conger greeted.

"Exhausting," Merry replied.

"Great," said Jake, opening the trunk.

Jake handed Conger one of the brim-full bushel baskets. He asked Jake for another. He watched in amazement as Conger climbed the steps, each arm half-wrapped around a basket.

Jake tugged the third basket out of the backseat and toted it by its wire handles. He wished he were wearing work gloves; the wire pressed remorselessly against the flesh of eight fingers.

"In the kitchen, please," Merry directed as she held the door.

On his way out, Jake paused momentarily in the great room to admire the artwork hung above the stone fireplace mantle: a three-foot by four-foot oil portrait of Mary O'Shae Muldoon astride her pinto horse. Though fully sketched, only a third of the canvas was painted. 'One of Sharon Gabriel DeCritt's signature works,' thought Jake. One of her smaller paintings, *Bluestem Egrets,* hung on the opposite wall above an inlaid, cherry wood game table. On the table sat a 1st Place chalice from the Waldoon Days scarecrow competition in 1930 and a framed black and white photo of the entry dressed in a tuxedo with devil's claws attached as the hands and feet.

Another Sharon DeCritt piece similar in size to Mary's portrait, a horse mounted spear-toting Indian on paper vellum, composed entirely of arrowheads collected from ranch grounds, hung in Waltsburg's Bruno Museum. By the cash register in the barbershop, alongside a Flat-top Specialist sign and the dark yellow ceramic bowl Doyle's mother fit over his adolescent head to trim his hair, hung two of Sharon's shadowbox arrowhead displays and a sketch of Viktor the gargoyle.

Merry thanked Jake profusely for being such good company. "Next trip, I'll tell you more about the Muldoons which, incidentally, was not their real name."

Jake gave Blanco a good rough-up before he hopped in his car and headed home. As he noshed on a peach, it occurred to him as if he had always known. 'Of course! The vision of the girl...atop the ladder...picking fruit.' He was sure there was a photo of nearly the same scene in a past issue of *Playboy* at his uncle's shop. He found KOMA out of Oklahoma City on his car radio; the opening fuzz box guitar riffs of Norman Greenbaum's *Spirit in the Sky* came in crystal clear. He turned up the volume. Later, Jake tossed and turned all night.

CHAPTER 20
SHAUNEE

Monday – July 20

Jake was out the door at daybreak. He rode his bicycle the eight blocks to the barber shop. As he wedged the bike's front wheel between the trash barrel and the shop's rear wall, he heard cock-a-doodle-dos in the distance. He could still see traces of the words: CALL ME! D …written in lipstick on the steel door he had scrubbed off the week before.

Inside, he fetched fresh water for Wally and assembled the collection of old *Playboy* magazines on the ping-pong table. Sorting through the dog-eared stacks, he thought he would recognize the one he was looking for. Unfortunately, the stash of magazines was not in any order. Last looked at was on top. The May 1965 issue with a bookmark caught his eye. Jake opened it to a Roald Dahl short story titled The Visitor, a piece Nonny had encouraged him to read. He remembered it well, but it was not the issue he sought. Minutes later, he spotted a second bookmark. The cover was familiar. Alas, it was an issue with the fold-out missing, the one formerly tacked to the back of the bathroom door.

Jake wandered to the front of the shop and vended himself a Coke. He adjusted the window blinds, swiveled the barber chair to face the front windows and sat. He watched the come-and-go traffic at the Beau Coup Café and the post office. Merry Belle and Nonny would be busy today peeling, pitting, slicing, canning, and baking, not to mention licking their fingers. Wednesday morning, there would be a sign taped to Beau Coup Café's entry door:

HOMEMADE PEACH PIE
One Slice per Customer
While They Last

He mindlessly watched a hummingbird dart about the feeder and the monotonous swirl of the barber pole. The forecast called for intermittent showers late-morning. He needed to mow the lawn before it rained. He could mow now, but the morning dew was too heavy. His thoughts turned to the girl on the ladder. How would she know where Waltsburg was? He had not written Kansas on the note. Who would be interested in an unshaven young man in bib overalls and a sweaty t-shirt? Would she recognize him without his sunglasses?

He had not had a girlfriend since junior high school. He was twenty-three and lived with his uncle. He earned his high school diploma from Granfield High and completed two years of General Studies at Ormestrong County Community College. So long as he stayed busy, thoughts of 'Now what?' that lurked in his mind more often recently did not grate on him. The vision of the girl perched on the ladder did.

He recalled the photo he was looking for was past the Playmate of the Month fold-out. He sorted the issues by date, every year of the '60's in a separate stack, ready for a systematic search. His undertaking was interrupted by Wally barking. From the doorway of the back room, he saw a figure peering in the front door. As he approached, a young woman called out, "Is Doyle DeCritt here?!" Jake unlocked the door and allowed her to come inside. She repeated her question in a normal tone of voice.

"No," said Jake. "We're closed Mondays."

Reeking of incense, she sported a boyish-style haircut crowned by a daisy chain of wildflowers, a tube top under an unbuttoned man's dress shirt, hip-hugger jeans, a puka shell necklace and bracelet.

"Who are you?" she asked.

"I'm Jake."

"You related to Doyle?"

"He's my uncle."

"I'm Shaunee. His granddaughter."

Jake knew little of the events that occurred in the late '40's. To the best of his knowledge, Doyle had no contact with either his daughter or his granddaughter since they parted ways. Off to one side, nearly out of sight, a young man smoking a cigarette leaned against an older Ford station wagon missing its hubcaps. Another person sat inside the vehicle. The guy wore Jesus boots, tinted granny glasses, and a graffitied Army field jacket over a gray t-shirt. His bushy hair contained by a red bandana.

"We're just passing through. I wanted to stop and say hi."

"They might've already left for Granfield."

Shaunee's male companion flicked his cigarette in the gutter and entered the shop. Wally approached him. He froze. "Whoa, man! Does he bite?" he said, flipping his glasses atop his head revealing bleary, bloodshot eyes.

"No."

"You got a bathroom?" he asked.

"Sure. Through that door, on your right. I'm Jake."

Ignoring Jake, the guy cautiously side-stepped Wally and grumbled to Shaunee, "How much longer?"

"What's the big fuckin' hurry?"

"Fuck you," he snapped and moseyed toward the back room.

"Nice talk, butthole."

Jake spotted Donna's car pull up across the street and park in front of the Beau Coup. "Be right back." He jogged across the street, reaching Doyle as he was getting out the driver's side.

"Morning, Jake. What's up?"

"You got company."

"Oh?"

"She says she's your granddaughter."

Doyle's eyes narrowed. His attention shifted instantly toward the young woman standing on the sidewalk, barefoot, flip-flops in hand.

"What is it?" Donna asked.

"Get a table. Be back in a minute."

Doyle extended his hand. "Hi. I'm Doyle DeCritt."

"I'm Shaunee. O'Neal. Shaunee O'Neal," she smiled, a smile that instantly reminded him of his wife.

"And you're here because…?"

"Just passing through. On our way to Chicago."

"From…?"

"The City of Roses."

"Where?"

"Portland. Oregon."

The young man shuffled out of the shop. Wally squeezed out behind him.

"Who's this?" Doyle asked.

"My friend, Kyle."

Kyle walked past them and got into the station wagon.

"Friendly sort," Doyle remarked.

"Been driving all night," she said. "We're a little spaced out."

"We're having coffee. Would you care to join us?"

"Far out."

Doyle turned to Jake. "What was he doing in there?"

"Using the bathroom."

"What're you doing in there?"

"Sorting through magazines."

"You gonna get the yard mowed before it rains?"

"Yessir."

Jake and Wally went back inside. He resumed his search for the ladder-girl, listening to his transistor radio. Doyle headed to the café where Donna sat at a yet-to-be-bussed table, smoking a cigarette. Shaunee followed and sat down.

"Hi. I'm Donna."

"I'm Shaunee. Can I bum one-a your smokes?"

Kyle and the third friend, a shorter, stockier female in elephant bell jeans and a New York Yankees jersey over a tie-dyed t-shirt, showed up, sat at the counter and ordered full breakfasts. Doyle and Donna ordered coffee and cinnamon rolls, Shaunee, a large orange juice, a bowl of oatmeal with raisins, and wheat toast.

"I think you were about one when your mother packed her suitcase and left."

"I can't identify with that. I...I have no memory of it."

#

Upon earning her art degree from Kansas State Teacher College of Hays, Sharon Gabriel applied for teaching jobs anywhere she could find a position open. As fate would have it, she was offered a part-time position at Granfield's high school. Doyle met Sharon during Waltsburg's

106

Waldoon Days celebration. She was exhibiting her artwork at the train depot among the crowd of vendors selling their wares. When he asked if she would like to have coffee sometime, she responded: "How about this evening?" Infatuation blossomed and the chemistry that ensued proved an unbreakable bond. Sharon took to heart her mother's advice. "If, one day, you think you're in love with a man and you think he might propose, ask yourself these three things: Do we laugh at the same things? Do we despise the same things? Do we avoid the same things? When you can answer yes to all three, marry him!

Doyle had neither seen nor heard from Shaunee's mother for over twenty years. Momentarily, it all raced through his mind. The undue losses and string of anxious highs and lows that haunted him for years flashed back as though it was yesterday. His teenage daughter, Sarah, along with eight other girls aged sixteen to twenty, pregnant by Sean Robert Muldoon, who practiced his cultish evangelism under the guise of The New Shalem Temple at Doona Falls Ranch he inherited. Embarrassment and shame compelled Doyle and Sharon, to place Sarah in Fairmount Maternity Hospital, in Kansas City, Missouri, a refuge for unwed mothers. On the drive back home from a Sunday jaunt to visit their daughter in December 1947, she got caught in a white-out snowstorm after dark, drove off the highway, rolled over in a ditch, and was not found till the following morning. His drive to Kansas City to inform Sarah of her mother's fate. His utter frustration at being denied permission to retrieve his wife's personal items and artwork from her studio in an upstairs bedroom of the Doona Falls manor house.

The following February, Sean Robert Muldoon was found shot to death on the third floor, site of his elaborate tabernacle, the murder still unsolved. In April, Doyle's daughter, Sarah, gave birth to a baby girl, Shaunee DeCritt. Restless and unhappy, Sarah stayed with Doyle less than a year before she packed a suitcase, all her mother's jewelry, Doyle's favorite photo of his wife and Mary Muldoon astride horses and eloped with an electrician thirty years her senior. Doyle reflected on his subsequent seven-year bout with alcohol, a period in his life he described as repeatedly begging a loan shark for more time. Eight-year-old Jacob Book, his sister's son, coming to live with him and his relationship with Ladonna Ramirez Pileaux were his salvation. By the mid-'50's, his life took a hairpin turn for the better.

#

"You must be what? Twenty-one, twenty-two by now?" Doyle guessed.

"Twenty-three next April."

"What's in Chicago?"

"*Hair.*"

"The play?" Donna asked.

"Yeah."

"Waltsburg's a ways out-a your way, isn't it?" Doyle said.

"Kind-a. Kyle's not real happy with me but he'll get over it."

"Think that jalopy of yours will make it there? It's a good day's drive from here."

"Believe it. We're crashing in Lawrence tonight. Someone Kyle knows has a pad there. Prob'ly let it all hang out tomorrow, then drive to Chicago. That jalopy is our motel. We're on a shoestring budget. One meal a day, no souvenirs, no Dairy Queen cones. A real downer."

"So, what d'you do in Portland?"

"Make jewelry. Like these," she said, fondling her puka creations. "Sell 'em to friends, head shops, boutiques, whoever. These are really big right now."

"May I see your bracelet?" Donna asked.

"Okay. Sure."

Donna looked at it closely, "Nice."

"It's for sale."

"How much?"

"For you, ten bucks. Shells are from Hawaii. I get fifteen to twenty back home."

"You don't say?" Donna responded, handing the bracelet back.

"Was that boy your son?"

"Jake? He's my nephew."

"He's cute. He looks a lot like Little Joe. That Ponderosa brother on TV."

"I've told him that before," smiled Donna.

"You going to school?" asked Doyle.

"Yes. I took an *origami* class last semester."

Doyle and Donna looked baffled.

"Japanese paper folding," she clarified.

Shaunee scarfed down her breakfast. Once the toast and oatmeal were gone, she poured the remainder of the complimentary milk into her bowl and tipped it up to drink. She asked Doyle why his hand was shaking.

"They're cold this morning," he said, rubbing his hands together.

"That shaking reminds me of Kyle's father. He has Parkinson's. Smokes grass to calm the symptoms." She produced a rolled joint from her shirt pocket. "You can have this. Best stuff you can get where we're from."

"I... uhm...I don't have Parkinson's," sputtered Doyle.

"It'll cure whatever ails ya. Lemme show ya the best way to do it."

Shaunee disappeared into the women's bathroom. Doyle gave the joint a sniff then handed it to Donna.

"The Harvey Wallbanger of the Me generation," she muttered.

Shaunee returned with an empty toilet paper roll and used her fork to make a small opening near one end of the flimsy cardboard.

"Where's the rocket?"

Donna handed her the joint. Shaunee inserted one end into the hole. "Cover this end with one hand, like so. Light up. Inhale. Hold it in ...forever. Zowie!"

She handed the gizmo to Doyle, who passed it to Donna.

"Someday you'll thank me for that. I'd take five for the bracelet," Shaunee said.

Donna pulled out her pocketbook. She held up three one-dollar bills. "This is all I've got till we get to the bank."

"Far out, it's yours," said Shaunee, removing her bracelet and passing it across the table.

Doyle picked up the check and left a two-dollar tip. He paid Luci at the register and filched a toothpick. "Whoops!" Donna pulled up short. "Left the bracelet on the table." Donna doubled back. Shaunee and Doyle exchanged a cordial handshake. She hastily said, "Take it easy."

On the drive to Granfield, Donna asked, "You okay? You're awfully quiet."

"Just thinking."

"About what?"

"Past stuff."

A couple minutes later, Donna broke the silence again.

"Didn't you leave a tip on the table this morning?"

CHAPTER 21
TA-WA-KO-NI

Jake sat on the front porch swing leafing through the new area phone-book. Earlier, he picked up the mail at the post office and deposited $42.00 of wages from Henry into his savings account at the bank. He chatted for a few moments with Parise and noted Darcy wrote CALL ME on his deposit slip. He picked up the dog poop and mowed the yard, but the rain arrived before he finished edging and trimming. Now, the shadow-gray overcast produced only a mizzle of moisture. Wally was curled up on the WELCOME mat. A load of laundry tumbled in the dryer. Jake left the front door ajar so he could hear the telephone or the dryer's buzzer. He watched robins and sparrows flap in a puddle. Two squirrels chased one another around the trunk of a pin oak across the street where Mrs. Brisby, clad in a canary yellow rain hat, floral housecoat, and galoshes swept her porch, steps, and walk. Jake often wondered about the colorfully painted red horse with the word *Välkommen* that hung from a porch column but never mustered the courage to ask. The five o'clock whistle sounded; Wally raised his head and harmonized.

During one of the rain interludes, Jake revisited the shop and spent another hour poring over the neatly sorted stacks of magazines looking for the photo he thought he remembered so well. The image of the girl on the ladder lingered like a dream-come-true. 'What if I sent her a letter? Would she remember me if I did?' His note was not signed. She did not know his name. He shared his peach picking experience with his uncle. In less than a fortnight many in town heard Jake had a girlfriend in Oklahoma nicknamed Peaches.

A yellow cargo truck lumbered past the house. Its side panel read:

KNAAKT & SONS
MOVING and STORAGE COMPANY
Residential and Commercial
Bonded and Insured
Free Estimates

'How could that be?! They went out of business last year. Who was driving the truck? It could not be either of the Knaakt twins. They were still together,' he reckoned, 'but not in that cab.' The truck's image produced a horde of unpleasant memories. The Knaakt twins were large boys, biggest in their class. They had fair skin, buzz cut reddish-blond hair, and by 8th grade were shaving. Seldom seen apart; where there was one, there were two. The twins paid Jake little mind till junior high.

#

It began on a two-day Waltsburg Boy Scout Troop summer sojourn to Camp TaWaKoNi near Augusta, Kansas. Champ Knaakt Senior was scout leader. Eleven, twelve to fourteen-year-old boys made the trip. One of the troop's two newest members, Jake looked forward to the outing. Unbeknownst to him, it was a rite of passage when the more experienced Scouts initiated the neophytes.

They arrived early Friday evening, set up tents, and built a fire. They cooked their first meal, skillet-fried bologna complemented by Wonder Bread, potato chips, and out-of-the-can baked beans. A snipe hunt began right after sunset under the guise of being a prerequisite to earn a merit badge. Jake and the other neophyte, Eric Carver, were given black eyes using campfire charcoal so they appeared more like snipes. Each was given a burlap bag and led to a wooded area bordering Santa Fe Lake. Instructions were explicit: hold the bag open while on their knees and remain perfectly still so the mess kit bowl did not fall off their heads. Scoutmaster Knaakt demonstrated how to whistle like a snipe, then admonished: No snipe, no merit badge.

Jake and Eric were left to their own devices, although a voice in Jake's head suggested something was amiss. The demeanor of the Knaakt twins was suspect. After a few minutes, Jake wandered back toward the camp site. On his way through the wooded area, he encountered the twins and another Scout. He shined his flashlight on them. All three held their hands behind their backs. Burning tobacco scented the air. They told Jake to get lost.

Jake sat by the glow of the campfire adding twigs to its dying embers. A mild breeze began to stir; lightning flashed far in the distance. The black sky above was clear and crammed with Milky Way stars. Minutes later, the twins returned, then Eric. Champ Sr. called the troop together. They recited the Scout oath, sang several songs, and listened to their Scoutmaster lecture them on character till it was time to sack out.

While scouts in another tent sang 99 Bottles of Beer on The Wall, the Knaakt brothers' tomfoolery with their Scout flashlights had Jake seeing spots before his eyes. In the dark confine of their cotton canvas tent, the palaver segued to sophomoric sexual innuendo. Banter included crude Rastas and Liza jokes from the twins, Eric's story he overheard from one of his dad's friends about a man asking a woman if he could park his Cadillac in her garage, and nominations as to who in Waltsburg had the biggest tits. That honor was unanimously bestowed on Angela Martinez, a Perky's Burger Stand employee. When the beer song singers went silent, the two look-alikes asked Eric and Jake if they knew the Ford Song. Champ Jr. snatched the flashlight from his twin brother's grasp. Waving the light sources like batons of a frenetic band leader, he, then Chase, broke into song:

> My eyes have seen the glory of the coming of the Ford.
> It is stamping out the competition when the foot-feed is floored.
> It has forged a faithful reputation and reaped its just reward.
> Its fame is marching on!
> Glory, glory hallelujah!
> Glory, glory hallelujah!
> Glory, glory hallelujah!
> It's the quickest off the line, it's so fine, my Boss 429.

Champ Sr. jerked the tent's flap aside. "BOYS! I mean it. Lights out." Four "Yes, sirs!" followed. All went quiet. Jake, then Eric, discovered grasshoppers stashed in the bottom of their sleeping bags. Panicked yelps erupted, to the twins' delight.

A loud crack of thunder startled Jake awake. Gusty winds and monsoon-like sheets of rain battered the tent. The entry flap whipped wildly in the wind; water seeped in on all sides. He discovered he was the tent's only occupant. He snapped up his sleeping bag and small suitcase and made his way barefoot through the dark to the Scoutmaster's tent with its waterproof fabric flooring. Jake was the last Scout in. Champ Sr. whispered loudly he would just have to make room somewhere. Jake's flashlight revealed a cranny between two sleeping Scouts. He wedged his way in, compelled to lie on his side. He felt the movement of a straggler grasshopper at the bottom of his sleeping bag and managed to crush it with his muddy toes. He had to pee. After several moments of deliberation, he decided to just let go. He was already sopped. What the heck? The misery of the moment, he calculated, would right itself in the morning.

At first light, Jake discovered his choice of spots to bed down for the night was between the Knaakt twins. Careful not to disturb the sleeping giants, he slipped away. Two tents were collapsed by the storm. He shivered in the bright morning sun as he picked his way through the campsite to the third tent to change out of his rain and urine-soaked duds.

First thing, Scoutmaster Knaakt had the troop re-establish the integrity of the tents. Soon after, the Twins resumed their taunts and dares. Jake and Eric resisted all gratuitous offers. They did not eat the wild mushrooms the twins picked to go with their scrambled eggs or drink the warm liquid offered them in an open 7-Up bottle or play a card game called Fifty-two Card Scout's Honor Pick-up. That evening, when the troop roasted hot dogs and marshmallows on coat hangers over a twilight campfire, Champ Jr. made sure Jake's first pair of marshmallows wound up in the fire. When Chase attempted the same maneuver with Eric, he got wise and shoved Chase to the ground. Before Champ Jr. could come to his brother's rescue, Mr. Knaakt intervened then braced his sons like a Marine Corps drill sergeant, "DID YOU NOT LISTEN LAST NIGHT! ABOUT CHARACTER!" echoed across the lake. "DOES DO UNTO OTHERS NOT MEAN ANYTHING TO YOU! After a few moments of silence …GRAB YOUR SHIT! YOU'RE SLEEPING IN MY TENT! Next morning the twins were assigned tasks typically reserved for neophytes: policing the grounds, loading the equipment into the scouting trailer, and filling in the latrine. The reason Jake gave Mr. Knaakt for dropping out of scouting: He simply did not like it, least of all his thirty-plus chigger bites.

#

Generally, the Knaakt twins were well thought of in the community. They worked hard, like stevedores for stevedore wages at their father's moving business in the former Jupiter Dance Hall. To their high school peers, they were just goofy, happy-go-lucky teenagers. One Monday morning in the boy's locker room before gym class, they showed off enormous hickey marks on their torsos from tormenting each other with bathroom plungers.

The September after the TaWaKoNi episode, the twins persuaded Jake to sit at a desk that was not his assigned seat. When he stopped by the barbershop on his way home, his uncle noticed a large stain on the seat of his khaki trousers. The duo had put a blob of Vaseline on the chair seat, and he spent the day at school appearing to have had an accident. All through junior high, they came up with up new taunts, knocking books from his grasp, snapping his bare buttocks with a wet towel in the locker room, and phoning him evenings at home chanting Jayboo. The summer after his sixteenth birthday, Jake bought a used Ford Falcon from Stuber's Used Car Lot. The second week of school he discovered his car had four flat tires in the school parking lot, the words BOO HOO JAYBOO scrawled in soap across the windshield.

Jake ended his junior year on a high note. He pitched the title game in the regional Class B baseball tournament in El Dorado, a five-hit, thirteen strikeout, shut-out performance that qualified the team for a shot at the state championship. An episode involving the twins the following June at the Sunset Drive-In Theatre in Granfield convinced him not to re-enroll at Waltsburg High. With his uncle's blessing, he completed his senior year at Granfield High.

Knaakt & Sons declared bankruptcy in December 1969. The following May, the twins went to work for a custom wheat cutting outfit out of McCook, Nebraska. Six weeks later, Jake faced the dilemma of whether to attend their funeral service. Was there such a thing as inappropriate happiness?

CHAPTER 22
THE EARTH SHALL INHERIT
THE MEEK

Tuesday – July 21

After closing, Jake finished sweeping, took out the trash, and set a wood crate of empty Coke bottles by the back door. The phone rang. Merry Belle asked if he would drive out to the ranch yet that evening, pick up a dozen peach pies and deliver them to Luci at the Beau Coup Café, and would he mind taking Nonny home? She said there would be two dollars and half a peach cobbler in it for him.

Wally whined and turned circles in the front seat as they turned off the county road onto the manor house drive. Fallen prey to weather, vandals and neglect, the once majestic stone gate columns to the eighty-six-hundred-acre ranch had not been tended in years. Neither had the wide cobblestone drive where moss, grasses and weeds filled most of the gaps. Its old, lichen-splotched Catalpa trees were gnarled and leafless. Blanco was waiting at the top of the steps. Wally bounded across Jake's lap when he opened the driver's side door and the two canines dashed off in the direction of the Falls.

Jake rapped the horseshoe knocker against the door. As he lingered, he studied the entry's exterior stonework. The large blocks of native Cottonwood limestone framing the entry were chock-full of fusulinid, crinoid and coral fossils. The tuck-pointing was flawless. Above the Gothic archway, centered in an octagon of mason-cut stone, a ring of inlaid arrowheads pointed outward. Jake guessed it to be a prairie flower or crude compass. He speculated as to which arrow pointed toward the Oklahoma peach farm. He knocked again and took a couple steps back.

Above the arrowhead display were two lintel beams that did not match the color or symmetry of the other stonework. Both were apparently inscribed once, now defaced, and illegible. The antique light fixtures on either side of the entry popped on.

"Young Jacob. How nice to see you," Nonny greeted. "Come right in."

Jake followed Nonny's measured pace into the immense kitchen where Merry sat on a bar stool at the large butcher block island, sipping from a teacup.

"Welcome to our fine mess," gestured Nonny.

"Can we interest you in something to drink?" Merry posed.

"I would have a small glass of milk if it came with a cobbler sample."

"I'll get it for him," Nonny offered.

"What did you do to your finger?" Jake asked Merry.

"A paring knife with a mind of its own."

"Another Battle of Jenkins Knob casualty," Nonny added.

"Why's it yellow?"

"She put G.I.M.P. on it. She puts G.I.M.P. on everything."

"It doesn't sting as bad as Merthiolate. We're exhausted, aren't we Nonny? Once we got started, it's like cleaning house. At what point does one know when to stop? Yesterday we picked apples in the orchard and sand plums along the creek. We baked pies and canned two dozen jars of peaches. Not to mention a two-hour Scrabble game after we cleaned up last night."

"Today we made Adam's Apple butter and put up sand plum jelly," Nonny interjected.

"Besides the pies, would you mind delivering a box of goodies to Luci for her Homemade on the Range display case, and a bushel of peaches for her own dessert ideas?"

"No sweat."

"Would you like your cobbler warmed up?" Nonny asked.

"Nn-no. Where did you come up with the name Adam's Apple?"

"It was the name of the speakeasy on the top floor of the Atlantic Hotel," said Merry.

"John was up there once."

"A pile of rubble now," said Jake, forking his first bite.

"It was <u>the</u> destination for dignitaries. An exclusive haunt patronized by men of means."

"The main attraction was Sophie's girls," said Nonny.

"Who?"

"Sophia Cervenka, the young, prim and proper madam who always had eight or more fifteen-to-eighteen-year-old girls for hire."

"She turned them into whores," added Merry. "Walt Bruno stopped orphan trains at the depot from time to time so Sophie could prospect among the itinerants, many of whom ran off. When orphan trains stopped running in 1929, Sophie boarded a train to Mexico, to border towns like Matamoros, Laredo Nuevo, or Juárez, and called on orphanages till she found what she was looking for. She concocted some story about adoption, made a generous cash donation, and brought the girls back to their new life in Waltsburg. The Mexican girls were a big hit. Business was never better, even during the Depression."

"Depravity at its finest, if you ask me," said Nonny.

"One afternoon, a week or so after Bruno and his bodyguard left for Chicago, three stylish thugs from Chicago showed up at the train station and took over management of the hotel. A month or so later, the top two floors of the Atlantic were gutted by fire. Townsfolk placed the blame on Sophie, rumored to have caught a west-bound train with her Mexican girls the same night as the calamitous event."

"That's amazing!" Jake exclaimed.

"Those stories won't grace the pages of any history book. Ours is a mix of remembrance and lore, infinitely more interesting than textbook accounts of events, personalities, places, and dates."

"The stories behind the stories," Jake offered.

"Romantics perfected fiction."

"Liars invented it, according to my dad."

"Ain't it so," said Nonny, as she plopped down on a bar stool and wiped her brow.

"We hoi polloi are quite durable," Merry continued. "We are a very large, inclusive club. We offer free admission, hymnals, and no guarantees. How is the cobbler?"

"Great!"

"Merry informs me you may have got snake bit down in Oklahoma."
Jake looked at Nonny, then Merry.

"The girl behind the counter at Redmond's."

"I plan to write her a letter."

"Don't be shy, Jacob," Nonny chided. "You need to drive back
down there and pick more peaches."

At that moment, two dogs trotted into the kitchen, panting like
winded steeplechase runners, followed by Conger.

"Better get these two hooligans some water, William," said Nonny.

"That's what I'm fixin' to do. Hey, Jake."

"I have a question," said Jake. "Above the front door, what was
carved in the stone?"

"Oh, that was Sean Robert's doing," said Merry. "The top one read
NEW SHALEM TEMPLE. The one below proclaimed The Earth Shall
Inherit the Meek. I had William deface them when we moved back to
the ranch."

"Are we ready to load up?" Nonny yawned.

Merry handed Jake two crisp one-dollar bills, a Pyrex dish half-full
of cobbler, and advised she would call Luci and let her know he was on
the way. Nonny took Jake's arm going down the front steps. The cicadas
were in full harp along Minnie's Creek. Nonny commented there must
be a thousand fireflies along the creek.

"More like a million," Jake embellished. "They light up the creek
like a Christmas tree this time of year."

"I am sure that is more accurate. I do not have my glasses on."

Jake angled Doyle's Cutlass around the turnabout, turned off the
radio, flipped on the air conditioner, and navigated toward town.

"Oh, that cool air feels good," said Nonny. "Big plans this evening?"

"Prob'ly won't hit the sack till late. Donna's coming over to catch
Phyllis Diller on Carson."

"Oh, I would love to do the same," sighed Nonny. "I suspect I will
be asleep by then."

"John and I plan to go fishing Saturday. You ever go fishing with
'im?"

"I never learned to swim. He would not enjoy my company."

"Never too late to learn."

"I am afraid I would find a way to drown. I was never comfortable around large bodies of water. My final nursing assignment was aboard the *USS Consolation* hospital ship during the Korean War. Much to my distress, I might add. I always kept my Mae West on or within arm's reach or in plain sight. There's probably a name for such a phobia."

"I'm afraid of anything with a mind of its own under my feet. Like roller skates, riding horseback, or icy sidewalks."

"Wait till you're my age, Jacob."

"Do you like apples, peaches, or sand plums better?"

"I've been piecing on them all. I will probably have the runs first thing in the morning."

"How did Merry come by all her food skills?"

"Trial and error, mostly. I think it was just after her nineteenth birthday Bearnard fired their cook and put Merry in charge."

As Jake pulled into Nonny's driveway, he puzzled over why she had never learned to drive. He assisted her up the porch steps. She thanked him for the ride home and encouraged him to go back down there and pick more peaches. He drove directly to the Beau Coup Café where Luci and Anthony were waiting.

CHAPTER 23
SING IT AGAIN

Saturday – July 25

John Griever often took Jake fishing at the eleven thousand-acre, teardrop-shaped Ormestrong County State Lake. About a three-mile drive from town over paved and unpaved roads and across the Corps of Engineers-built dam. They liked to arrive at the lake after supper and fish till an hour or so after dusk if the fish were biting, the mosquitoes tolerable, and the weather favorable. John brought all the gear and bait, a coffee can of nightcrawlers or a small bucket of live fathead minnows, or both, from the lean-to bait shop behind Stuber's Garage. Once word was out fish were biting, he was eager to haul a twelve-foot aluminum skiff on his homemade trailer out to the lake. Since September 1959, however, he never fished alone.

This evening, they did not get their lines in the water until sundown. From their launch site across the lake from the marina, they witnessed a divine Flint Hills sky, splashes of gamboge, carmine, and flamingo streaked cirrus clouds on the western horizon. John lit the Coleman lantern and combed through his tackle box. As he watched dragonflies hover and dart, Jake thought the dozen or so small, lantern-lit boats on the lake looked like giant fireflies at rest. John started casting for bass.

"Your dad used to bring you fishin' out here, didn't he?"

"From the bank. Wouldn't take me out here on the lake itself."

"Interesting man, your father. We'd run into each other occasionally. Didn't know 'im well. You know, when you think about it, you're a lot like him in some aspects."

"How so?"

"Don't drink or smoke, for one …but your mother liked to do both. I remember him tellin' me and Stimka once that the most special thing about the Flint Hills is its want of echo. He always liked bein' the center of attention. But he had a sense a humor that could leave scars."

"The invisible kind," said Jake.

"Yep. You know my meanin'. I remember one afternoon when him and your mother showed up at the Oasis Tavern and sat next to me and Lyla at the bar. He didn't say much but he did tell a story on you. The one about you losin' a tooth and puttin' it under your pillow. He and your mother forgot to trade the tooth for a quarter that night. Next mornin', after church, you showed them the tooth and asked why. D'you remember what he told you?"

"Yes. That the tooth fairy and God had a lot in common. You don't ever see 'em because they're very busy …going here, going there, doing this, doing that. God trying to answer everyone's prayers; the tooth fairy trying to look under all the right pillows. He told me to try again that night."

"When we got up to leave, your father raised his Coke bottle in our direction and said, 'Here's to the skeletons in our closets.'"

"D'you ever hear why my mom left town?"

"Nope. Never did. Your dad lost his job when the dairy plant shut down. That caused a lot-a hardship, money-wise. They was livin' off their savings just gettin' by when he finally found work at Boeing in Wichita, which meant they was livin' separated. He and another man in the area rented rooms and would carpool back here maybe every other month after gas rationing took effect end of '42. Everyone had to make do in those days. End of '45, your dad was paid a big year-end bonus. The following June, he and your mom spent a week in Acapulco on the honeymoon they never got to have. He showed us some photos of where they stayed. A place called *Las Brisas*. A bunch-a little pink and white cottages, each with its own private pool. You was the result, young man. I know she wasn't crazy about getting pregnant. Especially since your dad wasn't around most of the time to help out, to be there for her. Emerson got escorted out-a Barney's more than once for making a scene tryin' to apologize for somethin' while she was workin'. Troubles between 'em was always gettin' in the way."

"I know. They were always telling me things were going to get better."

"They prob'ly figured you was too young to understand."

"Remind me to tell you someday about finding my mom naked in bed with Jesus."

John cleared his throat. "Did I ever tell ya 'bout the time I was out here in '59 by myself. It was end-a September, I think. Stuber was supposed to come along but got tied up at his shop. The crappie was bitin' damn near as fast as I could take 'em off the hook and get my line back in the water. It got dark and I wasn't payin' no attention to where I was. Breeze drifted me toward the dam. I was about three hundred feet out from it when out-a nowhere the boat rises up on this big bubble-a water, like a whale had surfaced under me. The boat tips and slides off to one side and twirls around. I grabbed on to the sides. My rod slithers out-a my lap into the lake. Bait bucket spills. Minnows is floppin' all over the place. Lantern tips over and goes out. I see a bunch more giant heaves in the water, big as box cars. If there hadn't-a been a full moon, I'd-a never seen it."

"They say there's something like that out here," said Jake, watching his bobber ride Lilliputian swells.

"Sent shivers shootin' out my fingers and toes."

"D'you tell anyone?"

"Not till now. Put on my life jacket, motored back in, and drove home. Never allowed myself to get that close to the dam again. Jake! Your bobber just went under." Jake snagged a sun perch. He reeled it in, blessed it and released the fish back into the lake.

"Remember that geologist with the state geological society who thought the lake was formed by a meteor strike millions of years ago saying it's not the shape of something that formed naturally. It's more like a crater."

"That I would-a like to've seen."

"Been like a dozen Fourth of Julys," said Jake, as he rebaited his hook.

"If you knew it was comin', my guess is you'd wanna set up your lawn chair somewhere south of the Kansas-Oklahoma state line."

"God's confetti. Think those black arrowheads on Sharon's Indian at the museum are meteorites?"

"Could also be that black volcano rock 'cuz the Muldoon place is sittin' at the foot of-a ex-tinct oozin' volcano."

"D'you remember the Olsen's?"

"The ones who farmed out west-a town?"

"Yes."

"Didn't know 'em well. Why?"

Emboldened by Griever's heretofore untold tale, Jake described in detail the night of his carnal adventure with Susie Olsen during a 4th of July fireworks show. An event he had never revealed to anyone. John responded he would not want to go through that phase of growing up again. "That first thrill is one you never forget. If you ask me, it has an afterlife. Once you cross that line, it's damn near all you think about. Yer like a powder keg lookin' for a match. That person retchin' behind the clubhouse could-a been me. One year me an' Lyla and some of her friends from Whitfield overserved ourselves at the event. It wasn't pretty." John adjusted the lantern's brightness and started humming. Jake asked about the Adam's Apple speakeasy Nonny and Merry had mentioned earlier in the week.

"Oh, yeah. That was quite the place. I chauffeured Bear Muldoon into Waltsburg late one afternoon with a box-a fresh-butchered Angus steaks Bruno wanted for some shindig he was puttin' on. Muldoon had me to carry 'em inside and ride up the private elevator with 'im. The one that stopped only on the top two floors. Every gamblin' device ever invented was up there. The bar was stocked with whiskey I never seen before. Dining area had white linen tablecloths, napkins stuck in crystal glasses, chandeliers...fanciest place I ever been in. Muldoon pointed me to the kitchen past a long table where Bruno was with Miss Sophie, Karl Albrecht, and several fellas in military uniform with more brass than a Salvation Army band."

"You didn't stay for supper?"

"I got escorted back to the hotel entrance by Bruno's bodyguard."

"Was the brass from Fort Riley?"

"Prob'ly. At one time, Muldoon had himself a contract to supply all-a their beef."

"Eric ever fish with you?"

"Tried it once. He got spooked-out when it turned dark. He was imaginin' things that wasn't there, triggerin' bad reminders is what I gathered. His mind was jumpin' to assumptions. No rhyme or reason to it if you ask me. But I ain't walked in his boots."

"He say anything about flashbacks or nightmares?"

"Yep."

"I don't think they're bitin' tonight."

"Not right here, anyway."

"Maybe over by the dam," Jake teased.

"We ain't goin' there, young man. How 'bout over by the rock ledges."

"When's Deke gonna get your trolling motor fixed?"

"He's waitin' on a part out-a somewhere in North Dakota."

Jake set out the oars and started to row. He could still make out the high-banked shoreline to the southwest and silhouettes of the tallest yuccas in bloom along its rim. John set his rod aside. As he changed lures, he segued into song:

Jordan's river is deep and wide, hallelujah.
Meet my mother on the other side, hallelujah.
Jordan's river is chilly and cold, hallelujah.
Chills the body, but not the soul, hallelujah.

Michael, row the boat a-shore
Hallelujah!

Then you'll hear the trumpet blow
Hallelujah!
Then you'll hear the trumpet sound,
Hallelujah!
Trumpet sound the world around
Hallelujah!
Trumpet sound the jubilee
Hallelujah!
Trumpet sound for you and me
Hallelu…jah!

"Warming up for church tomorrow?"

125

"Naw. I just like the song. Choir don't sing the good stuff like that. Don't take me wrong, I like singin' The Old Rugged Cross, but what I really like is the folk stuff, Woody Guthrie, Zander Rhoades music."

"John Griever! That you singin'?!" came a familiar voice.

"Yessir!" John hollered back. "That you, Paul?!"

"Yup!"

"Catchin' anything?!"

"Yow! Moby Dick just broke Kristie's line!"

"Kristie's his granddaughter, right? You know Jimmy and Parise are expecting their first?"

"They didn't waste no time, did they? D'you know the first two times your mother got pregnant she miss-carried?"

"Uncle Doyle told me that. Yes."

"You can stop rowin'." John started casting again. Fourth cast toward the shoreline, he hooked and netted a largemouth bass he guessed was five pounds or better. "How 'bout that! This big fella's gonna see the bars on my grill tomorrow night. You might want-a go ahead and toss the anchor out."

Jake slotted the oars and dropped the anchor over the side, the anchor's chain sounding like a torque wrench as it disappeared over the gunwale into the tar face of water. A canopy of stars assembled overhead. A gibbous moon cleared the horizon. Its bright reflection gamboled along the quiet swells. Jake grabbed the thermos and poured himself a lid of water. While he watched a large sphinx moth orbit their lantern, he remembered fishing from the lake's bank not far from the public camping and picnic area and skipping flat rocks across the surface waiting for his bobber to dip. On one such evening Jake's father branded the lake Waltsburg's Walden Pond.

"What's this I been hearin' 'bout a girlfriend in Oklahoma?"

"She's not my girlfriend."

"You need to go pick more peaches, boy."

"Been looking for the *Playboy* with the picture of the girl on a ladder picking apples."

After a few moments of silence, John said, "I remember her. The one on the other side-a the foldout. She was blond. Standin' on a ladder in white cowboy boots. Had on some real skimpy short skirt, leanin' away from the camera, showin' lots-a cheek."

"Griever! You still there?!" they heard Paul call out.

"Yo!"

"Sing it again for us!"

"Yeah! Sing it!" came another voice.

"Yeah!" another chimed in.

John cleared his throat.

CHAPTER 24
THANKS FOR THE CHANGE

Tuesday through Saturday – August 4 to 8

Conger always accompanied Merry on her ventures to the Muldoon cabin in Manitou Springs. When he learned Jake had not seen mountains, he asked him to go along to share the driving. Merry determined their route, then fluffed her pillows, pulled a blanket over her shoulders, and instructed them to wake her when they were ready to stop for breakfast.

Jake woke a snoring Merry Belle as the trio neared Greensburg. Rounding the sweeping banked turn at the town's eastern city limit, Jake spotted a vintage WWII torpedo bomber parked on the tarmac of the airport where a windsock floundered in the breeze. Sadie's, a hamburger and fries joint sat silent at the highway's edge. Conger coasted through a green light at Main Street, past the Tucker Inn Motel, and a Big Well sign. After breakfast at Burke's Restaurant, they stopped at the World's Largest Hand Dug Well.

"William hasn't been here since he was a boy," Merry recalled. "Last time, I had to hold him up to look down the well."

#

Merry's comment instantly transported Jake back to an episode shared with his father.

The old well behind their home had long been dormant. Its four-foot high, ivy-covered limestone wall with its Asian *nón lá* shaped roof remained as décor in an otherwise featureless backyard. Jake guessed he was no more than six years old when his father lifted him up to peer into

128

the hole. Emerson Book held him firmly with one arm and pointed out the nest of brown thrushes at one end of the cross beam supporting the well's roof.

"Hear their cries? The babies are hungry." He urged Jake to "Listen carefully…" as he dropped a bird feather into the well.

'Listen for what?' Jake thought to himself as he watched the feather spiral downward, disappearing into the dark of the man-made maw.

A full ten seconds later his father asked, "Hear that?"

"Hear what?"

"The splash." Jake was utterly perplexed. "Hear the echo?" his father whispered. He listened as attentively as he could but heard nothing. "Those," said his father, easing him back down, "are the sounds of silence."

#

The threesome peered through the viewing windows' bars into the softly lit chasm of the enormous well. Jake felt the well's cool breath on his face as he took in the stonework and suspended zigzag metal stairs that one could descend for a nominal fee. They browsed the souvenir laden gift shop and paused at the 1,000 lb. Pallasite meteorite discovered on an area farm in 1949.

MULLINVILLE 10

FORD 27

DODGE CITY 44

Merry mandated a stop in Dodge City for a bathroom break. "The next hour or two may be the most boring part of the drive," said Merry. "There isn't any scenery you haven't already seen. Mary Muldoon used to tell us if we rose up on our tiptoes out here, we could see the postman coming for two weeks."

As Jake steered westward, telephone poles, fencerows, and highway foreshortened in harmony with indefinite vanishing points upon a level horizon, bounded by endless furrowed fields, after-harvest stubble, fallow pasture, milo and soybean crops. Oases of farmsteads with their machinery, barns, corrals, windmills, and canopies of mature shade trees dotted the landscape. Jake wheeled into a Sinclair station in Syracuse, Kansas, sixteen miles shy of the Colorado border, to gas up, scrape the insects from the windshield, and check the oil as a routine precaution. He vended Cokes for Conger and himself. On the next leg of their journey, Merry set her crossword puzzle book aside and reminisced. On a similar drive in 1932, Syracuse was the source of some colorful memories, not the least of which was her recollection of Teddy, the night clerk at the Ames Hotel. Her tone was wistful.

COOLIDGE 14

HOLLY, CO. 21

LAMAR 50

"It was an election year and the economy continued to languish. We'd had two flat tires since we left Waltsburg and were way behind schedule. Sean Robert was car sick. The wind was blowing a gale and the horizon was layered with cinnamon-colored haze. We stopped at the drug store in Syracuse. Mary picked up a couple of items and bought me and Caleb, William's father, something sweet to drink at the soda fountain. Back on the highway, blowing dust forced us to pull over before we reached the Colorado line. We were one of many vehicles sitting idle. Mary improvised dust masks from water-soaked handkerchiefs we tied across our faces. We looked like bandits ready to rob something. At one point, the wind shifted and blew right over us. It got so dark we could not see the hood ornament. Once the wind shifted back, the highway had disappeared, covered in drifts of dirt. The barbed wire fences on either side were packed with tumbleweeds. Like many other cars and trucks, we turned around and drove back to Syracuse. Bearnard stopped at the train depot's Harvey House Sequoyah Hotel. When he returned, his mood was sour. No vacancy. Eventually, Bearnard finagled two rooms at the Ames Hotel. We freshened up and drove back to the Harvey House for supper. Afterwards, Mary Muldoon, Robert, Caleb, and I went for a walk. Except for a train whistle, I thought it eerily quiet."

"Like Waltsburg, without the whistle," Jake commented.

"Or the ranch," Conger added.

"We cut our walk short. Everything was covered in a thick layer of dust. Caleb was fussy and not minding me. After I settled Caleb down for the night, Bearnard asked me to go down to the front desk to request an early wakeup-call and see if they had a newspaper he could read. That's when I got acquainted with Teddy, the night clerk.

WELCOME TO COLORADO

"When will we see mountains?" Jake asked.

"On a bright day, like today, we should see Pikes Peak before we get to Pueblo."

"Wish this idiot behind me would either pass or back off," Conger groused.

"He was only paid a dollar a night," Merry said.

"Teddy?" Jake questioned.

"Yes. He worked from six p.m. till six a.m. six nights a week."

"You fell for Teddy?"

"Infatuated would be a better word. He was a talker, full of stories. He'd quit college in Boulder after his junior year for lack of money but was good-natured about it. He was saving everything he could to finish his degree in electrical engineering."

"How do you save anything on a dollar a day?"

"He lived at home. Said he was also a lifeguard at the city swimming pool."

"When did he sleep?"

"I didn't ask. I did ask what he did for fun in Syracuse. He told me he and a friend of his trapped skunks. He claimed a good, narrow-striped pelt fetched as much as ten bucks. They often drove to Holly, Colorado, on Saturday nights to attend dances. He loved to fish, hunt, and play golf when he could. We didn't get to talk long; I needed to take the newspaper I borrowed from the coffee shop up to Bearnard before he or Mary came looking for me. Are you paying attention to the landscape, Jacob? The change in scenery?"

"It looks a lot like around Lake Ormestrong."

"Semi-arid is the correct term. Less green. More rugged. Rocks and prairie dog towns."

Just as Merry predicted, the muted, majestic silhouette of Pikes Peak appeared on the horizon before they reached Pueblo. By the time Conger began the ascent toward Manitou Springs, Jake was enthralled. The grandeur of irregular rock formations, conifer forests, and lenticular clouds was mesmerizing. "Anybody else's ears been popping?"

The Muldoon cabin was an unpretentious '20's-vintage house on a forested acre of land, a crooked half-mile off the highway as the crow drives, within the city limits of Manitou Springs. Merry was convinced there was at least a subjective connection between the mineral springs in Manitou and the natural spring water pool at Doona Falls. "Mary Muldoon was forever seeking an elixir to cure her lingering ailments. Since their arrival in 1919, she consumed bottle after bottle of Wasa-Tusa Home Remedy and Seelye's Fluorilla Compound hawked by a bogus health tonic maker in Abilene, Kansas. Manitou Springs was the perfect place for Bearnard to hire guides to escort him, Walter Bruno, and their invited guests into the interior to hunt big game. Cascade and Nevada Streets in Colorado Springs were the inspiration for Waltsburg's wide South Main boulevard."

Jake climbed out of the car and stretched. The aroma of pine-scented air filled his nose. Though it was still daylight, the sun retreated behind the Front Range and the temperature was forty degrees cooler than Pueblo. On the drive back to the cabin from a short trip to stock up on essential groceries, Jake marveled at all the random dots of light on the mountains. He and Conger gathered piñon by lantern light and built a fire. Merry lamented she forgot to pack her Scrabble game and turned in early. A short while later, Conger said good night. Slumped alone on the davenport, Jake stared at the fire, captivated by the pops, hisses, and sparky snaps. He soon fell asleep but not before a second well story crept into his thoughts.

#

Several days after his father's silent sounds tutorial, Jake, Eric Carver, and Kirk Michaels played hide-and-go-seek at Jake's house after school. Jake and Eric dashed off the front porch while Kirk counted, hands over his eyes. Jake chose to hunker behind the well. As he awaited his fate, two adult thrushes darted about, quite agitated. He guessed it was his proximity to their nest. Their erratic behavior was sure to draw attention to the well and give him away. Sure enough, Kirk called out, "Gotcha!" The thrushes continued to flit back and forth between the well and lowest limbs of an oak in a neighbor's yard. Jake watched one of the birds light on the well's craggy rim, cock its head sideways as if peering downward, then flutter to the opposite side and repeat the antic. It was then he thought he heard the cries, faint though they were. He told Kirk and Eric. All three stood on their tiptoes at the well's wall, listening.

"Hear it?" Jake had asked. They thought sure they did.

Jake's mother had already left for work, so Jake pleaded with the babysitter to come listen and bring a flashlight. Plopped in a recliner next to a radio tuned to a Top 40 station and reading a teen magazine, she was not the least bit interested. He wished his father were coming home this weekend. Jake opened his bedroom window a crack at bedtime so he could listen for the tiny cries, but a rainstorm passed through that evening and continued into the night. Next morning, when his mother woke him to get ready for school, Jake told her he thought a baby bird had fallen into the well.

Her response, "What d'you want me to do about it?"

He gulped his cold cereal and rushed out the door to the well. Same as the feather's splash and its echo, he heard only silence. No thrushes flitted; the nest was empty. By evening, a sense of loss and profound sadness brought tears to his eyes. It was not until a heart-to-heart discussion with his father a couple weeks later that Jake put the event behind him. Emerson Book hinted the baby thrush was in good company at the bottom of the well. The stuffed Pooh Bear and Dinky toy trucks little Jimmy Baguelt once chucked into the chasm shouting "Bombs over Tokyo!" would welcome the new arrival.

#

Most of their Colorado time was devoted to scraping and painting the exterior door frames and doors of the dwelling. Thursday, after lunch, Merry showed Jake two of the mineral springs downtown and remarked that Manitou was evolving into an artist's colony. Friday afternoon, they drove Jake to see the Garden of the Gods and Seven Falls. Cave of the Winds and the Pike's Peak Cog Railway would have to wait; there were hordes of tourists. Same evening, Merry treated the boys to a steak dinner at the Broadmoor in Colorado Springs. Next morning, they grabbed donuts and drinks to go at a bakery and drove home by the same route.

YOU ARE NOW ENTERING KANSAS

When they passed through Syracuse, Jake asked Merry if she ever tried to reconnect with Teddy. She said she had not. She asked William if he remembered stopping at Perkins Zoo at the east edge of the town. He shook his head no.

"They had the world's largest collection of squirrels," she said. "Surprised you don't remember it."

"Whitfield could make that claim, couldn't they?" quipped Conger.

Pushing eastward, the posted distances added considerable weight to Jake's eyelids. He wondered aloud if Merry had any other historical stops in mind before they got home.

"She's not feeling well," said Conger. "She hasn't been her usual, chatty tour guide self."

"She has been awfully quiet."

"She still asleep?"

Jake glanced over his shoulder. "Yup. Still dead to the world."

"Pretty sure it's the altitude. If she stays too long, she gets short of breath, dizziness, and stomach cramps. Surprised she didn't tell you about the time ol' man Muldoon went elk hunting and left his wife, Sean Robert, Mom, and my dad at the cabin for a couple days."

"Tell me."

"Early morning, after he left, Mom heard commotion on the front porch. She got out of bed and pulled the curtain back. A black bear stood on its hind legs tipping a hummingbird feeder, drinking the sweet water mix. Its cub was peering in the window Mom was looking out of. Nothing came of it, but she was terrified of going outside till they left for home. Her favorite snack on those trips was Boston Baked Beans they'd pick up somewhere. She also liked watching for Burma Shave jingles."

East of Syracuse, lulls in conversation grew longer. Jake noted highway mirage appeared as wet pavement, looked for animate cloud images, and studied billboard ads.

"Is Boot Hill worth a stop?" Jake asked. "I keep seeing signs."

"Mom took me there once. It is interesting. Especially the graveyard."

"D'you go to the Knaakt twins' funeral?"

"Just the church service. You went, didn't you?"

"Yeah."

"D'you want-a make sure they were dead?"

"I went to hear John sing."

"I never could figure out why they picked on you like they did."

"That makes two of us."

"Wonder if hell has visiting hours?" Conger speculated with a sneer. After several moments of contemplative silence, Conger yawned. "Can you take over for me here?"

The service station where Conger customarily stopped was packed with station wagons stuffed with vacation gear and vehicles towing campers on their way west. Instead, he pulled into a truckstop on the east edge of the town. Jake gently roused Merry from her sleep.

"Where are we?" she asked, rubbing one eye.

"Dodge City. Boston Baked Bean capital of the world."

"Oh, my. William's been telling stories. Are we getting gas here?"

"Yes."

Merry opened her pocketbook and handed Jake a ten-dollar bill. Jake got out of the car, stretched, handed the ten to Conger, and moseyed inside to use the restroom.

"I bought some Boston Baked Beans," said Jake, upon his return.

Conger paused for a long drink at the water cooler, paid a visit to the men's room, and picked up a small carton of chocolate milk. He was third in line to pay. He watched the cashier go through the motions of making change. She was a hefty girl, tall with unkempt brown hair and broad shoulders. He guessed her to be in her late teens.

"Hi! Can I help you?" she said. To Conger's utter astonishment, she had the same conflicted left eye as his, the same dark mole aside her nostril, and the prominent lower jaw, too. "Did you get gas?"

"Uh, yes...p-pump three, I think."

"Eight ninety-five."

"I wanted this, too," he said, showing her the milk carton.

"I got that," she said, with a quick smile.

He handed her the ten-dollar bill. She promptly made change and handed it back. He knew he was staring. She stared back.

"Do I know you?" she said.

"No. Thanks for the change."

Conger turned on his heel and left. 'Good grief,' he thought to himself, 'who says thanks for the change?' Jake had the car running and the air conditioning on MAX.

"Let's go," snapped Conger, latching his lap safety belt.

As Jake waited for a break in traffic to enter the highway, Conger flipped the sun visor down, removed his sunglasses, and looked in the visor mirror. When they arrived home, he confirmed with Merry that last she knew, Conger's father, Caleb, was still driving truck between Wichita and Denver. He wanted to believe the uncanny resemblance was just a coincidence. But, then again, she had the same snaggle tooth as his.

CHAPTER 25
THE SPENT CARTRIDGE

Sunday – August 9

The Impala's fuel gauge hovered in the red zone when they arrived home. Merry Belle went straight to bed with a headache and upset stomach. She suspected vacation snack belly. Cake donuts, Boston Baked Beans, and orange juice mixed with fried food over the past five days, strange bedfellows all in the hostel of a well-worn chassis.

Conger had skipped church the previous two Sundays, so he felt obliged to attend. Merry demurred. She concluded two Alka-Seltzer, another round of sleep, and a lazy day at home would be the best medicine. Conger left the house earlier than usual. The fish-face thermometer at the filling station next to Perky's showed 82°. Church bells echoed their familiar 9:30 peals. By the time he wheeled into the church parking lot, the wind was already gusting over twenty miles per hour.

Merry Belle woke from her dream in a cold sweat. *A bear was standing on the veranda looking in the window. A dog was barking, alerting her to the danger. It was snowing outside.* Her headache and upset stomach persisted. The alarm clock on the nightstand read 9:55. She had slept less than an hour. Indeed, Blanco <u>was</u> barking. 'She must want out.' Merry reluctantly threw on her frayed robe, or prom dress as Conger often referred to it. Brilliant morning sun shone through the gossamer veiling the windows either side of the foyer. The identical beams illuminated the room like stadium light. Merry's brain recoiled from the visual jolt, scattering photopigment like startled cockroaches. Blanco stood on her hind legs at the window, her head parting the sheers, wagging attentively. As Merry approached, she barked and raced to the front door. Merry peered out the window but saw nothing out of the ordinary. She let the dog out and watched her sprint toward the barn. 'Hope it's not a skunk.' Her headache shifted into throb as she wandered into the kitchen. 'Perhaps a strong cup of black coffee would help.' She rinsed the pot, measured a four-cup dose, and plugged it in. 'I hope William remembers to pick up a Sunday paper.' She plopped two slices of whole wheat bread into the toaster and set out the butter and sand plum jelly. She quickly surveyed the veranda from a kitchen window. No bear or snow, only the swaying tops of the trees across the fallow field between the house and the road. She refilled Blanco's water bowl, flipped on the ceiling fan, and scanned the pantry, thinking ahead to what she might throw together for supper. A chicken and noodle casserole came to mind. After setting out a frozen chicken breast to thaw, she noticed the counter in front of the narrow chuck wagon slot-door to the veranda was caked with dust. There was a time when only food and drink spills required her attention after all the cowhands and staff had been served.

'Those were the days,' she reminisced as she buttered her toast. Everyone was pleasant so long as she kept her mouth shut and did as she was told. The perks were agreeable. For her basic educational needs, Mary Muldoon hired a private tutor who, at Mary's insistence, placed strong emphasis on diction and elocution so the new domestic did not talk like an immigrant. She had her own bedroom and a new friend; a pet ornate box turtle, Mister Jingles, she found along Minnie's Creek. At least once a month, Mary invited her to go horseback riding. At the age of fifteen, Merry Belle was allowed to help herself to Mary's hoard of cosmetics for social functions. Life as a servant was tolerable. That is, until Bear Muldoon broke a cardinal ranch rule, one he himself had imposed. Three evenings a week, an hour of time was set aside for the women to bathe in the warm, natural spring water. During that time, the pool area was off limits to men. The week after her sixteenth birthday, Merry was paid a surprise visit at the pool by Bearnard Brace Muldoon, buck naked and aroused. "Mind if I bathe with you?" he asked.

As Merry noshed and sipped, she decided she would dust and do laundry; William could mop and beat the throw rugs. She placed a hand over her forehead and thought it felt warmer than normal. As she contemplated whether to lie back down, she was distracted. Her mind alternately processed the spirited, singsong chitters of a cricket somewhere in the room, the wind whistling past the house, and the dog's incessant barking. She decided to fetch Blanco back inside so she could have a more promising claim on peace and quiet.

From the top step of the front porch, she realized she did not have her glasses on and was still wearing slippers. The big barn, only a hundred and fifty feet distant, was something of a blur. She watched Blanco move side to side, to and fro, barking at something back of the stoic edifice. The dog paid no attention to her calls. She grabbed Conger's varmint rifle propped in a corner by the front door, donned her broad-brimmed straw hat, and strode in Blanco's direction.

"Blanco! Come!"

She could still hear barking, but the dog was not visible. Halfway to the barn, Merry saw a man chasing Blanco, then land two blows on the dog's hind legs with a cane-like object. Blanco's piercing yelps sent shockwaves through Merry. The man kicked the dog and stood over the groveling canine, poised for another strike.

"HEY!" Merry instinctively shouted and positioned the .222 Remington at hip level.

"WHAT'RE YOU DOING HERE?!" The man froze and slowly lowered his arms. As she approached, a gust of wind blew off her straw hat. She glanced as it flopped every which way toward Minnie's Creek. She blinked, shaded her eyes, then squinted trying to focus. The object in his right hand was a crowbar. He wore sunglasses and had not spoken. Nothing was right. 'Why is he here? What is he doing with a crowbar? Why would he harm my dog?' He began to sidle backwards.

"STOP!" she warned. "Who are you?"

He hesitated momentarily then resumed his retreat toward a white van parked at the opposite end of the barn.

"I said stop! Right there! Where you are!"

Ever so cautiously, he continued to back pedal. As Merry drew nearer, the man's backward flight quickened; he had no intention of heeding her commands. Merry flicked off the rifle's safety and fired a warning shot in his direction. The man abruptly stood still. Before the echo of the rifle's CRACK! faded, he dropped to his knees, arms collapsed at his sides.

When Conger arrived home, he saw Blanco at the foot of the front steps, her hind end partially covered with a blanket, her tail twitching halfheartedly. "What's wrong girl?" he crooned as he approached her. He entered the house and called out, "Mom! I'm home!" No answer. The smell of cigarette smoke pervaded the air. "Mom?!"

"In the kitchen!"

Conger dropped a Sunday paper on the butcher block where Merry sat, snuffing out a cigarette in a soup bowl.

"When did you start smoking again?"

"An hour ago."

"What's wrong with Blanco?"

"She needs to go to the vet as soon as we can get her there."

"It's Sunday."

"I called Darryl at home. He said he'd meet us at his office when we're ready."

"What happened? Why…"

"Sit down, William."

Conger removed his suit coat and loosened his tie. Merry helped herself to another half cup of coffee to which she added Irish whiskey.

"I shot a man this morning," she began.

"You WHAT?!"

"I said, I shot a man."

"Who?!"

"I didn't mean to. I…"

"Where? Who did you shoot?"

"Back of the barn. I don't know who he is," she said, sipping her coffee.

"When?"

"Sometime after you left."

"Where is he?"

"Behind the barn."

"He's still there?!"

"He's not going anywhere anytime soon. See for yourself."

"Why didn't you call Gene for help?"

"It happened in the blink of an eye. There wasn't time."

"Mom, do you realize…d'you know…good grief!" He stood up. "You okay?"

140

"I think I am," she said, squaring her shoulders.

"Call Darryl back and tell him we'll be there in thirty minutes. Where's my rifle?"

"Where it always is."

"What happened to Blanco?"

"Got clubbed with a crowbar. I saw him do it."

"Call Darryl. I'm going out there. For God's sake, don't call Gene yet. Okay?" Conger rolled up his shirt sleeves, retrieved his rifle, ejected the spent cartridge, and inserted a new one. "Help's on its way, girl," he said to Blanco, caressing her head and ears before making his way to the barn.

CHAPTER 26
WAS IT THAT SIMPLE?

Merry Belle held the back door open for William as he carried Blanco into the vet's building. Veterinarian Darryl Manning offered her a box of Kleenex as tears streamed down her cheeks. Conger reported the dog had darted in front of their car that morning then excused himself to call John Griever.

Conger had chatted with John after church. After he and Nonny grabbed their usual bite to eat and he dropped Nonny by home, he planned to pick up Jake to cut firewood they could sell in town. He called Nonny; no one answered, then Jake, who said he just heard John pull up. He told Jake to meet him at the vet's office right away. He would explain when they got there. Minutes later, John Griever pounded on the front door and was directed to the back entrance.

"What happened to Blanco? Jake asked.

"She had an accident."

"What you need us for?" Griever queried.

"We could use some advice. I think we might-a caught your barn wood thief in the act at our place."

"Gene got 'im locked up?"

"No. You need to drive out and see for yourself. It's a little hard to explain."

"We can go right now."

"Can't go right this minute. Gotta wait till Blanco gets doctored up."

"Well...," Griever hesitated.

"You want to see this. Trust me."

"I need to change out-a my Sundays. What makes you think it's the bastard what vandaled my barn?"

"You'll see."

Upon arrival, Conger led Griever and Jake to the back of the barn. The lifeless form of the perpetrator lay contorted in a mock fetal position. As Conger related Merry's account of events, Griever got down on his hands and knees and inspected the man's unshaven face. The entry wound was just above the bridge of the nose, slightly off-center.

"She got 'im in the cross hairs," Griever remarked.

"She intended a warning shot."

"You call Gene yet?"

"Nope. Wanted you to see it first. Come look."

"Know who he is?" said Griever.

"Nope. Haven't touched anything yet."

Conger led them to the white cargo van, its only windows surrounding the cab, its driver's side and rear doors open, just as Conger found it. "Take a sniff inside. Driver's seat is the worst." Griever poked his head inside the cab. The skunk odor was unmistakable. Conger showed them the jimmied barn door padlock and the items the man had loaded into the van including a turn of the century steamer trunk, two kerosene lanterns, a wood wagon wheel, a rusty scythe, barbed wire wreath, and antique medicine bottles. Also set aside were Mary Muldoon's custom-made Mexican saddle and horse tack. The man pried off a plank of barn wood and splintered the board into two oblong pieces. As the three lingered, they heard a truck pull up. Conger immediately stepped to the nearest corner of the barn. "Crap! Be right back."

Griever eyeballed the damage. "Imagine this guy's surprise when he realized it was tongue 'n groove constructed. Ain't no way he was gonna pry whole planks off-a here. Ever seen a real live dead man before? Ain't pretty, is it?"

"Wonder who he is?"

"You mean <u>was</u>. A thief is who he was. Back in the day, if we'd catch 'em in the act, lot-a times this is how it got taken care of. Lookie here, Jake. After all these years, you can barely make out the gaps between the planks."

"Heard a German built it."

"Called himself a pie-a-tust from somewhere out-a Pennsylvania. A carpenter by trade. Showed up in Granfield with his grandson. They was on their way to California. Some woman name-a Davis claimed she had a cure for the boy's autumnism by gettin' him to eat right."

"You mean autism?"

"That boy wasn't right in the head. Queer acting. Always smilin', though. We named 'im Happy. Called his grandpa Who 'cause no one could pronounce his last name. On their way west they got off the train in Granfield around supper time to stretch their legs and get somethin' to eat. Who got roughed up pretty good by some young thugs back-a the train depot after dark. Got his wallet, pocket watch, and train tickets stole. Railroad wouldn't make good on it. All they had left to their name was the change in Who's pockets an' a sawbuck he'd rat-holed in one-a the boy's shoes. Ol' Who was prob'ly in his mid-eighties, spry for his age, but didn't speak the good English. Karl Albrecht was at the County Assessor's Office in Granfield the morning after it happened and heard the story. He knew Muldoon had been lookin' for a bone-a-fide carpenter to do some work here at the ranch. When Karl found out Who'd built barns, he introduced them. Acted like a translator between 'em."

"There wasn't a barn here then?"

"There was a couple of 'em, but they was cowhand-built pole barns. Nothin' special."

"They get blown away in the tornado?"

"Splinter and nail. Muldoon wanted somethin' speck-tackuler. Somethin' he could show off, like the main house. Somethin' he could use for more than puttin' up hay and stablin' horses and milk cows."

"Was the horseshoe cross the Pie-a-tust's doing?"

"Don't recall it was. My guess, Sean Robert prob'ly done that."

Jake strode to the corner of the barn, curious to see who had shown up. Conger stood conversing with Jack Nagel and Bill Stimka. Jack's truck hitched to a horse trailer. Griever sauntered over to the open barn doors.

"Took every bit-a six months or better to build this mother. Can't tell ya how many truckloads of quarried stone, lumber, and gallons-a white paint we hauled out here."

"What happened to Who and Smiley?"

"When we was done buildin' the barn, Muldoon had me drive 'em to town, buy 'em tickets to San Francisco and give 'em some cash foldin' money. Never heard after that. One other thing he left behind, he showed Merry Belle how to make scrapple."

Jake spotted Nagel, Wild Bill and Conger standing over the corpse. "Wonder what Mr. Nagel thinks."

"Prob'ly same as me," said Griever. "Dig him a hole to go in somewhere. Next day or so, find a spot, maybe some big city parking lot 'bout a hundred miles from here and leave it set."

"And not call Gene?"

"Do that, it's gonna get complicated. Merry was just protectin' her property. Justice is done, if ya ask me."

Jake was conflicted. Was it that simple? Were they above the law? What if they got caught? If it were solely up to him, what would he do? His mind raced as the wind swirled the heat of a resolute sun around him.

"Jake! C'mon!" Griever urged.

"We're all in agreement," Conger said, as Jake joined in. "You want-a help or stay back here at the house?"

"What're we doing?"

"We're gonna dig 'im a hole in the ground."

"What about the van?"

"Park it in the barn. Worry about it later."

Jake felt the weight of all eyes upon him. He knew the difference between being compelled to act and choosing to act. Under the circumstances, he could not choose not to choose because, paradoxically, that was a choice. An unconstrained surge of camaraderie preformed his words. "I'll help."

"I knew you'd say that," Bill Stimka said, slapping him on the back.

Wild Bill off-loaded the horses and unhitched the trailer from Jack's truck. Jack, Conger, Griever and Jake rode the pickup to the Cemetary after loading the tools to dig a proper hole in the ground. Bill followed on his mount leading Jack's horse with the unknown perpetrator in tow, a knot of rope looped around his ankles dragging him to the site. Griever posited the best place to dig would be near Roxie Copeland Lassiter's grave and two nameless Depression era cattle rustlers, citing birds of a feather. Outlaws deserved to be eternal earth neighbors.

No one living knew the complete history of those buried in the private tract. During the construction of the manor house, Mary

Muldoon had the hallowed ground surveyed. Based on relics found at the site, Mary speculated it was a Lenape Indian burial ground, with several identifiable exceptions. The unsystematic layout sprawled in three directions away from a limestone rimrock that demarcated a change in ranch topography. She increased its size to include any grave sites not discernible by the naked eye, bordered it with a three-foot-high, white picket fence and commissioned an ornate wrought iron entrance. The letters across its arch read:

CEMETARY

The only man-made change since that time: Merry posted No Trespassing signs shortly after she and William moved back to the ranch.

It took them an hour to gouge a six-foot deep hole in the pristine prairie soil. They worked in shifts, alternately resting and browsing through the identification paraphernalia found in the man's pockets and the van. John Griever took keen interest in the most telling items. The man's driver's license identified him as Grayson E. Murphy, thirty-eight years old from Kansas City, Missouri. His business card implied he was co-owner of a retail store in the Westport neighborhood of the city. Dottie Dumpling's Dowry specialized in antiques, collectibles, imported gifts, fine art, and custom framing. Except for the Brahmin-esque red dot now on his forehead, the photo on the glossy card bore a remarkable likeness to the deceased. Conger and Bill lugged the cadaver to perch precariously atop an oblong heap of freshly excavated earth and rock at the edge of the cavity. With a nudge of Griever's boot, the lifeless body of the would-be thief collapsed into the opening.

"You guys go get on with what yer here for," said Griever. "We can finish up."

"Sorry what happened to Merry Belle," offered Jack.

"We came up eleven short of a herd by our count this morning," added Bill. "They're prob'ly down by Hoover's Bottom. Find strays there all the time." He offered Griever a Tareyton and lit up one of his own.

"There's some good shade there," Griever said, accepting a light from Bill.

"Don't do nothin' we wouldn't think-a doin'," grinned Bill as he mounted up, followed by his usual wink.

Jack leaned forward in his saddle. "We'll be back in an hour or so. We need to make goddamn sure we're all on the same page about this

…and be sure Merry isn't having any second thoughts about what happened. We can't mention this to nobody. Okay, guys?" Jack and Bill drifted eastward along Minnie's Creek. Griever strode over to the pickup and came back with a gas can and gallon bottle of Clorox. Jake stood leaning on his shovel just far enough back to not see the crumpled body. Conger sat on one of the mounds of earth and rock, head bowed.

"You havin' second thoughts?" Griever asked.

"Nope. Just thinkin' about Mom."

John Griever shook gasoline generously into the opening. He jerked a fistful of feather grass from its rooting and gave it a twist. Turning his back to the wind, he set the improvised torch afire and tossed it and his cigarette into the hole.

"You might want-a stay upwind," Griever advised.

Conger stood and moved next to Jake. Moments later, the flames rose above ground level then quickly burned lower. They watched the dark smoke rise and whisk on the stout breeze toward Minnie's Creek.

"Want a tour?" Conger offered.

"Sure," said Jake. "That smells nasty."

Jake had been around the Cemetary often enough, but never in it. The fatigued picket fence trellised macramé patterns of feral vinery complemented by ubiquitous sunflowers, coneflowers, thistles, and red cedar sprouts. An eight-foot jack-oak stood sentinel. A broad stand of wild oats grew along one side of the fence. As the two strolled toward the bank of variegated rock, Conger pointed out the sites identified by Merry Belle. The upright, matching marble headstones of Bearnard and Mary Muldoon were the largest and most prominent; both died the month of April 1944, but not on the same day. Robert Muldoon's flat, unpretentious stone, demarcated by an artfully arranged cross of fist-size stones, read:

SEAN ROBERT
1948

His formal headstone, a half-ton granite monolith he himself commissioned, with its Latin epitaph NON OMNIS MORIAR and all but a date of death, languished in a corner of the Pennsylvania barn gathering dust and barn swallow droppings. Jake lingered long at Sharon Gabriel DeCritt's grave. The year she died; same year he was born. Of the three ranch hands killed in the tornado, the names of two, Dooley and Pasqual, were still legible on makeshift limestone markers. Also discernible, the names of two Muldoon dogs, Thor and Sampson, and Tuffy the cat that perished in the 1944 twister, though none of them were ever found. Merry Belle's pet box turtle, Mr. Jingles, and Ben Whitewater's wife, Snow-in-Her-Hair, were also at peace in the designated plot.

"No one's been buried here since Robert that we know of. Mom has a backstory for most of 'em."

"Who notched out the rock on the ledge?"

"Robert. It was his pulpit. Mom said he would sit here for hours in one of his robes reading Mary Baker Eddy and shouting scripture. See that dark rock below it, to the right? Mom thinks it might be a chunk of meteorite."

Jake stooped down and ran his fingers along its exposed surface.

"Boys!" Griever hollered. "C'mon. Let's finish 'er up!"

As Conger and Jake retrieved their shovels, Griever poured bleach over the smoldering corpse.

"Why do that?" Jake asked.

"Makes it less likely the critters out here will dig 'im up."

Jake consciously avoided eye contact with the cadaver as they shoveled. Enormous white thunderheads blossoming far to the north silhouetted a Mississippi kite perched on an upper limb of a spent cottonwood. Two feet shy of filling the hole, Griever vaulted into the indentation and stomp-compacted the new fill. Conger lent him a hand to climb out. Jake shed his sweat-soaked Baltimore Orioles t-shirt, wiped his face, neck, and upper body, and draped it on the fence. When they finished, Conger collected the shovels, picks, and rake, and chucked them in the bed of the pickup. Jake tossed the empty gas can and bleach container in with the tools and slammed the tailgate shut. They watched John Griever wipe his eyes, head bowed, transfixed over the newly formed mound.

"What's he doin'?" said Jake, under his breath.

"Maybe he's having second thoughts."

After an awkward couple of minutes, Conger and Jake rejoined Griever who stood motionless as a post rock fence post.

"Never seen you get so shook up over something," said Conger.

"Ain't that. Must-a been the smoke and them Clorox fumes what got to me."

"You having second thoughts?" Conger asked.

"Hell no," Griever said, clearing his throat. "The son-of-a-bitch stole my Philco radio. I give eleven dollars for it at a farm sale. First thing I ever bought with my cowhand wages. Franklin Delanor Roosevelt came over that radio," he said, wiping his brow on his sleeve. "Boxin' matches. Jack Benny. Glenn Miller. All them reports about the Earhart woman gone missin'. D-Day news. Amos and Andy. Eisenhower gettin' elected. After Mom died, there was times when that machine was my only entertainment, the best friend I knew in the world." Griever wiped his nose again on his sleeve and fidgeted with his hat.

"You got Roger now," wisecracked Jake.

"Some Sundays, Mother and I'd hear Pastor Lowman preach the gospel on WLS. And I recall listenin' to the last half of the Giant-Dodger game on that radio, the one where Bobby Thomson clinched the pennant for the Giants with a three-run homer in the bottom of the ninth."

"When was that?" asked Jake.

"October 1951. I can still hear The Old Scotchman shoutin'…it's going, going, GONE! The Giants win the pennant!"

"I didn't know you were a baseball fan," said Jake. "You ready to go?"

"Not just yet. I think we might ought-a say somethin'. To make it right."

"Like what?" Conger asked.

"Just gimme another minute."

Jake looked to Conger who shrugged his shoulders. Except for an occasional bird call or rustle of wind, the three united in the silence. On a distant hill, Jake spotted a herd of Black Angus cattle that looked like a sprinkle of coarse ground pepper. He surveyed the tamped down grasses, chert nodules, leftover clods of fresh dug soil surrounding his shadow, and more thunderheads billowing up to the north. At long last, John Griever blew his nose one-handed in a red kerchief and cleared his throat again.

"May God have Murphy."

CHAPTER 27
THE ORMESTRONG OPEN

Saturday – August 29

"JAKE! Telephone!"

'Who calls this early in the morning?' Jake thought as he shuffled to the kitchen and picked the receiver up off the counter.

"How would you like to be beer cart girl at the golf tournament?" asked Reverend Cage. Darcy Cage had committed to take Natalie's place this year, the Reverend explained, but she had spontaneously taken off to Lawrence late last night. Parise was not the least bit interested and Ramona had to work all day. Jake had already volunteered to help John Griever grill post-tournament hamburgers at the country club midday. They would really appreciate him filling in. How soon could he be there? While Jake showered, Doyle phoned Donna and conspired. If Jake was going to be the beer cart girl, he needed to look the part. On his way to the club, and at Doyle's suggestion, Jake swung by Donna's home. She asked if he had a preference as to which wig, blond or brunette?

Converted from sand to grass greens in the early 50's, mature trees, a meandering creek, and strategically placed ponds rendered the Waltsburg Country Club 9-hole golf course postcard picturesque. The course's signature feature, a silo from the acreage's farming days transformed to resemble a golf bag with four larger-than-life golf clubs protruding from its top, towered near the clubhouse. Over time, three clubs disappeared. The sports page editor of the *Granfield Daily Dispatch* proclaimed that the converted silo looked like a Paul Bunyan cocktail with a swizzle stick. The country club's Saturday prime rib dinner night, open to the public, was still a popular destination for area residents.

Since its inception, the club's annual golf tournament, The Ormestrong Open, had been a big hit with golfers. In the early years, the tournament featured quality prizes, generous sponsor giveaways, and a four-star steak dinner afterward. Its rich tradition memorialized with plaques and photos on the flocked wallpaper walls of the erstwhile pro shop. When, despite a shotgun start, the teams were stacked three-deep at each tee box, the tournament adopted a two-day scramble format. The *Waltsburg Journal* once described the tournament's ambience as "more testosterone than a samurai locker room." This year, the Double-O had twelve teams entered, eight fewer than the previous year, for the half-day event.

In harmony with the growing popularity of the sport, thanks to expanded television coverage, Granfield redesigned and expanded its 9-hole public course to eighteen holes. Over time, it became the more popular destination for golfers in the county. Now, fewer looked forward to the Open for the golf. Most came just for the fun, raffle and prizes, others for the mesquite-smoked burgers, chips, bar-b-que baked beans, potato salad, and chocolate sheet cake included in the registration fee. Still catching his breath, Police Chief Eugene Lassiter joined Paul Baguelt waiting in line at the check-in table.

"You missed the putting contest," said Paul.

"I'm lucky to be here."

"Crime wave?"

"Two carloads of students sellin' magazine subscriptions door-to-door. Happens 'bout twice a year. They drop 'em off in town. Start knockin' on doors sayin' they're tryin' to put themselves through college. Then, our phone starts ringin' off its rocker."

"That a misdemeanor or a felony?"

"Just another pain in the ass. They claim they never heard-a the Green River Ordinance."

"So, you do what?"

"Find the adult sponsor. They're usually on Main somewhere havin' coffee. Spot the out-a-state tag and unfamiliar face. Tell 'em they got thirty minutes to round the kids up and get on down the road."

"Where they out of?"

"Athens, Georgia, this time."

"You're riding with Allen, by the way."

"The hell you say. If I'd known that I might-a found some paperwork to catch up on.

How come Dan couldn't make it?"

"Don't know. Said he'd fill me in later."

"Where is Allen?"

"Out scouting the course."

"Like he's never played here before."

"You know Allen."

As they moved up in line, Gene and Paul watched tournament director Leland 'Icky' Skalicky and his wife, Nedra Knaakt Skalicky, cradling Wicket, her toy poodle, go through the motions of checking in players. They assigned a starting hole and passed out small, white paper sacks of tournament goodies: a dozen tees, a sleeve of Maxfli golf balls, logoed plastic ball markers, a divot tool, and other knick-knacks. Nedra nibbled on sunflower seeds. Leland snacked from a giant bag of Cheeto Puffs. Paul pictured the Skalickys as sumo wrestlers. Nedra looked like an overweight Betty Boop with a rococo makeover; her mate, a ponderous heap of warmed-over *jaternice*.

"Too bad Natalie ain't around this year," Gene said.

"Oh, yes, it is. She made over a hundred bucks in tips as cart girl last year."

"No kidding? Geez. I'm in the wrong line a work."

"Not if you grow a pair."

"Who won the putting contest?"

"Don't know."

"I take that to mean Allen didn't?"

"He didn't enter. First prize was a Nicklaus White Fang putter from Granfield Sporting Goods. Allen said if you win a putting contest with the putter in your bag, why would you want a different one?"

"Good point. You been playin' much lately?"

"Not as much as I'd like to."

"Me neither. My recovery game just ain't what it used to be."

Gene stepped up to the check-in table. Wicket yapped at him. Nedra clamped her hand over the dog's mouth and crooned, "No, no, sugar-bullet."

Icky did not look up and simply asked, "Name?"

"Barney Fife."

Icky checked the roster. "Don't see that name here."

"Baguelt's group. I'm subbing for Bruner."

Icky looked up. "Haw-Haw-Haw. Good one."

"Sorry what happened to Chase and Champ," Gene said to Nedra.

"Me, too. They're in heaven now."

Gene stepped aside. Icky sucked down some of his large soft drink and stuffed another handful of Cheetos in his mouth. Paul stepped up. Wicket whined. Icky sipped again at his drink, half-covered his mouth, and belched audibly.

"That the Skalicky mating call?" Paul queried.

Paul and Gene exchanged a glance as the corpulent tournament chairman scanned the roster and chairman's obese wife scooted two goodie sacks across the tabletop.

"Your group starts on six," said Icky, his orange fingers groping for more Cheetos.

As the two golfers headed in the direction of Paul's golf cart, Paul remarked, "That man's definitely a bump looking for a log."

"Ain't that the damn truth. Hey, Paul. Look. Isn't that Jake?"

Paul squinted. "Think so. Yup. We got us a blond Eric Carver."

Unbeknownst to Jake, his image would soon take its place among tournament winning team photos, Hole-In-One commemoratives, and beer cart girl legends as the unpretentious blond in sunglasses and a Baltimore Orioles ball cap alongside Angela, Ramona, and Natalie Martinez, Parise Bruner, and others before them.

CHAPTER 28
BLACK MOON

Monday – August 31

On a dare three years ago, the group had performed their skiffle music at the Scorpio Lounge. John Jefferson Griever, Lyla Witte, and her two young adult offspring, Indy and Briley, practiced every chance they got, often in the music room of the Bruno mansion. The song selection was eclectic, relying largely on old familiar favorites recognizable by even the most disinterested listener.

The Scorpio Lounge changed hands in March. A 3.2 beer joint north of the tracks, it survived numerous ownership and name changes over the years. Originally, it had been O'Sullivan's or Sully's. The new proprietor renamed it the Tackle Box hoping to cash in on the fishing and boating crowd that passed through town to and from Ormestrong County State Lake. Eager to attract area residents, he spent the better part of three months and a considerable sum of money converting it from a dive to a more respectable destination. The themed decor related to fish, area fishing, and paraphernalia. From sunup Friday through sundown Sunday, patrons could order a basket of cornmeal crusted, deep-fried catfish and chips.

A word-of-mouth campaign supplemented by a dozen strategically posted, hand-lettered notices promised something out of the ordinary. To the annoyance of Tackle Box regulars, a bank of lights remained on to illuminate the makeshift stage set in a back corner. Ceiling fans turned just fast enough to keep cigarette smoke from layering. Decked out in chaps and his finest cowboy regalia, Wild Bill Stimka addressed the half-empty venue first. Over the intermittent click-clacks of billiard balls, cha-chings of the cash register, and occasional raised voice or laugh, he asked if there were any talent scouts present. He announced he would recite a cowboy poem and read from a library book he checked out earlier that day.

"We didn't know you could read!" shouted a Tackle Box regular.

"Hey! Bear with me," Bill shouted back. "It ain't that long."

"That's what Lyla's been tellin' everyone," another called out.

The selected poem portrayed a cattle drive in a rainstorm. Wild Bill yelled and gestured, over-shouting his would-be hecklers. He ended his five minutes of fame saying that having bad breath is better than having none at all. Jake stepped forward wearing John Griever's black cowboy hat every bit two sizes too big. Tilting his head back he hollered "Howdy, howdy. Look at me. I'm a cowboy." Jake introduced the musical troupe as The Broken Buckboard Bumper Band and sat at a front row table with Doyle, Donna, and Nonny. Next to them were some of Lyla's friends and family from Whitfield. At one end of the bar, stood Eric Carver and Darcy Cage with another college-aged couple in *de rigueur* counterculture apparel.

John Griever took the microphone and, after thanking the Methodist church for the use of their portable sound system, announced their first number, an original Zander Rhodes ballad *My Little Cherry from Tucumcari*. Woody Guthrie's *This Land is Your Land* and *So Long It's Been Good to Know Yuh* were next, followed by *Camptown Races* and Stephen Foster's original *Old Folks at Home*. Washboard, musical saw, kazoo, tambourine, acoustic guitar, banjo, spoons, *maracas*, Jew's harp, and harmonica harmonized. All added vocals whether solo, duet or as a group. Not every song was introduced by name. *Somewhere Over the Rainbow* needed no introduction nor did *Michael, Row the Boat Ashore*. *Turn Your Radio On* and *Shady Grove*, however, were announced. *Dem Bones* and *When Johnny Comes Marching Home Again* rounded out the program. John Griever grabbed the mic and announced, "Show ain't over yet, folks."

Eric and his male counterpart drifted over to the jukebox and began to study its menu. A couple of minutes later, someone hollered, "What're we waitin' for?!" Straightaway, the 1946 film version of Irving Berlin's *Puttin' on the Ritz* sprang from the band's sound system. Indy Witte in top hat, bow tie, cane, and skimpy black sequined leotard tap danced to the song. Part way into her act, the jukebox uncapped *I-Feel-Like-I'm-Fixin'-To-Die*. Eric Carver and his unidentified comrade, beers in hand, sang along in dissonant voices and started yelling "Give me an F...." Without hesitation, John Griever approached the music machine's sing-a-longs, taking exception to their utter lack of respect. Lyla bolted out of her chair and unplugged Country Joe and The Fish from the wall outlet.

Eric and pal stopped singing and impulsively headed out the door trailed by their female companions. Eric's top of his voice rant "WHAT THE FUCK ARE WE FIGHTIN' FOR?!" resounded like bamboo wind chimes in a monsoon. Indy did not miss a beat. Her performance drew the only significant applause of the evening. She took her bows and blew kisses at those who clapped. Lyla strode over to the bar and had words with the bar's owner.

Guitar in hand, John Griever stepped up to the mic, "Show's over now, folks."

CHAPTER 29
STUBER'S GARAGE

Friday – September 4

Labor Day weekend

In addition to serving as a used car lot and live bait source, Deke Stuber's garage offered Waltsburg residents quality repair on domestic cars and trucks. Business for Deke boomed after Waltsburg's Chevrolet/Pontiac/Buick dealership closed in 1965. Jake made some good spending money washing, waxing, and detailing cars the past few years, a service Anthony suggested to Deke his second day on the job.

Stout-built like a fireplug, Deke was sixty-eight. Known as a man of precise gestures, he carried on conversation by contorting hands and fingers to fully illustrate his narrative, especially when it involved the repair, installation, or function of something mechanical, like a carburetor or new spinning reel. Although plagued by arthritis since his mid-fifties, he conscientiously tended to his wife's multiple sclerosis issues. When Charlene, originally the office manager and the driving force behind opening the business, became incapable of doing her part, her younger twin sisters from Wundchen took turns looking after her weekdays.

Although the front door was locked and a CLOSED sign dangled in place, the office's window air conditioner droned. Neither Deke nor Anthony had watered the raised planter beds either side of the main entrance; whatever was planted in them now withered past the point of no return. Three consecutive weeks of oven-like, curb-buckling temperatures hovering around the century mark tested the hardiest of native flora. Predictably, the dog days of summer in Kansas were, as John Griever often over-simplified, "…hotter than a June bride."

Opening the back door, ready to tackle his weekly cleaning chores, Jake was met by fume-tainted air. As his vision adjusted to the semi-dark, he noticed shades pulled in Deke's office on the opposite side of the garage. He hoped Deke read the note he had slipped under the office door last week saying they were low on floor sweep compound. Anthony's Ice Cream Truck was missing from its usual spot. Catharine Mixx's Lincoln convertible, a Thane's A-1 Propane truck elevated on a hydraulic lift, a Dunker Baptist Brethren Church minivan, and Leland Skalicky's tricked-out Harley-Davison golf cart sat idle. 'It's a perfect day for Lone Cloud to be out peddling cold treats,' Jake thought. Inspecting Icky's cart, he wondered why anyone would have racing stripes, curb feelers, shag carpet, bucket seats, eight-track tape player, stereo speakers, and CB radio on such a vehicle. He grabbed the push broom and cranked out two casement windows on his circuitous route to the office. Before knocking, Jake peeped through one of the small tears in the brittle shade of the office door. What he witnessed generated more questions than answers.

Catharine Mixx in a sleeveless Persian blue sun dress stood behind Mr. Stuber who was seated at his desk blindfolded with a shop rag; head tilted back. Intermittently, Catharine leaned forward and spoke next to his ear. She tugged at two strands of string running from either side of his neck down the front of his work coverall, converging toward a location hidden by the desk as if she were manipulating a marionette. He heard their low voices but could not make out the words. Sherman, Catharine's boxer, picked up Jake's scent. She leapt to her feet, barked, and scratched at the door. Jake stepped away and began to sweep. Catharine appeared, restraining Sherman by her collar.

"Jake! It's… Well… You startled us."

"Sorry. I clean Saturday afternoons."

"I… we know that. You're early, aren't you?"

"No, ma'am. It's five o'clock."

She glanced at her watch and let Sherman loose. Deke appeared in his stocking feet, pencil tucked behind one ear, cleaning his eyeglasses with a shop rag.

"Guess we lost track of the time," Deke mumbled.

"D'you get more floor sweep? You know you're about out."

"Matter-a-fact, I did." He disappeared momentarily and returned with an unopened drum.

"I can take that, Mr. Stuber. D'you want, I mean, I can come back later."

"No-no. We're done in here."

"Says you," Catharine muttered, then turned and walked back inside to retrieve her purse.

She ran her fingers along Deke's arm and repositioned her sunglasses, "Talk at you later."

As Jake lugged the drum of compound to the rear of the shop, Catharine punched the overhead door's control button, ordered Sherman into the back seat and drove off. Jake flipped on the overhead fluorescents and tied a clean shop rag around his forehead. 'Good thing I waited before interrupting this time,' Jake thought to himself, as a chapter from his boyhood flashed through his conscience.

#

School was dismissed at noon one day after a neglected hot plate pan in the teacher's lounge caught fire and scorched a wall, ceiling tiles, and melted a stockpile of Styrofoam coffee cups. Though actual physical damage was minor, smoke and noxious fumes permeated the building.

Jake, Eric Carver, and Kirk Michaels walked to Jake's house. His mother slept afternoons, so the boys would quietly self-entertain or play at the park till 4, then watch *The Pinky Lee Show* till the babysitter showed up and changed the channel. Today, quietly entering the house, they heard unfamiliar noises. They followed the sounds to his parent's bedroom. They stood in the doorway and witnessed a lively demonstration of the reverse missionary position. The second time Jake said "Mom?" he got noticed. They heard JESUS! at least three times during the panic that followed. "JAKE! WHAT'RE YOU DOING HOME?!" Then, "GET OUT!" Off they ran. With school milk money burning a hole in their pockets, they paid a visit to the Ben Franklin store to resupply their PEZ dispensers before they split up. Jake took refuge in his uncle's barber shop. He told Doyle the school fire story and matter-of-factly stated he had observed his mother in bed with Jesus, neither of whom had clothes on. The following week Mrs. Book filed for divorce.

#

While completing his chores, Jake discovered two mousetraps with snagged prey and tossed them out. As he swept the front walk, he heard Native American drumbeats in the distance, triggering his memory of the girl in the orchard. Both he and Merry Belle surmised she had Indian blood. That, he reminded himself, was seven weeks ago. How many times had he composed a letter to her in his mind? Was there a snug harbor for notions not acted upon. If so, how crowded could it be at age twenty-three?

CHAPTER 30
WHAT BRINGS YOU
TO WALTSBURG?

Saturday – September 5

Labor Day weekend

"How'd you do that?" Jake asked.

"Cleanin' out the kitchen closet last night. Tryin' to make me some more room to put stuff an' dropped my bowlin' ball on it," John explained, wincing as he slipped his sock and boot back on.

"Didn't they give out medals at Jenkins Knob for that sort-a thing?"

"If they did, I'd be the most decorated dumbass in the county. It'll feel better when it stops hurting. By the way, I told Henry to include a square of their cheapest asphalt shingles."

Jake took a long swig of his lukewarm Coke, set it down on the dilapidated picnic table, and resumed picking at a splinter embedded in his index finger. The shade of a massive sycamore tree provided little relief from the heat. Two of John's nannies stood nearby eavesdropping on their conversation. Replanking the thief gaps and patching the roof of John's barn would use up the hottest half of the day.

"Here," said John, handing Jake a pocketknife. "This might help with that. Never see the end of them Jenkins Knob kind-a wounds. Got anything else planned for the weekend?"

"Not unless you want-a go fishing."

"Too crazy out there Labor Day weekend. Whole different crowd shows up. A man could get seasick from all them ski boat wakes. You goin' dove huntin' with us?"

"Maybe." Jake said, as he slipped the small blade's point under his fingerprint to dislodge the irritant. "Heard from Eric lately?"

"Not a peep. He might still be pissed 'bout what happened at the Tackle Box. I'd guess he's back in Lawrence. There's a whole new crop- a freshman girls moved into that town over the past week or so."

Jake handed back the pocketknife, squeezed then sucked a drop of blood from his finger.

"Your phone's ringing."

"I hear it."

"Might be Henry."

"Nonny, more likely," John guessed, wiping the sweat from his brow. "Know what this reminds me of? August-a last year. Middle-a the month if I remember right. Me sittin' in my choir robe sweatin' like I was bein' grilled for supper."

"Long sermon?"

"That and the air conditionin' was on the fritz. I'm gonna go grab me a cold one. You want somethin'?"

"No, thanks."

John returned with a can of Coors. He downed three quick swallows and sat back down. "That's what the doctor ordered."

Jake watched a half dozen houseflies jockey for position on the lip of his Coke bottle and re-inspected his minor surgery effort. A large flock of starlings took to the air from the weed-filled pasture by John's entry drive, twisting in unison into geometric shapes known only to nature, a miniature murmuration. Henry drove in, kicking up a rooster tail of dust that wafted in the same direction as the vehicle. John's phone was ringing again. Jake looked to John, who took off running at a hop-skip to answer. It occurred to John that perhaps it was Nonny. What if she had fallen? Jake shooed a goat from the truck's path and directed Henry to park inside the barn. He wiped another drop of blood on his jeans and slipped on his work gloves. John returned to help them unload.

"Was it Nonny?"

"Nope. Doyle. You had a visitor come by the shop to see ya. He said she left a pair of white cowboy boots with silver stars on 'em."

Jake froze. "She still there?"

162

"Didn't say. That the Indian girl from the peach farm you was writin' a letter to?"

"Never sent one."

"Well, young man, if I was you, I'd haul ass to town."

Jake dropped four oak planks on barn's dirt floor, doffed his gloves, and shed his carpenter's belt. "Be back!"

Jake pulled up in front of DeCritt's Barber Shop next to a late model Lincoln Continental Mark III with Oklahoma tags. Inside, Doyle was winding up a trim on D. Darryl Manning.

"They're on the shoeshine stand."

Upon inspection, there was little doubt the pair belonged to Kimmy.

"Where'd she go?"

"She might be over at Luci's."

Jake headed across the street. What would he say to her? He had absolutely no memory of the ten-minute drive from John Griever's place. His mind preoccupied, reassembling her like a jigsaw puzzle. Was she Indian? If so, what tribe? Should he ask? The moment Jake entered the café he was unsure of himself, self-conscious to the core. He spied Luci talking with a dark-haired girl in a booth.

"Here's Jake," said Luci.

The girl turned her head. It kind of looked like her.

"Hi. I'm Jake."

"I-I know. I'm Kim." The black currant shade of hair, the colorful beaded bracelet and epicanthic fold of the eyes all registered true. Luci asked Jake if he wanted a Coke and asked Kim if she wanted more iced tea. They nodded. Jake took his place across from her, trying his damnedest not to stare.

"Nice lady," Kim said.

"Yes, she is." He averted his eyes as a fish-out-of-water feeling washed over him. This was not the character he encountered in Nowata County, Oklahoma. Apparently, that was just the bud; this was the bloom. He drew in the fresh scent of her perfume. She appeared poised in a ruffled, sleeveless lavender blouse, white cotton short-shorts, and manicured nails. Her hair pulled to one side revealed pierced ears with hoop earrings. Her smile exposed a chipped front tooth and single wire orthodontic retainer. He was glad he had not sent the letter he did not write. As conceived, it did not fit this young woman.

"What brings you to Waltsburg?" he finally managed.

"My car." Kim opened her small leather purse and withdrew a crumpled slip of paper. It was the handwritten note he had given her at Redmond's Peach Haven.

I live in Waltsburg
Come by barber shop
I will polish your boots

"I'm on my way to Manhattan to visit a friend. Is your offer st-still good?"

"Absolutely."

"Can I pick them up Mm-Monday on my way home?"

"Uh…sure."

She stuttered. He was tongue-tied. He watched his uncle and Darryl chatting outside the shop and the campers and RVs headed to Ormestrong County Lake with a variety of watercraft in tow.

"Where's home?" he queried.

"Bartlesville."

As Kimberly Anne Fitzgerald talked about herself, Jake began to relax. Unable to have children of their own, Kim's parents adopted her in 1955 at the age of three through a fledgling international agency. Kim was Korean, not Native American. Her adoptive father, a Korean War veteran, owned and operated an electrical contracting business with his brother. He specialized in commercial installations; his brother directed the residential side.

Throughout her first-grade year, the public school had not responsibly addressed the taunting and mean-spirited mimicking of her stuttering and non-Caucasian appearance. Kim's parents sent her to Monte Cassino Catholic boarding school for girls in Tulsa where the same issues persisted. "Only in the eyes of God are all Catholics created equal," Kim heard her aunt tell her father. Over his objections, Kim's Aunt Nell took matters into her own hands mid-term and enrolled her at Tulsa's private Holland Hall. Kim moved in with her aunt and, over the years, became a reliable helping hand and close companion.

Jake introduced Kim to his uncle Doyle and Wally, and paid Donna a visit. The chit-chat, in each instance, was brief and cordial. Jake and Kim established noon Monday as a good time to meet up again and retrieve her boots. Their parting was awkward; neither seemed to know what to say to the other. As he watched the Lincoln glide north on Main, that half-empty feeling reared its head again. He wondered if he had made a good impression. He wondered what she thought of Waltsburg. He wondered if the friend in Manhattan was male or female.

CHAPTER 31
YEOP CHAGI

Monday – September 7

Labor Day

Waltsburg's noon whistle sounded. The lunch hour came and went. Initially, Jake sat on the pew outside his uncle's shop. His anticipation languishing under the tenacity of a late summer sun, he retreated to the first barber chair, blinds minimally parted, ceiling fan on high, to wait for Kim. Her boots, on the seat of the first chair by the door, were as white and supple as he could make them. He stuffed a handwritten receipt inside one of the boots:

No charge. Courtesy of Jake's Bootblack Palace

He shaved and splashed on Aqua Velva, wore a striped Banlon shirt and a clean pair of Levi's. His freshly washed, waxed, and vacuumed car looked the best it had in months. He waited to vend himself a Coke in hopes she might like one also. The Beau Coup Café closed for the holiday. Main Street was quiet ahead of lake-goers on their way home. He watched occasional swirls of leaves, paper, and dust scud northward. The hummingbird feeder rocked back and forth on this, the second straight breezy day. A car pulled in next to his. Doyle and Donna walked in.

"She not shown up yet?" Donna queried.

"Nope. How was the lake?"

Donna faced the back-bar mirror and finger-combed her hair. "Way too much wind for me. Not a good day for a picnic."

"Lake was white-capping everywhere," added Doyle. "It's like a blowtorch out there. Lot-a people out, though. We drove down to the

166

nursing home in Houray to see Deke's wife. She didn't recognize either of us, so we didn't stay long. A nurse's aide brought her a snack and glass of water. She took a sip and asked what it was. The aide said, 'Water.' Charlene said something like, 'I've never had this before. It's delightful.'"

Donna asked, "Weren't you supposed to meet your friend at noon?"

"That was the plan. Did you hear the fire horn? It went off just after eleven."

"We did not. D'you hear yet where the fire is?"

"No."

"That's twice already this month," said Donna.

"We need rain."

"Haven't had any since that day your granddaughter and her friends blew into town. We're headed home to watch the telethon."

Straight up two p.m., Kim arrived. Her car bumped the curb and rocked backward, her turn signal still blinking. Jake shoved his hands in his jeans pockets and went outside.

"Hi. I am s-so ss-sorry I'm late." she said, exiting the car. "You had lunch yet?"

"No. You?"

"You c-can c-call me K-kim."

"Okay. You can…"

"Jacob," she interrupted.

"Or Jake. Or shoeshine boy."

"Are my boots ready?"

"Of course," he said, leading her inside.

"W-wow!" she exclaimed, holding them up. "I hardly recognize them."

"Ladder ready."

"Where c-can we eat?"

"Barney's Restaurant and Perky's are open."

"What's Perky's?"

"Burgers. Fries. Shakes. You know."

"Let's go there."

They ate in Jake's car, windows down in the shade of the carhop canopy. Kim spoke freely about life in the Maple Ridge suburb of Tulsa with her Aunt Nell, a well-to-do woman who oversaw a very lucrative commercial real estate portfolio inherited from her entrepreneurial father.

When not attending school, she assisted her aunt with most routine functions of day-to-day living. "She's not an invalid. It's the arthritis in her hip. S-she broke it years ago when s-she fell off a ladder in the orchard. S-some days s-she needs a c-cane." Kim was also full of questions. Did he grow up here? Where did he work? Was there anything interesting to see or do? Did he have any hobbies? Why was mistletoe above the barber shop's front door in September? Ultimately, Jake asked if she was ready to get back on the road and head home. She said she was not in any hurry. He suggested they go to Memorial Park and asked if she would object to Wally tagging along. She grinned and wondered aloud if three would be a crowd. Jake said no, Wally was a great tour guide.

As they strolled across the backyard of the modest two-bedroom, wood frame house on Newberry Street where he and his uncle lived, Kim fawned over the yard's hub, a splendid nine-foot Rose of Sharon loaded with lavender blooms. Encircling its base, a low stem wall of blond brick corralled a dense planting of pink Sweet William. "Lavender's my favorite c-color," she remarked. Jake showed her his secret passage, a shortcut to the park he had devised and maintained since he was eight, through the thicket of Osage orange trees that long ago over-whelmed the chain link fence. The park was abuzz with activity. The pair sat on a bench out of the wind on the shady side of the shelter house and sipped at their large Perky's soft drinks. Jake asked if she remembered anything about where she came from. She had only vague memories of the orphanage. She had no idea who her natural parents were or what became of them during the war. Kim remembered the train ride from Los Angeles with a man in military uniform who would become her father. At the train station in Oklahoma City, she met the lady she would call Mother.

Jake empathized. He intimated he knew his parents but circumstances between his mother and father effectively made him an orphan at age eight. His father, Emerson Book, a maintenance foreman, lost his job when Waltsburg's dairy shut its doors in 1940 and eventually found second shift work at Boeing in Wichita. When the war started, the aircraft manufacturer maintained round-the-clock shifts to meet the insatiable demand for bombers. He rented a room in Wichita and commuted only if his gasoline ration stretched.

#

Promoted several times, Jake's father sent home enough of his wages so that, monetarily at least, they were a solid middle-class family with little debt other than their mortgage. At war's end, Emerson's efforts to convince his wife to sell their Waltsburg house and relocate to Wichita were met with defiance. Jake's mother worked split shift as a waitress at Barney's Restaurant. Tips were best during breakfast and supper hours. She slept afternoons. As a result, Jake spent much of his after school and summer vacation time at his uncle's barbershop where Doyle introduced him to shining shoes, sweeping floors, and running errands.

Theirs was not, however, a happy home. According to his uncle Doyle, Jake's dad's quirky sense of humor drove Jake's mother nuts. Two months after Jake's eighth birthday, she withdrew all the family money from the bank, including Jake's savings account and sent Jake to stay with Doyle for the Memorial Day weekend. Relinquishing any claim to their home in the divorce agreement, Jake's mother rationalized the eventual sale of the house would more than make up for any financial hardship she caused. No one heard from her again. The following week, the produce manager at Wyatt's IGA unexpectedly quit his job and skipped town leaving no forwarding address.

Not long after, Jake's father was promoted to a middle management position with Boeing and transferred to Seattle, Washington. Emerson arranged to send a monthly check to Doyle to compensate for Jake's general welfare. He included Jake on his health insurance policy and paid for Jake's college. Jake had not seen his father for eight years.

#

Kim placed her hand on his arm and empathized. Jake recounted the history and high-lights of his peach-picking trips with Merry Belle omitting, of course, the visual of looking up her skirt. Kim had an orchard story of her own to tell of the summer she was fifteen. She asked if he remembered the large woman who loaded their pick onto the four-wheeler. She was Aunt Nell's much younger half-sister, Georgianna, who lived near the orchard. The one, quizzed Jake, who talked out of the side of her mouth? She nodded.

She began her tale, but hesitated and asked, "You have Indians here, too?"

"Yes, but that's not one of them."

As Lone Cloud's snub-nosed Divco approached, Native American drumbeats and chants blaring, children and adults alike lined the parking area. Jake abbreviated the backstory then, asked if she liked ice cream. "I'm ss-still pretty full," she said, wiping jewels of sweat from her forehead. She suggested they move to the other side of the shelter, facing the wind. The view was the backside of a World War I American M1905 Light Field Gun pointed towards the town of Whitfield. Even with the gusty breezes, the heat was uncompromising. Jake suggested they walk down to the river. They climbed the earthen embankment and picked their way across the riprap rock to the river's worn-smooth stone bank. Jake offered his hand for her final steps. Wally eagerly stepped into the cool, shallow water and slurped noisily.

"You c-call this a river?" asked Kim.

"We do."

"It's not exactly...I mm-mean, it's not very big."

Jake removed his shoes and socks, rolled up his pant-legs and waded into the purl. "C'mon in," he said. "Water's fine."

A short while later, Kim continued her orchard story. Georgianna oversaw the day-to-day operations of the orchard in tandem with Hayden who had been associated with the peach enterprise from its inception and could fix about anything. When Kim was fifteen, Aunt Nell arranged for her to reside with Georgianna and help during peak peach-picking time. Late one night, after a grueling twelve-hour workday, Kim was abruptly awakened by someone on top of her kissing her ear and cheek. When she struggled to see who it was, the unknown individual kissed her full on the mouth. Because she felt confined, Kim said, she panicked and pushed back against the weight with such force, the intruder tumbled to the floor. She rolled to the opposite side of the bed and stood. When the somebody came around the foot of the bed toward her, she scrambled across the bed trying to escape but was blocked by a chair-back wedged under the room's doorknob. Her eyes, adjusted to the dark, perceived the assailant lunging toward her. Instinctively, Kim executed a *yeop chagi*, a defensive, thrusting side kick, simultaneously with a *kihap* shout. The heel of her right foot landed with everything she had on the intruder's face. The intruder collapsed, writhing in pain. Kim hastily wrestled the chair aside and dashed out of the house. She ran up the road to Hayden's residence and pounded on his door. "I told Hay-Hayden what happened. He grabbed a sh-shotgun and headed back across the road. Halfway there, he s-saw Georgianna's car back out and ss-speed off. He discovered the front door locked but found the back door wide open. Hay-Hayden ss-searched the house. No one was there. When he returned, we c-called my father and Aunt Nell."

"Lucky kick, huh?"

"Not s-so much luck. Aunt Nell made me take *tae-kwan-do* lessons from a Grandmaster at a private *dojang* ss-since I was ten."

"Was it the woman who loaded our peaches?"

"Yes. I broke her jaw, ch-cheek bone and two teeth. Aunt Nell and my father drove up early the next morning. They talked to me and H-hayden then went to Georgianna's place. S-she would not let them in so Daddy k-k-kicked in the door. He told me on the drive home the whole left s-side of her face was black and blue, her left eye ss-swollen sh-shut. They s-sat her down in a chair. Aunt Nell pulled a s-snub-nosed .38 Ss-special out of her purse, pressed the barrel against her forehead and ss-said s-something like, 'You ever touch our K-Kimmy again, I'll blow your gawd-damn brains out.'"

"And you still work there?"

"I s-stay with Hay-hayden and his wife when I do."

"That's just crazy."

"You should try and k-kiss me ss-sometime and ss-see what happens."

Jake looked her in the eye. Was it a dare? A warning? An invitation? Tears crept down her cheeks. She sniffled, turned her head, and wiped them away.

"What's wrong?"

"Nothing. Just …s-something that happened in Manhattan. I'll tell you about it one of these days. S-see this?" she said, exhibiting her chipped front tooth. "I fell flat on my face running barefoot in my underwear through the dark to Hay-hayden's house that night." She glanced at her watch. "I sh-should probably be going."

On the short drive back to the shop Wally licked her ear. "Wally. No!" Jake admonished.

"Does he do that to everyone?"

"Just the ones he likes. Wally has very good taste."

After trading addresses and phone numbers Kim thanked him for showing her such a good time and apologized again for being late. She backed the Lincoln out but hesitated. She powered the passenger side window down and motioned him forward.

"Thanks again. V-very much." She waved and drove off.

Jake opened his driver's side door. Wally leaped in. The five o'clock whistle sounded. Wally howled in his best dog alto. Traffic on Main had picked up considerably as the lake shed its windblown, water-logged, sunburnt enthusiasts. As he backed out, he spied Kim's white boots just inside the front door.

CHAPTER 32
THE RED DOG INN

September 9th through 17th

It was the unintentional brainchild of Jacob Book. An editorial in the *Granfield Daily Dispatch* near the end of August discussed the ongoing repercussions of the U.S. military invasion of Cambodia and the Kent State shootings in May. The writer quoted anti-war activists at Ormestrong County Community College and the Reverend Cage who in turn cited a Directive adopted by their Board of Christian Social Concerns: "…this carnage cannot be the will of God and we must, with all our energy, demand that it cease." The article also mentioned the day-long war protest scheduled for September 19th in Lawrence, Kansas. Jake brought up the subject while fishing with John Griever the week after Labor Day.

"Too bad," Jake commented, "we couldn't give 'em that thief's van to bash."

John was silent for a few moments and then proffered, "Who says we can't?"

The next day, Jake, Conger, and Griever hatched a plan to dispose of the van. Conger tracked down one of the organizers in Lawrence, who jumped at the idea of a vehicle to bash as part of their protest. Conger offered it delivered at no cost, explaining it had been skunked and the owner was unable to eliminate the lingering odor. Griever visited with Deke and Anthony to be sure they would be willing, on such short notice, to strip the vehicle of its engine, radio, reusable parts, and identification features in exchange for the use of Stuber's tow truck. Once the van was parked inside Stuber's Garage, Jake and Conger disguised it by adding a four-inch wide, wrap-around red stripe. On both side panels, they stenciled the name:

Arbuckle Bros. Plumbing
AMherst 3-5452

When the paint was dry, they abraded the name and number rendering it virtually unreadable. In addition, they crumpled one front fender with a sledgehammer.

Though John Griever opted to take secondary roads on the cheerless outing under overcast skies, Jake still worried someone might recognize the van. Escorts Jake, Conger, and Griever towed the van to the front entrance of the Red Dog Inn at 7th & Massachusetts Streets. The sponsors insisted on early delivery to allow time to tag the vehicle with anti-war symbols, slogans, and graffiti.

Organized by a loose-knit coalition of student and national anti-war groups, the rally was backed by Students for a Democratic Society, Vietnam Veterans Against the War, the Black Student Union, Women's International League for Peace and Freedom, empathetic area churches and businesses. Proceeds from the bash were to benefit the families of two students slain in July, both the result of confrontations with local police.

The Red Dog Inn manager's office was small and cramped. Its limited wall space was adorned with Chamber of Commerce plaques, licenses, and autographed photos of bands that performed on stage here. Jake noted images of regional groups that included The Fabulous Flippers, Spider and the Crabs, Mike Finnigan and the Serfs, The Dinks, and the Rising Sons, interspersed with more well-known acts: The Drifters, Fleetwood Mac, The Kingsmen, Wilson Pickett, and the Ike and Tina Turner Revue with the Ikettes.

After a round of perfunctory first-name introductions, handshakes, and weather-related comments, John Griever handed the protesters' spokesman the keys to the van saying, "You won't need these." The ad lib one-liner seemed to ease the awkward atmosphere. The four motley student representatives excused themselves and left. Phil, the Inn's manager, and his bouncer, Munk, an ex-KU football offensive lineman from Chicago, visibly relaxed.

"You coming back Saturday?" Phil asked.

"Don't know," said Griever. "Ain't thought that far ahead yet."

"We just hope this thing doesn't get out of hand."

"I read where someone set fire to the student union last spring."

"Yes. But it wasn't near as bad as that arson fire someone set on K-State's campus a year or so ago."

"Fuckin' niggers and hippies are behind most of it," Munk added.

"All hell broke loose here in July. Fires set, cars rolled, shootings. We had it all goin' on. We got our own Kent State and Jackson State all rolled into one."

"We had two get shot to death," said Munk.

"They been extorting money from local churches. In June, the cops found twenty-three sticks of dynamite under a propane truck in town. Saturday morning, our doors here stay locked. All our fire extinguishers will be in the lobby. You have no idea what some of these radical assholes might do when they got a crowd cheerin' 'em on. This grassroots movement they call the New Left, if you're on the receiving end, it's more like what's left? ...if you get my drift."

"You got a right to defend your property," Griever remarked.

"Not sure I want He Defended a Dance Hall as my epitaph," said Phil, as he snatched a tissue, sneezed, and blew his nose. "Sorry. Allergies. Right now, they're not that well organized. Their agendas differ but the war in Vietnam has been a catalyst, a cause they can all rally around. Personally, I'd just-a soon all these foul mouth, fist-pumpin', Che-lovin' Lefties would pack up their soapboxes and move somewhere else. You know? Like Cuba."

"Where do you draw the line?" tested Conger.

"That is the $64,000-dollar question. Where, indeed? How much ground do you give up to keep 'em from settin' fires and shootin' at ya?"

"They ain't never gonna be satisfied, if ya ask me," Griever said.

"The Black Power and anti-war groups are the loudest voices. Name a cause, any cause, they want-a be heard."

"Got a bunch-a outside agitators comin' here, too," Munk inserted.

"A witch's brew," said Griever.

"I say it's about time for us to go," urged Conger.

"Monday, I got a call from the FBI wanting to use this place as a staging area Saturday. I said no. <u>That</u> would be bad for business. Know what I'm sayin'?"

"You should move to Waltsburg," said Jake.

"Ha!" Phil chuckled. "Don't think the small-town lifestyle hasn't crossed my mind. My wife wouldn't need any encouragement. She grew up in Humboldt, Kansas. I tell her, find me a decent paying job, we'll pack up and go."

"Our IGA is looking for sackers and stockers," Conger mentioned.

Phil laughed and rose out of his chair.

"They just installed lights on the tennis court at our city park," Jake added.

Phil grinned, "My wife and I'll have to dust off our tennis rackets and come visit one of these days."

"Where'd you get that?!" Jake blurted. "On the wall. That picture."

Phil turned to look, "Oh, that. Got that off some hippie-types one night, uh, a month, or let's see, maybe closer to two months ago. Two chicks and a guy came in on nickel beer night. They bellied up to the bar. Ordered draws and a tub of popcorn. Just as they were leaving, Munk spotted the guy snatch the March of Dimes collection card off the counter by the cash register and shove it down the front-a his pants. Munk grabbed me and we followed 'em to their car, some crappy ol' Ford station wagon with Oregon plates. The guy had just opened the tailgate when we confronted 'em."

"It's my uncle's," Jake said. "They stole it, our collection card, and TV fund money from the shop back home."

"Under a blanket, back-a that station wagon was full of those cards. Most of 'em with coins removed. That picture was in among 'em."

"I shoved that skinny little twerp up against the car and asked him if he liked the fuckin' face he was born with," said Munk. "He was scared shitless. Didn't give us no trouble. Gave the card back. Said sorry about twenty times."

"He offered us the picture," Phil said, sitting back down. "So, we took it."

"Should-a called the law on 'em," Griever interjected.

"Like I said, local cops had more 'n they could handle last July. Petty larceny would-a been the least of their worries. You know?"

"Can we have it back?" Jake asked.

"How do we know it belongs to you?"

"It's my uncle's. His wife was the artist. It's signed SGDeCritt, isn't it?"

Phil removed the 6" x 8" drawing from the wall and took a closer look at the gargoyle caricature with its lightly shaded red tongue, then flipped it over. "What's on the back?"

"Its name, the title," said Jake.

"Which is…?"

"Viktor."

"What else?"

"A Bible verse."

"From the Book of Ephesians," Griever specified.

"Do you know it?" Phil quizzed.

"Put on the whole armor of God so we may be able to stand against the wiles of the devil," Jake quoted.

"That proof enough for ya?" challenged Griever. "Yer in possession of stolen goods."

Phil glanced at Munk who shrugged a shoulder. Phil handed the rendering to Jake with a smile. "Sorry for your loss. Should-a let Munk beat the snot out-a the scrawny little hippie-punk when we had the chance."

"They stole collection cards from other businesses where we're from," said Griever, "and walked off not payin' for two breakfasts."

"What a coincidence. Their kind is twelve for a dime nowadays."

All doors of the ill-fated van stood open as John Griever navigated the tow truck away from the Red Dog Inn. Two of the four students who attended the meeting earlier sat on the curb. The overcast sky had convalesced to mostly cloudy. Welcome shanks of sunlight dappled the landscape. Jake mused over the framed pen and ink sketch as he watched the hypnotic sway of a St. Christopher's pendant dangling from the rearview mirror. He reminded himself he needed to touch base with Kim about her boots. How could he get them to her? Why was he procrastinating giving her a call? Except for directions how to get through town to Interstate 70, none of the three spoke until they were outside the city limit. John Griever was first to break the silence.

"I never seen so many martin houses in one place in my life."

"Bunches of 'em, wasn't there?" Conger responded.

"Where'd you see purple martin houses back there?" Jake asked.

"He meant all the big apartment complexes and dormitories," Conger answered, then turned to Griever, "Didn't you?"

CHAPTER 33
POWER TO THE PEOPLE

Saturday – September 19

"One, two, three, four. We don't want your fucking war!"
"One, two, three, four. We don't want your fucking war!"
"One, two, three, four. We don't want your fucking war!"

Jake, Conger, Griever and Bill Stimka stood on the sidewalk in front of the Lawrence National Bank directly across the street from the Red Dog Inn, maintaining a respectable distance from the van being bashed non-stop by anti-war protesters. Slogans, bumper stickers, and tagger art, like the "X" in NIXON replaced by a swastika, covered the van. Repositioned perpendicular to the curb, the air let out of its balding tires, it looked submissive, cowed like a luckless Inquisition martyr.

Frat boys, hippies, middlebrow adults, children, sorority chicks, Haskell Indian Juco students, and a priest were among the identifiable van whackers. Black, white, short, tall, bald, bottle blond, and afro alike stood in line to drop their dollar bills in a five-gallon bucket, step forward, and take their best shots at the redecorated vehicle. Eric Carver strode up to the target and landed five blows on the driver's side door. Jake wondered if the others noticed Darcy Cage on the opposite side of the street, restraining Rocky on a short leash.

"Hey, hey. Shout, shout. Tell Tricky Dick to pull us out!"
"Hey, hey. Shout, shout. Tell Tricky Dick to pull us out!"
"Hey, hey. Shout, shout. Tell Tricky Dick to pull us out!"

Many rejoined the chants orchestrated by a colorfully garbed,

179

middle-aged black activist with a bullhorn standing atop the van. He exuded the charisma of a rehearsed speaker and spewed the clichéd rhetoric of a cause. His voice roller-coastered from 'war and politicos' to 'black power and civil rights' to 'military-industrial complex' to 'rant-chant' again. Jake thought he looked a lot like Jimi Hendrix. In less than ten minutes, the profanity-laced themes became repetitive, much like the chants themselves.

Circulating through the large crowd, a host of busybodies distributed copies of the day's scheduled activities, anti-war literature, underground newspapers, area *cause célèbre* flyers, and discount coupons for local fast food and dry-cleaning businesses. Others sought signatures for assorted petitions. Jake watched monarch butterflies gamboling over, through and across 7th and Massachusetts on their annual migration south.

The ubiquitous media with their 35mm cameras and telephoto lenses milled about recording the event for posterity's footnoters. The curious, the conflicted, the silent majority lingered elbow to elbow with the antic-spiced, anti-establishment din makers. Merchants in the immediate vicinity attempted business as usual but tacitly held their breath. Local law enforcement maintained a low profile, directing traffic around the demarcated two-block zone on Massachusetts Street. More than a hundred sheriff deputies, local police officers and reserves, Kansas highway patrolmen, Civil Air Patrol, Kansas Bureau of Investigation, and FBI agents stood by, either out of sight or incognito, in the event they were needed. All University of Kansas campus security and maintenance personnel and City of Lawrence firefighters were also called to duty and placed on high alert.

Like a misdirected running back's stiff-arm, the Hendrix look-alike pumped a clenched fist skyward shouting:

> "We shall overcome!"
> "We shall overcome!"
> "We shall overcome!"

The Red Dog's marquis promoted The Soul Express rock group. A hand-lettered banner of butcher's wrap END THE WAR extended the length and height of The Dog's multiple-door entry. In the intersection of 7th and Massachusetts, a group of twenty or so locked arms and shouted a separate cheer as they danced a crude circle around a burning American flag crumpled on the street. In less than an hour, the Waltsburg foursome had seen enough. They hiked back to their car as another chant resounded above the throng:

"Hell, no! We won't go!"
"Hell, no! We won't go!"
"Hell, no! We won't go!"

CHAPTER 34
JUNE 1964

Wild Bill announced he had an idea in mind for lunch if they did not mind taking a different route home.

"How different?" Griever queried.

"Take 59 Highway south till I tell ya to turn west."

"How far is it?"

"Less than an hour, prob'ly."

"It better be good. I got shit I gotta get done today."

As directed by Bill, Jake turned onto Grant Street in Hoxspur, Kansas.

"Ain't nothin' to this town," Griever observed.

Encircled by thirsty grassland, it was a paradigm of a tiny prairie community without any reliable notion of a business district. The Hideaway Tavern was nothing short of ordinary till one bit into a slab of their smoked ribs wrapped in foil and newspaper.

"How many would you guess were there this morning?" Conger asked.

"A thousand, maybe more, if ya ask me," Griever speculated, wiping his hands for the third time on his crumpled napkin.

"Anybody know what the black armbands mean?" Jake asked.

"I'll ask Eric next time I see 'im," Griever offered.

"What'd he weigh when he got back from 'Nam?" Bill asked.

"130," said Griever.

"That ain't healthy."

"He weighed 205 the last year he played football," said Conger.

"Nobody gets better eatin' hospital food. You seen what Darcy done to his car? Couple weeks ago, she took a ball bat to the hood."

Bill nudged Jake with his elbow. "You want yer beans?"

"You can have the rest of 'em."

Bill helped himself and channeled more bar-b-que sauce onto his plate.

"How do you get more beer?" Conger grumbled.

"Most people go up to the bar an' ask," said Bill.

Conger scooted his chair back and stood. "Anyone else?"

Wild Bill and John Griever each forked over enough cash for a second round.

"Jake…another Coke?" Jake shook his head no as he gnawed a rib.

"There a bathroom in this place?" Griever asked.

"Back yonder," answered Bill. Griever wiped his hands and mouth and headed in the direction of yonder.

"We ought-a get you to our next Antler Club meeting," Bill said, finishing his beer. "We could use some new blood."

"When's the next meeting?"

"Ain't heard."

"Could you hand me a couple more napkins?"

Bill passed Jake the napkin dispenser and reached across the table, helping himself to Griever's side of baked beans. "Man, these beans is good today."

"How'd you hear about this place?"

"Lyla's mother told me about it."

Conger returned with three longneck bottles of cold beer. Bill scooped another spoonful of beans from Griever's serving.

"I saw that!" said John, sitting back down. "There's more where them come from. Git yer own."

"Trade ya my beans for your slaw," Conger offered.

"Eric had a bout with malaria, too, didn't he?" Jake said to John.

"Laid 'im up for weeks."

"He damn sure ain't the stud he used to be," said Bill.

#

Wild Bill's comment spurred Jake's vivid recollection of a warm June evening in 1964 when he, Kirk Michaels, and Eric Carver, along with Lyla Witte's fifteen-year-old daughter, Indy, went to the Saturday night double feature at the Sunset Drive-In Theatre in Granfield. Jake drove. Kirk rode shotgun. Eric and Indy took over the backseat, by design. Eric placed an ice chest full of beer in the trunk and a blanket on the backseat floorboard. On the drive to Whitfield to pick up Indy, Eric made two things clear: They were not to turn around during the movie and they were to keep the portable speaker volume on loud.

They arrived early enough to claim a back row niche. Jake thought Indy, attired in tight jean short-shorts and a halter top, looked much older than her age. Eric raided the ice chest for a six-pack. He, Kirk, and Indy church-keyed their Hamm's. Minutes before twilight, Kirk and Jake meandered to the concession stand and purchased two tubs of fresh popped popcorn and a king-size Coke. On their way back, Jake spotted the Knaakt twins' blue and white Ford Custom Ranchero with its rusted-out rocker panels. He had neither seen nor heard of the twins since school let out for the summer. An uneasy feeling coursed through him but, he reminded himself, he was not alone; he was in good company.

The raspy, reverberating speaker voices blared from Kirk's side of the car. In every feature length film, breaks occur in character dialogue and background music. *Dr. No* was no exception. Neither Jake nor Kirk had to imagine what the sounds emanating from the backseat implied. Predictably, the windows fogged up. Jake rolled down his window, switched on the ignition, and turned the defrost fan to HIGH. They had finished their tub of popcorn and all but devoured the nearly full tub from the backseat when Jake spied the Knaakt twins advancing in their direction.

"Lock your door," Jake urged, crunching ice with his molars.

"What?!" Kirk replied, talking over the speaker and defrost blower.

"Lock your door!" he repeated, locking his and rolling up the window.

Jake pointed out the approaching twins in their bib overalls and faded yellow Knaakt & Sons Moving tees. Champ Junior had a large drink cup in one hand, Chase, a carton of popcorn. They halted directly in front of the car. Both brothers feigned masturbation and shouted. Kirk turned down the speaker volume.

"Jayboo! Jayboo! Jayboo!"

Champ splashed the drink on the windshield and hood. Chase followed with the popcorn.

"Jesus Christ!" Kirk hollered.

Jake honked his horn, blinked his headlights, and turned on the windshield wipers. The twins broke and ran, disappearing into the maze of vehicles.

Eric's head popped up over the seat. "Hey! What gives?!"

"The Knock-Knock retards just trashed Jake's car."

"Where are they?"

"Ran off. Toward the concession stand."

"Those candy-ass cowards," Eric snarled.

Jake shut the ignition off, got out of the car, and started brushing popcorn from the hood. Kirk joined in. Eric stepped outside, barefoot, shirtless, jeans unsnapped, and half zipped. His athletic, sculpted six-foot-two physique reminded Jake of the Charles Atlas ads in the comic books he had collected as a kid. Eric Carver was the only other boy in school who could challenge Conger in the weight room; Eric often bench-pressed more.

"I gotta pee," said Eric.

"Me too," echoed Indy. "Wait up!"

"Sorry about your car," Kirk offered.

"It'll wash off," Jake muttered.

"Should-a told me they were out there," Eric declared.

"You were busy," said Jake.

"Oh, yeah! C'mon, Indiana, hurry up."

"I am. I ain't comin' out there with no clothes on."

Indy slipped out of the backseat. "You want my comb?" Eric teased.

"Want me to shove that beer up your ass?!" she said, roughing up her hair.

They strolled the short distance to the privacy fence that defined the outer limit of the drive-in's parking area. Planks had been removed by others before them. Separate guys and gals unlighted areas to urinate in harmony with nature circumvented walking all the way to the concession stand. Eric tossed his empty beer can toward others along the back side of the fence. After, he fetched an ice-cold six-pack from the trunk and waited for Indy.

"What time does she have to be back?" Jake asked.

"She doesn't have a curfew."

"I do," said Kirk.

"You kiddin' me?!" exclaimed Eric.

"Nope. One a.m."

"What time is it?"

"Two freckles past a mole," Indy quipped, coming up behind Eric and sliding her hands into his front jeans pockets.

"11:30," said Jake.

"Okay. Twelve-fifteen we head home."

Back in the car, Kirk turned up the speaker. Alternating between a bad and so-so connection, it produced static and an advertisement for a local new car dealer. Out of the corner of his eye, Jake watched Indy guzzle her beer, shed her halter top, shimmy her upper torso and say, "Like this?" Kirk asked Jake if he wanted to go up to the concession stand and get another Coke. Jake shook his head no. The second feature's title *From Russia With Love* flashed on the big screen.

"You seen this?" Kirk asked.

"Yeah."

The opening credits and James Bond theme song had just ended when Kirk turned down the speaker volume. "Twins are leaving," said Kirk, pointing to Jake's left.

"Hey guys!" Eric barked, sitting up.

"They're gonna come this way," Jake predicted.

"Move over," Eric said to Indy. He hastily pulled on his jeans, crawled across the seat, and opened the door. He stood, toes crooked over the edge of the car door's threshold then stepped down and fumbled for an unopened can of beer on the floorboard.

"They comin'?" Kirk asked.

"Could be. Where's the church key?"

Indy popped up wrapped in the blanket. "What's going on?"

Jake slumped down in the seat. Eric made his way along Kirk's side of the car, ducked under the speaker cord and crouched down. Champ Knaakt Jr. navigated the truck inches from the front end of Jake's Falcon and stopped. All they could see was Chase Knaakt's giant bare ass completely plugging the passenger window frame. Eric notched a small opening, shook the can vigorously with his thumb over the hole and sprang toward the truck's window. The geyser of cold beer scored a direct hit. Chase Knaakt yelped and nose-dived into his brother's lap. The truck lurched forward, erratically swerving left, then right. Eric trotted alongside, alternately shaking the beer and spewing it in the open window. As the twins' truck pulled away, he pitched the can in the truck's bed.

"COOL!" Kirk cried out. "How cool was that?!"

They dropped Kirk by home in Waltsburg. Two blocks from Kirk's house, Eric ordered Jay-cob to pull over, quick. Jake no sooner stopped the car than Indy puked out the window. It took less than five seconds for Eric to say good night on her porch. There was no question there would be hell to pay come September. The bar had been raised.

#

Bill and Jake stood on the wood plank walkway outside waiting on the others to pay. "D'you see all them photos on the walls? This town used to be full of life. Back in the day, this place was a saloon. That boarded up buildin' 'cross the street was a dance hall called the Hot Fish.

Lyla's mother told me the town came alive when they struck oil 'bout three mile east-a here durin' the Great War. When the oil boom fizzled out, so did the town. During Prohibition, she said Hoxspur was a haven for grifters and bootleggers. What'd you think of the grub?"

"I'd come back. How much longer before Waltsburg looks like this?"

"It won't happen in my lifetime ... but it's comin' sure as the all hat, no cattle crowd."

Back on the highway, Wild Bill slumped against the door in full siesta mode. All agreed Stimka's surprise destination was worth the detour.

"Mom told me Abraham Lincoln once labeled Lawrence the Cradle of Liberty."

"Liberty don't come cheap," John imparted. "You two ain't old enough to remember, but the *Waltsburg Journal* newspaper office got fire-bombed in '41 over-a anti-Germany story they wrote up claimin' Hitler was the devil turned inside out. That fire burnt down the newspaper, City Hall, the bank, and damaged two other buildings. Lot-a town records burnt up in that fire."

"Jesus H. Christ!" Griever exclaimed. "Was that you, Stimka?!"

All three rolled down their windows.

"Hey!" he said, jostling Bill.

Wild Bill lifted the hat from his face. "Wh-what?"

"D'you just fart?"

"I believe I mighta," came the answer, fanning his lap with his hat. "Hoo-boy. I think them beans must-a went right through me." Griever punched him in the arm. Bill punched back. They started to scuffle.

CHAPTER 35
JAKE GETS AN OFFER

Friday – October 2

Dan Bruner asked Jake to stop by his office. Upon entering the bank, Parise waved him over. "Go on in. He's expecting you."

"You hungry?" Dan asked, glancing at his watch. "How 'bout we walk over to Luci's and grab a bite."

Arriving early enough to be seated in a booth, Jake asked if there was a problem with one of his accounts. Dan said no. After some token chit-chat and placing their orders, Dan requested their conversation be kept confidential. "Darcy gave her notice yesterday. Her last day will be October 16th."

"I didn't see her when I came in."

"She called in sick. Just between us leprechauns, did you know she's pregnant?"

"Uh…no. Did not." Jake wondered who the father was. His second thought, 'Why is Dan confiding in me?'

"You know Parise and Jimmy are expecting their first. She'll be leaving end of the year. She's more interested in raising a family. Valoise and I are very much looking forward to being grandparents. Bottom line, I'm losing two very good employees over the next three months."

"Darcy getting married?"

"She didn't say. I'm not one to pry unless you are behind on your payments or something like that. You ever given any thought to what you plan to do with your life workwise? Think about being something other than a Jake-of-all-Trades?"

"Not lately."

"Would you consider working for me at the bank?"

"I guess, sure. I would. I think."

"I need someone who gets along well with people."

The server brought their house salads and topped off their ice waters.

"What Waltsburg needs are jobs," Jake commented.

"True. Don't have any good news on that front. In fact, there's more bad news coming. The Ben Franklin store plans to shut down after the holidays. I spoke at length with one of Franklin's vice presidents after I heard. They're closing a number of their stores in towns with populations under a thousand. He used the term 'under-performing' a half dozen times. Have you heard Luci's thinking about expanding into the Franklin store? She thinks the area would support a venue for special occasions, meetings, reunions, one-time events, those sorts of things. If she knocks a hole in the wall, rearranges her kitchen layout and adds some new equipment, she could easily cater them."

"What-a you think?"

"I think it has merit. She can sublease from Ben Franklin. They've got over five years left on their lease. The rent's dirt cheap. I hate to see another vacant storefront on Main. I asked her for a business plan and five-year income projection. D'you see her new slogan on the window?"

"Didn't know she had one."

BEAU COUP CAFE

Order what you like. Like what you get.

"By the way, the best news we've had at the bank in years happened a couple-a weeks ago. Just by chance, Merry Belle came across both her baptismal and adoption certificates, the pieces of the puzzle we've been missing for almost ten years."

"Cong mentioned that last week."

"I think now we can finally get the Muldoon estate settled. She'll soon be a very well-to-do woman and the rightful landowner, not a tenant-at-will."

Jake knew from Conger that the old travel trunk the would-be thief uncovered in the Pennsylvania barn produced a treasure trove of artifacts.

The most significant finds were the certificates sought by Merry, the bank, and the bank's legal counsel, Preston Carver. While there were still some in Waltsburg who knew most of the story, few knew all the details.

#

After numerous disappointments, an irreversible rift had developed between Sean Robert Muldoon and his parents. Robert had no interest in raising cattle in no man's land as he often referred to it. Sent to Kansas State College of Agriculture and Applied Science in Manhattan to study animal husbandry, Robert, unbeknownst to his parents, enrolled instead at Manhattan Bible College. His first-hand exposure to evangelism at the Aimee Semple McPherson revival when he was eight left an indelible impression.

During the spring semester of his first year at Bible College, Robert became carnally involved with one of his instructors twice his age, Waltsburg native Bernadette Lowry. When she let him know she was with child, they secretly married. She resigned her position with the college before their relationship was discovered. The newlyweds' first visit to the ranch sent Bearnard into a rage. Revelations of Bible College enrollment and a pregnant wife a generation his senior, plus Robert's obvious lack of contrition were more than his father could stomach. Robert and his father had never been close; Bearnard never again spoke to his son. Mary Muldoon was more empathetic but wore her disappointment on her sleeve during the newlyweds' tenuous two-day stay. Before he left the ranch, Robert packed all the clothing and personal items he could transport. It was the last time he saw his parents alive.

The upshot of the subsequent estrangement, Bearnard and Mary placed the ranch in a trust. At the suggestion of bank president, Archibald Bruner, Waltsburg State Bank was named Trustee. Robert and Merry Belle were the designated heirs. It was explained in detail to Merry shortly after it was finalized. When Robert moved back to the ranch after the tornado took his parents' lives, he disavowed his religion, deeming Catholicism obsolete. In his opinion, the Church was preoccupied with the ancient dogma of damnation, preparing one from cradle to grave to ascend to an imagined paradise if one obeyed the Rules. He invented his own inspirational message. He devised a formal ritual, available to believers of any faith, to cleanse or unbaptize souls. According to Merry, he practiced the ritual in the Falls pool. He imagined the New Jerusalem and thousands of followers; his mark left for eternity. In Sean Robert's mind, come hell or bad weather, he would be the next Billy Sunday.

#

"You know it took us years to locate Merry? When Bearnard and Mary were killed in the tornado, Merry Belle and Robert came back to the ranch, but he ran her and her son off in no time. Without the adoption papers, Merry didn't have a legal leg to stand on."

"Conger said they hated each other."

"Robert treated her like a doormat."

"She became a teacher, right?"

"Accepted a position in Follett, Texas, we later learned. She legally changed her name to Shay and went by Frances M. B. Shay. She never considered herself a Muldoon. If it were not for Jack Nagel and Bill Stimka, we'd-a never been able to keep the ranch afloat financially. Over time we wound up selling off thirty-four hundred acres to pay the back taxes and upkeep."

"How soon you need to know about the job?"

"The sooner the better, Jake. If you sign on with us, it will mean working pretty much a set schedule. Forty-hour weeks. Evenings, weekends, and holidays off. Two weeks paid vacation annually. And I can pay you four-fifty a month to start."

"Is there a signing bonus?"

Dan laughed aloud, "Of course. I pick up the tab for lunch today."

"Uncle Doyle know about this?"

"Nope. Just you and me."

"Who's gonna clean the bank's windows?"

"You, I guess."

"At the usual rate?"

Dan wiped his mouth with a paper napkin, crumpled it and dropped it in his empty soup bowl. "Sure. Why not? Tell me about this girl friend of yours in Oklahoma."

CHAPTER 36
FIRST CALL

Monday – October 5

It was 7:45 p.m. Jake stood frozen still in the semi-dark of the barbershop, hovering over the phone as if choosing between life and death. Next to the phone sat a list of topics he had jotted down, topics they might talk about. He looked in the mirror, put a comb through his hair, and dialed her number.

"Hello?"

"Is Kim there?"

"Who's calling?"

"Jacob Book."

"She has a math class at the junior college this evening but should be home around eight. Can I give her a message?"

"Can you have her call me?"

"Does she have your number?"

"Yes."

"I'll let her know you called. Bye now."

Jake fidgeted. Nine o'clock came and went. Did she get his message? Had she lost his number? Should he try again? At 10 he gave up. When he got home, there was a message taped to his bedroom door.

Kim called at 8:15

Of course! When exchanging addresses and phone numbers on Labor Day, he had given her his home number.

CHAPTER 37 - CALL #2

Tuesday evening – October 6/7

"Hi! Ss-sorry I missed your call," Kim gushed. Their small talk streamed like they were longtime friends until Kim had a meltdown. "I had an algebra class last night. When the instructor called on me to answer a question, s-speaking out in a classroom packed with nobody I knew caused me to s-stumble over more ss-syllables than usual. After class, three walking behind me mimicked my ss-stuttering and s-started giggling. By the time I got to my car, I was crying. My ss-speech therapy s-sessions are helpful, but I s-still can't s-shake the problem entirely." Between snivels, she told Jake she tries to ignore such events but, on occasion, it gets to her. "I'm cursed. Ss-sometimes I feel like a cat's s-scratching post."

"You're not." He intimated that as they got better acquainted Labor Day, he did not hear it. "It doesn't bother me."

"It does me. I get s-self c-conscious about it. Remember at the peach farm when Georgianna told you I ss-stuttered? After you left, s-she and I got into an argument about her telling people I ss-stutter. It's not her place …none of her damn business telling people that. Boy, was I mad. Fact is, I drove home that evening. Haven't been back s-since."

Jake tried to change the subject when she started apologizing. He asked if there was a focus group she could join like Alcoholics Anonymous. Kim laughed. "Do you realize how long group ss-stuttering meetings might last?" Jake asked if he could call again Sunday. After they hung up, Jake knew he needed to go to the library and see if they had any books on stuttering.

#

Next day, Jake paid a visit to Waltsburg's Carnegie Free Library. Jake's appointment with Joan Lowry was short and to the point like the sign on her office door: 'HEAD HONCHO.' "We are out of space here," she opined and apologized for the mess in her office. He asked if they had any books on stuttering? Offhand, she could not think of any. She said if he had trouble finding a book to ask for help. If there were not any under the stutter heading, he could try looking under stammer. Jake found nothing useful under stutter or stammer. On his way out, he asked Mrs. Lowry if she knew of any famous people who stuttered. "You might look up King George the Sixth, Queen Elizabeth's father. He's the only one who comes to mind. He had a debilitating stammer. He dreaded giving speeches."

CHAPTER 38
THE ORME RIVER VALLEY
QUILTING CLUB

Sunday – October 11

Though Joan 'Hanky' Lowry had swept her front porch, steps, and walk that morning, molting deciduous trees supplied a fresh scatter of leaves like Dust Bowl migrants caught up in the spirit of let go. All in harmony with the earth's orbit and first autumn shiver. As the quilting club's president and hostess, she set her thermostat at 72° and put out a fifth of Jameson to defeat the chill for the get-together of the Orme River Valley Quilting Club.

A holdover from the Mary Muldoon days, the ORVQC was a quasi-charitable circle that raised money and solicited donations of second-hand clothing, blankets, and winter coats to be donated to charities for orphaned and abandoned children. The original group met twice a month and turned out two quilts annually, sold at public auction for Mary Muldoon's favorite charity the Little Red Stocking campaign. Prior to her death, Mary and other Waltsburg women drove to Wichita each year to deliver donated goods to the Phyllis Wheatley Children's Home.

After Mary, Bernadette, and Sharon passed, the group strayed from its charitable enthusiasm. Meetings became infrequent and the group disbanded. Merry Belle re-established the club upon her return to Doona Falls Ranch. In the interim, charter member Violet Brisby saw to it that a WCTU crusading quilt was displayed in the town's museum. Quilting and charity no longer interested the group. The purpose of the semi-annual gatherings was to discuss their lives and everyone else's business. As membership grew and familiarity flourished, gatherings were the forum for first-hand backstories that brought the past to life.

This day, members noshed on Luci Bertolini's assortment of finger food creations and leafed through an old photo album. The ladies raved about Luci's cream cheese-honey-walnut spread and Donna Pileaux's new eyeglass frames accented with rhinestones. A scrapbook photo of members celebrating the anniversary of Luci Bertolini's first year in business sparked a confession from Luci that Waltsburg was not her first choice of locations. Her heart was set on opening an eatery in Council Grove, Kansas, her father's family's hometown, but the bank turned them down for a loan. Fortunately, Luci explained, she and Anthony were accustomed to living frugally. After his discharge from the Army, and prior to moving to Kansas, they spent two years in San Diego. She enrolled in culinary school and tended bar weekends. He turned a wrench at a reputable automotive shop within walking distance of their studio apartment.

"You met in San Diego?" Parise asked.

"No, Australia. Summer of '63. In Sydney, when he was on R&R."

Luci told the backstory of her father's calling with the China Inland Mission that landed him in Nanking, China, in the summer of 1935. Fall of 1937, Luci was six months along in her Chinese mother's womb when her missionary father decided to return home for the Thanksgiving holiday and remain state-side until the child was old enough to travel. Circumstances in China had taken a turn for the worse. The Japanese Army had invaded the country and was advancing in their direction. Safe passage arranged, on October 4th they left for Shanghai.

Over the years, Nonny alluded to the loss of her soldier husband. "I long ago concluded it was not meant to be," said Nonny. "The whole world was upside down. Who could say what might come next? We set our alarm clocks, put one foot in front of the other, and carried on."

"What became of him?" Parise queried.

"It took years for me to completely dismiss the fancy he was coming back."

"From where?"

"Burma."

Merry presented several new photos to be added to their collection. They were discovered in a steamer trunk stashed in the big barn. Two were photos of Mary Muldoon astride her horse, Sheba, one with a handsome young Robert Muldoon holding the reins. He looked more like his mother, no conflicted eye, prominent lower jaw, or mole aside his nose like Bearnard. Claire Nagel mentioned she was sure she had spotted Sheba in the pasture across the road from their place the week after her mother's funeral. She mentioned her husband's ongoing struggle with the Veterans Administration to treat the wounds he received during the closing days of the Battle of Okinawa in June 1945. The left side of his body was riddled with artillery shell and coral rock fragments while serving with the Seabees. She asked if any of them ever noticed Jack's left eye, nostril, ear, and lip were out of alignment with his right side. He sported a large handlebar mustache to draw attention away from the asymmetry.

Another snapshot passed around stirred Merry's memory. In it, John Griever, Wild Bill Stimka, Zander Rhoades, and Dutch Dooley cavorted in front of the old Doona Falls Ranch bunkhouse during their cowboying days. Zander played banjo, Griever guitar, and Dooley harmonica while the somewhat blurred image of Wild Bill danced. Nonny commented it was Zander who taught John guitar. He told me Zander could incite a corpse to sing. "They called themselves The Lighthearts," Merry said, alluding to the Saturday night parties in the big barn that lasted well into the small hours of the morning. She recalled Bearnard Muldoon's obsession with polka music and dance. No one could remember the name of their accordion player but did remember he was from the town of Wundchen.

"As I recall," Merry continued, "Nonny spent more than her share of Saturday nights in the Falls pool with men."

"I was in my prime! I never experienced so much unbridled joy."

"John told me that every Sunday evening in back of the bunkhouse, Zander made up the best campfire stone soups he ever tasted," Merry noted. "Zander's Appalachian recipes were a welcome change to the ranch menu. He was unusually fond of wild ramps."

"Oh," Hanky interrupted, "before I forget, Valoise and I drove down to Houray yesterday to visit Charlene Stuber. I'm afraid she's not long for this world. She's been in a coma for a week now."

Merry handed Donna an envelope addressed to Doyle. Donna warily lifted the flap.

Inside was a black and white photo of a posed semi-nude woman Merry found among the trunk's trove of relics. Though the woman's face was turned away from the camera, a teacup-size birthmark was apparent on her left shoulder blade. Merry was sure it was Sharon DeCritt, taken in her studio at the Doona Falls house. "I'm not surprised," Donna replied, as she slipped the photo back in the envelope. "Doyle has a nude self-portrait she sketched for him hanging over the dresser in his bedroom that's much more revealing than this. Thank you. He will be grateful."

"Anyone here remember the closed-door meetings Bearnard held in the barn?" Merry asked. "As many as forty men attended those gatherings. Politically, he was a socialist, a carry-over from his days as a thug in Glasgow. He subscribed to a popular socialist newspaper out of Girard, Kansas. I found a handful of those papers in that trunk."

"D'you know Upton Sinclair's *The Jungle* was originally serialized in that Girard publication?" Hanky interjected.

"Dan told me you found an original, notarized copy of your adoption papers in the trunk," said Valoise.

"What else was in there?" Ginny asked.

"Oh, my. Let's see…my baptismal certificate. Some of Robert's baby things. A headless doll. A very fancy blue dress I suspect was Mary's wedding dress. Irish tatted lace. Recipes. Rosary beads. Brass knuckles. A book of nursery rhymes. Oodles of postcards and Valentines."

As Lyla Witte studied the bunkhouse photo, she recalled the first time she met Bill Stimka at a church-sponsored covered dish supper. "He asked me what I did for a living. I told him when I wasn't moving dirt around with a dozer somewhere or picking at my banjo, I was a certified taxidermist. I mounted animals. He took a step back, thought for a second, and announced that in a previous life he was a Brahma bull named Stiffy."

The group hooted, agreeing that sounded like something Bill would say.

"We've been friends ever since."

"Very close friends," Nonny added with a wink.

"You bet," said Lyla. "He told me it's in his last will and testament, the day he croaks, he wants me to stuff him, track down that ghost of a pinto horse, saddle it, and mount him up. Bind his boots to the stirrups, cinch his wrists to the saddle horn, sew the reins in one hand fisted like a bull rider, and let the pieces fall where they may."

"Bill sired Indy, right?" Nadine Baguelt said, with a grin.

"Yup."

"And Briley's John Griever's son?" Donna Pileaux offered.

"Yup."

"And yawl are still friends?" asked Parise.

"Yup."

"Ever consider marryin' one of 'em?" Ivy Butterbaugh asked.

"Never."

"I didn't know any of that," Parise said, nibbling on her fourth comfiture-filled pastry and brushing crumbs from her new maternity top.

"When's your due date?" Claire asked.

"End of March. I have a question. Up to what point can Jimmy and I still have sex?"

The group exchanged glances.

"Till it's uncomfortable," Nadine tendered.

"Great answer," Valoise Bruner added.

"You hoping for a boy or a girl?" Jenna Fairchild asked.

"'Long as it's healthy and got all its fingers and toes, we don't care. Well, Jimmy did put a baseball glove in the crib. So, I guess, you know…. Has anyone heard that Jake might go to work for my dad at the bank?"

"When did this happen?" Donna asked.

"Over lunch about a week ago."

"News to me."

"It's ten till," Hanky announced.

"Almost time," said Nonny.

The doorbell rang. Hanky answered and ushered in Catharine Mixx. "Ladies, I invited Catharine to join us today."

"Sorry I'm late. Had an open house in Granfield."

"Is Marti not coming anymore?" Donna said to Nadine.

"We're not her cup of tea. She and Kristie are in Kansas City this weekend with Marti's folks. If Marti had her way, they would move there. Tomorrow."

"Allen didn't go?" Donna asked.

"He's in Lawrence at a pledge class reunion of his fraternity at KU. Jonathan has a chest cold. He's staying with us."

"Did Horse Face ever officially resign?" queried Lyla.

"No. She just stopped coming," said Hanky.

"She give a reason?"

"She decided it was not in her best interest to mingle with a group of women who add hell-broth to their coffee."

"The Polka Queen of Waltsburg," Hanky elaborated.

"She and ol' Pere Gustafson. Remember him?"

"They were a pair, weren't they? Pere could cut a rug in his day."

"Violet can be so bloody judgmental," Nonny inserted.

"Intransigent would be more like it," said Hanky. "Ladies, before we adjourn to the back porch, I would like to offer a prayer for Charlene." They stood and joined hands.

As if on cue, the group drifted toward the back of the house. Six members hung back. They had observed the ritual multiple times. Nonny asked Nadine if Catharine could borrow her opera glasses. "What're we doing?" Catharine whispered at Nonny, the strap of a pair of binoculars now looped around Nonny's neck.

The group assembled on Hanky's screened back porch. It was a ritual about to come to an end. Henry Yost's small clapboard home's backyard sat directly opposite Joan Lowry's. Over the years, his screened porch fell into disrepair. Stripped of all but its perimeter load-bearing supports, his washer and dryer, small chest freezer, stacked patio chairs, bar-b-que grill, and accumulated junk sat in open view. Building materials to enclose the porch lay strewn on the ground. By week's end, Henry and Jake would enclose the porch, complete with a new aluminum storm door and two small windows.

In the distance, the town whistle pronounced straight-up five p.m. The low angle of the sun fell on the backside of Henry's house like a spotlight. As he had for years, Sunday evenings at this hour Henry Yost would launder his clothes. Right on cue, he appeared in his skivvies, laundry basket in hand. Lean and wiry, he was in great shape for a man in his late fifties.

"There he is," announced Hanky in a stage whisper. All raised their binoculars. He went through the motions of starting a first load, unaware of the peeping Godivas.

"Looks like he's doing a light load first," murmured Ivy.

Task completed; Henry started to go back inside but hesitated. He strode back over to the washer, lifted the lid, shed his skivvies, and tossed them in.

"Oh, my word," Hanky mumbled.

Ogling in complete silence, one could hear a pin drop. When Henry stepped back toward the door, Nonny could not restrain herself. "Good morning, Henry!" He turned about, shaded his eyes, and then waved in their direction before disappearing into the house.

"Nonny, you are incorrigible!" exclaimed Merry.

"*Bravo*, Nonny!" Lyla cried.

"Show's over," announced Hanky.

Everyone headed back inside except Nonny and Catharine.

"He's not circumcised, like my Daddy." Catharine remarked. "Is he married?"

"Never has been that I know of."

"How long before he puts 'em in the dryer?"

CHAPTER 39
MR. ROGER

The two ambled back inside. "Okay, Nonny. You still need a ride out to the nanny goat ranch?"

"I do. Preferably before it gets too dark."

"What are you doing at John's?"

"I am taking this cardigan for Roger."

"I love the colors. Who's Roger?"

"John's imaginary friend who lives in the shelter belt."

"He taken to drinking?"

"No. It's a story I cannot tell you about just yet."

"How do you dress something imaginary?"

"Very prudently."

"Have you met this Roger fellow?"

"I am hopeful he will allow me that privilege this evening."

"John knows you're coming?"

"He does."

"Does he know why you're coming?"

"Not precisely."

"Will he bring you home?"

"I believe Jake will. They are painting the barn this weekend."

As the big car crossed the railroad tracks with nary a jounce, Catharine asked, "What do you know about Henry?"

"He's always friendly but not altogether gregarious. He works hard at whatever he does. Keeps to himself mostly. He comes from a Mennonite background. Spent I do not know how many years looking after his elderly parents in Moundridge. Why?"

"I think he and Jake repaired the termite damage to my front porch and steps a couple years back. Right after I moved in."

"You had termites?"

"Yes. A bit ironic, isn't it? A real-a-tor having a termite infestation?"

"Did you complain?"

"Wouldn't have done any good. You know, *caveat emptor* and all that."

Catharine slowed to turn onto the dirt road leading to John Griever's place.

"Does the name Porfirio Rubirosa ring a bell with you?"

"No. Why?"

"My nurse comrades and I religiously followed his escapades in gossip columns from the forties through the mid-sixties. He was a Dominican diplomat, a continent-hopping playboy who was immensely popular with famous women. As the story goes, he had a peter so large, Parisian waiters named over-sized pepper mills *Rubirosas*."

"Do tell!"

"We often fantasized over his apparent sexual prowess. In our opinion, if it was good enough for heiresses and movie stars, it was good enough for us. Cath'rin! You turn here!" Catharine hit the brakes but overshot the entrance by two car lengths. Nonny reflexively braced herself, arms outstretched, hands propped against the dashboard.

"Sorry. My mind was elsewhere. You okay?"

"Yes. I believe so."

Catharine backed up and drove into the yard very slowly. Nonny retrieved the aubergine, pink and orange striped cardigan from the floorboard and refolded it.

"You expecting company?" Jake hollered to John.

"Maybe," John called back from the far corner of the barn. Oversized paint brush in hand, he stepped down from his ladder and headed in Jake's direction. Several of John's ever-curious goats gravitated toward the vehicle.

"You expecting Miss Mixx?"

"She might be bringin' Florence Nightingale for a visit."

Nonny thanked Catharine for the lift and made an unhurried exit. Catharine waved, executed a turn around and left.

"Welcome home," John greeted.

"Thank you. I see you are sprucing up the barn."

"Can you stay for supper?"

"I would rather not. Is there a good place to pick wildflowers close by?"

"West side of the barn," Jake answered.

"I should like to pick a small bouquet to lay at my father's grave."

"I can pick some for you," Jake offered.

"Suppose you want us to put 'em on the grave for ya, too?"

"No. I will. I brought this for Roger," Nonny said, holding out the colorful cardigan.

John took the garment and unfolded it. "Might be too big. Roger's lost a lot-a weight."

"It will have to do. I think it's time we met."

"He's pretty fussy 'bout what he wears."

"I assume you will accompany me so I can be properly introduced?"

"Where d'you get this?"

"Ginny's close-out rack."

"It's a woman's sweater?! You want Roger to…"

"It'll have to do."

John handed the garment back. Jake returned with a fistful of fall wildflowers: goldenrod, Queen Anne's Lace, and blue sage.

"C'mon," John sighed. "Let's get this over with."

"Want me to keep painting?"

"Let's call it a day. It's gonna be dark soon."

As Jake sealed up the paint cans and cleaned their brushes with turpentine, he remembered he had promised Kim a call today. John opened the barbed wire gate to the pasture.

Four nannies followed along.

"Friendly little buggers, aren't they?"

"That and they might-a got a whiff-a the rag top on Mixx's limo."

He asked if she planned to split the do-it-yourself bouquet and pay homage to their mother whose grave and marker were on the opposite side of a once-magnificent box elder tree split by lightning when Nonny was a teen. She snipped he knew damn well that required she bring her mother's Bible with its bookmarked verses. She took John's arm, and they strolled out to the site; a crude, fieldstone marker tilted over time, flanked by a salt lick remnant. Nonny laid the bouquet at the marker's base, the name I. J. KRAVCHUK still legible.

"Do I remember there being dates on the stone?"

"Not that I recall. We can have 'em put on there."

"I do not know the year he was born. He joined a self-defense unit during the First Russian Revolution. I remember him telling mother about some of his adventures. But he had land and a family to tend to."

"You never told me he was in the Army."

"I do not know if he ever wore a uniform or just became disillusioned. Famine and all the warring factions compelled them to emigrate. He was a good father. A good provider. I am ready to meet Roger now."

They strolled along the shelter belt that defined John's west property line. Jake tagged along. It was he who discovered the skull a few feet from the tree where John erected his deer stand. As time permitted, Jake and John scoured the area for other skeletal parts. While some teeth and many small bones of the hands and feet were missing, they were able to reconstruct roughly eighty percent of the skeleton using bailing wire, fishing line, electrician's tape, and an illustrated anatomy book from Waltsburg's library. Upon completion, and at Jake's suggestion, John christened the unknown person Roger, after the Jolly Roger flag flown by some Caribbean pirates. He placed a ball cap on its head to conceal the conspicuous damage, and probable cause of death, to its forehead. Roger sat upright, propped against the trunk of a tree. He was posed, legs crossed, a Methodist pew hymnal in his lap.

"I borrowed that from church," John said of the hymn book. "Roger likes me to sing to him sometimes."

"I'm sure he is a good audience."

"You moved his head," Jake noticed.

"Thought he was better off lookin' at the hymnal than starin' up at me."

"Have you any idea who Roger was?" Nonny probed.

"My guess is some sod-buster that got his head bashed in by a tomahawk."

"How do you know it's a man?"

"Common sense, ain't it? If it's a woman, I'd have to mind my manners. Couldn't swear. Couldn't spit..."

"Who would she tell, John? Have you reported Mr. Roger to the authorities?"

"No. Why would I?"

"Just curious."

"Jake thinks it's a man. He even has some idea who it might be." Nonny's eyes snapped toward Jake. "Tell 'er, Jake."

"Al Jolson doing white-face."

John laughed. Nonny chuckled, nervously. Jake commented he needed to head home soon.

"Can we dress him now?"

"No. Need to treat the garment with pesticide or moths will make quick work of it. Jake and I can do it later this week."

"It ought to be done before winter."

"We got 'im strapped tight to that elm. He don't much like bein' tinkered with."

"Promise me he will wear the cardigan before it gets too cold?"

"I give ya my word, didn't I?"

Jake opened the passenger door for Nonny. On the drive back to town, she made Jake swear he would see to it that John kept his promise. Otherwise, Nonny remained pensive and quiet. In her mind, Roger was what remained of Fergus Griever resurrected and reconstructed. She chose not to tell John the truth. In her mind, they were back together. Enjoying each other's company, the way it should have been all along. To Nonny's way of thinking, anything that might upset such a relationship was not worth revealing. As she heard John say many times, 'There's some things don't need fixed.'

CHAPTER 40
THE INVITATION

Jake drove directly from Nonny's to the barber shop and dialed Kim's number.

"Hi. It's me again."

"Hi, me!"

"I had a thought."

"Really? Is this s-something new for you?" she laughed.

"No. That didn't come out right. A thought about us."

"Tell me."

"What if you came to Waltsburg for Thanksgiving?"

"What if I did?"

"That's what I'm asking."

"I need to think …about that."

"I know. It's just a thought I thought."

"It's a good one. Where would I s-stay?"

"Uhm… with Donna maybe? She has a spare bedroom."

"I was hoping you'd s-say motel so we could sh-shack up."

Jake went silent.

"Just k-kidding."

"We don't have a motel in Waltsburg."

Kim laughed. "Too bad. Let me know what Donna s-says."

"I will."

"Cool! What else have you been up to besides thinking?"

CHAPTER 41
WHAT ARE FRIENDS FOR?

Tuesday – October 13

It was Jake's first invitation to an Antler Club gathering, the congenial vestige of the Bruno-Muldoon-Albrecht summits at the Atlantic Hotel. Six four-top tables were arranged to seat the like-minded group. Cinnamon rolls and coffee were ordered all around. Jake alone ordered homemade soda biscuits with Amish sausage gravy and a glass of milk.

John Griever stood, spoon-tinked his water glass, and addressed the group. "We have a new guest among us this mornin'. Mr. Jacob Book, who I think you all know, told Stimka a few weeks back he might like to become a member. So, without further to do, I suggest we take the vote on 'im. All in favor of lettin' Jake join the group, raise yer right hand." To Jake's astonishment, no one did. "All opposed?" All raised a hand. Momentarily nonplussed, Jake wondered if he would have to leave.

"Okay, Mr. Book ...yer in."

Topics of conversation simulated an oral bulletin board among those present. Dan Bruner had the latest scoop on the search by the State of Kansas for a new prison location. The list had been narrowed to six sites in the northeast quadrant of the State. Two were Waltsburg-specific: the former high school property and the erstwhile United States Air Force ordnance plant six miles west of town. Dan Bruner knew the area was in desperate need of jobs and was confident that the 1970 census would confirm Waltsburg's population still in decline. Davis Spellmeier confirmed their staff had been in touch with the Governor's office, but no decision yet made.

Several commented on Eric Carver's grooming, counterculture attire, and give-a-shit attitude. Jake added that Eric was dogged by flashbacks from his tour of duty in Vietnam. Collin Fairchild wondered if he had sought counseling. John Griever noted that Eric's mother was a psychologist and student counselor at the University of Kansas. Jake was quizzed about his new girlfriend from Oklahoma. Jake made it clear Kim was not hot to trot nor had he made it to first base yet. Davis Spellmeier mentioned that cattle rustlers cut fence at the Zimmerman place the first of the month and made off with five yearlings. D. Darryl Manning shared a story about the sick cat that neither he nor its owner could retrieve from under a car seat. He rolled up a shirt sleeve to show his souvenir scratches. Jack Nagel announced that wildcat driller Butch McGrath from Wichita was seeking permission to drill for oil on Doona Falls Ranch property. "He ain't the first an' he won't be the last," Wild Bill added.

Tony Bertolini talked of Luci's intent to expand her business into the Ben Franklin space as a venue for special occasions and overflow seating when the German or Mexican ladies served up their popular ethnic fare. Doyle said he planned to raise the price of a haircut twenty-five cents effective January 1st. The most astonishing revelation of the session, however, came from Paul Baguelt. Sunday evening, he fired his son Allen.

"He stickin' around here?" Griever asked.

"No. Moving to Kansas City."

"What's he gonna do there?"

"Count beans for someone else, I guess. Bottom line, Allen is no longer employed with us," Paul stated with finality.

#

Over the next couple of weeks, the story leaked out. In addition to padding or turning in bogus expense reports, Allen had been soliciting cash and gifts from suppliers, wholesale reps, and sub-contractors for years. In return, they got Baguelt Custom Homes' business without having to sharpen their bidding pencils. Paul became suspicious of his oldest son's honesty when Lyla Witte's off-the-cuff remarks from the driver's seat of a bulldozer led him to investigate his company's relationship with other subs and suppliers.

Driven by his desire to appease an unsettled wife and envious of her well-to-do parents' lifestyle, Allen dressed like his in-laws, talked like them, and acted like them. Those behaviors, alone, rendered him a misfit in Waltsburg. Unduly influenced by his wife's unwillingness to sever the umbilical cord of her only-child status, Allen and Marti drove to Kansas City every other weekend, leaving Friday afternoons and returning Sundays. From the day they settled in Waltsburg, Marti did not belong. She was ill at ease among groups of locals whether PTA, quilting club, Campfire Girl or Cub Scout meetings and activities. Marti silently loathed its lack of sophistication. She missed shopping on the Country Club Plaza, having coffee with her friends at Putsch's coffee house, first run movies, and living the upscale lifestyle her parents enjoyed in the Mission Hills suburb. Marti was a big city girl, a creature of the suburban lagoon. Allen looked forward to their Kansas City jaunts as much as Marti. He relished the rounds of golf at the Mission Hills Country Club and hobnobbing with his father-in-law's affluent friends in the club's grill afterward. Life was keen in the land of privilege, propriety, and Ralph Lauren.

#

Marti's mother arrived Monday evening. They spent two days packing and labeling boxes. On Thursday, Marti, her mother, and the kids drove to Kansas City so Marti and her father could start house hunting. Allen stayed behind to wait for the movers to arrive Friday morning. After work on Thursday, Paul paid Allen a visit.

"Oh, hi," Allen greeted, upon answering the door. Paul let Allen know that he was fully aware of the fling with Natalie Martinez and her pregnancy. Allen remained silent as if exercising his Fifth Amendment right, neither confirming nor denying. In less than ten minutes, Paul was out the door.

#

At the conclusion of the group's get-together, John Griever stood and proposed a toast. "Here's to friends. May God Almighty hisself give us the strength to put up with 'em." Except for Jake, they responded, "Hear, hear!" or "Amen!" The final act of those gathered involved a coin flip. By process of elimination, the last man standing picked up the tab for the group. Unbeknownst to Jake, it was an initiation rite, rigged in advance, the price of admission for a new member. Flipping a coin in the air, catching it, and slapping it on the back of one's wrist was not complicated. Responding to a declaration of heads or tails was a matter of honor. Invariably, Jake was asked to declare first. He had no reason to doubt the veracity of any member of the group. On the final flip between him and Davis Spellmeier, they wished Jake better luck next time. Later that day Doyle told Jake he was predestined to be odd man out. After all, what are friends for?

CHAPTER 42
THE BELCH HEARD
'ROUND THE WORLD

Saturday - October 17

At Donna's suggestion, Jake asked Kim if they could meet somewhere between Tulsa and Waltsburg to plan a Thanksgiving visit. Ultimately, they agreed upon the Emmett Kelly Museum in Sedan, Kansas. Jake arrived twenty minutes early. Kim was parked out front. She was slumped down in the driver's seat, head against the window, eyes closed. Jake rapped on the window. "Sorry" she said, yawning. "I got here way too early."

Kim was not in a talkative mood. While they meandered about viewing the memorabilia and exhibits, scarcely a word was exchanged. Jake asked the docent if Mr. Kelly lived in town. "No. He lives in Florida." Once outside, Jake asked Kim what was wrong. "Nothing," she answered. It was almost noon so he asked if she would like to get a bite to eat. She shrugged then said "Sure." He went back inside and queried about a good place to eat in town. It was suggested they might try The Green Door Café down the street. Kim hopped out of the car and went inside before Jake could open the door for her. They sat opposite each other at the last two-top table available. A waitress delivered menus, ice waters, and asked what they would like to drink. Kim chose coffee, Jake a coke.

"Sorry I'm not very good company," said Kim, blew then wiped her nose with a napkin.

"Do you have any Midol?"

"I don't even have any aspirin with me. I think I'll try their biscuits and gravy."

"And wash it down with a coke?"

"Why not?"

"You don't drink coffee?"

"Not old enough."

Kim smiled. "Think I'll have a half-order of toast." From the container of assorted Smucker's jellies on the table she picked out an orange marmalade. "We don't have any silverware," Kim noted. Jake's glib coffee comment produced only a hairline crack in her ice-like demeanor. How could he perk her up? He asked what she had planned for the rest of the day.

"Bet you didn't bring my boots, did you?"

"Totally forgot. Sorry. You thought any more about coming to visit over Thanksgiving?"

"No. Not really."

She was not making eye contact. He repeated himself, asking about what the rest of her day looked like.

"I'm sure Aunt Nell will think of something when I get back."

"You grew up in Bartlesville, right?"

"Yes."

"What did you do for fun when you were growing up?"

"Self-entertained mostly. I didn't fit in well with the other neighborhood kids. The dolls my parents bought me didn't look like me. I eventually decided I was the babysitter, not their mother. I didn't really start having fun till I went to Holland Hall. That's where I met Chana who's my best friend now." Kim pulled out her wallet and produced a small photo taken in a photo booth and handed it to Jake. "That's us at the Oklahoma State Fair last year."

"Wow! She is beautiful."

"What about me?"

"I'd say it's a toss-up."

"Don't get any ideas. She has a boyfriend."

"Is she Korean?"

"No. Her family is from Goa. She's who I was visiting in Manhattan over Labor Day."

"I had hoped it wasn't a guy."

"It didn't turn out well. Chana's boyfriend set me up with a blind date who talked a lot about himself, his fraternity, and wasn't interested in me at all. We went someplace for pizza then to a bar in Aggieville. Later we drove to a place called Bluemont Hill that overlooks the city of Manhattan and parked. Apparently, it's the 'in place' to go if you want to make-out."

The waitress brought silverware, served their drinks, and took their food orders.

"I was in the back s-seat with this guy who finally s-stopped talking. He put his arm around me, pulled me to him, and s-started k-kissing me. He tasted like beer. I tried to resist. I mean, I hardly knew this guy. He was all over my front porch. I'd push his hand away. It would come right back. I put up with it five minutes longer than I s-should have. He wouldn't take 'n-no' and 'don't' for answers. Finally, I yelled "N-NO! Chana told him to s-stop whatever it was he was doing, traded places with him, and had her boyfriend drive us home."

"You should've kicked him like you did what's-her-name at the peach orchard."

"We were in a Volkswagen, or I might have. You're not like that are you?"

"Yes. I was hoping when we're done here, we could get a room at that motel I saw on the highway on my way into town," Jake grinned.

Kim frowned. "In your dreams."

"Just kidding."

"I know. I'm OTR now anyway."

Jake told her the last time he had a girlfriend was in 9th grade. Her name was Susie Olsen. Their budding relationship changed course on a 4-H group hayrack ride late one spring evening when they were able to kiss and pet non-stop. End of July her family moved to Minnesota. They wrote letters until she did not write back. Kim asked if he was heartbroken. Jake said he did not know what to feel.

"And …after we got home that night, Chana said s-sometimes sh-she feels like we girls are little more than what boys want us to be. You know? What did you do in Waltsburg for fun when you were a k-kid?"

"Go to the park. Ride bikes. Play pinball. Tumble in dryers at the laundromat with my friends. Have belching contests at the local hamburger stand."

"Contests?"

"Yeah. We'd take a gulp of pop. Then take turns to see who could belch the loudest."

She smiled, swallowed a gulp of air, and broadcast the loudest belch Jake had ever heard. Heads turned and necks craned all around them. Kim slumped in her chair and covered her mouth with both hands, her eyes wider than a six-lane expressway, then wriggled back upright.

"Sorry. I didn't know it would be that loud."

#

Jake and Wally sat on the couch watching clips of today's Vietnam War on the 6 o'clock news when Doyle and Donna walked in. Jake was brooding. His 'What did I do wrong?' thoughts lingered, replicating a labyrinth he had not experienced since his mother abandoned him when he was eight.

"What time did you get back?" Donna asked."

"3:30. 4."

"How'd it go?"

"Okay. Sorta."

"There are some TV dinners in the fridge if you're hungry," said Doyle.

"I ate at Perky's."

"She coming for Thanksgiving?" Donna queried.

'Don't know,' Jake shrugged.

CHAPTER 43
THE TANG OF SMOKE

Friday – October 30

Dusk feigned an early arrival; a blanket of dark clouds smothered the horizon. A Canadian cold front was expected to arrive in the area at any time. On the drive to Doona Falls Ranch, Jake and Nonny saw sporadic ricochets of lightning illuminate cloud cover skulking in their direction. They were greeted at the manor house steps by the flickering scowl of a jack o'lantern as a muffled roll of autumn thunder settled across the landscape.

Nonny sat with one leg elevated on a foot stool. A charley horse aggravated her right hamstring, the occasional muscle spasm disrupting her concentration. She was low man on the tally sheet, their Scrabble game past the halfway point.

"You gonna play anytime soon?" Conger implored. "I gotta go to work Monday."

"I'll play when I'm good and ready," Merry responded, eyeing the game board.

Conger asked if anyone needed anything from the kitchen, grabbed his empty glass, and excused himself.

"You don't get trick-or-treaters this far out from town, do you?" Nonny queried.

"No."

"Cong and I have decided to trick-or-treat as adults this year," Jake announced.

"Indeed," Nonny responded. "Is there no age limit?"

"First I've heard of this," said Merry.

"Atticus Finch and Boo Radley," said Jake, with a smirk.

217

Merry laughed. Nonny appeared baffled. Conger returned to the table.

"Jacob, you two are too old for Halloween treating," Nonny insisted. "You should be ashamed."

"We are ashamed, aren't we Jake?"

Jake rubbed his shoulder. "Been feeling it right here, all week."

"Same here. Mine started last year when we costumed up as Dr. Jekyll and Mr. Hyde."

Nonny looked both boys in the eye, "I believe you are pulling my leg."

"Just the good one," winked Jake.

"Next year you can recruit Jimmy Baguelt and go as The Three Stooges," Merry offered.

"Don't make me laugh," Conger replied.

"We should drop by Ginny's Halloween Sale tomorrow," Merry remarked to Nonny.

"We should, yes."

"Mom, you want me to play for you?"

The telephone rang. Conger rose to answer it.

A lightning strike ignited a grass fire on Isaac Zimmerman's land. He and his five boys were unable to contain it; their efforts foiled by gusty winds. The fire was spreading swiftly in the direction of Doona Falls. Zimmerman contacted Jack Nagel, who phoned Chief Lassiter, who, in turn, sounded Waltsburg's fire horn. The foursome stepped outside.

Converging boundaries of cloud cover flanked the star-smitten sky directly overhead, ebony as Wally's coat. An orange contour glowed on the southern horizon bisecting heavens and earth. The tang of smoke tainted the air. Occasional embers of native grass flew overhead. They glimpsed five whitetail deer bound toward Minnie's Creek. The air was flush with winged insects and dissonant chords of thunder. A flatbed truck and pickup drove in. Jack and Claire Nagel, Bill Stimka, Collin and Jenna Fairchild jumped out.

"Get some water on the barn!" Jack shouted at the boys.

Jake sprinted to the cast iron pump and cranked the handle as fast as he could. Conger snatched buckets from the barn. Jack yelled for Merry to hose down the grassy areas around the house. As Nagel and Stimka lit a backfire with firesticks, Jake spotted a coyote dashing toward the creek. The aura on the horizon grew brighter, the drifts of smoke thicker, the star-spangled sky dimmer. The pasturemen stood silhouetted against the line of fire set as a buffer to the rogue blaze. John Griever drove in and immediately joined Conger, scooping water from the stone trough, and slinging it on the barn.

Jake spotted two patches of fire east of the barn. He filled a bucket, ran to the nearest one, doused it with water, and stomped out the remaining flames. Claire Nagel, Collin and Jenna Fairchild tended to the other, larger area. John handed out wet gunny sacks. Moments later, Lyla, Indy, and Briley Witte pitched in. It took eight of them to defeat the rapidly spreading burn. Jake hustled back to the pump. He was aware both land and air teemed with life. All sizes and shapes, winged and grounded, scurried through the pall of smoke, away from the conflagration, a silent exodus in the direction of the creek. Jackrabbits, field mice, and a rafter of jakes scampered through the English turnabout. Another coyote broke cover and raced northward.

Less than a half mile from the backfire, flames topped the rise, spreading toward them with the shifting wind. Jake saw more patches of fire flaring in the direction of the Cemetary. It was obvious they needed more manpower to contain all the outbreaks. Jake felt the strain on his arms and shoulders from the non-stop pumping. Gene Lassiter, out of uniform, pulled up in his black and white. He hollered Waltsburg's fire truck was on its way.

"Holy shit!" Griever exclaimed. "Look!"

Swirling winds and intense heat had conflated to create a fire devil. A vortex the shape of a phonograph needle, fifty feet high, dazzled brilliantly, twisting scarlet, orange, and yellow grassland chaff. Spinning, bobbing, shifting at whim, it alternately grew and shrank, leaned then straightened. Suddenly, it dissipated, summarily dispatching a fiery poof of embers on the wind. Isaac Zimmerman pulled in with two of his sons. Gene Lassiter relieved Merry of her grass watering duty. Nonny and Merry sat on the top step of the porch. They spotted possums, a raccoon, and a red fox scampering toward the creek. The incandescent glow of the front porch lights and bright barnyard light hosted cults of winged creatures churning in frenzied flight, soundless as necropolis mice. The clash of weather fronts sparked a sudden downpour of cold, gravity-mad rain from a featureless sky. Merry and Nonny retreated inside. John Griever labeled the fortuitous downpour an Act of God.

"Does a cup of hot tea sound good to you?" Merry asked.

"Oh, yes. Please. I could murder a spot of tea right now. Could I trouble you to bring me a chair?" Merry fetched a dining room chair from their Scrabble table and Nonny sat, just inside the entryway's threshold, door open, an afghan draped over her shoulders. Spectators-at-large, they awaited the kettle's whistle.

In minutes, the temperature dropped twenty degrees. The inversion produced a foggy translucence. Steam, smoke, and dust hunkered like a collapsed cloud. Nagel and Stimka navigated the flatbed truck eastward to check pastures and locate the herd of cattle they guessed fled to Hoover's Bottom. When the fire engine pulled in the drive, the others abandoned their efforts and assembled near the front of the house. D. Darryl Manning, Bob Copeland, and Francisco Martinez drove up in full fire-fighting gear and clambered aboard the firetruck. Gene directed them to sweep the pastures to the south in their tank truck as far as the Zimmerman place. When Whitfield's firetruck pulled in, Gene directed the crew to support Nagel and Stimka.

Covered in soot, dank and redolent of prairie fire smoke, Jake and Conger sat on the curb of the turnabout where those remaining huddled. A light drizzle replaced the hard rain then shifted to wisp-like waves of mist brushing over the landscape much as one would feather dust Steuben glass. Through the haze, backlit by the barnyard light, the part-time firefighters witnessed a feeding frenzy. Brown bats, swallows, nighthawks, crows, and wrens collectively gorged themselves on the diaspora of grassland insects driven from the burning pasture. The birds snacked at will on bugs snagged mid-air or plucked squirming off the ground.

As crows hectored from their apple tree lecterns, a box turtle made its way along the stone curbing at top speed, its shell scraping the curb every other stride, its neck stretched impossibly forward. The spectators stared numbly as the reptile passed under Jake and Conger's legs, past the cast iron, horsehead hitching posts in the direction of the creek. Conger suggested it might be one of Mr. Jingle's shirttail relatives. Shivering and covered with goosebumps, Jake traced the odor of burnt rubber to the amorphous soles of his sneakers. Snow, thick as a fresh-shaken snowglobe, began to fall from the heavens.

CHAPTER 44
THAT MARE'S
LONG DEAD BY NOW

Sunday – November 8

Collin Fairchild and his wife, Jenna, planned an early morning drive to Fort Scott, Kansas, for their grandson's birthday party but he first needed to check on the cowhand-constructed bridge at Meyer's Crossing for his boss, Jack Nagel. Meyer's Wash was a watershed creek that wove its way among the hills to meet up with Minnie's Creek, the confluence known as Hoover's Bottom. It was still dark as they crept along the make-do pasture path, over the crest of a rise, toward the slapdash bridge. Collin engaged his high beams and stared ahead.

"What's that?!" Jenna exclaimed.

Two hedge posts, barbed wire still intact, blocked their way. Collin angled his headlights toward the gaping hole in the fence line. He grabbed a pair of work gloves off the dashboard and got out of the truck. Crows protested loudly from the opposite side of the road. As Jenna watched her husband drag the hedge posts from their path, she saw a white horse with dark spots grazing in the distance. Collin's door stood open; the boisterous birds vied for her attention. She got out and walked around the front of the truck in search of the cause for the ruckus.

Collin brought the pickup to a stop just shy of Meyer's Crossing. The bridge looked fine. Jenna flicked on the dome light and glanced at her watch. She knew they had to stop by Jack Nagel's place now, to let him know what they had discovered. Collin breathed a sigh of relief as he spotted Jack's flatbed Ford and lights on inside the immaculate doublewide mobile home. Hans and Greta, Nagel's German shepherds, noisily announced their arrival. They greeted Collin at the gate of the white picket fence and anxiously licked his hands. Jack appeared, coffee cup in hand.

"Morning!" Collin greeted as he opened the gate.

"Back at ya, Collin. There a problem with the bridge?"

"No, sir. Saw something else, though. Fence is out 'bout a quarter mile shy of the bridge. Posts yanked out-a the ground on the south. Two snapped in half. More down to the north."

"See any tire tracks?"

"No, sir. Looked like something headed north was scrapin' the ground."

Jack's wife, Claire, stepped outside. Jenna joined in.

"Could be the cattle got spooked by the wind last night," he guessed aloud, fiddling with one end of his handlebar mustache. "Maybe went right through it?"

"Nothin' tramped down. No hoofmarks."

"It's pitch black out there," Jenna offered. "We heard crows makin' a racket other side of the road but couldn't see 'em."

"Got coffee made," Claire said. "You two like some?"

"Got a drive ahead of us. We need to be gettin' on down the road if that's okay."

"Supposed to be half decent weather today. You two go on, get out-a here while you can," Clair said.

"Who owns the pinto horse around here?" Jenna asked.

Claire stiffened, tilted her head a notch sideways, and folded her arms.

"Nobody I know of," said Jack.

Collin looked to Jenna, "Where'd you see a pinto?"

"Down the fencerow you were workin'."

Jack knew the backstory about such a horse. The Fairchilds were new to the area and unaware of the legend. Claire was silent. She had not told her husband about her sighting of a pinto this past spring.

"Go on, you two. I expect Wild Bill to show up any time now. We'll head over that way."

Collin circled, avoiding the bigger puddles, and turned onto the highway. No sooner had he shifted into third gear than Bill Stimka passed him from the opposite direction. Collin watched Bill's brake lights flash in his rearview mirror then disappear. Claire insisted on accompanying Jack to check fence. Breakfast could wait. He might need an extra pair of hands and she was no stranger to ranch work. Catching another glimpse of the pinto piqued her imagination. She knew tales had been bandied about among area residents for over two decades. Sightings were rare, the opportunity too good to pass up. Claire unplugged the coffee pot, threw on a sweater, and grabbed their work jackets.

First rumble of the flatbed's engine, Greta and Hans hopped on the back. Jack quickly scraped the rime from the windshield. Claire and Wild Bill squeezed into the cab. Claire asked Bill how he was doing, mostly to elicit the familiar response, "Lookin' mostly at the same shit, different day," followed by his signature wink and impish smile.

Minutes later, they turned off the highway onto Meyer's Crossing Lane, a narrow ten-foot path between the fences of two separate landowners.

"I saw what Jenna saw," Claire said.

"The pinto?" Jack presumed.

"The week after my mother's funeral. I was pulling bedding off the clothesline when I saw it. Out in the pasture, across the road. I turned my head to watch what I was doing. When I looked up again, it was gone."

"That mare's long dead by now," said Bill. "Back in '44, when that tornado tore up the Muldoon place and killed ol' man Muldoon and his wife. Killed three ranch hands and all the horses in the stable 'cept the pinto. Sheba, they called her. Muldoon's wife's horse they bought off an Indian in Oklahoma."

"I know what I saw," Claire countered.

"Hell, if I wasn't down to El Dorado at the auction that same evenin', I'd-a prob'ly been at the Pearly Gates singin' for my supper with the rest of 'em," Bill continued. "Day after it happened, me and a buddy-a mine from Houray drove up there to help pick through the pieces. We saw that mare a couple-a times. Wouldn't let nobody come near it. We figured its brains was scrambled." After a short pause, he added, "Too bad Sean Robert wasn't there when it hit."

Jack focused on the fencerows in his headlights. He heard the dogs' claws search for footholds on the flat metal bed in sync with the uneven contours of the narrow lane as they cleared the rise that sloped toward the cattle crossing.

"Power go out in Houray last night?" Jack asked.

"Yep. Wind was blowin' a gale. Couple gusts rocked my trailer."

"We were watchin' tee-vee when the power went out at our place just before Lawrence Welk came on," added Claire.

"Wonder if Whitfield went ahead with their big plans last night," said Jack.

"Ain't heard."

"Lyla go?"

"She wasn't plannin' to. What'd you say Collin said about fence down?"

"Right along here, somewhere. Both sides of the road."

Claire's hands were cold, and she could see her breath. She turned to Jack, "Heater working yet?" He fumbled with the controls. A blast of tepid air came out at foot level. "What's that? In the road?"

"Crows," said Bill.

"Got to be right here close," Jack said, as the crows took flight.

"There's your down fence. See it?" said Bill, rolling down his window.

Jack angled the truck's lights toward the gap in the fence, set the parking brake, and let the engine idle. Bill pulled on his gloves and bounded out of the truck. On his zigzag route back, he noted shreds of red, white, and blue fabric snagged on the barbed wire and kept his eye to the ground looking for clues. Jack got out and fetched a high intensity light from behind the driver's seat, plugged it into the cigarette lighter socket, and surveyed the prairie opposite side of the road. Claire rolled up the passenger side window and tucked her hands under her thighs.

"I seen buffalo take fence down like that," Bill said, "but there ain't no tracks. Whatever caused it left-a skid mark."

"What-a you make-a that?" said Jack, referring to a large gathering of crows hopping about, landing atop of, and picking at an object roughly the size of a bowling ball.

"Keep the light on it," said Bill. He whistled and motioned to the dogs he knew were itching to get down off the metal bed. Both dashed toward the noisy birds, scattering them. They watched him hopscotch his way over the downed barbed wire fence. He walked around the object, then squatted down and stared.

"You ain't gonna believe this," Bill called out. "It's a head. A human head near as I can make out. Looks like a pair-a goggles shoved back in the eye sockets." Claire felt goosebumps erupt on her arms and tingles race down her legs. "It's sittin' middle of-a patch-a prickly pear cactus …face up," Bill added. "God-damnedest thing I ever seen."

"For Christ's sake," Jack mumbled under his breath. "Hon, grab that tarp behind the seat." He passed the light to Claire. "Keep the light on us while we cover that thing up."

Back at the truck, Jack grabbed his twenty-gauge shotgun, a nearly empty box of shells, and a long-handled flashlight. He told Claire to take the dogs back, call Gene Lassiter, and load up eight steel T-posts, the pounder, pickaxe, and sharp-shooter shovels. "Here's your coat," she said as the dogs climbed in front with her. Over the rush of warm air from the heater vents, she heard Jack yell BRING COFFEE! At the crest of the first rise, she abruptly swerved attempting to run over a crow, tossing Hans into Greta and Greta into the door.

Bill removed his hat and ran a hand through his hair. "I seen some things in my time but never nothin' like this."

Jack had on Okinawa, in 1945.

CHAPTER 45
THE HUNT

Jake was up at an ungodly hour. This was opening weekend for hunting pheasant and quail. He and Wally, Doyle, Griever, Paul Baguelt, Dan Bruner, and Dan's brother-in-law Carl from Kansas City always hunted Doona Falls Ranch. The indigenous trees and shrubs that flourished along Minnie's Creek were consistently quail-rich and a haven for wildlife, a meandering mix of the vibrant and untamed, engulfed by hardy Bluestem grasses, wildflowers and thistles that earned their thrive on the prairie. They met at the ranch early Sunday morning with the wholehearted approval of Merry Belle Shay. As usual, they planned to walk the creek to the draw at Hoover's Bottom and retrace their path. Spirits were high for the hunt and the promise that upon their return, Merry would have breakfast waiting.

As Doyle turned into John Griever's place, Wally stood up, shook, and looked out the window. Traversing a cattle guard, the car's headlights revealed the shell of a '37 Chevy coupe tucked in the overgrown fencerow corner. Puddled ruts led to the skirted singlewide mobile home with its concrete block steps and makeshift awning over the entry lit only by a 60-watt bulb. Doyle pulled in behind Griever's pickup, dimmed his headlights, and left the engine running. From out of the dark, a goat appeared on the opposite side of the car and stared Wally in the eye. Wally barked. Griever poked his head out the door and waved, then disappeared back inside. Jake climbed in the back seat. Moments later, John Griever wriggled out toting his shotgun, a box of shells, a grocery sack, and a thermos.

"Right on time," Griever greeted. "We should get there right about daybreak."

"I take it Roger's not coming with?"

226

"He don't get all that excited 'bout bird huntin'," Griever responded as he unscrewed the lid of his thermos and poured himself a ration of coffee. "Jake, you a coffee drinker yet?"

"Not old enough."

"What's in the sack?" Doyle asked.

"Goat's milk for Merry Belle. Tradin' her for one-a her homemade pies."

Doyle doubled back and turned onto the blacktop that led them past the unlighted billboard at the edge of town:

WELCOME TO WALTSBURG
Home of the Demons
Class B State Baseball Champions – 1964

Jake glimpsed Eric Carver playing pinball inside the 24-hour Loads of Fun laundromat. The marquis on the shuttered Cozmos Theatre read:

Go Demons
Beat Whitfield

The only other signs of life were lights inside Barney's Restaurant spilling out onto the bleak avenue, highlighting a contorted tabby grooming itself on the curb. Doyle decelerated to cross the railroad tracks and dodged several large tree limbs and a variety of debris strewn along the wide, rain-glossed boulevard.

"Wind blew a howl last night at my place," John commented. "Blew one-a my barn doors off its hinges."

At the south edge of town, the last street sign read:

BRUNO MUSEUM ▶
◀ MEMORIAL PARK

Doyle engaged his bright headlights and accelerated. Jake perceived a glimmer of light on the eastern horizon as they sped over the Pegram truss bridge that spanned the Orme River.

"Get much rain at your place last night?" Doyle queried.

"Some. Felt wind mostly."

"Radio said Granfield had gusts over 60 miles per hour."

Halfway to the Doona Falls Ranch turn off, Doyle glimpsed flashing red lights in his rearview mirror growing closer by the second. He eased off the accelerator, angled onto the grassy shoulder, and came to a full stop.

"What is it?" Griever asked.

"Law coming up behind us."

A Waltsburg police black-and-white flew past and quickly disappeared over the next rise. Doyle maneuvered back onto the highway and picked up his speed. Turning onto a dirt road, he headed toward a softly glowing horizon through patches of gauzy ground fog, apparitional across the graceful, undulating contours of the Flint Hills. Much of the pastureland blackened by fire a fortnight earlier. Jake heard small rocks ping the underside of the car while Doyle and Griever nattered about last year's hunt.

"They're already here," Jake said.

Doyle pulled up behind Dan Bruner's station wagon at the front of the house. Griever rolled down his window and chucked out his coffee.

"Hey, Dan!" Griever hollered. "Made any bad loans lately?"

"Not since you were in last."

'There it is,' thought Jake. 'The jawing.' His favorite part of the hunt. Ribbing and telling lies over a Merry Belle Shay breakfast was the entertainment highlight of the outing.

"Jake, can you let Merry know we're here?"

Jake and Wally were at the bottom step when Merry opened the door. "Good morning!" she called. Blanco squeezed out and began her familiar sniff and wrestle routine with Wally. Wally broke away and made a dash around the manicured hedges and flower beds surrounding the weathered Madonna-and-child statue, stopping long enough to lift a leg at its base.

"Go right ahead and do what you got to do," she offered.

Griever bounded up the steps and handed her the sacked containers of goat's milk.

"Thank you, John. I'll have your pie baked 'fore you leave."

Sunbeams lit the tops of the tallest trees. The reddish Spanish roof tiles of the stately home blushed as the delicate veneer of frost evaporated like vapor from a block of dry ice. "Time to lock and load," Doyle barked. Shotshells chambered, cleck-clack. Jake pulled his skull cap down over his ears and slung a game pouch over his shoulder. As a boy, his father would not allow him to carry a loaded gun. Jake had not cared at the time; now it was a conscious choice.

#

In their early teens, Jake and Eric Carver frequently tagged along with Jimmy Baguelt who would borrow a Baguelt Custom Homes pick-up and slip out to Ormestrong County State Lake to fish, skip rocks, or plink at prairie dogs with their slingshots. One afternoon, pockets full of marbles, they laid patiently in wait for another p-dog to expose itself in the sprawling prairie dog town on the south side of the reservoir. It was a futile exercise that seemed like great fun at the time. That is, until Eric hollered, "I think I got one!" He sprang to his feet and raced in the direction of his line of fire with Jake and Jimmy in close pursuit. Sure enough, to their complete amazement, Eric's projectile had found its mark. A p-dog slithered on its back, circling a mound. The boys watched in awe as the helpless noncombatant, knowing its fate, staged its agony, communicated by throes, a cats-eye marble lodged in its gullet. Though nothing was agreed, none mentioned the event afterward, nor did they ever again go prairie dog plinking.

#

Past the Pennsylvania barn, Carl, Dan, Paul, and Griever forded the rock-bottomed creek and formed a skirmish line. Jake and Wally weaved through the timber along either side of the creek itself. Doyle walked the near side skirting plum thickets and tall stands of switchgrass. From experience, they knew once a covey flushed, the birds sprangled in the trees and tallgrasses.

Jake and Wally occasionally disappeared among the trees and foggy mist that hunkered as far as the eye could see. A quarter mile into the quest, Griever commented that he had not heard so much as a Bob White whistle or a meadowlark warble. Another couple hundred yards, he asked Jake to ask Doyle if he could hear anything. The answer came back he did not but wasn't that the quiet after the storm. They could still see the sharply defined back edge of the storm front, its cobalt blue cloud bank well to the northeast, angling toward Kansas City and St. Joe.

Griever's ears buzzed as he listened for any familiar sound. Although they often spooked a deer or coyote from this veritable nature sanctuary, he had yet to spot any wildlife. The mist along Minnie's Creek slowly dissipated in harmony with the sun's ascent.

Dan Bruner spotted a turkey buzzard circling above and called out to John asking if he could see all the crows up ahead.

Paul asked, "Can you see that red and yellow stuff in the trees from your angle?"

"Yeah. What the hell is it?" said Dan, shading his eyes.

As they drew closer, they heard a cacophony of caws. Crows tree-hopped and occupied limb upon limb like blight. All sizes and shapes of yellow, white, royal blue and red streamers hung snagged in the trees. Other colorful remnants spilled over into the meadow. John Griever angled back toward the tree line.

"DOYLE!" Griever shouted. "YOU SEE WHAT'S UP AHEAD?"

"WHAT?"

"UP AHEAD. YOU SEE ANYTHING THAT AIN'T RIGHT?!"

"LIKE WHAT?!"

"Jake, you see anything from in there?"

"Hedge apples."

Griever, Paul, Dan, and Carl walked side-by-side now. As they approached the scene, wave upon wave of crows took flight, their screeches annoying as fingernails on a chalkboard.

"I SEE IT NOW!" Doyle cried out. "GOT COYOTES RUNNING EAST OF ME!"

Mid-shelterbelt, one exceptionally large, colorful stretch of fabric emblazoned with a cartoonish smiling sun, hung hopelessly tangled in a large cottonwood tree, billowing like a sailing ship's square sail. Beau d'Arc and hackberry trees, blackjack oak, red cedar, and sand plum thickets snagged their share of fabric as well.

"It's a hot air balloon," Carl said. "What's left of it."

Jake found the balloon's wicker gondola halted dead in its track by a barbed wire fence, two propane tanks and remnants of a Confederate flag still intact. Griever raised his twelve-gauge and fired a shot in the air sending the crows clambering into flight. Doyle assumed Wally was barking at the giant sheet of fabric billowing in the light breeze that had begun to stir. To Doyle's horror, however, he spied the lifeless form of a human body wedged high up at the 'Y' of two limbs amid a maze of broken branches and nylon ropes that dangled like tentacles. As the five surveyed the wreckage, they discovered the mangled remains of two adults, one female, and one missing its head, as well as two children, one with an arm wrenched from its socket.

Griever broke the silence. "Jesus H. Christ! What hell did this come from?!" He removed his outer hunting jacket and covered a young girl. The others followed Griever's lead, shedding their outer wraps to cover up the corpses as best they could. Carl commented that the headless body he covered had been gnawed. The group gathered around Doyle and stared up at the third adult, a contorted chalk-white cadaver clad in a gray frock coat adorned with a double row of gold buttons, epaulets and missing one boot.

"Someone needs to call the law," said Carl.

John Griever picked his shotgun off the ground and twice fired into the shelter belt. "Goddamn crows!"

"How about we hike back to the house and call Gene?" Doyle said.

"How 'bout I stay here and keep the buzzards off," Griever volunteered. "Root around a bit. Maybe find some-a the missin' body parts."

Dan offered to stand guard with Griever who lit a cigarette, stood his shotgun up against the cottonwood and turned his back to pee. The others trooped in pursuit of their shadows through prairie grasses shimmering with thaw. They had not hiked forty paces when another shotgun blast rang out.

CHAPTER 46
THE PRINCE VALIANT LOOK

Thursday – November 19

A respite from Jack Nagel's seven-day-a-week ranch work routine was something he subconsciously put off looking forward to. Nestled in Doyle DeCritt's barber chair's ringside seat, he had a view of the Ben Franklin Five-Ten store and early morning traffic at the Beau Coup Café, post office, and Donna's beauty salon. A very small world, he concluded, where he might think about something or nothing at all. Two nondescript, out-of-state-tag cars pulled in and parked diagonally in front of the Beau Coup Café. Four official-looking, coat-and-tie types went in.

"Know what gripes me?" said Doyle. "They all ask the same questions. Reporters, Highway Patrol, FBI, KBI, FAA...all the same questions."

"Bill and I been going through the same drill. Hard to get anything done the past ten days. I hear Whitfield's infested with 'em."

"Talked to Gene late Sunday afternoon. Said he got a call from Whitfield's sheriff around nine Saturday night about what happened. Wasn't much either of 'em could do till the storm blew over. Half the county's electricity went out. They both had their own set of problems to deal with. What's Claire been up to?"

"She's been researching into pinto horses. Been to the library. Paid a visit to the vet. Just cannot get it off her mind. Jenna Fairchild claims she saw the mare."

Jake finished buffing Jack's boots, toss-juggled three shoe polish tins, then set the boots at the foot of the cash register counter. He plopped down in a reception chair and thumbed through the latest issue of *Esquire*. Doyle handed Jack a mirror then lightly brushed the hair from his shoulders and neck. Jack handed the mirror back, "Now show me the big picture." Doyle swiveled Jack 90° to face the backbar mirror. Jake looked up from his read.

"And on the sixth day, God invented men like me!"

Doyle removed the tissue, then the cape, and waggled it. Jack eased out of the chair and stretched his arms over his head with a groan. Jake jumped up, retrieved the long-handled push broom, and began to herd the human and dog hair across the tile floor.

"Here comes big trouble," said Doyle.

In barged John Griever, clanging the bells above the door so hard the *faux* mistletoe attached above dangled precariously. "Mornin'!" Griever hollered, holding the door for Eric Carver clad in a tatty, graffitied Army field jacket and bell-bottom jeans shuffling five steps behind with his dog, Rocky, allowing a surge of chilled November air to cross the threshold as well. Wally enthusiastically greeted the newcomers.

"Got you your re-supply of J. J. Griever's Fresh Smoked Down-Home Country Deer Jerky," Griever announced, waving a brown paper sack. "Nonny's on her way. Dropped her off at Donna's to pick up somethin'."

Jack pulled on his boots and handed Doyle a ten-dollar bill. Doyle made change including a fifty-cent piece. Jack promptly dropped it in the TV fund jar and ambled over to the plate glass window.

"When did your sister start using a cane?"

"End-a August. Bursitis in her hip's been actin' up on 'er lately."

"She moves along pretty good for her age," Jack said, then scratched at a spot on the glass with his fingernail. "When's the last time you cleaned these windows? You got spider webs, mud dauber adobes, June bug barf …looks like molted cicada lingerie outside, there on the glazing."

"We got a bucket, sponge, and squeegee in back, if you got time."

"I'll do it," Jake volunteered.

"What time's Henry picking you up?" Doyle asked.

"When he gets here."

Griever and Carver headed toward the back room. Nonny arrived at the window, shaded her eyes, and peered inside, an oversized Beau Coup Café coffee mug gripped in one hand. Wally stared up at her, wagging unreservedly. Jack Nagel opened the door. "You comin' or goin'?" Jack donned his jacket and hat, then stooped down to scratch Wally's ears. "You need to twist Eric's arm into making an appointment."

"It's the 'in look' for a young man nowadays, is it not?" said Nonny.

"Ask Donna if she can perm it for him," Jack said, as he headed out the door.

Jake took Nonny's cane, coat, and scarf. "How thoughtful of you, Jacob."

"Take that coffee for you?" Doyle offered.

"Oh, thank you. I may have slopped a bit on the walk."

Doyle set Nonny's coffee aside and adjusted the chair as low as possible. She accepted his hand of assistance and plopped down with a sigh. Doyle tossed the used cape into a hamper and pulled a fresh one from a utility drawer. The pick-pock tones of a ping pong game filtered into the front of the shop.

"Would you mind facing me toward the window?"

"I assume you'd like the usual little pick-me-up in your coffee?"

"Yes. I would."

He fetched a nearly empty pint of Jameson from a bottom drawer, poured the remainder into her cup, and handed it to her. She stirred it with an index finger, licked the finger, and cautiously raised it to her lips.

"Trim it up, same way?"

The Prince Valiant look, her half-brother John Griever called it. Nonny had been a loyal patron for fourteen years, ever since she officially retired from her nursing career. She weighed the same as she had when she entered the Army Nurse Corps as an RN, but, as she freely admitted, everything sagged a bit these days. Those fleshy slings under her triceps, the damnable new wrinkles under her eyes and the spider veins on her thighs were an affront to her vanity. Nonny's vibrant blue eyes and clear complexion accented her salt and pepper hair. She was still an attractive woman, sporting a demeanor suggesting a young girl may still be trapped inside.

"Take your glasses?"

"No. I could not see the world go by if you did."

Jake appeared with a bucket of soapy water, sponge, squeegee, and step stool. A lima bean green Volkswagen pulled up in front of the shop as he headed outside.

"You ever sample John's jerky?"

"Will not allow it on my person or my property under any circumstance. Least of all in my mouth. I'm afraid he's trying to inflict that *base cuisine* on everyone in town." As Doyle began to comb and snip, they watched Jake sponge-scrub the first large window. A pig-tailed brunette climbed out of the Volkswagen. She had a 35mm camera slung over one shoulder, an oversize leather purse over the other, and a small notebook in her hand.

"I don't know this person. Do you?" Nonny ventured.

"Nope. Looks like another reporter."

The young woman repositioned her sunglasses to the bill of her cap and stepped inside. Jake stared after her as she pulled the door shut at odds with the pneumatic closer's resistance. She surveyed the interior of the shop unaware of Wally sniffing her pantlegs.

"Help you?" DeCritt queried.

"I'm looking for a Mr. Doyle DeCritt."

Without warning, Wally raised up, planted his front paws squarely on her chest, and knocked her back against the door.

"Oh! My…hello! I didn't see you."

"Get down!" Doyle commanded.

The young woman offered a hand. Wally licked it kindly. "What's her name?"

"Walter. It's a he."

"I love dogs," she said. "I have a chow at home named Mao."

"Wally, go get in your chair. Go on." Wally trotted back to his blanketed, Naugahyde loveseat and sat. Griever, Carver, and Rocky came out of the back room.

"You'll pick me up at noon?" Nonny asked.

"Yup." Griever stiffened to attention and saluted. "God Save the Queen!" He executed a Royal Fusilier left turn and the threesome traipsed out the door.

"He can be such an irritation at times," Nonny grumbled.

Donna Pileaux entered the shop and stepped directly over to Nonny, handing her a sealed Mason jar. "You forgot this," she said. "Morning, Doyle."

Nonny took the jar and peered at it over the top of her eyeglasses. "O yes."

"Busy place you got here," the young woman said, stepping aside for Donna to exit.

"I'm Doyle DeCritt. What's on your mind?"

"Oh. I'm with the *Emporia Gazette*. In Emporia. I'm covering the hot air balloon story in Whitfield. Got your name from Mrs. Shay. She said you were one of those who found the balloon. I was hoping you might have some time to...."

"Just a minute," Doyle said. "Can I put that somewhere for you?"

"It's not for me. It's for you," Nonny said, handing over the jar. "They're pickled beets Merry Belle and I put up last May. Formanova Long variety from my garden."

"Thank you. I'm honored."

"You should be. It was damn hard work."

"Sorry," Doyle said to the young woman. "Do you have a name?"

"Oh, yes. Molly. Molly Reed."

"Do you have a card?"

"I do," she replied, digging into her purse.

"I've got five more coming in this morning and six more later this afternoon that I know of. You might drop back by around two."

"I can do that," She glanced at her notebook. "Would you happen to know how I can get in touch with a Jacob Book?"

"He's working today."

"Where?"

"Wherever he can find it."

"Where's the best coffee in town?"

"You might try Barney's Restaurant. Just up the street, across the tracks."

"Okay. Thanks."

"I hope you have some new questions," Doyle chided.

"Oh, I do! I focus on human interest stories," she gushed. "On the living. Not the headline stuff. I'm more interested in the Leo Beuermans of the world, or Patsy, the basset hound orphaned when her owners were killed last month in the Wichita State football team plane crash, or why cemeteries in Manhattan are segregated. Bye."

Jake came back inside. "She was in Lawrence. Taking pictures at the anti-war rally. What did she want?"

"Same-ole," Doyle muttered.

"The *Emporia Gazette*," said Nonny. "William Allen White's anti-KKK paper."

"Who's Leo Beuerman?" Doyle asked.

"I haven't the slightest."

"John's told you about the hot air balloon wreckage we came across, hasn't he?"

"No. I read about it in the Granfield paper."

The phone rang. Doyle answered. "That was Henry. He's on his way." Doyle turned back to Nonny. "What's your schedule like today?"

"Me? O' I have a delightful day planned. Next, a therapeutic neck and shoulder massage from the woman with whom you frequently sin, then the transformation of my hair color back to what it used to be. I'm not ready for the Grandma Moses look just yet. John, God bless his sovereign soul, will pick me up at noon. He will escort me to the post office, then home. I plan to have a good lie down before Catharine picks me up for a spin in that magnificent automobile of hers. We plan to run out and pick up Merry Belle and take a drive in the Flint Hills. I believe she's entitled to a break from all the attention of late."

"Heard from Ginny lately? I hear she plans to open her new store in Granfield day after Thanksgiving. The day she closed her shop she told me she had more customers driving here from Granfield than she had in Waltsburg. She complained the only time Waltsburg women darken her door is when she has a sale."

"I hadn't heard that."

"When's the last time you bought something at Ginny's?"

"Last month. I purchased a stylish knit sweater for Roger on sale for half-price."

Jake finished the inside door glass on his hands and knees. He leaned back on his heels, inspecting his work then carried the WELCOME mat outside, shook it, gathered his things, and disappeared into the back room.

"Made any plans for Thanksgiving?"

"I have. No cooking, baking, or relatives."

"John aware of this?"

"He's my little brother. I do not think of him as a relative."

Henry Yost pulled up parallel to the shop and honked.

Jake reappeared. He popped the till of the cash register and removed two one-dollar bills.

"Bootblack money," he said, waving them at Doyle. "I'm out-a here."

"Jacob…"

"Yes, ma'am?"

"You must drop by the house soon and tell me about this exotic girl friend of yours."

"Do you remember King George the Sixth from when you were in Britain during the war?"

"As if it was yesterday. Why do you ask?"

"Tell you later. Gotta go."

Doyle and Nonny watched as Wally and Jake climbed into the front seat of Henry Yost's well-used pickup, YOST SERVICES still legible on the door panel.

"Henry is a proper gentleman, if you ask me." Nonny offered.

"He's been like a father to Jake the past couple of years. Jake's developed a work ethic you don't see much anymore in young men his age."

"Merry Belle says Henry works like he's killing snakes."

"So I've heard." Doyle faced his subject and quickly surveyed his work. "You might meet her over Thanksgiving."

"Meet whom?"

"Jake's exotic girlfriend."

"She'll be in Waltsburg?"

"He'll know for certain Sunday. Are you ready for a look at yourself?"

"If I must. Cheers!" and downed the last swallow of her tepid cocktail. He traded her empty coffee mug for the mirror. She moved it slowly from side to side. "I see I have some strays. Are those March hares or split ends?"

Doyle wet his comb and artfully drew it carefully down one side, then the other. "Static electricity."

"Oh. That is much better. Any suggestions as to how we might somehow improve on the rest of me?"

"If I were you, Nonny, I wouldn't rearrange a thing."

She handed the mirror back. Doyle removed cape and tissue.

"Do you realize the more we get on in years, the more of a caricature of our former selves we become?" she said.

"You needn't remind me."

"Could you get your fee from Donna? I suspect I've left my pocketbook at her place."

Doyle replaced his OPEN sign with BACK SHORTLY. As he locked his front door, he envisioned a five-inch square, fresh-baked frosted Beau Coup cinnamon roll with a hot cup of Luci's fresh ground coffee. He caught himself staring at the spiraling blur of red, white, and blue ribbons on his barber pole. His reflection in the door's glass, however, was crystal clear.

CHAPTER 47
BAD DECISIONS
OFTEN MAKE GOOD STORIES

"Bad decisions often make good stories, Miss Reed. Coffee?"

The café officially closed at 2:00. Except for employees accomplishing clean-up chores, the Beau Coup Café was empty. Doyle fetched the coffee pot and poured them both a cup. He and the young *Emporia Gazette* reporter, a recent graduate of the University of Kansas with a degree in journalism, sat in a booth near the back of the café.

"Mmm. By the way, this coffee's way better than that other place this morning. Before we get started, I had lunch with a highway patrolman in Whitfield yesterday. He offered to tell me what happened. Off the record, of course."

"I'm all ears."

"Oh. Well …basically, they were belatedly commemorating the town's 100th anniversary and unveiling a statue of the town's namesake John Wilkins Whitfield, a pro-slavery advocate who had twice been fraudulently elected to represent Kansas in Congress before we became a state. During the Civil War he served in the Confederate army as a Brigadier General. Hundreds turned out for the event. The hot air balloon operators balked at going up because of the windy conditions, but the mayor was insistent. He persuaded one operator into tethering his balloon just long enough for the ceremony, maybe ten minutes, to a height of twenty feet or so. The mayor Mr. Beaufort, his wife, three grandchildren, and the operator went up in the gondola."

"We heard ol' Estes Beaufort paid the guy extra to do that."

"They hadn't been up but a few minutes when, in the middle of the mayor's dedication speech, a sudden burst of wind swayed the balloon so hard to one side, two of the tether ropes snapped. When the wind let up, the balloon swooned in the opposite direction. With a second gust, it began to twist and twirl. Another tether ripped a bolt-anchored park bench right out-a its cement base and started flailing back and forth, slamming into things."

"Jesus," Doyle mumbled.

"One person told him they saw the balloon do almost a 90° arc down, and then up, flinging the youngest grandchild out of the basket like a catapult. She landed on her head…split it open like a watermelon. People were screaming, running for cover like something out of a horror movie. Then, the last rope snapped. The balloon knocked over a light pole, hit a tree, and away it went, spinning like a child's top."

"TV weatherman labeled it a *derecho* wind. Sounds to me like Hollywood could not have scripted it better. Anyone take pictures?"

"Apparently, but those have all been collected by authorities as evidence."

"Pending an investigation into how people can be so stupid. We can put a man on the moon but…," Doyle sighed, "still no cure for stupid."

"I have a question for you. How is it that on one side of the tracks Main Street is four lanes wide but only two on the other?"

"I take it this is your first time in Waltsburg?"

She nodded.

"Mmm. I know some of the story."

"Oh. Could you excuse me?' she said, grabbing her purse. "I need to powder my nose."

CHAPTER 48
GOTT MIT UNS

It was 2:15. Catharine was running late yet Nonny was not ready for Catharine to pick her up. Where were her eyeglasses? 'Maybe they were where I opened the mail?' She probed the drop-front writing desk of her heirloom secretary. The turned down corner of a letter protruding from her diary grabbed her attention. Something she had not thought of in years. It was postmarked August 1946, addressed to "Nurse Wilson" c/o International Red Cross Headquarters in Geneva, Switzerland. She read or, rather, had it read to her just once. The letter was from Kurt, the Heinkel He 111 *Luftwaffe* pilot, who required special, intensive care. His plane's nose glazing was shattered by a flak burst on a daylight bombing raid over Southampton in May 1940. He and his crew miraculously survived a forced landing in a field outside Netley Marsh.

Kempton Park Prisoner of War Camp, Sunbury-on-Thames, Surrey, England, on the south edge of London, was a reception camp. It was a large complex with guard towers enclosed by a double perimeter fence. Blackout status during non-daylight hours was mandatory.

Not many of her nurse comrades were anxious to succor enemy combatants as the war was not going well. In her mind, it was what she trained to do. She was a soldier's nurse. As the newest nurse on site, her Brit and Canadian counterparts assigned her the dark schedule, 8 p.m. to 8 a.m.

Nonny's first encounter with Kurt was in the camp infirmary. Except for narrow slits to facilitate sight and breathing, the patient's head was covered in bandages. A fractured sternum, multiple contusions, and several broken ribs restricted his mobility. Severe lacerations to his groin and forearms required frequent dressing changes. Their familiarity was based solely on voice and touch. He spoke broken English; she, no

German. By lume of lantern, or torch, Nonny diligently tended to the man as she did others, often seeking to pacify her charges by humming her mother's favorite Ukrainian lullaby.

A week after his arrival, during the wee morning hours, while Nonny replaced the dressings around his groin he developed an erection; he said, "I smile now." She tilted her head, contorted her face, stuck out her tongue, and looked at him cross-eyed. He shook with laughter, then convulsed in pain, stifling the amorous urge. The pair's happenstance rapport lasted less than a fortnight. Newspaper headlines extolled the Miracle of Dunkirk. Nonny and other nurses were hastily transferred out of Kempton Park.

The letter arrived while she was temporarily in the post-war employ of Sir Guy Croftingsham, a former MP and sole heir to a shipping fortune, who enjoyed a life of privilege on a sixteen-hundred-acre estate near Oxfordshire whose only son had lost both legs to a land mine during the war. The return address on the back of the envelope was Kurt's in Baden-Baden, Germany. It took nearly a year to reach her and another two days for her to find the courage to open it. The hand-penned letter was written in German thanking her for her hospitality. Nonny silently repeated to herself, '*Gott mit uns*,' his words, spoken after each ministration.

The doorbell chimed announcing Catharine's arrival. Nonny took one last glimpse at herself in a mirror before opening the door. She liked what she saw. Notably, her misplaced eyeglasses were attached to the pearlescent beaded chain around her neck.

"Oh, good!" Catharine greeted. "You are here. I was afraid you gave up on me, or your doorbell wasn't working."

"I'm ready. How many times did you ring?"

"Like they say, third time's a charm. Shall we go for a ride?"

"Yes. By all..." Nonny's cat squeezed out the door. "Tommy!" she exclaimed. "Come back here!" The cat bounded over the rail, off the side of the porch.

"Want me to try to catch him?"

"No. He's been cooped up for over a month now. I had him neutered. He's such a fighter, that cat. He hardly has any ears left."

"I could use a salesman like that," Catharine said, as she stepped inside.

"The vet also gave him a hormone injection to short circuit his instinctual grit."

"I would pass on that one. You might want to bring a sweater."

CHAPTER 49
JUST WHAT THIS TOWN NEEDS

"Okay. Let's see. Where was I?" she said, scanning her notes. "I find it curious the railroad tracks divide the town into two rather distinct segments. Was that intentional?"

"North of the tracks is the older part of town, built above the floodplain. When they passed the Flood Control Act in 1928, Bruno used his influence to persuade the Army Corps of Engineers to build a dam on this side of Ormestrong Lake. Flooding problems solved; the town expanded. Bruno and Karl Albrecht platted everything south of the tracks."

"Why is Main Street wider on the south than the north?"

"They modeled it after boulevards they saw in Colorado Springs while on hunting trips. They were determined to keep the industrial uses like cattle pens, brick factory, salvage yard, beef and dairy processing plants separate from the new residential areas, or so I heard. Contain the saloons, theaters, and dance halls in the same general area as well. Make the one side, south of the tracks, more appealing to homeowners. The commercial development along Main on this side of the tracks didn't happen till after the bank burned down in '41 and relocated."

"I love the planted median strip this side of the tracks. So, who were they, these urban visionaries?"

"Bruno showed up in the late 1800's, about the same time as the railroad. Some said he came from Chicago. Others said Boston. There's even evidence suggesting he may have grown up in Argentina."

"I can research that. Are there any photos of him?"

"Our museum, the Victorian mansion that was his home, has a couple that might be him. An oil portrait in the music room is a good likeness. All the furnishings, art, mirrors, most everything, are the way they were the day he left."

"I'll have to stop by there."

"Go by the library and ask for Joan Lowry. She or a volunteer will have to let you in."

"Did this Bruno guy work for the railroad?"

"Not to my knowledge. He had big plans for Waltsburg. Without the railroad, it would have been a waste of time to invest much time or money in a place like this. You been to the city park yet?"

"No. Why?"

"The raised mound east of the ball diamond was a railroad bed. You can still see the two trestles for a bridge across the river that was not completed. Bruno talked the railroad into constructing a rail spur to Doona Falls Ranch so they could ship cattle direct. That raised bed goes on for another quarter mile, but for some reason was never finished."

"He must've been quite the diplomat?"

"If it lined his pockets."

"A robber baron type, then?"

"I have no idea how he acquired his wealth."

"What became of him?"

"He and his bodyguard boarded a train for Chicago in the mid-thirties to straighten out problems they were having with whiskey shipments. They were never heard from again."

"Wasn't that during Prohibition?"

"Just after they repealed it. 1933 maybe? Or '34."

"Kansas has a long history of anti-liquor laws. Why here, do you think? Why Kansas?"

"My guess, at the crux of it, all the do-gooder, well-intentioned, holier-than-thou types."

"Like Carrie Nation. Do you know she described herself as 'a bulldog running along at the feet of Jesus barking at things He didn't like'?"

"It's a shame she didn't show up in Waltsburg. Bruno would've had her tarred and feathered and put on the first train to the South Pole."

"Maybe they should have banned Bibles."

"Maybe they should've just left well enough alone."

"Was he mixed up in organized crime?"

"Bruno? I have no idea."

246

"That might make a great story if I could tie him to someone like, say, Al Capone."

"I'm not positive but I think at the time of Bruno's disappearance, they already had Capone behind bars."

"D'you ever meet Mr. Bruno?"

"No."

"See him?"

"Once or twice. He was a very private man." Doyle had no intention of revealing to Molly Reed the extent of his knowledge from numerous, up-close encounters with the man, or that the oil portrait in the music room of the Bruno mansion was painted by his wife.

"Okay. What about the cattle baron, this Burnard Muldoon fellow?"

"It's Bear-nard, not Bur-nard."

"Bear-nard," she repeated, as she wrote. "Where did he come from?"

"Most people thought he was from Scotland. But he talked like an Irishman."

"Are you saying it doesn't add up?"

"I'm saying there's probably more there than meets the eye."

"Like the war in Viet Nam. Their claims don't always match the facts. Okay, Bear-nard Muldoon. When did he arrive on the scene and why Waltsburg, of all places?"

"1919. He wanted a place to raise Black Angus cattle."

"So, he bought the big ranch where Mrs. Shay lives?"

"No. He started that place from scratch, adding to it every chance he got. At one time, it was over twelve thousand acres."

"Oh. That is big. The house. That barn. Did he build those?"

"Yep."

"What did he do before he immigrated here?"

"No idea. He wasn't no cowboy, but he knew Angus cattle. If you really want to know about Muldoon, you should talk to Merry Belle Shay."

"I interviewed her and her son, William, for about forty-five minutes yesterday. William is kind-a creepy, I thought. That one eye of his. Very distracting. I don't know why, and I know it sounds crazy, but he reminded me of Quasimodo."

"William is a very fine young man," Doyle demurred. "But he's not her son."

"Oh. I just assumed he was. He called her mom."

Anthony approached the table.

"You look pretty snazzy in an apron," Doyle remarked.

"Luci wants you to know she'll be closing up in about ten minutes."

"We'll be out-a here by then. This is Molly Reed, a reporter for the *Emporia Gazette*."

"Nice to meet you," Anthony said, extending his hand.

"Not busy at the garage?"

"Plenty busy. The regular dishwasher has jury duty. Just filling in. Then, back to the wrench works."

"Nice meeting you," Molly said, as Anthony excused himself.

"Okay. Who was Karl…Albreckt?"

"The son of German immigrants, who became a sort of step-'n-fetch-it for Bruno. Over time, he oversaw Bruno's real estate interests."

"I assume he's passed on?"

"Yes."

"Any family left in Waltsburg?"

"No. His wife died before he did. His children have since scattered with the wind. His estate never did locate one of them."

"Children do tend to scatter after they leave the nest."

"Especially when it comes to small towns like ours. There aren't many good reasons for them to stick around anymore."

"Tribune's the same way."

"You from Tribune?"

"Yep. Greeley County, U-S-A. Least populated county in Kansas," she meted out, with a hint of pride."

"That's a long way from nowhere. You going home for Thanksgiving?"

"Plan to. But I have to be back in the office Friday afternoon. For some reason, more people kick the bucket around holidays. I'll have more four-score-and-sevens than usual to edit over the next month or so."

"You got a lot of hours on the road ahead of you."

"There's I-70 now. I can make pretty good time most of the way."

"Ha! Western Kansas looks pretty much the same whether you're going seventy or a hundred and seventy," Doyle said as he toyed with his coffee cup. "So, you graduated from KU in May?"

"Cum laude, if I may brag."

"You majored in journalism?"

"Yes. I worked for the *Gazette* the past two summers. They all but promised me a job when I graduated."

"You planned ahead."

"I work cheap. I like meeting and learning about people. I like to explore as many nooks and crannies as the world has to offer."

"No shortage of those. Gotta start somewhere. Underbelly of glamour, so to speak."

"Kind-a. Truthfully, though, anyone with a Smith-Corona can call himself a writer."

"Anyone with a mouth can call himself a critic according to my high school civics teacher. Did you have some questions about the hot air balloon?"

"Oh, yes. I understand you found it while you were hunting. There were six of you. Is that right?"

"Yes. And a dog. You met Wally. Do they ever let you be creative?"

"Not really."

"I was going to suggest you interview Wally. Type arf, bark and woof two hundred times as your story about us finding the balloon."

"I like your thinking, but they would question my sanity," Molly giggled.

"Do you like what you do?"

"So far. My dream is to go back to school and work on my Master's."

"The sooner you do that, the better. Routine and debt shape your life before you know it."

"Depressing, isn't it? We better get going, huh?"

"Yes. Where you headed next?"

"The bank. I have a three o'clock appointment with Mr. Daniel Bruner."

"He was there. He can fill in the gaps. Coffee's on me."

"Thanks. I appreciate you taking time to talk to me," she said, placing pen and paper in her shoulder bag.

"If you make it over to the museum, my wife's arrowhead depiction of an Indian astride a horse is hanging over the fainting couch in the parlor."

After a polite handshake, Molly Reed headed out the door. Doyle ambled over to the serving window.

"Tony! How much for the coffee?"

"It's on the house, if you'll turn off the burner out there and bring me the pot."

"No problem. When you're done here, I got a floor needs swept across the street."

"Just what this town needs," Anthony hollered back. "Another comedian."

CHAPTER 50
I WANT TO TAKE YOU HIGHER

Tuesday – November 24

"Sorry for the short notice," said Catharine, as she slung her coat on a chair that promptly slid off onto the floor. "Crap!" She draped it and her purse on the coat tree just inside the front entrance to Hair by Pileaux salon.

Donna said, "Floor's clean. Jake just finished wet mopping a few minutes ago." She switched on the red neon SALON sign in her front window above the flecked three wise monkeys decal.

"I need to slow down," Catharine groaned, bending over, rumpling her hair.

Donna took a drag off her cigarette. "Claire's running late. Sit. Take a load off."

"Don't ask me how I am."

"Holiday stress?"

"Got a speeding ticket yesterday. He said I was doing 48 in a 20."

"Gene get ya?"

"No. Officer Spellmeier."

"D'you hike up your skirt?"

"Yep. About four inches shy of taking his picture."

And…?"

"He gave me directions to City Hall, as if I didn't already know."

Jake darted out of the back room toting a large waste can and transferred the contents from four smaller wastebaskets. Catharine plopped herself down in a styling chair. Donna's circus pink Hoffman Solaradio played so softly that only the melody to the Carpenters' *We've*

Only Just Begun was audible. Jake disappeared into the back room. Donna inhaled the last of her Marlboro and snuffed it out in the oversized ashtray on the backbar counter.

"Jake!" Donna hollered …"Dump this for me, will you?" she said, handing him the ashtray brimming with butts.

"Why do the holidays have to get here so early?" Catharine complained.

"They're sneaky that way. Head down," Donna instructed, as she initiated a ritual neck and shoulder massage. "Relax. Close your eyes. Hands in your lap, please. That's it. Pretend you're spaghetti. Right out of the package. I'm the hot water. Okay?"

Jake reappeared, handed Donna a clean ashtray, and fetched his jacket from a salon chair.

"Where's Sherman?" he asked.

"Home. Prob'ly curled up on my bed. Would you bring me a magazine?"

"Which one?"

"I'll get you one in a couple minutes," Donna said. "You finished?"

"Yes, ma'am."

"D'you get the coffee started?"

"It's perkin'."

"Leave the seat down on the stool?"

"Shore did."

"Shake out the mats?"

"Sho' nuf, Miss Pillowtalk. I shakes 'em hard. Real hard. Right outside the door, there."

"Did the devil make you do it?"

"Sho' did, honey. What you see is what you get. Eeeyow!"

"I heard your Oklahoma Peach will be here for Thanksgiving," said Catharine.

"Yep. Her name's Kim. I gotta go. Got-a dentist appointment in Granfield at nine." He wriggled into his well-worn Demons high school letter jacket, pulled up the hood of his sweatshirt, and shoved his hands in his jeans pockets as he jogged across the street.

"I've never seen him act silly like that. He's usually so shy."

"We stayed up late last night to watch Flip Wilson do his Geraldine on Carson. You should hear him do one of his Eddie Haskell impressions sometime."

Catharine shifted in the chair and rolled her shoulders. "I heard he's going to work for Bruner at the bank."

"Yep. Starts next Monday."

"I think that fits him perfectly."

"Jake's been on cloud nine the past few weeks. Last couple months he's run up over two hundred dollars in long distance charges."

"The boy's in love."

"Yep. It's all new to him. And he found out she's Korean, <u>not</u> an Indian. A war orphan adopted by a family in Bartlesville. Cute as can be."

Catharine went silent, allowing herself to be manipulated by a pair of practiced hands. Donna ground her fingers into Catharine's flesh as if kneading a fresh ball of bread dough. They listened to the tinny expansion ticks of the duct work as warm air channeled through its obstacle course, out of sync with the conspicuous 'thock...throck... thock ...throck' of the brass pendulum in the salon's seven foot, thirty-hour longcase clock.

"It's cold in here," Catharine declared, popping her knuckles.

"My old furnace needs about twenty minutes to do its thing. Used to take longer than that till we dropped the ceiling and put in insulation."

"Mmm. That feels good. Can I let you know when to quit?"

"Price might go up. I read in the new *Reader's Digest* where cracking your knuckles can promote arthritis."

"Sorry. Bad habit of mine. Maybe I should take up smoking instead?"

"Personally, I wouldn't recommend it. Unless you're real hard up for a hobby."

"When did Jake start cleaning for you?"

"Week after Natalie got killed. Besides pedicures and nails, she did general clean-up. On weekends, usually. Did the same for Baguelt Homes twice a week."

"D'you know she was pregnant?"

"Nonny told me that. Yes. Oo...right there. Oo..."

"I need to find some competent help. Being in here by myself gets really old some days."

"I'm looking for a sales associate."

"Talked to anyone around here about it?"

"Gene Lassiter."

"No kidding? Mr. Top Cop. How funny."

"Don't repeat that. Okay? After he retires. He knows more people in the county than most, has a good reputation, and doesn't take shit off anybody."

"No argument there."

"Commission-only pay isn't for everyone."

"Interesting Gene might become a real-a-ter."

"Real-a-<u>tor</u>," Catharine rectified. "What time is Claire's appointment?"

"Now."

"What's her problem?"

"Greta killed one of her chickens this morning. There. That better?"

Catharine dramatically rolled her head side-to side. "Much. I really appreciate you squeezing me in this morning," she said, rubbing her eyes.

"Allergies?"

"Nope. Had a meltdown last night."

"Sorry to hear. Anything I can do?"

"Nope."

"Going anywhere for Thanksgiving or staying home?" Donna queried, as she fastened and adjusted a cape.

"Staying home. Just me and the dog."

"Your mother still live on base at Fort Riley?"

"Nope. Moved to North Carolina. We don't talk much anymore. Good day for me to get some quiet time. Curl up with my new book."

"Which is…?"

"*The French Lieutenant's Woman.*"

"Good read?"

"I'm only on chapter two. I'll let you know."

"You going to Luci's this morning?"

"I'm going there, but not for myself. Luci's making up a quart of her chicken soup I can take to Nonny."

"Nothin' like Jewish penicillin for what ails ya. Nonny not feeling well?"

"Says she's feeling a bit under the weather, maybe running a fever."

"Have Nonny call me. If she's running a fever, I might be able to help. Something Papa used to do when we were kids. You take an egg from the refrigerator and rub it on the sick person's face and body, making the sign of the cross. Then, place the egg in a glass of water and put it under their bed overnight."

"Sounds like voodoo."

"Folk medicine. A *curandero* remedy Papa practiced on us kids. Okay. What're we going to do with this today?"

"Shampoo and set? Nothing fancy. No big plans this weekend."

Though neither noticed, intermittent snowflakes began to fall, whipped about by a north breeze. Donna turned up the radio and lathered Catharine's hair. Their conversation centered on Donna's uncertain plans for Thanksgiving Day. Scheduling a live-alone father, three brothers, four sisters, spouses, and children ranging in age from learning to crawl to high school graduate had its challenges when the holidays rolled around.

"I was in charge of bird-day last year," Donna said, as she towel-dried Catharine's hair. "Papa insisted we have Thanksgiving at his home. Same one we all grew up in. Wood-frame, two bedrooms. One bath, tiny kitchen, formal dining room. Largest room in the house was the sunroom upstairs. We called it *un solario grande*."

"Sounds like an airplane bungalow. And there were how many of you?"

"Ten. And two gerbils. We girls got the sunroom. No such thing as privacy."

"Packed like sardines."

"Last year we needed one bedroom just for coats."

Donna discarded the towel, faced Catharine toward the backbar mirror and began combing out her shoulder length hair.

"We probably ought to do color and a haircut next time."

"Okay by me."

"Oh, I just remembered. You wanted a magazine." Donna stepped over to her magazine rack. "We got *Ladies Home Journal, Reader's Digest, Good Housekeeping, Better Homes…*"

"Got a *TIME* or a *Newsweek*?"

Donna delivered a *TIME* and resumed the comb out.

"Looks like it's starting to snow a little out there," Donna commented.

"Know what they forecast on the news last night? Up to one inch or maybe less."

"Brought to you by Madame Ouija and… Oh! OH! I love this song!" Donna exclaimed.

"Me too! Turn it up!"

> *I want to, I want to, I want to take you higher*
> *I want to take you higher*
> *Baby, baby, baby light my fire*
> *I wanna take you higher*

Donna stopped combing. The comb became a mic. She faced Catharine, head bobbing, eyes bulging like a dairy cow being machine-milked for the first time.

> *Boom laka-laka-laka, boom laka-laka-laka, boom*

Catharine leaned forward, seized her mic hand and, nose-to-nose, they sang:

> *I wanna take ya higher*
> *Boom laka-laka-laka, boom laka-laka-laka*

Catharine rolled up the magazine as her own microphone and stood in the chair. Together they gyrated and waved their arms, sang, and snapped their fingers. Neither of them noticed Claire walk in. When Donna spotted Claire, she stepped quickly over to the counter and lowered the volume. Catharine eased herself down and sat primly.

"Morning, Claire," Donna greeted, blushing slightly.

"Morning! Am I interrupting?"

"Not at all. We were just, you know, being our unprofessional selves."

"Need me to pull the blinds?"

"Not this time."

"Sorry I'm late," Claire said, as she hung up her jean jacket and adjusted her cable knit mohair sweater.

"No problem. Grab a mag. Be with you in a few."

"Could I use the bathroom first?"

"You bet. Coffee's on."

"Morning, Claire," said Catharine, with a crooked grin.

Catharine thumbed through her magazine. As Donna applied setting solution and rollers by rote at an Indianapolis 500 clip, she caught sight of Doyle tending to his first customer across the street. His next-door neighbor to the north, Ginny's Fashions sat dark, WE HAVE MOVED painted on the storefront windows. The empty two-story structure once known as Gibby's Bakery & Confectionery Shoppe, abutted the barber shop on the opposite side. A casualty of the '58 recession, its display cases, fixtures, and equipment were still intact. Its dingy display windows featured an All Bright Realty FOR RENT sign. Donna recalled when they first started seeing each other, Doyle took her to Gibby's on a snowy, blustery cold Saturday afternoon and bought her an Apple Brown Betty topped with real whipped cream and a charitable sprinkle of heart-shaped Red Hots for Valentine's Day. Later, he remarked that her red tongue made her an official Waltsburg Demon.

"D'you ever hear from your daughter?" Catharine asked.

"I'm sorry, what?"

"Don't you have a daughter?"

"No, but I had a cat once."

"Your daughter. Do you ever hear from her?"

"Not since I wired her two hundred dollars bail money."

Claire reappeared, selected the latest *Good Housekeeping*, and sat across from them.

"You might as well sit over here. I'm almost finished."

Claire stood and stretched. "You wouldn't care if I unsnapped my jeans, would you?"

"Hell, no," Donna said. "Make yourself at home."

"They won't fall off, will they?" Catharine posed.

"Not off a butt this size."

"You're being way too hard on yourself," Donna said. "You look great in jeans."

"They're so much tighter when I got my long johns on."

"Okay, young lady. <u>You</u> are ready for the dryer."

Catharine sat quietly under the dryer, but not before spiking the *TIME* in a wastebasket declaring she, for one, hated the war. The one she was compelled to hear about Every. Goddamn. Day. The one she watched every evening on the television news. Was there no end to the revolving door of politicos? Hawks, doves, draft dodgers, sit-ins, and protesters? She silently fumed over last night's brief, unexpected phone call from her mother. It was obvious her mother had too much to drink, not news to Catharine. What was there to be said between the estranged over the death of her father, Lt. Col. Quentin Mixx, a West Point grad on his third tour? He was confirmed KIA in May. Friendly fire, Battle of Kham Duc, Quang Tin Province, Republic of South Vietnam, meant little to her. Catharine's mother waited six months to tell her Daddy's dead and that she had since remarried and moved to North Carolina.

'Great timing,' she thought. 'Three days before the Great American Holiday.' Stark images resurfaced: her mother postured as a tormented hostage in her own home, her father frequently depicting her mother as Satan's Quartermaster, and her own irrepressible tantrums and sobs last night. Was she her mother's daughter, after all? Finding Sherman cowered under her bed was sobering. Catharine was not ready to confront or divulge the erotic, blissful moments she remembered vividly; the ones shared with Daddy as a pre-pubescent girl. The periodic, one-sided private sessions with Deke Stuber were not what she longed for. The initial rush of cold air from the dryer on her damp head raised goosebumps on her arms and sent shivers down her legs. 'Maybe there was something worthwhile in this *Reader's Digest*.'

As Donna washed and rinsed her hands, Claire removed her boots. Customer number two ducked her head in anticipation of Donna's artful two-minute massage.

"What's with Catharine this morning?" Claire asked.

"Not sure. She's really uptight about something."

"Could you work that right side a little harder? We put up hay yesterday."

"Need something to bite down on?"

"No," Claire chuckled, reflexively crushing the magazine. "Does Doyle ever get this kind of treatment?"

"If he behaves himself. What's on your docket today?"

"I've got to clean house. I keep putting it off."

"Same here. Do you hire out?"

"On a cold day in hell, maybe."

"Isn't that what long johns are for?"

Claire laughed out loud. Donna shifted her focus to Claire's temples.

"Doyle said Jack told him you have an anniversary coming up."

"Yes. Sunday will be our twenty-fifth."

"Congratulations! Family coming in?"

"Starting tomorrow evening."

Catharine slung the *Reader's Digest* across the room in the direction of a wastebasket but missed. She stalked over to a waiting chair, got down on all fours, retrieved the magazine, and calmly placed it in the rack. She picked the TIME out of the wastebasket, put it in the rack, and resumed her post under the dryer, arms folded like a petulant child.

"Heard you were in on fighting that fire at Doona Falls."

"I was. Never any rest for the weary out there. Like Jack says, if the sun didn't set, we'd never get any sleep."

"I see you're wearing the pendant," Donna remarked.

"Yes. Got it from Merry Belle the week after Labor Day."

"Where'd you see it?"

"In the pasture across the road from our place last spring when I was hanging out laundry. I got one for Jenna Fairchild. She saw it a couple of weeks ago. I checked with Darryl. He said it is possible for a horse to live that long."

"Makes you wonder, doesn't it?"

Claire breathed a deep sigh and stretched her legs as the longcase clock chimed its half past the hour.

"Where'd Jenna see it?"

"Near Meyer's Crossing, where we found fence down and the head of that balloon operator out in the field."

"Two of my sisters called me after they saw the story on the news. Okay, then. What're we going to do with this today?"

CHAPTER 51
THE MULDOONIES

November 26

Thanksgiving Day

Light snow was forecast. No hint of wind, only calm beneath the homogeneous shroud of overcast that sagged low enough to stir longings for open sky. Jake, Kim, Conger, and Portia wandered toward the Cemetary, their every breath apparent, their bellies full of Merry Belle's traditional Thanksgiving turkey and trimmings dinner. A noticeable limp in her gait, Blanco trailed the group. Wally led the pack with his usual weave, stop and sniff. Jake offered Kim quiet commentary on ranch features: the Madonna and Child statue, the nine apple trees that survived the tornado, the footings of the old bunkhouse and pole barns. Kim stopped momentarily to remove a rock from her shoe, grasping Jake's arm. Much to his delight, she slipped her cold hand into his.

Minnie's Creek was the primary topic as they strolled through Bluestem pasture mottled by fire less than a month earlier. The austere refuge was freckled with exposed squirrel and bird nests. Conger pointed to the quarter-mile long disparity in tree height; evidence of a tornado's path, and the twisted remnant of a creep feeder left where it landed. As they approached the hallowed ground Jake wondered if they might see colorful remnants of the hot air balloon still snagged in trees. Portia told Kim her grandmother was buried here. Wally reached the rock ledge first and started barking. Below, six adults and three children sat yoga style, holding hands, heads bowed, encircling Sean Robert Muldoon's gravestone.

"I know these people," grouched Conger.

"Who are they?" Jake asked.

"Mom calls 'em the Incorrigibles. Be right back."

Conger eased down the abrupt sedimentary barrier and approached the group. Almost immediately, the outsiders gathered their things, strolled out the gateway, and headed toward the creek. Conger returned and assisted Kim and Portia down the rock bank. Jake slithered down behind them and repeated his question.

"Robert Muldoon disciples," said Conger. "They show up out here several times a year to tend his grave. They usually park a quarter mile north and hike in. We've warned them. Put No Trespassing signs where they park and here on the fence but apparently none of 'em ever learned to read."

They followed Conger to Robert's grave. Store-bought cut flowers, two 303 cans of cranberry jelly, and a manila envelope addressed to Sean Robert lay at the base of the gravestone.

"Weird," said Jake. "That was what, twenty-some years ago?"

"Who was he?" Kim asked.

"Tell you later."

They watched the devoted disappear into the trees and brush along the creek. Portia took Kim's hand and led her to her ancestor's grave. She repeated the story of Snow-In-Her-Hair, Ben Whitewater's wife, as it had been told to her. She briefly narrated how her relative lost both her parents to smallpox, and later contracted typhoid from the Grasshopper River, now known as the Delaware, the primary source of drinking water on the reservation. When prayer proved ineffective, Ben brought her to Doona Falls Ranch hoping the geothermal waters might have a healing effect. Two days after their arrival, she passed away in her sleep.

"Too bad all the wildflowers are gone," said Kim. "We could pick s-some for her."

"There's still a chance you might find something along the creek," Conger suggested.

"Let's go," said Kim, grabbing Portia's wrist and leading her away.

"They did a bang-up job on his grave," noted Jake.

"They always do."

"They always bring flowers and mail?"

"Always something."

"Ever read any of it?"

"Once," Conger admitted. "Last Christmas, it was holiday sheet music, a Monkey Wards catalog, and a barbed wire wreath."

Jake angled over to the barn wood thief's burial spot. "Can't hardly tell anyone's buried here."

"We did good."

"Think what we did was the right thing to do?"

"Absolutely! Same day we buried this guy, Mom told me about the cattle rustlers they caught red-handed and lynched out here during the Depression. Said she will never forget the sight of two men dangling from tree limbs where the creek and Meyers Wash meet. Bearnard made everyone go out there to see 'em twist in the wind."

"I had a dream the guy was loitering outside Stuber's Garage. His body charred black from burning. Kim walked up to him and asked if he wanted his library card back."

"That's weird."

Jake gazed toward the creek but did not see either of the wildflower seekers. "You gotta go to work tomorrow?"

"No. You?"

"I start full-time at the bank Monday. Between now and then, I gotta keep Kim entertained."

"She's nice. Where's she staying?"

"With Donna."

"You ask her to marry you yet?"

Jake chuckled, "Haven't even kissed her."

"What're you waiting on?"

"Think it's too cold to hike to Hoover's Bottom?"

"It's not getting any warmer. Why?"

"I'd like to show Kim the buffalo wallow there."

"Not sure Blanco can make it that far and back."

The first snowflakes began to fall, gravity obedient, perpendicular to Earth like textbook geometry. Jake pulled up the hood of his sweatshirt, blew warm air into his cupped hands then buried them inside the pockets of his new World Series Champions Baltimore Orioles jacket.

"Here they come," said Jake. "Looks like they found something."

"Look what we found!" exclaimed Kim.

"These are devil's claws," said Conger. "What're those?"

"Rose hips," said Portia, of the bright red berry-like buds. "They're medicinal."

"And that?"

"Portia says it's watercress and you c-can eat it."

Portia arranged their finds atop Snow-In-Her-Hair's grave.

"I think she will be overjoyed," Portia smiled.

"Anybody ready to go back?" Conger pressed. "It's getting colder."

"In a moment," said Portia, whose gestures and words in her native tongue enchanted the others. On their way back to the house Portia noticed Blanco was not among them. She was sitting about twenty paces behind. "C'mon, girl!" Conger coaxed. Blanco took two short steps and stopped. Conger backtracked, lifted the 70-pound canine, and carried her.

"She's not back to being herself yet," lamented Conger as he rejoined the group.

"What happened to her? Kim asked.

"Hit by a car," Jake offered, as he took Kim's hand.

Kim patted the dog's head and murmured, "Poor baby."

On their trek back to the house, Conger asked Portia if she would translate her words. She said she preferred not to and commented her grandfather planned to be interred next to his wife when the time comes. She added Ben Whitewater suspected one reason his wife died was the fact that they, and many others on the reservation, converted to Christianity. He deduced, therefore, any tribal animistic rituals, talismans, or ceremonial dances no longer had any force or effect; elixirs passed down from their ancestors, such as willow bark and brewed chicory root, replaced by bogus white man's remedies like *Sagwa* hawked by the Kickapoo Indian Medicine Company in their traveling medicine shows. As they approached the house, Kim commented she had never seen such a magnificent barn. Jake spun an overview of its history as he knew it from John Griever. Conger filled in additional details.

"Mom said it used to have a cupola with a weathervane before the tornado. Squint your eyes. You can still make out where they replaced the middle section of the roof."

Conger took Blanco to the top of the steps before setting her down.

"I'm going to show Kim the Falls," said Portia, snugging her coat collar.

Jake and Conger opted to go inside where it was warm. They joined Ben Whitewater, John Griever, and Doyle in the parlor while Merry Belle, Nonny, and Donna completed their post meal tidy-up.

"Girls get lost?" Ben queried.

"Portia's showing Kim the Falls," said Conger, shedding his parka.

"Eden on Earth," sighed Ben.

Nonny plopped herself down on the sofa. Donna entered the room carrying a sterling silver tray with saucers, cups, cream, sugar, and a half-empty fifth of Jameson. "Who would like coffee?"

"I would take a cup," said Ben.

"I know Nonny wants one. Doyle?"

"None for me, thanks."

"John?"

"Yep."

"Would you boys like to make some cocoa?"

Portia entered the room, whispered in Conger's ear, and they left.

"Were you a big help in the kitchen?" Doyle asked of Nonny.

"Not really."

"Donna said you tripped over your cat?"

"Yes. I believe it was intentional. Tommy has not been friendly towards me ever since I had him fixed."

"D'you break it?"

"Yes. I was told I have to wear this confounded sling for six weeks."

"It'll heal," John said. "Never should-a had 'im fixed."

"All he ever did was whore and brawl with his mates."

"No wrong in that if you know Mother Nature. Now look what ya got."

"I cannot win for losing."

"Last Sunday I stopped by to…"

"You do not need to tell this story, John," Nonny interrupted.

"…stopped by to pick Olga up for church."

"I do not go by that name. You are being an arse."

"Anyway, I walk up the porch steps and there's eight, nine toms there."

"John...."

"Now, it ain't till later I find out what she had done to the cat," John laughed. "These ol' boys is taken turns humpin' ol' Tommy. Yowlin', mountin', and pawin' him somethin' terrible. He's crouched down, covered with spit. That hormone shot Darryl gave 'im makes his ex-runnin' mates think he's a girl."

"He's a house cat now," said Nonny.

"He's a sissy," John snorted. "Turned 'im into a real sissy what don't fight back."

Conger stepped back into the room. "The pool is off limits. The girls are taking a dip."

"What did Portia want?" Jake asked.

"Towels. I'm going to put more wood on the fire."

Blanco and Wally lay sprawled on the Oriental rug in front of the stone fireplace. After Conger placed more split logs on the fire and realigned the fire screen, he caught himself staring at Mary Muldoon's portrait above the mantel. 'Such a way to die,' he reminisced. As related by Merry, her body was riddled with shards of glass imploded and swirled about the interior of the manor by tornadic winds. She miraculously survived for three days while townsfolk held their breath and prayed. Most thought death was the best outcome as she had also broken her spine and lost sight in both eyes to the maelstrom's razor-sharp debris. Merry was away, finishing up her teaching degree at Kansas State College under the aegis of Mary Muldoon. She and her son, Caleb, returned to the ranch immediately when they heard the news. She was holding Mary's hand when the matriarch drew her last breath. Merry told William she lost her best friend in the world. Donna and Merry joined the circle. Jake returned with steaming cocoa. Drinks in hand, the conversation turned to the uninvited guests in the Cemetary.

"Sometimes there's only two or three. On occasion, we've encountered as many as fourteen," said Merry. "Was that short, heavy-set woman with knee-length hair in this group?"

"No," Conger replied.

"She's the most outspoken of the lot. She believes they're entitled to do whatever they damn well please whenever it suits them. The same month William and I moved back on the ranch, she and three others showed up. Sped right through the turnabout, past the barn, on out to the burial ground. William and I hiked out there to see who it was. I told them I didn't mind if they tended Robert's grave so long as they checked in with us first to let us know they're out there, as a matter of courtesy. A month or so later, that mouthy, long-haired tub-o-lard and several others were out there one night holding some sort of candlelight vigil."

"In white satin choir robes," added Conger.

"They'd piled up stones at the foot of Robert's grave."

"Looked like some sort of shrine."

"It almost came to blows over us disrupting their mysterious little ceremony. I told her if they ever lit a candle out here again, we'd shoot first and ask questions after."

"D'you remember your words?" Conger asked.

"I'm afraid I do not."

"And I quote 'This ain't Stonehenge, Rapunzel!'"

"I was mad! The nerve of these Muldoonies and their mystical mumbo jumbo. I told 'em to get the hell off our land and stay off."

"Muldoonies? I like that," John said. "You should dig 'im up and bury 'im in another cemetery."

"Don't think that hasn't crossed our minds. I've grown more cynical with age. I know too much."

"Mom?!"

"I'm referring to the Muldoons, William. All the bits and pieces I overheard while working here, especially when Mary and Bearnard got into arguments, which was often. They slept in separate bedrooms. They basically led separate lives. Their true last name, I am sure, was O'Shaughnessy. Both were as Irish as the Blarney Stone. The ranch's registered brand is a *triquetra*."

"How'd they come into being so rich?" Jake asked.

"Bearnard learned from his mother on her deathbed that he was the bastard son of a well-to-do whiskey distiller from the Speyside region of Scotland, a toff whose family traced its bloodline as far back as Robert de Brus. She was an Irish immigrant forty years the man's junior and worked as a domestic on the whiskey family's estate. She was let go once it was discovered she was pregnant, so she moved back to Glasgow with family. Bearnard took his mother's name and had nothing to do with his

Scot father. I know he was raised in the Gorbals district and joined up with a street gang. Because of his size and reputation as a formidable street fighter, he was welcomed into the gang's hierarchy as an enforcer for their sizeable gambling, prostitution, and protection rackets. The gang placed their abounding cash profits with a priest who stashed the money in accounts ostensibly church related. For years, Bearnard was the go-between, the trusted straw man who conveyed the funds weekly. The priest had a younger sister named Mary. She and Bearnard were introduced, courted, and eventually wed."

"Mary Muldoon confided in you then?" Doyle asked.

"Yes. She would become especially chatty when we were bathing in the Falls pool or on horseback rides. She loved the Hoover's Bottom area. She declared it the most peaceful place on Earth."

"Can't argue that," John concurred.

"Bearnard's mother eventually found work in a Singer sewing machine factory in Glasgow. When the company boosted workloads and cut wages, she openly supported women workers' strikes. She was among the hundreds fired by Singer to break the backs of the strikers and labor unions. After that, Bearnard supported her and her family. She died in 1918 of consumption."

"What made them think of coming here?" Donna asked.

"Bearnard was a wanted man," Merry maintained. "Slumlords often raised rents in the Gorbals district tenements crowded with immigrants. Those who could least afford to pay. There were organized rent strikes and scores of bitter confrontations when non-paying tenants were forcibly evicted. Bearnard, or whatever his name was then, and his cohorts kidnapped the owner of the tenement where his mother and extended family lived. According to Mary, they bound and blindfolded him. Threatened, starved, and tortured the man till he promised not to raise their rent.

Once released, the man went to the police and demanded the thugs be arrested and punished. Bearnard was easily recognizable because of his large stature, a prominent mole on his face, and conflicted eye. After two of his accomplices were caught; Bearnard went into hiding, leaving Mary and child to fend for themselves. She was continuously watched and harassed by the police. Then, Red Clydeside came to a head."

"Never heard of that," said Ben.

"Most people haven't, at least not in this country. At the end of January 1919, a rally organized by the socialist and Marxist-leaning trade unions drew as many as ninety thousand protesters to Glasgow's city center. It was a defining moment for the country. Things got out of hand. It turned into a riot the police could not contain. The government feared it was a Bolshevist uprising. They invoked the Riot Act and deployed soldiers and tanks to maintain order. Bearnard embarked on a course of action he'd planned for all along."

"He absconded with the gang's money," Nonny interjected.

"The chaos brought about by Red Clydeside provided the perfect cover to escape Glasgow. With phony identity papers and a boatload of money withdrawn from accounts set up by Mary and Mary's brother, Bearnard booked passage on a luxury liner from Liverpool to New York. Mary was pregnant with their second child; the war was over, so no U-boat worries. In their minds, the timing was better than perfect."

"Where the hell did he get his know-how for Angus cattle?" John asked.

"Around the age of fourteen, he worked as a laborer on a farm midway between Edinburgh and Glasgow. According to Mary, he cleaned stables and barns. Bearnard learned to shovel shit early on. Something we Irish were predestined to do, according to Protestants."

"Ah'll be," John sighed.

"Fascinating," said Donna.

"You in charge of the chamber pots when you came to the ranch?" Ben asked.

"Yes. The slop jars were my responsibility," Merry said. "Cleaning hearths. Meal prep. Washing dishes. Dusting. Doing laundry. Scrubbing floors. Shooing chickens off the veranda. You name it, I did it."

"What happened to her brother? The priest?" Jake asked.

"He disappeared. Mary said she never heard from him again. How could she? They had new identities in a new country."

"I do not believe Sherlock Holmes could have found them," Nonny commented.

"Can I pour more coffee for anyone?" John asked.

"If you leave ample legroom for the Jameson this round," said Nonny.

"Same for me, John," Merry said.

Both Merry and Nonny again added whiskey to their coffee. John cautioned Nonny about consuming too much alcohol in light of her condition. Nonny responded by comparing herself to Gibraltar in some indecipherable way.

"Doyle and I want to thank you for such a wonderful Thanksgiving dinner," said Donna.

"Me and Kim, too," Jake said.

"The best ever," added Ben.

"Thank you. I enjoy doing it. Sorry for getting off track," said Merry. "I, well, never mind. My blood pressure spikes every time I think about those people. That obnoxious, long-haired Muldoonie woman is the one I should-a shot."

"Mom!"

"Fiddlesticks," Merry muttered.

Conger glared fiercely at Merry and discreetly shook his head at her.

"Anyone ready for another slice of plumpkin pie?" Nonny offered.

"I'm more stuffed than a Lyla Witte animal mount," said Doyle.

"No more for me," Ben answered.

"Those girls are gonna freeze out there," Donna remarked.

"Jack and Claire not available this year?" Ben inquired.

"Sunday is their twenty-fifth wedding anniversary," said Donna. "They got family in from all over."

"Which reminds me," said Merry. "I need to call Claire. We're out of eggs."

"You should raise your own chickens," Ben hinted. "Mary Muldoon had quite a flock here back in the day."

"There won't be a chicken on this ranch as long as I'm alive. They're predator magnets."

A lull befell the conversation. Hands folded in his lap, head nodded like an idle pump jack, Ben Whitewater dozed in his armchair. Jake collected the empty cups and transported them to the kitchen. Doyle stood and announced he and Donna ought to be heading home.

"I hope all the hot air balloon stuff is behind us now," said Doyle.

"Amen," said Merry. "We got dead bodies all over the place out here."

"Mom...!"

"As God is my witness, the way I felt after Bearnard had his way with me, time and again. I felt like one of them."

"Nobody wants to hear about poor little Frances," Conger admonished.

"At least I didn't have to look the son-of-a-bitch in the eye when he bent me over and..."

"Mom! That's enough!"

"Can't you see I'm tired?!"

"Then go lie down!" Conger rejoined.

Merry went silent. Doyle and Donna said their good-byes and left. Ben began to snore. Roused by Conger's tone of voice, Blanco ambled into the parlor. John advised Nonny to fetch her coat and a large slice of pumpkin pie to go. He enticed Merry off the sofa and gave her a hug.

"I am sorry for being what I am," Merry said. "And, for what I said. I apologize."

"Bruner tells me they might have your ownership problem straight by sometime soon. Nothin' but good comin' your way."

Tears streamed down Merry's cheeks. "I am sorry."

"If we don't trouble about each other, we ain't friends," said John.

CHAPTER 52
A WALTZ AT WALTER'S
IN WALTSBURG

Friday/Saturday – November 27/28

Kim made no mention to her parents or Aunt Nell of her trip to Waltsburg. They were clearly disappointed she would not be among them Thanksgiving Day. In their view, why couldn't she spend Thanksgiving with family and then drive to see her girlfriend on Friday? She beg-bargained the timing of her outing in exchange for a cross-my-heart promise to spend the Christmas holidays at home. Kim's story: She was driving to Manhattan, Kansas, to spend Thanksgiving with her best friend, Chana Da Silva.

The Friday after Thanksgiving, Jake spent the day introducing Kim to Waltsburg. In addition to becoming better acquainted with Doyle and Donna, they had tea with Nonny at her home, staying much longer than Jake anticipated. She reminisced about the war and only true love of her life, Captain Cransford Wilson, a Royal Military College grad, and proper gentleman. "It was quite nerve-wracking, especially during the Blitz. I escaped London every chance I got. Nonny showed them the Celtic earrings she had purchased in Blackpool while on leave. When I retired and moved back here, our tornado sirens bring back those dark days."

"How did you and Mr. Wilson meet?" Kim asked.

"At a bottle party club in London in December 1939. I fell in love the first time he asked me to dance. Six weeks later, we married." She told them that in April 1940, Captain Wilson was among the British Expeditionary Force deployed to France to counter a German offensive

271

they knew was imminent. "He survived the beaches at Dunkirk without a scratch. Not long after, he shipped out to India. I received a letter from him weekly until his unit was deployed to Burma."

"What happened to him?" Kim asked.

"You two have better things to do than listen to an old woman waffle."

"N-not today we don't," Kim encouraged.

After visiting with Nonny, Jake drove Kim out to John Griever's where she was introduced to Roger, Pee Wee, and most of John's goats. Over lunch at the Beau Coup Café, Jake told her about the remnants of the hot air balloon they discovered along Minnie's Creek, omitting the grisly details. They took a drive around Ormestrong County State Lake, stopping briefly so Jake could show her the cove where they launched John's boat. Under the watchful eyes of a pair of very vocal killdeer, Jake skipped flat rocks over the lake's mirror-like surface to show off one of his left-handed skills. As they wound their way back to town, he showed Kim The Hump, a geological anomaly along one of the lake's back roads, with its abrupt four-foot drop. Since the 1920's, it posed an irresistible dare to thrill-seeking drivers to go airborne. The unofficial Hump Jump distance record holder was Jimmy Baguelt's '67 Camaro, now serving a life sentence in Waltsburg's salvage yard.

That evening, Donna prepared *pozolé blanco* with fresh lime, complete with *tortillas* and *queso fresco*. Kim, Jake, and Doyle declined the after-supper tequila shot offered by Donna who, upon tendering a toast to her pantywaist *gringo* guests, imbibed. They watched television through *Love American Style*. On the drive home, all Jake thought about was another day with Kim. Donna offered to trim her hair around nine. Afterward, Jake planned to show her through the Bruno mansion.

Built during the Gilded Age, Walter Bruno's gated Victorian home on ten acres of prime real estate at the west edge of town now served as the town's museum. Kim and Jake strolled through the sprawling five-acre rock garden, a labyrinth of shaped hedges and pollarded trees, fountains, sculptures, gazebos, and Asian carp ponds that flanked the home on two sides. From beneath a twelve-foot tall, rough-hewn cross, they caught a sunny glimpse of the Orme River's rocky bluffs on the opposite bank. Jake had been here many times over the years but never as a tour guide. A docent was not required. Joan Lowry trusted Jake with a set of keys. As they approached the home along one of the flagstone paths accented by elfin drifts of new snow, Jake commented the best time to visit the estate grounds was late spring when most of its flora was abloom. Kim dallied at a life-size bronze sculpture, the embrace of two nude young lovers.

She admired it from three sides. "I hope they lived happily ever after. Don't you?"

"Yes. My…uh, my father called it the Statue of Puberty."

Kim laughed. "Excellent title."

"That's the millstone from the old grist mill," he pointed out, as they neared the steps to the front entrance. Much of the home's wraparound porch and screened pergola still glistened with frost. The five brick chimney stacks were impressive from any angle. He pointed out the barley-sugar columns of the *porte cochère* and said they were slated for a new coat of paint in the spring. Jake was about to try the third choice from the keyring when the pedimented, stained glass paneled front door abruptly opened. There stood Violet Brisby, the odd neighbor who lived across the street from him and his uncle, the one who occasionally danced with a broom on her porch; behind her stood Reverend Cage.

"Hello, young man," the tall woman offered with a smile.

"H-hello," said Jake. "We were just coming in."

"Such a coincidence," she said. "We were just leaving."

Mrs. Brisby was attired in her turn-of-the-century Edwardian get-up. Accustomed to seeing her with her hair bundled atop her head that accentuated her long face, Jake noted her hair was down. Her perpetually parted lips and toothy understated smile betrayed her identity. There were still some in town who, behind her back, dubbed her Horse Face.

"Who might this be?" Violet asked.

"My friend, Kim. From Oklahoma."

"Cherokee?" Violet guessed.

"Korean," Jake corrected.

"American," Kim adjusted.

"I'm Reverend Cage," the man said, offering his hand to Kim. "Bit of a chill in the air this morning, isn't there?"

"Sun's back out though," Jake countered, as he and Kim slipped inside.

"Such a splendid sun it is," Violet replied. "Our plants here love the morning sun. We just finished giving them all a drink."

'Makes sense,' Jake thought. Her eccentric nature notwithstanding, Violet Brisby was a museum docent, one of the remaining few in town interested in preserving the past. Jake told the pair they had just completed a walk of the grounds and were now ready to tour the mansion.

"The aristocracy that was," Violet commented. "Enjoy your visit. Be sure and show your friend our crusading quilt in the sitting room."

Mrs. Brisby and Reverend Cage took their leave. Jake mulled over where to begin. He plucked a brochure from one of the matching demilune tables in the foyer, glanced about, and handed the piece to Kim.

"What k-kind of tile is this?" she asked, stooped down, running her fingers over the colorful tiles.

"Imported. Marble, I think."

"It looks like blue s-sky."

"It's there in the brochure. I can't pronounce it."

Kim found the reference and took a stab at the pronunciation, "*Azul cielo.*"

"What would you like to see first?"

"You pick."

"How about we start upstairs and work our way down?"

They wandered into the interior; the air seasoned with a hint of mustiness. At the bottom of a broad spiral staircase, Jake punched the mother of pearl light switch buttons several times, to no avail. Over the past couple of years, he and Henry made some minor repairs to the knob-and-tube wiring, but only as the museum budget permitted. As they ascended the stairway in semi-dark, Kim commented, "Wouldn't it be fun to ss-slide down this banister."

Top of the stairs, he punched another light button. Third punch, five of six lights came to life illuminating a cavernous hall. Kim asked where Walter Bruno was from. He repeated what he had heard from others: Chicago, Boston, Argentina? A preponderance of circumstantial evidence supported all three. Jake headed in the direction of the master bedroom. She paused to examine a verse embroidered on matted fabric hanging on the wall, framed in tiger maple, flanked by outsized oil paintings of a lighthouse and clipper ship.

> "And this is good old Boston,
> The home of the bean and the cod,
> Where the Lowells talk only to Cabots,
> And the Cabots talk only to God."

"Did he have a wife and children?"

Jake did an about face and sidled up next to her. "Not that anyone around here knew of."

"When did he die?"

He related what he knew from the hand-me-down scraps of local lore. In the mid-'30's, the week after Walter Bruno and his bodyguard boarded a train for Chicago, three dapper businessmen showed up one afternoon at the Waltsburg train depot and produced official-looking documents stating they were the new owners of the Atlantic Hotel and all else previously owned by Mr. Bruno. "No one knows what happened to them."

"He lived in this place all alone?"

"He had servants. C'mon, I'll show you the master bedroom."

As they approached the end of the corridor, Kim saw her reflection in a wealth of mirrors. Jake restated Joan Lowry's supposition that Bruno was a collector of mirrors. According to the brochure, there were 144 in the house. "My dad told me mirrors are like flies on the wall," he recounted. "They see what we can only imagine." He opened the door to the master suite.

"W-Wow!" Kim exclaimed.

"Fit for a king, huh?"

Drawn to a collage of framed photographs, Kim stepped over to the north wall and studied each attentively. "Is your Mister Bruno in any of these?"

"Mrs. Lowry thinks he might be one of the children pictured."

She removed a photo, brushed off a cobweb, glanced at the backside and then carefully re-hung it. "You think these were taken in this c-country? It reminds me of New Orleans."

"You been to New Orleans?"

"Yes. Two years ago during Mardi Gras with my parents and Aunt Nell. It was like being in a foreign c-country. What's in there? Where the light's on?"

"Master bath."

Kim drifted inside for a closer look. Jake held back to take advantage of the opportunity to sneak a peek at himself in a three-way, full-length dressing mirror.

"There's four more mirrors in there," she said, exiting the bath. Kim sauntered over to one of the bay windows, parted the sheers and mouthed 'wow' as she assimilated exceptional views of the Orme River's rocky bluffs. Jake turned out the bathroom light and followed into the shallow alcove till he stood immediately behind her to share the view. When she about-faced, they were belly button to belt buckle. She looked up.

"You ever going to kiss me?"

He hesitated just long enough to take her hands in his.

"Would now be okay?"

"Yes."

"Promise not to kick me?"

"Yes."

She elevated to tiptoe height; eyes closed. The kiss lasted until Jake could no longer hold his breath. He wondered how many mirrors in the room witnessed the event. Did those mirrors also have ears? Did they eavesdrop on her sighs that tempted like an unopened, defenseless Whitman Sampler? Did they foresee her revelation later that evening this was the first time she had kissed a boy she liked. Or his disclosure of what he saw peering up her skirt in the orchard? Emphatically contradicted by her insistence she <u>was</u> wearing underwear, a thong.

As the tour progressed, so did their closeness; intimacy as prescient as it was inexpert. She favored locking her arms around his neck, running her hands through his hair, and pulling him close. His hands preferred to caress and gently stroke her arms, shoulders, and back. In an embrace at the bottom of the staircase to the servant's quarters, they explored the contour of each other's hips. Under the gaze of a bighorn sheep head mount in the billiard room, Kim's hands found their way under his sweatshirt and caressed his bare back. While viewing post-Impressionist artwork in the ballroom, their hands learned the shape of each other's buttocks. In the library, she studied the map and summary of the Battle of Jenkins Knob, a pre-Civil War stand-off between area Free Staters and a marauding band of pro-slavery border ruffians. The reported outcome was that one drunk literally shot himself in the foot; the recorded version was that one man got shot in the foot. Jake approached her from behind. He found her hands and kissed the nape of her neck. She responded by raising his hands and crossing them with hers across her chest. While in the parlor viewing Sharon DeCritt's oil portrait of Angus cattle and egrets, Kim slipped up behind him and wriggled her small hands into his front pockets, sending a shiver coursing through his body. Almost an hour passed before they stood facing a pair of majestic, hand-carved mahogany pocket doors to the ground floor music room. Jake determined it fitting as the tour's grand finale.

"This can be difficult sometimes," he said, wrestling a thumb latch twice the size of his thumb. "Henry says it only works if you hold your mouth just right." Latch disengaged; Jake rolled one of the doors part way into its cove.

The largest, most magnificent room in the house, nearly three stories high, the music room featured a southern exposure and windows on three of its six sides. More than two dozen large, live potted plants and palm trees infused hues of green throughout the space, greatly enhancing the room's three-dimensionality. The sun in its seasonal slump created an array of distorted window shapes stretching up the room's north wall obligating its twelve-mirror décor to reflect light in opposite directions. Walter Bruno's oil portrait in full Napoleonic mien hung suspended in their midst. She asked if the black Persian cat in the crook of Bruno's arm had a name. Jake shrugged and pointed out a football-size meteorite. She admired the damask furniture. The dark red settee with carved head arm rests was nearly a twin to the one in her Aunt Nell's home. It was, however, the room's centerpiece, a late 19th century Victorian Broadwood grand concert piano of Indian rosewood that captured her attention. Situated on a raised dais beneath a crystal chandelier, its faded red dust cover intact, Kim could not resist.

"C-can you help me pull the c-cover off?"

Their final tug at the cover sent up a small cloud of dust. A glittering swirl of specks, illuminated by invasive shafts of autumn sunlight, roiled like a mushroom cloud.

"Pixie dust!" she proclaimed.

Together, they propped open the lid, revealing its inner mechanism.

"Oh, my gosh! There's a bird nest in here."

Jake leaned closer to inspect. He scanned the compilation of odds and ends and recalled seeing similar nests in Stuber's Garage. "Pack rat," he declared.

"Is it s-still in there?"

"Don't see 'im."

Kim settled herself on the bench and scooted it forward slightly. She depressed several of the piano's keys and generated a series of D-flat major chords. "This is really c-cool," she cooed.

"It looks ancient."

"It has issues. When was it tuned last? Oh, well, find a s-seat. No applause or autographs till I'm finished."

The piece was not familiar to him. He marveled at her dexterity, her self-confident manner. Neither of them was aware of Joan Lowry standing in the doorway, listening in on the impromptu concert. Upon the last chord having been wholly absorbed by the plaster and lath walls and exposed walnut beams, Kim stood on the piano bench and took a formal bow. Joan entered the room, applauding enthusiastically, "*Brava!* Chopin's 'Minute Waltz'," she heralded. "My sister's all-time favorite piece to perform." She approached Kim and extended her hand. "I'm Joan Lowry."

"I'm Kim," she responded, stepping down from the piano bench with an assist from Jake.

"How long have you been playing?"

"Since I was seven."

"You must be the one from Oklahoma everyone calls Peaches."

Kim arched an eyebrow and looked to Jake.

"Yes," he blushed. "But she has a real name."

"Has Jake been a satisfactory tour guide?"

"He has."

278

"Perhaps we should promote him to docent status. That would make you something of a legacy, Jake. Sharon DeCritt served on the Museum's Board for years as our docent coordinator.

Oh, well, sorry to interrupt. Today is plant watering day."

"I think they've already been watered."

"Oh?"

Jake recounted their happenstance encounter with Violet Brisby and her comment that they had given all the plants a drink.

"They? She had a helper?"

"Yes."

"Sounds like I might be on a wild goose chase."

Joan Lowry stepped over to the potted palm next to the piano and burrowed her fingers into the soil. "They missed this one." She strode over to a feral looking schefflera and finger tested the soil. "0 for two."

"Maybe they didn't come in here," he postulated. "Getting that dumb door latch to work can be tricky."

"Do I know who she was with?"

"Yes. I'm sure you do."

"Male or female?" she said, rotating the schefflera one hundred eighty degrees and harvesting a yellowed frond.

"Male."

"She wearing her hair up or down?" Joan quizzed, ambling back toward the couple.

"Down," said Kim and Jake in unison.

"Hmm…sounds like Violet is up to her old tricks. Do you have any questions about this place?" Any gaps I can fill in?"

"No, ma'am."

"Okay, then. Finish your tour. I'm through interrupting."

"We're done," said Jake. Joan told Kim she was glad they met, that she was welcome anytime and hoped she was enjoying her visit to Waltsburg. He handed Joan the set of keys and informed her of the unresponsive light switch and showed her the pack rat's nest. He and Kim lowered the piano's lid and replaced the dust cover. Curious, Jake checked the dun-colored soil of a philodendron in the foyer on their way out. '0 for three,' he deduced. Kim paused, peered into a gilded, oval mirror and reapplied lipstick.

"Ready?"

"Always," Kim answered, fronting him. "Do you like the c-color?"

"Sure."

"Hold s-still. I think you have s-some, too," as she traced a thumb across his lower lip.

He ventured a quick look in the mirror. "I don't see any."

Kim threw her arms around his neck and kissed him full on the mouth. "N-now you will."

That afternoon, Kim phoned her mother and Aunt Nell but not before calling her friend Chana to make sure family had not called to check on her. Early Saturday evening, they drove to Granfield for bowling and pizza. Both occurred after Doyle's six o'clock closed AA meeting in Bowl-O-Rama's all-purpose room. On the drive home, Doyle informed that Eric Carver's dog, Rocky, had been hit by a truck on Main that morning. The story, as he heard it from Dan Bruner, who heard it from Parise, who heard it from Jimmy, the dog impulsively bolted across the street in pursuit of a stray cat. An eyewitness fetched Eric from his pinball play with Jimmy and Kirk at Loads of Fun. Eric and Jimmy carried the dog to the vet's office, but Dr. Manning pronounced the injuries untreatable. Rocky had to be euthanized to transcend the suffering.

Though Kim had yet to mention Jake to anyone back home, she planted the thought of him visiting her and her family over the Christmas holiday. Jake reminded her he would be working full-time at the bank. She pointed out Christmas Day fell on a Friday this year. Surely the bank would be closed for the holiday till the following Monday. Maybe even close early on Christmas Eve? They agreed to work something out. How Kim would break the news to her family she had a boyfriend was another matter entirely.

CHAPTER 53
NIGHT SHIFT

Sunday – December 20

Parked in front of the Waltsburg State Bank, Davis Spellmeier kept his patrol car's heater on low and sipped at his last half lid of thermos coffee. He made a mental note of the burned-out streetlight at the corner of Corrientes Street and Main. He glanced at his watch. It was 3:35 a.m. Five hours from now he would be home eating two eggs sunny side up, bacon, two slices of wheat toast with strawberry jam, and sipping fresh-made coffee served up in his *Have Gun Will Travel* souvenir mug.

Davis hailed from three generations of family farming. He had no interest in agriculture after high school graduation. Following his second semester at Ormestrong County Community College where he met the girl he would marry, he opted to pursue a career in law enforcement. Completing his academy training second in his class, he was hired by Eugene Lassiter the week following formal graduation ceremonies. Gene took him under his wing and spent many spare hours seeing that Davis's on-the-job training was thorough.

This early morning, he patrolled residential neighborhoods enjoying Christmas lights, nativity scenes, and sundry holiday décor. His drive through the pitch-dark parking lot of Memorial Park reminded him of the third line from Clement Moore's oft recited seasonal poem, "...not a creature was stirring..." By the time he pulled into the country club's lot, he was humming *Silent Night* as he could remember only six lines of Moore's ditty. Driving by DeCritt's Barber Shop evoked memory of a comment made by a youthful ride-along one Saturday evening about this time of year. At age twelve, Jake Book thought he might like to be a policeman one day. On a cruise along Main, Jake naively quoted his father on the town's Christmas décor "…like putting costume jewelry on a corpse."

Two blocks north of the barber shop, Davis spotted an approaching vehicle in his rearview mirror northbound in the southbound lane. He doused his headlights and made a U-turn. The car pulled up in front of the post office and parked parallel to the curb. He watched its driver step inside, leaving the driver's side door open and car running. As he drew closer, he recognized Violet Brisby's gold Buick Electra. He pulled alongside and rolled down the passenger side window. Clutching a fistful of mail, out she came clad in a housecoat, topped by a vintage mink stole with heads and feet; her hair coiled in a maze of curlers, her face white as grade school construction paper paste.

"Morning, Violet!" he greeted, startling her.

"Merry Christmas!" she responded and drove off.

To Davis, Waltsburg resembled the quiet inside a mausoleum this time of morning. Then it struck him as if he had stolen something. Were not the uniform, stacked rows of mailboxes inside the Post Office like miniature mausoleum vaults? And wasn't the postmaster tantamount to God, there to receive all those in need? He shook his head, 'Too much idle time on my hands when I dream up weird things like that.' He rolled up the passenger window and decided to swing by the Bruno Museum.

Spellmeier swiveled his door-mounted spotlight across the Bruno acreage. He picked up several pairs of green eyes in the distance, critters running errands that mattered, no doubt. As the beam of light swept the front portico of the mansion, a raccoon stared back at him and scampered out of sight. It reminded him again of the ride-along years ago when Jake chattered non-stop. The stories recounted from the previous summer's Boy Scout outing at Camp *TaWaKoNi* with the coon-like blackened eye sockets, harassment by the Knaakt twins, and lingering chigger bites. He recalled commenting to Jake that childish pranks were a part of growing up but thought better of relating any of his own experiences. In his opinion, Jake was too young to make the connection between 'boys-will-be-boys' and 'grown-men-can-be-ridiculous'. How could he forget the chuckle at the October Antler Club meeting when members rigged the coin flip, so Jake had to foot the group's tab? Davis took a swallow of his coffee infused with grounds. He stopped outside the gated entrance of the Bruno estate and poured it out. He yawned, gripped the steering wheel, stretched his arms forward pushing himself back against the seat, and rotated his head side-to-side. He secured the squeak-squealing iron gate, adjusted the heater up a notch, and backtracked along Orme River Drive to the stop sign at Main.

Cruising the double wide boulevard at a marching band's pace, he noted the blinking red light atop the six-barrel Orme River Valley CO-OP grain elevator and lighted clock on the bank building. He crossed the tracks where the train station was trimmed in traditional holiday lights. The yet lifeless Barney's Restaurant appeared defunct as the Cozmos Theater. The site of the recently razed Atlantic Hotel stirred the sensation that something should still be there. Where the boulevard narrowed to two lanes, Davis stifled a yawn driving past the former Albrecht butcher shop, its ground floor windows shuttered with plywood. Back left, a vacant lot, site of the town's tornado siren tower, then the former Knaakt & Sons Moving and Storage Company building. Catty-corner, across the street, a dark Tackle Box Tavern, alley, and fluorescent lighting from inside Loads of Fun Laundromat that illuminated the sidewalk. Davis coasted to a stop. Rhythmic, strobe-like flickers emanated from inside the building. Owner Leland Skalicky was renowned for procrastinating repairs. Davis knew, however, a flickering fluorescent bulb tended to emit irregular flashes. 'Better have a look,' he thought.

CHAPTER 54
ROCKY DID NOTHING WRONG

Though details were scant, Waltsburg was abuzz as people learned the news. The closed-door meeting in Chief Lassiter's office with Preston Carver and his wife began as soon as they arrived from Granfield. Officer Spellmeier would repeat the story to Preston's ex-wife, her closest friend, and Darcy Cage over the noon hour when they arrived from Lawrence.

"Tell Mr. Carver what you saw, exactly as you saw it, from the time you entered Icky's place," Gene said to Davis.

"We not gonna wait for Darryl?"

"He's on his way."

Davis related that when he entered the laundromat, he found the pinball machine tipped over, shattered glass everywhere, and still connected to the wall outlet. The light behind one of the hula dancers on a remnant of unbroken backglass emitted throb-like flashes. "It was humming, making a loud clicking noise. I unplugged the machine thinking it might be a fire hazard. I found a metal folding chair thrown through the window of Icky's office."

Gene interrupted, "ROCKY DID NOTHING WRONG" was scrawled on the back wall."

"I headed back to the office to call Icky. Thought he ought-a know what happened as soon as possible."

Someone rapped on Gene's door. Darryl Manning entered. Once Darryl was settled, Davis continued. "As I drove past Darryl's building, something struck me as odd. I backed up and noticed a light on inside, toward the back, where the exam rooms are. So, I pulled into the parking lot and drove to the rear of the building where I observed a car with Douglas County tags."

"Eric's car," Gene interjected.

"Darryl's back door was open."

Spellmeier concluded there was little doubt Eric Carver committed suicide by intra-venously injecting pentobarbital. The empty vials on the exam room counter and size of the syringe yet embedded in his forearm suggested a self-administered dose large enough to euthanize a horse. Naked, the words BULLET SPONGE tattooed across his chest, Eric lay splayed on an exam table.

Subsequent interviews with Kirk Michaels and Jimmy Baguelt uncovered a plausible explanation of Eric's Loads of Fun vandalism. The week before Thanksgiving, Leland Skalicky banned Rocky from the premises after a customer complained the dog had barked at her children. The morning Rocky was run over by a truck, Kirk and Jimmy listened to Eric rant. He placed the blame for Rocky's death squarely on Icky's shoulders. In Eric's mind, had Rocky been allowed inside as he had been for years, the cat chase would have never happened.

CHAPTER 55
IN MEMORIAM

Wednesday - December 23, 1970

Bordering Waltsburg's country club golf course, Pierce Village Cemetery lay nestled in buffalo grass and wild brome. Salient windswept juts of granite, marble, and fieldstone memorialized the reckoning. A sequestered Manifest Destiny roster of pioneers, immigrants, sodbusters, and following generations rested, swallowed by a remorseless prairiescape. The names and epitaphs from a leonine yore mostly forgotten, blunted by each successive generation's fixation on the then-and-now or tomorrow's forecast.

The metal handles of the casket were cold as freezer rime. Jake talked Conger out of his right-hand glove. The amateur pall bearer drill team toted the casket to the grave site, avoiding errant golf balls along their path. Reverend Cage presided. The assembled listened, then bowed and prayed to the Invisible on behalf of the deceased. Eric Carver's angst preserved like the fossil of an extinct mammal, as questions churned in the minds of those left behind.

Under his breath, Kirk Michaels called her Carver's whore. Jake hardly recognized Darcy Cage as a bleached blond. Gravid with Eric's child and big as a partially inflated dirigible, Darcy stuck close beside Eric's mother and another woman. Along with the couple he had seen with Eric at the Tackle Box Tavern the eve of Black Moon Monday, they huddled near the freshly dug rectangle opposite Preston Carver and his wife. Darcy's face was flush with grief. She wiped her eyes and nose time and again with a handkerchief and made eye contact with only the ground. The mood of the small gathering was stoic, same as Jake's grandmother's graveside service when he was eleven. He remembered his father's comment on the drive home that death is a blacksmith of tears.

The sentiments espoused by the pastor meant little to Jake, until "...but Eric's spirit lives on in the collective memory of kith and kin," moved him to recall his last Eric Carver sighting nearly two months ago playing pinball at Loads of Fun the morning of the quail hunt. Since Eric's return from Viet Nam, all their encounters had been brief: the country club the evening of the July 4ᵗʰ fireworks show, Eric's last slow-pitch softball game the night of the tornado warning, their pinball play that ended badly on Jake's birthday, and the morning the Emporia Gazette reporter showed up at his uncle's shop. Jake considered Eric a long-time friend. His sorrow peaked during the prior evening's visitation in the mortuary's chapel. His tear ducts momentarily irrigated his eyes as he overcame the lump in his throat but bereaved, he was not. His tears refused to fall. Eric was no baby thrush. Except for the blanched expressionless face, now clean-shaven, and his hair groomed in a college-boy Princeton cut, Eric looked like the Eric he knew best from their high school days.

On the short drive back to town, Kirk recounted the scene from the vet's exam room. Mesmerized, he and Jimmy Baguelt watched Rocky lick the tears from Eric's face as Dr. Manning euthanized the canine with a lethal injection of pentobarbital. Kirk recalled watching Rocky's tongue stop, still on Eric's cheek. It was the only time he ever saw Jimmy tear up.

After dropping Kirk by home, Jake confessed to Conger that he'd had another dream about the barn wood thief. "This time I was browsing the obit section of the *Kansas City Star* when my eyes were drawn to a blank space headed only by the thief's name." Conger remarked he hadn't given a second thought to the event and said in his opinion, it was not worth worrying about. He got what was coming to him. If it was any consolation, Blanco felt the same way. Jake wondered if his dreams were anything like what Eric Carver experienced. Did Jack Nagel and T. Robert Friscote still dream about their war experiences? Maybe Nonny had them too? Would they ever go away?

Driving back to the bank, Jake's thoughts turned to his father's reply to his high school graduation announcement. Still neatly folded in its original envelope in his top dresser drawer, the philosophical ramble resonated with the moment. 'Every day is a new beginning,' he wrote, 'from the moment one opens his eyes. Subconsciously surveying one's surroundings to verify all is in the same order as the night before: clothes slung over the back of a chair, curtains pulled shut, and miscellaneous clutter in prior arrangement. We take for granted that dawn comes after dark, baseball after winter.' Insignificant as it seems, it all matters, according to Emerson Book. 'Each day we are escorted toward the inevitable by happenstance, choices, and change that shape our lives more than we would like to admit. From start to finish we strive to maintain the balance between our feelings of being lost in the crowd and at a loss without it. What quality of life can be devised by merely reacting to stimuli? As a child, didn't you learn quickest when you took risks or challenged authority?' Hence, his father summarized, 'we plea, we reach out to a greater power to affect outcomes. We thrive on routine, know from experience, and worship that sixth sense of order especially during periods of uncertainty.' In that same dresser drawer was an unopened Valentine postmarked February 1965 addressed to Susie Olsen stamped: Return to Sender / Addressee Unknown.

During a lull at his teller's station, Jake remembered he and Donna planned to do some last-minute Christmas shopping in Granfield that evening. She needed to redeem a layaway and he was still undecided about a gift for Kim. The bank posted its Christmas Eve close as 3 p.m. Shortly thereafter, he planned to be on the road to Bartlesville with Kim's white cowboy boots boxed-wrapped-ribboned-and-bowed riding shotgun.

#

"Hop up here, we got time," said Donna. "Stores are open till nine tonight."

"How about just around the ears?" said Jake. "I don't want-a look like a new haircut."

Donna draped a cape over his shoulders. "How did it go this morning?"

"Okay. I guess."

"Very many show up?"

"Nope."

"Darcy there?"

"Yep."

"That had to be awkward for Reverend Cage. Don't you think? Word is she's living with Eric's mother in Lawrence. Want-a grab something to eat in Granfield? I'm starved." Together, they closed the salon and got into Donna's car. "The first place Doyle ever took me was to Gibby's," Donna reminisced as she turned onto the highway.

"Was he sober?"

"Yes. He was. I figured it was payback for me driving him home a week earlier when he was too drunk to drive."

"That's how you met?"

"Yep. At the Oasis. You know it as the Scorpio or Tackle Box. I was the new girl in town, working as a stylist at the Palace Salon. Had my divorce decree, a beauty college diploma, a four-year old daughter, a Siamese cat named Gung-ho, and not much to look forward to.

#

Donna and Jake sat in a booth at Wong's Cafe in the heart of Granfield's downtown business district.

"Lot-a people out tonight," said Jake.

"Last minute shoppers, like us. So, what do you have in mind for Kim?" she queried, chop-sticking her first bite.

Jake accepted Donna's advice as if she were a parent. Her no-nonsense, reassuring approach: Keep it simple. It's not the gift *per se*. It's the thought. Kim would like whatever he chose because it was from him. Would the petite bracelet with diamond chips he picked out be enough? He kept his fingers crossed.

CHAPTER 56
AND HEAVEN AND NATURE SING

Friday/Saturday – December 25/26

Days in advance of Jake's visit, Kim made sure select Oklahoma refrigerators were amply stocked with Coca Cola. On Christmas Day, he overcame his trepidations of meeting the Fitzgerald family members with his 'yes sir, no sir, yes ma'am, no ma'am' skill set. He helped himself to the roast turkey, bread stuffing, clove studded baked ham, mashed potatoes, gravy, buttery sweet carrots, jellied cranberry sauce, and homemade rolls. For dessert he could choose either mince pie or Christmas pudding, all of which were more welcoming than the barrage of questions directed his way. 'Where are you from?' 'Where's that?' 'How was the drive down?' 'What do you do for a living?' 'Are you a Notre Dame football fan?'

Kim later intimated to Jake, the war, the recession, and a stranger in the family midst tempered the festive occasion. To her, the atmosphere was too restrained. That did not keep her from placing her hand on Jake's thigh under the table every chance she got. Upon finishing his pie, Jake excused himself to use the bathroom. When he came out, Kim was waiting, pulled him back inside, and shut the door. She threw her arms around his neck and kissed him full on the mouth. "I really missed you."

After dinner, Kim jumped at the opportunity to take three young cousins and Jake to a nearby park playground. That evening, while her father sipped his Jack Daniel's, more pointed queries were directed Jake's way. Asked if he attended church, Jake answered jokingly he was a lapsed closet Methodist. Kim's father, Owen, launched into a comparison of his sister Nellie and Jake. Kim countered saying Aunt Nell went to church.

"When she gets a wild hair up her ass."

"Daddy!?"

When Owen poured himself another two fingers of whiskey, Kim's mother begged off saying it had been a long day, she was tired and going to bed.

"Then we got the devil's spawn there on the peach farm in Nowata," he continued. "We should-a filed charges against her when we had the chance."

"Daddy…"

He drained his drink and set the glass down hard on the coffee table. "See you two in the morning."

On the drive to Tulsa the next day, Kim apologized for her father's surly behavior. She explained Aunt Nell and her father were more like business partners than brother and sister. Nell relied on him, an electrical contractor, to service the commercial properties in the family portfolio. Those jobs provided a steady workflow in the iffy economy, but not enough to prevent him and his brother from having to lay off three F & F Electric employees recently.

"I'm glad you came," said Kim as she snorkeled the last drops of her cherry limeade under the canopy at Pennington's Drive-In. "Did you like the movie?"

"I liked the company I was with."

"You're not into war movies?"

"They're tough to watch right now."

"Ss-sorry about your friend."

"Thanks. He was a completely different person when he got back from Vietnam. Completely different."

"I love my bray-bracelet," she said, holding her arm out. "Do you like the watch I picked out?"

"Very much."

Kim handed him her empty burger basket. "You must be a lucky charm. Finding a place to park here on the first drive through is a first for me."

"Don't see traffic like this at home. Is it always this crazy?"

"I think the whole ss-city of Tulsa is out today."

Jake glanced at his new watch. "Shouldn't we better get going?" he asked as he placed the remaining scraps and trash on the window tray.

"I told her we'd be there by s-six. <u>Do not</u> tell my aunt we came here to eat, okay? Sh-she'll be upset I didn't bring her a ss-slice of their Black Bottom pie."

"Got time for a belching contest?" Jake grinned.

"Nn-no." Kim waved a car hop over. "Let's go," she said.

As they pulled into Nell's drive, Jake asked if she ever got lost in such a large home.

"Of course not, one room leads to another." She explained Aunt Nell inherited the home from Kim's grandmother whose husband had purchased it from a wealthy oil company executive. Entering the front door, Wags, a snarky, eight-year-old Yorkshire terrier, tried to convince Jake the WELCOME mat on the front porch did not mean him. Kim whisked the dog off to her aunt's bedroom and shut the door. After showing Jake to an upstairs bedroom and copping a kiss and a grope, they joined Aunt Nell in the kitchen and Kim prepared her aunt a light meal. When Nell finished, they adjourned to the great room. While Kim fetched her aunt's usual after-supper scotch on the rocks, Jake appraised his surroundings. He noted house plants conspicuously outnumbered furniture and Kim was clearly more at home here. Nell apologized for her dog's behavior and lamented her bridge group decided to postpone their card playing till after the holidays. Kim asked her aunt if she planned to attend church tomorrow. Nell responded no.

"Oh, good," said Kim, "we can ss-sleep in."

"How was the movie?" Nell queried.

"Good," answered Jake.

"I've not been to a movie at The Brook in ages," said Nell.

"Jacob's not into war movies," Kim added. "Kimmy told me about your friend. Such a waste."

Nell was curious about Doona Falls Ranch she had heard so much about. Jake invited her to visit someday. He would personally make time to give her a tour. Kim told her she would have to buy hiking boots, a cowboy hat, and learn how to sss-spit in the wind. Kim announced she and Jake were going to take a short walk around the neighborhood and invited her aunt to come along. Nell declined and asked Kimmy to replenish her drink and put Wags out back before they went. Their stroll mimicked the stop-go pace of Waltsburg's Fourth of July parade.

Frequent pauses to hug, smooch, and caress cut into Kim's narratives of the stately homes. The grandeur reminded Jake of the Bruno mansion.

"Getting chilly out there," Kim commented upon their return.

"Air smells like it might rain," said Jake.

Wags immediately objected to Jake's presence, so he was again remanded to his owner's bedroom. The three chatted till nine-thirty. Nell excused herself, announcing it was time to retire and listen to some New Orleans jazz. Kim let Jake use the bathroom first to get ready for bed as she planned to take a shower. Jake asked if she wanted company. "I wish," she responded, saying the shower stall contained barely enough room for one. Jake grinned from ear to ear. She called him a tease.

The night light next to the bed created an assortment of vague shadows. Wide awake, Jake wondered if he had made a favorable impression with Kim's parents and Aunt Nell. Had he followed Donna's advice to just be himself? He fluffed his pillow and turned on his side. Tomorrow was the long drive home; Monday, another back-to-work day. A highlight of arriving home tomorrow afternoon would be gifts to open under the tree. His bedroom door opened and quietly closed.

"Jacob? You awake?" Kim whispered aloud.

She tiptoed across the room, turned her back, and hiked up her nightgown. "Remember what a thong looks like?" Jake squinted trying to make out as much detail as possible. She let the gown drop, unplugged the nightlight, and told him to scoot over.

CHAPTER 57
THE DREAM
AWAY FROM HOME

Sunday – December 27

Jake pried the door open with a crowbar. He picked his way through the cheerless crowd to the open, second story bay window on the far side of the master bedroom. Momentarily aware his shoulders served as a carpenter's level parallel with the window's sill, a surge of crisp air ambushed his senses. He sneezed. "Gesundheit!" Someone blessed him.

Across the way, chime echoed from a church spire upholstered with hard frost. Its hula hoop size lighted clock the shape of a bottle cap lettered 'It's the real thing' intrigued him. Below, men in fatigues and boonie hats, weapons slung, waited at parade rest. They lined the approach to the edifice's main entrance, backs turned. The wreath-bedecked doors stood open. Light glowed yellow. Jake's first impression: a Currier and Ives lithograph, its greeting card snow glistening anew. He searched for a Nativity scene but did not see one. 'What's the occasion?' On command, the soldiers sang 'When Johnny Comes Marching Home Again,' the melody blaring from the Divco's loudspeakers. Trailed by a graffitied white cargo van with no driver, the converted milk delivery truck lumbered up the double-wide boulevard on the wrong side of the median. The word VET embossed on its side panels; it came to a halt in front of the church.

*'The old church bell will peel with joy.
Hurrah! Hurrah!
To welcome home our darling boy
Hurrah! Hurrah!'*

A blond, winged angel robed in garlands of rose hips, stepped forward trailed by a small herd of goats. She stopped at the edge of the top step and set down the handbasket of apples she carried on her arm. Heels of her polished white boots together, toes apart, she saluted the Stars and Stripes. Lone Cloud, in red and black war paint, jumped out and opened the Divco's rear doors. Six white-frocked attendants with black armbands carted an iron lung coffin down the church steps at a calculated cadence and loaded it onto the truck. The music stopped midstanza. A man with a bullhorn appeared. Clad in black, topped with a cleric's collar, he resembled a Black Cow sundae with a marshmallow dollop. The silence was deafening, the narrative brusque.

'Let it be said …he volunteered to serve. He learned to crawl. He trained to kill. Conditioned to obey, he answered curtain calls on command. All the King's forces were brought to bear. So young these men, able bodied and all. From the here and now. We humbly beseech. Hear us O'Lord. Tears to dust. In God We Trust.'

A choral Amen sealed the ceremony. Rocky howled from inside the corner phone booth. The goats lingered but the rose-hipped girl with wings had disappeared. 'Where did she go?' Jake turned to ask if anyone in the room knew where she went. No one was there. But of course. The Bruno mansion had been vacant for more than thirty years.

*'We'll give him a hearty welcome and then
Hurrah! Hurrah!
The men will cheer and the boys will shout
The ladies they will all turn out'*

Alone in the room, Jake heard his father's voice, 'Hurry up and get dressed!'

'Dressed for what?' he deliberated. The door burst open, ripped from its Victorian hinges by a kihap shout. The girl with wings stood arms akimbo, elegantly rendered in Marvel comic book ink. He blinked and rubbed his eyes with cold hands.

'D'you brush your teeth yet?' Jake heard his father holler. 'It's getting late. I only have time to read one Dr. Seuss before I drive back tonight.'

'Can she listen, too?' Jake urged, as he donned his pj's.
'Who?'
'Her!' he opined, pointing to the figure in the doorway.
'I'd rather go to the park,' she responded in a bubble of comic-speak.
'Now? It's dark out.'
'I like to play in the dark,' she bubbled.

> *'Their choicest pleasures then display.*
> *Hurrah! Hurrah!*
> *And let each one perform some part,*
> *To fill with joy the warrior's heart...'*

'Race you to the top,' she challenged. 'Ready?' At the count of 'on your mark, get set,' they shimmied up the smooth fourteen-foot steel support poles of the playground's swing set. Halfway there and in the lead, Jake felt an internal smolder building in that place between his legs. The more energy he expended edging upward to achieve his goal, the more he repressed outright laughter.

> *'Get ready for the Jubilee*
> *Hurrah! Hurrah!'*

Within an arm's length of victory, he was consumed by the primal burn of la petite mort. Vitality sapped, savoire-faire nonplussed, he slithered back to square one, embarrassed. On the other hand, his cheery counterpart folded her wings and effortlessly glided back down. Jake concluded, 'Maybe it isn't the same for girls...'

> *'...when Johnny comes marching home.'*

When he woke, Jake was addled by unfamiliar surroundings. The second-floor bedroom in Aunt Nell's house was warm enough to melt butter in nothing-flat. He held the phosphorus flecked face of his new Timex up to his nose. It was 2:11. When he cranked the dormer window open, he could hear the patter of light rain and a dog barking in the distance. He retrieved his underwear from the tangled sheet and crawled back into bed.

CHAPTER 58
ACCORDING TO JOHN

Saturday – January 31, 1971

"Psst! Hey, Rodge! You awake?"

John Griever got no response.

"See anything yet?" Only arias of silence accompanied the cold. "Atta boy!" he whispered loudly. "You remembered what I told ya. No talkin' 'less absolutely necessary." Roger was an agreeable sort, a good listener, a near-perfect hunting companion.

At first light, John surveyed the line of timber before him from his crow's nest. Not one leaf twitched, or bird called in the frigid January air that was as still as a puddle. He yearned for a seat cushion from one of his dining room chairs; the deer stand was not built for comfort. Ol' man Teichgraber, his closest neighbor and most enthusiastic deer jerky customer, phoned the night before. He had spotted a white tail buck and five does grazing his land at sunset. The buck, in his opinion, sported a trophy rack. It was exactly two weeks after deer hunting season officially closed. According to John, however, what was on his land was his.

In the absolute absence of live movement around him, John wondered how many others like Roger lay expediently buried in hastily marked or unmarked graves. He imagined the prairie as a potter's field of the forgotten, of voices silenced, destinies short-changed, and hearts denied their throb. Had anyone words to say upon Roger's interment? Was he excited about Nonny's choice of sweaters, or would he rather exchange it for something more masculine? Would he laugh at Jake's Al Jolson one-liner? Did he mind being on display? Might he be happier if he were returned to the elements to decompose in private, the tickle of a tree root at his ribs? John meditated on the closing line of Reverend Cage's New Year's sermon, "Forever may not be as long a wait as we think."

Griever's thread of conjecture was broken by the sound of movement, the scrunch of footfalls across a mantle of brittle leaves. He stiffened and rotated his head ever so slowly. A version of hunter's joy set in as he watched a rafter of wild turkeys forage for food.

CHAPTER 59
CLOUD NINE

Monday – February 16

"Remember when you treated me to an Apple Brown Betty at Gibby's on Valentine's Day?" said Donna, out of the blue.

"I do. What made you think of that?" Doyle asked, as he prepped Donna for a trim in her salon.

"Not sure. Time of year, maybe? I have the craves for something sweet," she said, stifling a cough. "I need something to soothe this sore throat."

"Okay, Miss Pileaux, what are we going to do with this today?"

"I'm letting it grow out."

"Elizabeth Taylor's Cleopatra look is still popular in some countries."

"Oh, aren't you Mr. Funny this morning? Last time home, Papa told me I look too grown up with it short."

"He wants his little girl back. In that case we'll need to do color, or you'll have to hold <u>very</u> still so I can snip out the gray."

"Trim the bangs."

"That's it?"

"You heard from Jake yet?"

"Called last night about 9:30."

"And you're just <u>now</u> telling me?! What's the verdict?"

"Her father said yes. He proposed. She said yes. He gave her the ring. Said he'd drive back this evening."

"Yea! Three for three. He's on a roll."

"Floating on Cloud Nine somewhere over Oklahoma."

"Good for Jake. They set a date?"

"June something. You'll have to ask him. Think Jake's kicked the tires and looked under the hood yet?"

"Yes."

"Taken a test drive?"

"No."

"How short do you want the bangs?"

"We'll have to celebrate."

"Yep. How much shorter do you…?"

"I need to run to the store. What can I fix? We need to pick up some champagne, shouldn't I?"

"Donna?!"

"Just so they don't hang in my eyes. June what? Didn't he say? That's only three, four months from now." Donna could hardly contain herself, let alone sit still or follow directions. The thought of Jake getting married was the thrill of rowing a boat merrily down a stream. As Doyle lightly combed and snipped, she mind-shopped for a new dress.

"Aren't you going to wave?" Doyle asked, breaking her train of thoughts.

"What?"

"Outside. In the window."

Catharine Mixx in sweats and a red knit skull cap jogged in place, waving at them exaggeratedly. Donna waved back.

"Want me to let her in?"

"No. Look busy. You know she and Henry are an item now?"

"So I hear."

"I think it's a good match. Don't you?"

"No more Howdy Doody performances at Stuber's."

"What's that supposed to mean?"

"Nothing."

"You know the best thing about the engagement? It might take Jake's mind off Carver."

"That would be a good thing."

"I can make flan for dessert tonight."

"Jake would love that."

"Hold on a second." Donna hopped out of the salon chair.

"What're you doing?"

"Pen and paper. I need to write some things down before I forget," she said, re-settling herself and slipping a Sucrets lozenge in her mouth.

"I can't finish this with your head down."

"How long does it take to snip bangs?"

"Another minute. Assuming you sit still." Twice, Doyle placed a finger under Donna's chin and gently coaxed her head up. "When's the last time you sharpened these scissors?"

"You'd have a glass of champagne with us tonight, wouldn't you?"

"A swallow. Yes." He handed Donna a mirror. "How's that look?"

"It'll do."

Donna continued to write on the back of the spiral notebook that served as her appointment book. Doyle poked through her backbar drawers in search of a whetstone.

"By the way, I got a message from Jake's mom. She wanted to know how Jake was getting along."

"What did you tell her?"

"It came through her lawyer. I told him he had graduated from college, has a new job at the bank, and still likes to...."

"Bet she'll want her bride's maid dresses to be lavender."

"You're not listening."

"I've heard every word you said."

"Hearing and listening are two different things."

"I'm listening."

CHAPTER 60
NOBODY IS PERFECT

Sunday – March 14

Waltsburg's Whist Club had shrunk to four members. Like the Orme River Valley Quilting Club, frequency of get-togethers was haphazard. Only Violet Brisby and her long-time playing partner, Mrs. Eunice Hartwell, retained any genuine enthusiasm for the game. As a spur-of-the-moment substitute, this was Jake's first time ever to play whist and he felt more than a little awkward in the group.

Taught by a temperance/suffrage crusading mother as a way to pass the time while sequestered in various jails or makeshift detention centers, Violet was an artifact of passions and pastimes past. An only child, she saw little of her father, the Reverend Bertrand Brisby. An ardent member of Kansas' Anti-Saloon League, he spent inordinate amounts of time away from home. Ultimately, the firebrand politics of her parents led her down a non-conformist's path. When Violet came of age and began to entertain thoughts of marriage, she was well aware of the deft navigation skills required in a male-dominant culture. Four years ago, she legally changed her surname back to its original, the sixth name change overall.

"Were it not for marriage, I believe men would spend their entire lives thinking they had no faults whatsoever," said Violet, as she took her first trick, then led the king of diamonds.

"Nobody's perfect, Vye," Eunice mumbled.

"Phooey," Hanky exhaled under her breath, tossing the queen of diamonds that skittered across the table into Jake's lap.

"So, Merry's not feeling well?" Eunice asked, following suit with the trey.

"Apparently," Hanky said.

"Diamonds are trumps, right?" Jake asked.

"They are," replied Violet.

Jake followed suit with the nine spot. Violet scooted the cards her way, smartly gathered and bundled them as her second trick and studied her hand. The foursome noshed on a peanut and M & M's mix courtesy of their hostess. Jake nipped at the ice water he requested once he learned Violet had only tea, Sanka, and Green River soda to choose from. Whist reminded him of 10-point pitch *sans* bidding. Between hands, Jake reflected on Hanky's earlier explanation of the fierce rivalry between the Brisby/Hartwell duo and Hanky/Merry Belle combo. He knew how determined Hanky and Merry could be. Eunice was competitive but had a genial personality. Conversely, Violet was often arrogant to the point of being overbearing. She wore her emotions on her sleeve and hated to lose. Jake was no stranger to Violet's haughty disposition.

#

Though the Earth had completed three trips around the sun since the incident, Jake was sure she had not forgotten, let alone forgiven him or Wally for the unpleasant episode. Violet Brisby's exceptionally groomed, AKC registered King Charles spaniel *Miss Hoop-Dee-Doo*, nicknamed Doodle, lay quietly in the yard across the street tethered to a porch rail. She was in heat. Jake lolled in his front porch swing wholly absorbed in his college sociology text prepping for an exam. Violet pruned her trellised rose bushes, weeded, watered, and tended her late spring flora. When she toted a bushel basket of clippings to the trash barrel at the rear of the house, Wally pounced. Violet's panicked screams broke his concentration.

"That boy's dog should be shot!" Violet yowled at the three male guests in her formal living room. "I know how to operate a gun. I'll do it!" she fumed and disappeared into the hallway. Gene looked to Jake who was soaking wet, "We might have to cuff Wally and haul 'im in for questioning." Jake read Gene's twisted smile and relaxed for the moment. As he glanced about the room, Jake noted the baubles, stained ceiling plaster, and upright Victrola. A row of five urns arranged on the fireplace mantel roused his curiosity. Violet reappeared toting a hammered double-barrel shotgun. Suspecting Violet knew little about

303

guns or gun protocol, Gene asked her if it was registered with his office. Her furrowed brow betrayed her confusion, so he continued the ruse.

"Where'd you get this?" he asked as he coaxed the firearm from her grasp.

"My husband."

"Which one?"

"Mr. Gustafson. He was a crack shot in his day."

Davis Spellmeier leaned forward, "Looks like an antique."

Gene broke open the breach and held it up toward the window to inspect the inside of the twin cylinders.

"When's the last time it was fired?"

"When he was alive."

Gene switched on a bridge lamp with its red and gold embroidered silk *chenille* and bead shade emitting a flamboyant glow in the otherwise dismal setting and checked the gun's provenance. "W. Powell & Son. You familiar with that maker?" Gene asked.

"That a twelve gauge?"

"Ten gauge. Here, feel how heavy it is," handing the firearm to Davis. "I remember ol' Pere Gustafson. That man had more up-'n'-at-'em than Pete Rose. He was quite the dancer I recall."

"The best," Violet sighed.

"My father loved to polka," said Gene.

Jake perceived a mood swing in Violet's face, her stern countenance softening.

"Afraid I'm a little rusty," she said.

"That makes two of us," Gene responded. "Where's Wally?"

"Home. In the house."

"Where's your dog, Violet?"

"In her box. In the bedroom. She's not happy."

"How do we know this?"

"She won't talk to me. Just lies on her blanket, not moving."

"How'd you get so wet?" he asked Jake.

"I tried to separate them."

"And..."

"They were stuck together. When I lifted Wally up, her dog wouldn't come off."

Davis turned his back trying to stifle a laugh.

"I sprayed them with the garden hose," Violet interjected.

"Did that do the trick?"

"Kind-a," Jake mumbled.

"That mongrel violated my Doodle!" bristled Violet.

Davis stepped over to the front door, hand over his mouth, index finger and thumb pinching his nostrils shut, trying his damnedest not to burst out laughing. Jake warily back-pedaled toward the door.

"This is not a laughing matter," said Violet.

"Indeed, it's not, dear," Gene consoled, gently touching her arm. "I'm sure Jake feels badly about what happened. Don't you Jake?"

"Yessir. I'll be on the porch."

"Spilt milk won't clean itself up now, will it?" said Gene.

"I want that dog's pecker on a platter!"

"Be right back," said Davis and quickly slipped out the screen door.

"Violet, we can't change what happened. Can we?"

"Where's he going with my gun?!"

"We need to register it, photograph it, add it to our...."

"When do I get it back?!"

Davis placed the shotgun in the trunk of his patrol car. He motioned to Jake and together they crossed the street and sat on the top step of Jake's front porch. Davis told Jake an official report would be made but assured him nothing would come of the incident. He further advised, however, Jake ought to consider having Wally neutered and quoted the old Ben Franklin 'ounce of prevention, pound of cure' saw. He asked Jake how school was going. Then, faint though it was, they heard the music:

Roll out the barrel, we'll have a barrel of fun
Roll out the barrel, we've got the blues on the run...

Moments later, Gene and Violet were dancing on her front porch. Violet's hair was down.

Davis's right foot tapped time on the step. Jake listened to Davis mumble under his breath, 'One and two, three and four...' as they watched the odd couple polka.

"Ol' Pere Gustafson was the man, the one husband who taught her how to live a little," Davis said. "Gene says he would dip the sugar cubes she put in her tea in *akvavit* for digestive purposes. Violet became very fond of the habit and would fix tea for herself three, four times a day. She never suspected for a moment she was consuming alcohol. You ever try it?"

"No, sir."

"According to Gene, Pere use to make claim that after three shots of *akvavit*, anyone can speak Swedish."

After several moments of reflection, Jake asked, "Why would anyone around here want to speak Swedish?"

Davis chortled and asked Jake if he noticed the five sealed urns arranged on Violet's mantel. He explained each one represented a former husband but only one, Pere Gustafson's, contained ashes.

#

Violet led the ten of diamonds. Hanky discarded a club.

"Have you and Kim set a date?" Hanky asked Jake.

"Yes, ma'am. June 5th."

"You're getting married?" Violet probed.

"Yes."

"She from Waltsburg?"

"Oklahoma," said Jake, playing the jack of diamonds.

"She that Indian girl with you at the museum?"

"She's not an Indian," Hanky corrected.

"She's Korean," Jake added. "Adopted by…"

"I know an Indian when I see one."

Jake and Hanky exchanged a glance. Eunice played the seven of diamonds. Jake reached forward and pulled the cards toward him.

"That will be your only trick, young man," Violet asserted.

Jake's only break from the card game was a trip to replenish his ice water and use the bathroom. The bathroom was tiny. Bold stenciled white lettering across the top of the medicine cabinet mirror read: Proverbs 31. The scent of gardenia and lilac instantly reminded him of his mother. He spotted the source, a White Shoulders perfume bottle on a wall-mounted glass shelf. Sitting on the pot, his knees nearly touched the cast iron clawfoot bathtub. To cover the scent he left, after washing his hands, he spritzed the perfume then fanned the air with a hand towel, a practice his father used if a book of matches was not handy.

Returning to the table, he reflected on John Jefferson Griever's theory about card games in private homes, a latent card shark's *feng shui.*

306

For good luck, you and your partner should seat yourselves parallel with the home's bathtub. He and Hanky were aligned perpendicular to Violet's. He groaned inwardly, ready to be home. The last hand of the evening, Hanky twice finessed Violet and took all thirteen tricks. Her composure bordering on collapse, her brow knitted into a 'V,' a distraught Violet Brisby declared the evening's match over. Hanky could not restrain her elation. Rising from her chair, she remarked, "So, Vye…why the long face?"

CHAPTER 61
WILD OATS

Friday – May 22

"I'm closer than a phone call," Kim teased when she phoned Jake at the bank to let him know she had arrived. Wedding reception planning was in full swing. Conger, Jake's best man, took temporary quarters with Francisco Martinez to make room for Kim's mother, Aunt Nell, and Portia. Kim and Chana planned to spend the night at Donna's house. The Saturday morning planning session at the ranch included Luci Bertolini, the caterer for the occasion; Donna, acting as wedding reception coordinator; and Nonny, designated head step-and-fetchette. The wedding party broke for lunch at 12:30. Merry gave the newcomers a tour of the Falls and Pennsylvania barn. Afterwards, Portia, Kim, and Chana hiked out to the Cemetary. Though breezy, it was a clement 80° under a mostly sunny sky. Halfway to their destination, Chana twirled, arms outflung, and exclaimed, "I could really live out here!"

"There's much to love about the prairie," said Portia. "But it rarely loves you back." Standing atop the rocky escarpment that formed one boundary of the weathered burial plot, the three observed a pinto grazing on the broad stand of wild oats outside the picket fence. Its tail swishing, the horse nickered then snorted at the strangers in friendly greeting.

"Is that Conger's horse?" Kim asked.

"No," said Portia, certain they had happened upon Mary Muldoon's storied mount.

Once in the Cemetary, Portia gathered a fist full of wildflowers, knelt at her grandmother's grave, weeded the plot and arranged the handpicked prairie flora in an oval pattern. Kim repeated for Chana what

308

she learned about Snow-in-Her-Hair from their visit last Thanksgiving. The pinto grazed and observed the three visitors with interest. Portia calmly approached the mare. The horse hung her head over the fence and allowed Portia to stroke her jowl and forehead. Kim and Chana listened to her talk quietly to the mare in her native language. Up close, it was clear the pinto had not been cared for. Her coat was coarse, her mane matted, raw puncture wounds were evident on a thigh, and one of her hind hocks was swollen.

"C'mon," urged Kim. "Let's hike ow-out to the most peaceful place on Earth."

"Where would that be?" Chana asked.

"Hoover's Bottom."

As the they left the Cemetary, the pinto followed along at a distance then quickened its gait and angled toward Minnie's Creek. Even at a relaxed pace, the horse hobbled painfully. The mare disappeared into the thicket along the creek. As the trio strolled through thigh-deep prairie grasses, Portia stumbled but regained her balance short of a fall. She had been more interested in keeping an eye on the pinto than watching her step. Surveying the line of growth along the creek, she spotted movement. Quick, shadowy bursts of skulk and slither paralleled their path sending a shiver down her spine.

"You okay?" Kim queried.

"Hold still a moment." She continued her gaze toward the creek, using Kim's shoulder as an arm rest to balance as she wriggled her ankle. She spotted more flashes of movement advancing in the same direction as the horse. "Think I might have turned my ankle," she said, feigning a limp. "Let's head back."

Upon hearing of their pinto sighting, Merry was amazed Sheba allowed Portia to touch her. She explained that the stand of wild oats was the remnant of a Sean Robert Muldoon ploy to lure the animal. Several months after the tornado struck the ranch, one of his acolytes spotted Sheba in the Cemetary. Robert often left a pail of oats for the horse hoping to catch a glimpse. Merry presented the three with the last of her pendants. Later that evening, Portia intimated to Merry the legendary horse was being stalked by a pack of coyotes.

CHAPTER 62
THE SECOND
WEDDING RECEPTION

Saturday – June 5

Much to the dismay of Kim's parents, the formal marriage ceremony was celebrated at the First Methodist church in Tulsa, Oklahoma, just after 10 a.m. Although initially brought up in the Catholic faith, Kimberly Anne Fitzgerald adopted her Aunt Nell's nonchalant approach to religion. Actual church attendance occurred at Easter and Christmas. Devout pragmatist that she was, Nell griped she had yet to find a church, any church, with good parking.

The couple's second wedding reception was held at Doona Falls Ranch. The five-car caravan arrived ahead of schedule, leaving enough time for all to stretch their legs and freshen up before guests arrived. The newlyweds greeted guests on the arbor-adorned veranda of the manor house and posed for photos with nearly every possible combination of kith and kin. Among other finger foods, Luci Bertolini's bite-size feta cheese and spinach pastries baked in phyllo dough were savory champagne companions.

As the sun waned on this late spring evening, a hybrid assortment of guests congregated in and around the Falls pool. While John Griever, Nonny, and Ben Whitewater basked in the pool's warmth, the less ardent of the group settled themselves on its rim soaking their feet. Parise sat apart on a tree stump, back turned, breast feeding their eight-week-old son.

Knowing it would be ill-advised to attempt the prank himself, Jimmy Baguelt mumbled in Kim's ear while wading in the natural spring water above the pool. Upon a mere moment's reflection, she suddenly

310

leaped from the Falls' rock lip into the pool, body compacted, legs tucked under her wedding gown, a parachuting cannonball. Jake could have sworn he heard Jimmy yell, Geronimo!

"KIMMY! Shame on you!" Nell scolded.

"O' how glorious!" Nonny exclaimed, wiping the splash from her face and eyes. "I do believe you may have ruined that lovely gown."

"It's only good once," Kim responded as she climbed out with an assist from Henry Yost and Catharine Mixx.

Ben Whitewater launched into his boyhood tale of how his parents cured him of chasing chickens. No disrespect to Mr. Whitewater, but Jake had heard the story. He suggested the younger group take a walk. A sopping wet Kim, along with Jake and the bridal party wandered out to the Cemetary enjoying a late spring breeze, a sun postured to set, and a thin veil of clouds on the western horizon flaunting hues of charcoal and orange peel.

As if a dark blanket were pulled over its erstwhile *dramatist personae* one millimeter at a time, the rock ledge cast its shadow over the hallowed ground, same as it had since the first of its wards were interred. The wedding bunch chatted briefly with Claire Nagel and Jenna Fairchild as they sat in wait on either side of Robert Muldoon's pulpit-notch, fantasizing the phantom pinto might encore, an Instamatic camera and pair of binoculars within reach. Portia did not tell them about the pack of coyotes she spied stalking the spavined mare a fortnight ago. She knew in her heart the pinto was gone for good, but still venerated in the moment by the presence of five wearing its pendant. Kim was anxious to shower and change into something comfortable. "Let's go," she whispered in Jake's ear. By the time they returned to the house, it would be dark, followed by prairie dark.

Earlier, while the newlyweds greeted guests on the veranda, Jimmy and Kirk decorated Jake's new air-conditioned Chevy Nova. Jake anticipated the tomfoolery. Doyle's Oldsmobile sat out of sight in the big barn, fully packed and gassed up, ready to roll. In the dimly lit barn, Jake opened the passenger door for Kim but not before pulling her close. Arms embraced, lips joined, hands explored. They were not alone. From the cavernous dark came sounds of uninhibited lust.

"Let's get out of here," Kim sighed.

Jake tuned the radio to KOMA as they drove out of the barn. Kim sat next to him, as close as she could get.

"Wonder who was in the b-barn?"

"We might not want-a know," said Jake, as they passed under the old stone archway. It was more than a three-hour drive to her family's cabin on Grand Lake O' the Cherokees where they would honeymoon. Jake asked Kim what she did with her wedding dress. She said she left it in the barn, commenting it might make a good scarecrow one day. Kim asked if he was disappointed his father did not attend.

"Didn't send him an invitation."

"You're going to tell him though, right?"

"Thought I'd wait for our wedding pictures and send him one with a note."

"Did you ever consider moving to Sea-seattle with your dad?"

"Before he remarried, I thought about trying it. He said Boeing was hiring, summers were pleasant, lots of good-looking girls, and the coffee nothing short of *primo*."

"How come you didn't go?"

"I don't drink coffee."

"Oh, yeah. I forgot. Ss-seriously, why didn't you go?"

"Because we were an accident waiting to happen."

"How ss-sweet. If I'd known that, I'd of visited Waltsburg ss-sooner. You sh-should've s-sent me that letter you didn't write."

"Think your aunt can get along without you?"

"Sh-she's already hired a housekeeper. I'm expendable. Thank God!"

> *"And it's one, two, three, what're we fighting for?*
> *Don't ask me I don't give a damn.*
> *Next stop is Viet-nam…"*

He snapped off the radio. The Eric Carver Tackle Box Tavern Black Moon episode coursed through his memory. He intuitively applied John Griever's advice: 'If yer havin' bad thoughts, think about somethin' good, somethin' that'll put a smile in your head.' Jake conjured up Ben Whitewater's chasing chickens story.

#

Four days later, Kim and Jake returned. As they pulled into town, Jake said, "I hope you don't mind sharing the house with Uncle Doyle until we find a place of our own."

"I have a surprise," Kim announced. "Aunt Nell bought the house on Newberry Street and gave it to us as a wedding present. Your uncle moved in with Donna while we were gone."

"No kidding? When's the wedding?"

Kim yawned, nestling closer to him.

# # #

Made in the USA
Monee, IL
27 October 2023

45312277R00177